Hidden in Plain Sight:

A Translation of the Dào Dé Jīng
Based on Bronze Inscription Glyphs
and Reimagined as a Secret Autobiography

by
Betsy Pearson

**Hidden in Plain Sight: A Translation of the Dào Dé Jīng
Based on Bronze Inscription Glyphs
and Reimagined as a Secret Autobiography**

Cover design:
David Huebner, Back of Beyond Media, Sheridan, Wyoming

PUBLISHED BY SUNWARMED SAGE PRESS

1635 WEEPING WILLOW LANE

SHERIDAN, WYOMING 82801

SUNWARMEDSAGEPRESS.COM

Ordering information:
sunwarmedsagepress.com/ordering
sunwarmedsagepress@gmail.com

ISBN: 978-1-7357931-9-1

For Lǎozī,
One and the Same,
always.

"Those who speak do not know, the wise are silent,"
These words I hear from Lǎo Zī.
If Lǎo Zī is wise,
why did he write the 5,000 words?

> *~ Bǎi Jūyì, Poet, 772–846 AD,*
> *(1,400 years after Lǎozī)*

Because I carved my life in those words, and it was…
complicated!

> ~ Lǎozī might have answered

Hidden in Plain Sight: A Translation of the Dào Dé Jīng Based on Bronze Inscription Glyphs and Reimagined as a Secret Autobiography

Table of Contents
(The chapters are sequenced as in the oldest known, the Mawangdui Silk Text [MWD], Manuscripts.)

Translator's Note
An Introduction by Lǎozī

The Dào

Chapter 1: Introducing the Dào, its mysterious two-wings, and the conception that started it all
Chapter 2: The reason for this dual identity
Chapter 3: It sounded better to play small and function as a low-ranking local official in this new, dual role rather than to rise up through the ranks.
Chapter 4: This debate was interrupted by a medical emergency and some help from an outside source
Chapter 5: Timely advice for me, along with a challenge
Chapter 6: The Good News and an introduction to A Certain Someone
Chapter 7: "You can't create 'this place' for the heavenly spirit in your earthly womb by being 'you,'" she said.
Chapter 8: "You need to be one of the elite."
Chapter 9: "But you don't have to, nor should you, get carried away or do this forever."
Chapter 10: A succinct description of my task and the name we gave it

The Dé

Translator's Note

The main body of this book is a new English version of
the *Dào Dé Jīng* in which each Chinese character has one
consistent and unique translation that blends descriptions of
Zhou Dynasty glyphs with historical definitions. I chose this
approach to get as close to Lǎozī as possible. Since Chinese
languages are pictorial in origin, I decided it was worth
considering what images Lǎozī chose to draw in his classic
text. And because he couldn't know how language would
evolve in the future, I didn't include modern meanings when
they differ from meanings dating closer to Lǎozī's time.

As I assembled the objective pieces of this translation, I
started connecting the images into a sort of mind movie, and
that movie turned out to be a surprising biopic of Lǎozī's own
life. I've framed that rather heretical historical fiction as
Lǎozī's autobiography and put those wild bits into the
introduction, the chapter titles, and Lǎozī's "editorial
comments" which you'll find scattered throughout the book.
You can recognize the fictional parts because they have no
line numbering and are in italics.

I love to imagine Lǎozī himself scripting this biopic. I love
the possibility that he not only discovered and distilled
wisdom so profound that it's been valued for millennia but
also managed to hide an autobiography in plain sight, right
there inside the very characters he used to share that
wisdom. On top of all that, Lǎozī crammed his text full of
rhythm, rhyme, alliteration, imagery, and all the other tools
of tremendously pleasing, rich, powerful poetry. What a
genius—and what a generous, playful friend—winking at us
across the years.

I absolutely do not claim to have found the one true meaning of Lǎozī's work or the one true story of his life. I wouldn't even want to do that. I personally don't believe it's that kind of a text, and even if it were, I don't have the background to act like any kind of authority on Chinese language or Taoist thought. But I always enjoy a new way of looking at a classic, even when I don't agree with it, and especially when it opens my mind to a wondrous kind of unknowing. I hope you do too. If, however, you simply prefer to enhance your favorite translation of the *Dào Dé Jīng* by considering some of the images that Lǎozī drew, you can ignore the lines that contain my fictional imaginings and stick with the main body of this book.

~

Sima Qian, court historian around 85 BCE, during China's Han dynasty, and a native of the ancient state of *Liáng*, described and evaluated several versions of Lǎozī's life story including the most traditional one:

> Renowned imperial advisor Lǎozī was born in
> the 6th century BCE during the Eastern Zhou
> Dynasty's Spring and Autumn period. When
> he was an old man, some say in *531 BCE*, Lǎozī
> tired of toxic politics and decided to emigrate
> west. A border guard named Yinxi recognized
> the sage and beseeched him to write some
> words of wisdom before departing. Lǎozī
> granted Yinxi's request, wrote the *Dào Dé
> Jīng*, then disappeared forever.

Over time, theories have multiplied as to where, when, and even *if* Lǎozī lived and wrote the *Dào Dé Jīng*. Most scholars don't agree with the traditional explanation and in fact believe the *Dào Dé Jīng*, originally referred to as *The Lǎozī*, wasn't written by one single author at all. Taoists of course disagree.

Likewise, there have been many versions of the book itself, both in Chinese and in other languages. It's known as the second most-translated book in the world. By 1998 there were thought to be 250 English translations, and many more have been published since. No two versions of the *Dào Dé Jīng* agree on particulars or even on the big themes. Over the last forty years, I became increasingly interested in understanding the differences between translations and trying to get as close to the original as possible. I grew absorbed in the characters, then in their etymology, and finally in the author himself. As I went deeper, I grew evermore amazed by the elegance, humor, and craft of the *Dào Dé Jīng*… and puzzled by its mysteries.

I like the idea of investigating Lǎozī and the *Dào Dé Jīng* from inside the book itself. Traditionally, that meant analyzing the "received" texts that have come down to us over time. But that changed early in the 20th century when archaeologists began unearthing ancient copies of the *Dào Dé Jīng*. In 1973, the *Mawangdui Silk Text (MWD)* manuscript was found in a tomb dated to 168 BCE. In 1993, an even older tomb, dated to 300 BCE, revealed the *Guodian Bamboo-Slip* version. Most recently, in 2009, Peking University announced a bamboo-slip manuscript known as the *Beida Lǎozī*, dated by script and style to 141–87 BCE and said to have been donated to the school after being recovered from a foreign collection. The most similar to our received version in many ways, the *Beida Lǎozǐ*'s provenance isn't publicly known.

The only things we can know for sure about these three most ancient versions of the *Dào Dé Jīng* are that they differ from each other, they're probably not identical to any original that existed, and they're not exactly like our received texts—there are gaps and variations in characters, chapter divisions, and sequencing. But they share one important similarity. In the received version of this *Jīng* ("classic text"), Chapters 1-37 describe the *Dào* (commonly translated as "The Way"), and Chapters 38-81 describe the *Dé* (sometimes translated as "Ethics"). All three of the oldest manuscripts reverse that order and place the *Dé* before the *Dào.*

The day I learned that the *Dé* most likely came before the *Dào,* was the same day I first encountered a *Dào Dé Jīng* etymology reference that went back further than the clerical/seal scripts or Warring States period... back to Bronze Inscriptions from earlier in the Zhou Dynasty. I started to ponder the implications of the fact that almost all of the *Dào Dé Jīng* translations I'd been reading were based not only on modern sequencing but also on modern Chinese characters, whereas the original was of course written in an Old Chinese script. I don't know why it had taken me so long to internalize such an obvious truth. But once the light came on, I immediately wanted to see the ancient glyphs and learn about the pictures within those characters.

All writers' word choices are important, and since a picture is worth a thousand words, it seems to me that Lǎozǐ's character choices are particularly vital. They give us a glimpse of authenticity that the modern definitions can't provide, especially given that the meanings of words change over time. Consider how English words were so different even a few hundred years ago when, for example, *quelling* something meant killing it and not just calming it down.

It's even more complicated in a pictorial script. As the written aspect of Old Chinese evolved, it adapted to the increasing quantity, complexity, and abstractness of words by placing several images together to form compound characters. Often one sub-component's image seems to give the word its semantic meaning, and another seems to provide its phonetic sound. But I believe the phonetic component's image also contributes to and refines the meaning. After all, there's always more than one character that could carry any given phonetic sound, so there's a reason for choosing a character with that precise image to do that work in that place. And as Lǎozī surely knew, we can't un-see or un-feel an image. That's why my interpretation for each character includes descriptions of its sub-components.

To further confound matters, Old Chinese scripts had regional differences. And several kinds of scripts were evolving simultaneously in each region for different uses and socioeconomic classes. Scholars find it difficult to piece it all together because of the sporadic sampling of texts we've found. Most of the original writing that survived the Spring and Autumn period as well, as the Warring States period that followed, is in the form of bronze inscriptions. Though the bulk of writing took place on bamboo and wooden slips bound together by silk thread or leather thongs, bronze castings were more durable. Almost all the slip texts that managed to survive the elements were burned later during the Qin dynasty. Some texts, however, were copied and handed down through the ages. They were re-written in each new era's script and evolved into the received classic texts we read today.

Many scholars and devotees have compared the various ancient manuscripts to one another as well as to the received texts. In doing so, they've generated hypotheses about chapter sequencing, correlations between ancient and modern characters, and whether the original was oral or written. There are also a large number of opinions as to how to go about posing and testing such ideas: Contextually? Personally? Traditionally? If so, through which Taoist lineage?

And then there's the real meat of the matter: what is the *Dào Dé Jīng*'s topic anyway? Is this a book about politics, mythology, mystical experience, socioeconomic realities, philosophy, how to live an individual life, physics, ultimate reality, or some combination of these topics? What does it say about its topic? In fact, what's the meaning of any one chapter, line, or character?

So much of any "answer" depends on one's assumptions. You've already noted some of my assumptions as well as the questions I've chosen to ignore completely. I like to believe that Lǎozī existed and authored the *Dào Dé Jīng*. The visual beauty, internal structure, and flow of characters suggest to me that it was written (rather than simply oral). And based on what I've found in my research, as well as on my personal preference and sense of the thing, I choose to believe the traditional origin story and dates.

Why do the dates matter to me? Because of my interest in getting as close as I can to the characters that Lǎozī himself penned. It's hard to know what kind of writing system a Lǎozī of 531 BCE would have used to write down an epic poem mid-departure at a border station. During this time, the Small Seal script was organically developing from the script of the earlier Western Zhou dynasty (1066 – 770 BCE). As far as we can tell, the evolving seal script was not yet fully developed or codified, and during the 500's BCE, it coexisted with a rougher, popular "vulgar" writing. Not only are the Western Zhou Bronze (WZB) Inscriptions the immediate etymological precursor of whatever script Lǎozī used, but also, they likely were known to Lǎozī since he was a court clerk and historian. That's why, if there's no Spring and Autumn period character known for a word, I looked to those bronze inscription characters for my translation. When no WZB character is known for a compound character, I assembled the WZB versions of its various sub-components into one drawing. When no such images exist, I used the earlier Oracle Bone Script characters.

Once I assembled a character's images, I sifted through definitions to find the oldest meanings and layered those in with descriptions of the images. Although I value the completeness of this approach, it means my translation for one character is long—very, very long in many cases! Chinese manages to convey all this information in one character and one syllable. That's one more thing that awes me about this language and also makes it impossible to fully, accurately translate it across eras or cultures. We are forced to leave out some of the details and nuance of the original in part because there's no choice and in part because we want to make it lyrical and easy to read. We want to simplify it.

When we run into a word, sentence, paragraph, or chapter that seems to contradict a previous point or simply doesn't compute, it's human nature to try to "make it make sense." I think this phenomenon is behind the biggest differences between translations.

Another cause for divergent interpretations is the simple fact that in most, if not all languages, words mean different things depending on context. Consider the various implications of a fork in the road, the fork you use to eat, a forked tongue, or, in very recent slang, "that forking jerk." When they know a lot about these contextual differences, translators assign various meanings to one character in various places. Unfortunately, when this happens, we readers are deprived of seeing when and how someone like Lǎozī chose to repeat certain characters or perhaps even develop his own "technical" lexicon. The other side of this coin is that if we translate one or more characters in the exact same way, the result looks like Lǎozī chose to use the same word in places where that's not the case.

There are other differences between English and Chinese that make translation hard. For example, in Chinese, you don't necessarily have to choose past or present tense for a verb or know the number of the subject. You don't have to choose a gender for pronouns. One word can be a noun, a verb, or an adjective. And the list goes on.

Another big issue, maybe the biggest one you'll find as you read my translation, is syntax. Consider the hypothetical phrase: "cat angry talk you luck good." You might decide it means: "it's good luck if an angry cat's talking to you" because the pauses and inflection upon delivery, as well as your ear for your own language, would make you decide on punctuation and phrasing. Not only is word-order different between languages, but the *Dào Dé Jīng* has almost no punctuation, and the little in-between words used to connect ideas in a certain way are sometimes absent, unrecognizable, or unclear to our modern ears. It can be frustrating.

But when we try to make it more comfortable or certain, we layer more of our own ideas onto the translation. For example, if it makes no sense to you that a cat could be talking or that this would be good luck, you might translate that sentence as "when a cat's angry, you should talk about good luck."

Native Chinese speakers have an incalculable advantage in translating Old Chinese. But it's also true that there is a lot of variety between native Chinese speakers' translations. It's just a mystifying text for who knows how many reasons. I think the glyphs are both complicit in and able to shed some light on this enigmatic nature.

That's why my goal was to assemble the most objective and complete description of the glyph components as possible while also incorporating the oldest translations of each character. In this way, I hoped to let Lǎozǐ's own evocative nature shine through.

I've already mentioned my most important rules: I never translate two different characters in the exact same way, and I use the same translation for a character every time it appears.[1] However, when a character appears more than once in a chapter, I often shorten its translation after the first appearance for the purposes of flow and brevity.

I decided to present the characters in the same order as the *Mawangdui Silk Texts*. I start a new line for each character, and I start a new paragraph for each line.[2] Unlike my previous versions, in this book, you'll see places where I included a few little transitional words for example, "and" or I put something in the past tense based on time-specific words in that chapter. The only things I unabashedly improvise are indentation, capitalization, and punctuation— the oldest versions have nothing of the first two and very little of the latter.

~

I figured once I assembled a strictly consistent, bare-bones pictorial version, then I could stop, step back, look at the book in a form that I believe to be closer to how Lǎozī wrote it, and then… then have an experience more like that which Lǎozī intended. I trusted something would happen in and to me, and it did. That experience is what I used to write the fictional autobiographical notes. I hope it will be a springboard from which you can have as much fun reimagining Lǎozī's life story as I've had.

---

[1] Exception: For the character *zhī*, 之, the most-frequently used character in the book, I prefer the translation "what it has, stepping on from this footprint, it has this" but sometimes use only a part of that or even "its" or "apostrophe-s."
[2] Exception: When I translate *zhī* as "'s," then it's on the same line as, and attached to, the previous word.

A companion website, thedaooflaozi.com, is in development. It will give you a place to engage with the text more easily. You'll be able to see my interpretations alongside others, choose or compose the definition you prefer for each character, and then, with a click, compile them into your very own complete translation.

Meanwhile, I hope you use this book to do that very thing. There are 5,297 characters in this version of the received text. Chapter-line-and-character numbering, along with the Modern Chinese characters and Pinyin transcriptions, appear in the main text so that you can use the 812-character Glossary to see each character's reconstructed glyph image and a list of every spot where that character occurs in this book. I hope to have this indexing system and glossary available for public use online as soon as possible.

The close reader will notice some changes from my earlier published translations. I am always refining my understanding, and I invite you to join me: search a character online, dive into its history, explore its etymology, and compare other translators' versions of the word with your own sensibility.

Have your own personal encounter with Lǎozī and the images and ideas in the *Dào Dé Jīng*, and interesting things will happen. That's what I want for you and for Lǎozī, to whom I offer this book with the greatest of thanks.

*An Introduction by Lǎozī**

When I approached the western front of the kingdom of Chu, weary of corrupt and harsh politics, I'd settled on a plan to leave behind politics and war forever. Quickly. But a border guard named Yinxi recognized me as the emperor's famously sage advisor and begged me to pause and put down some words of wisdom, "or perhaps even your own story," he added. Like most people, he'd heard rumors that I'd been "discovered" by the emperor when I was a roaming clerk-for-hire with some undefinable charisma and little regard for convention. He'd also heard even quieter rumors about the nature of my relationship with the emperor. But the truth was that no one knew much about me.

I was known by a lot of names… which conveniently doesn't really clarify anything! It was said that my childhood personal name was 李耳 or Lǐ Ěr, which translates as plum tree ear. You will not find this plum tree character in the Dào Dé Jīng, but most of the components in my other names do make appearances. My formal adult courtesy name was 伯陽, Bó Yáng. I translate Bó as "a count—an acorn like an eldest brother or paternal uncle," but it also is a general honorific. Yáng is well-known as "the male principle, like sun shining on a big soil mound." So yes, I sometimes called myself "Sir Manly!" Too on the nose?

But more commonly, during my adult life, I was called something much less impressive: 老聃, Lǎo Dān, or honorable loose-haired elder bent over an arrow as a cane with long hanging-down ears. The "long hanging-down" part doesn't appear in this book, but you will find the old man character here and there if you keep an eye out. Prominent ears were considered signs of long life and wealth, so… lucky me. I wouldn't say I was "all ears," but, as you'll see many times in this book, I always did "keep an ear out." My posthumous honorific name is of course Lǎo Zī, that same honorable loose-haired elder, 老, bent over an arrow as a cane, but accompanied by 子, *a little baby with arms open wide and legs swaddled.*

But back to Yinxi's request. Why did I agree to write the book? Well, I really liked him, plus I do so love words and word play. And puzzles. And that's how an idea occurred to me. Could I write a many-layered poem that had rhyme, rhythm, beautiful lessons for the good life plus glimpses of the secret, often wonderful, and also sometimes scary and difficult circumstances that allowed—actually, forced—me to discover a spacious way of living? As you'll find out in this book, I longed for the real me to be known. Alas, telling the truth about myself had gotten me into trouble, but because the Chinese languages have a pictorial base, I wondered if I could embed that truth in the text by choosing words drawn with images that, coincidentally, provided literal glimpses into my story. Could the book be one long double-entendre? I resolved to try. I thank you, dear reader for taking the closer look necessary to refocus and really see those pictures.

I first wrote 42 chapters on what I'd taken to calling Dé (the heart-aligned straight path) and how I planned to embody this way of living a humble life after crossing the border. My past figured into those 42 chapters but in a disjointed manner. Maybe writing those safer chapters warmed me up and emboldened me, for then I was able to write 37 chapters dedicated to the backstory that brought me to that border station. This is where I got clearer and more direct—you could say it's the revised, final draft. It focuses on the seemingly more abstract and mysterious concept I called Dào, "the path of a mythical wild-haired head buck." Versions of my text handed down over the years have placed the Dào section first, and I've done the same thing here. It is, after all, the correct chronological order of my story. And, since I introduce the entire cast of characters more clearly in the Dào section, the Dé section makes much more sense when read second.

You'll notice that in the body of the text, I've translated most verbs for you in the present tense, often using the gerund form with an -ing suffix. That's partly because in the Chinese languages, these verbs don't need a tense the way they do in English and sometimes they're used as nouns. But it's also partly because, even though I'm telling you my story, this is first and foremost a book with truths about anyone's life, especially yours. Please always use it for yourself in whatever way feels most honestly and helpfully true. That's always been my first goal.

- *Fictional!*

<u>*The Dào*</u>
Walking With the Footprint
of the Loose-Haired Head Buck

Chapter 1: Introducing the Dào, its mysterious two-wings, and the conception that started it all

Dào, that is to say, walking with the footprint of the loose-haired head buck	1.1.1	dào	道
—that lip-smackingly genuine	1.1.2	kâ	可
walking with the footprint of the loose-haired head buck—	1.1.3	dào	道
wrings to backward the two wings of	1.2.4	fēi	非
a conventional royal administrator wearing a men's headcloth as a skirt	1.2.5	cháng	常
walking with the footprint of the loose-haired head buck.	1.2.6	dào	道
That personal name given in childhood and still whispered by moonlight	1.3.7	míng	名
—that lip-smackingly genuine	1.3.8	kâ	可
personal name—	1.3.9	míng	名
wrings to backward the two wings of	1.4.10	fēi	非
the conventional royal administrator	1.4.11	cháng	常
personal name.	1.4.12	míng	名
A shamanic dancer with animal tails flowing from her wrists, *"Wú,"* that is to say, *"Not-Having,"*	1.5.13	wú	無
that personal name given in childhood and still whispered by moonlight:	1.5.14	míng	名

the heavenly from high above this
great big person
now down here in this earthly womb,
stepping on from this footprint had this
    conception in a woman
    kneeling, happy, speaking of
    gathering herself from three
    sides.

1.5.15	tiān	天
1.5.16	dì	地
1.5.17	zhī	之
1.5.18	shǐ	始

The flesh-and-meat-handling *"Yǒu,"* that is to
say, *"Being,"*
that personal name:
    the medicine-dancing-scorpion insect
    swarm of
    matter outside one's body, "cut from
    the cow" by a bloodied blade,
stepping on from this footprint had this
    suckling by a woman kneeling
    with breasts full of milk.

1.6.19	yǒu	有
1.6.20	míng	名
1.6.21	wàn	萬
1.6.22	wù	物
1.6.23	zhī	之
1.6.24	mǔ	母

This tapped lightly with a tutoring cane and left a mark
on the solid shield of the past:
The conventional royal administrator,
    shaman-dancing "Not-Having"
    missing, kneeling with a yawning mouth before
    a ravine eroded between two mountains,
    wanting, lacking,

1.7.25	gù	故
1.7.26	cháng	常
1.7.27	wú	無
1.7.28	yù	欲

cultivates like a plow
someone with one big eye for a head kneeling on a
stork-like temple or watchtower to keep lookout for
    what that holds a basket of,

1.8.29	yǐ	以
1.8.30	guān	觀
1.8.31	qí	其

a young woman kneeling in a mist, four tiny
drops belittled as a rich young master, that
subtle, ingenious, exquisite aura.

But the conventional royal administrator,
    flesh-and-meat-handling "Being"
missing, kneeling with a yawning mouth before
a ravine eroded between two mountains,
    wanting, lacking,

cultivates like a plow
someone with one big eye for a head kneeling on a
stork-like temple or watchtower to keep lookout for
what that holds a basket of,
    a person carefully tracing a frontier border line,
    walking with the footprint of a musical
    instrument, like an acorn atop the wide side of
    a blade, lightly plucked or hit by hand, moving
    slowly, with just the left foot leading the way.

1.8.32	miào	妙
1.9.33	cháng	常
1.9.34	yǒu	有
1.9.35	yù	欲
1.10.36	yǐ	以
1.10.37	guān	觀
1.10.39	qí	其
1.10.39	jiào	徼

*This part of my word game made Yinxi pause. Was I
saying that "when we are in a state of not-wanting, we
contemplate the subtle mystery of creation, and when
we are in a state of wanting, we contemplate the visible
path?" Yes. That's how this passage usually is
translated, and that's one of the important truths I
learned as I moved through the hard conditions you'll
find in my story.*

*But was I also saying that "if a dancing girl gets
pregnant and goes missing, then someone like me
would make sure that every watchtower will be on the
lookout for a young woman carrying the aura of a little*

*master; whereas, if a logistics guy goes missing, they'll
be watching for a notably large guy walking along a
remote border, much like where we were standing?"
Yes indeed. No wonder Yinxi looked at me sideways
under his lashes.*

This here—the foot stops a person here on this
footprint!—   1.11.40   cǐ   此
these two, this pair of traditional, adult, gendered
head-cloths covered by "The One?"   1.11.41   liǎng   兩
This is boiling sugarcane with fire as follows!   1.11.42   zhâ   者
*When speaking as ordinarily and generally as any
commonplace bucket, they're known as "Fán, one and
the same,"*   1.11.43   tóng   同
stepping out of their cave,   1.11.44   chū   出

   yet now, bearded, "Ér," you're   1.12.45   ér   而
   a person wearing a mask, hiding   1.12.46   yì   異
   that personal name given in childhood and still
   whispered by moonlight.   1.12.47   míng   名

*Those two personas were one until that person
emerged from hiding with a simple disguise. The power
of a beard can't be overstated—though I am going to
spend a whole book trying!*

"Fán, one and the same,"   1.13.48   tóng   同
by the nitty-gritty, grinding gizzard of a fowl, what
that's called,   1.13.49   wèi   謂
stepping on from this footprint had this,   1.13.50   zhī   之
   this hard-to-see structure of a double-looped,
   figure-eight skein of string-dyed-black. 1.13.51   xuán   玄

This hard-to-see structure of a double-looped, figure-
eight skein of string-dyed-black,   1.14.52   xuán   玄
stepping on from this footprint had this,   1.14.53   zhī   之
    again, on the right hand,   1.14.54   yòu   又
    this hard-to-see structure of a double-looped,
    figure-eight skein of string-dyed-black.   1.14.55   xuán   玄

Yes, this dark double-looped thread happened twice.
More on that later.

The sun, shining down like an eye on the people, sees
all this, sees   1.15.56   zhòng   眾
a young woman kneeling in a mist, four tiny drops
belittled as a rich young master, that subtle, ingenious,
exquisite aura,   1.15.57   miào   妙
stepping on from this footprint had this   1.15.58   zhī   之
    two-winged gateway.   1.15.59   mén   門

Chapter 2: The reason for this dual identity

Folks started making harsh judgements about what
that baby would be like once he was born, labelling him
before he was even born.

Regarding the heavenly from high above this great big
person,   2.1.1   tiān   天
now here down below,   2.1.2   xià   下
gossip, comparing two people like there was something
oh so sweet in their mouth, said: 2.1.3   jiē   皆
    "Speaking as a great big person to a baby,
    distinguishing, imparting, and administering
    wisdom confidently and intimately,   2.1.4   zhī   知

an admired beauty, a person wearing a ram's
horn headdress...   2.1.5   mâi   美
what do they have stepping on from this
footprint,   2.1.6   zhī   之
creating something by hand, carving an
elephant likeness of good fortune and royal
power?!   2.1.7   wéi   為
    The admired beauty,   2.1.8   mâi   美
    what it holds a basket of is lopped off,
    thereby defining whatever remains as
    'not-that' but rather as   2.1.9   sī   斯
    a tomb constructed over the heart,"   2.1.10   è   惡
    already finishing it in the womb.   2.1.11   yǐ   已

Gossip said: 2.2.12   jiē   皆
    "Speaking as a great big person to a baby,
    distinguishing, imparting, and administering
    wisdom confidently and intimately,   2.2.13   zhī   知
    the traditionally virtuous, offering up a ram's
    head while speaking back and forth, tongues
    waggling,   2.2.14   shàn   善
    what do they have stepping on from this
    footprint,   2.2.15   zhī   之
    creating something by hand, carving an
    elephant likeness of fortune and royal power?! 2.2.16   wéi   為
    The traditionally virtuous,   2.2.17   shàn   善
    what it holds a basket of is lopped off,
    thereby defining whatever remains as
    'not-that' but rather as   2.2.18   sī   斯
    the husk of the initial false guard-petals
    but not really the true flower of   2.2.19   bù   不
    the traditionally virtuous,"   2.2.20   shàn   善
    already finishing it in the womb.   2.2.21   yǐ   已

This tapped lightly with a tutoring cane and left a mark
on the solid shield of the past...
flesh-and-meat-handling Being
and a shamanic dancer with animal tails flowing from
her wrists, Not-Having,
    like a seen tree and the eye seeing it (or like a
    well-tended lord and his attentive attendant),
    when taken together, create this singular
    phenomenon...
    sprouting a bud from the ground.

*And so it happened: the cave, the beard, the two new
identities. It turned out that they had complementary
traits well-suited for the job at hand...*

Solid (like that hard yellow earth with two little grass
tufts next to River Han where "short-tailed birds" find
no food)
and easily changeable (switching from saying "don't,"
as serious as three drops of blood on a blade, to shining
like the sun),
    together the two of them created this singular
    phenomenon...
    completing that final "nail" in a weapon on a
    pole;

lengthening (as long as hair that has to be tied with a
brooch, like a loose-haired old man)
and short (an arrow so small it fits in a bean-shaped
food container),
    together the two of them created this singular
    phenomenon...

2.3.22	gù	故
2.3.23	yǒu	有
2.3.24	wú	無
2.3.25	xiāng	相
2.3.26	shēng	生
2.4.27	nán	難
2.4.28	yì	易
2.4.29	xiāng	相
2.4.30	chéng	成
2.5.31	cháng	長
2.5.32	duǎn	短
2.5.33	xiāng	相

shaping as finely and level as two shields side
by side with measuring lines of three hairs'
breadth;   2.5.34   xíng   形

way up in a two-story building outside the city, high
above what's faced with admiration and echoed in
there,   2.6.35   gāo   高
and now here down below,   2.6.36   xià   下
        together the two of them created this singular
        phenomenon...   2.6.37   xiāng   相
        a person leaning toward that loose-haired head
        buck, separated by an arrow, adoring,
        emptying all their resources (a king!);   2.6.38   qīng   傾

singing one tone from your mouth   2.7.39   yīn   音
and the many sounds you hear when hitting chimes
with a weapon in your right hand, going right through a
person,   2.7.40   shēng   聲
        together the two of them created this singular
        phenomenon...   2.7.41   xiāng   相
        warming, wetting, and stickily kneading
        together, harmonizing like breath blown into a
        reed-pipe mouth organ;   2.7.42   hé   和

at the front, that place in battle where a step could
mean your feet get cut off as punishment,   2.8.43   qián   前
and walking slowly with just the left leg leading the
way, leaving behind this tiny silk thread footprint like a
knot in a thread, a descendant, at the end,   2.8.44   hòu   後
        together the two of them created this singular
        phenomenon...   2.8.45   xiāng   相

        accompanying one another single file near soil
        mountains, slowly walking with the footprint of

flesh-and-meat-handling Being, the left leg
leading the way.   2.8.46   suí   隨

Ideally, this new hybrid life would look like this…

This baby footprint on bamboo-slip pages,   2.9.47   shì   是
this is cultivating, like a plow,   2.9.48   yǐ   以
an ideal grounded sage known for his civilian petition
to authority, standing straight, speaking, and being
listened to,   2.9.49   shèng   聖
that person: 2.9.50   rén   人
when *disappearing like a tiger head at home*, footprint
pointed back down by a table, staying here, chaste,
rather than accepting a government position or getting
married…   2.9.51   chù   處
    they'd be shaman-dancing Not-Having   2.9.52   wú   無
    creating something by hand, carving an
    elephant likeness of good fortune and royal
    power…   2.9.53   wéi   為
        what they have, stepping on from this
        footprint,   2.9.54   zhī   之
        their task, what they do with a
        weapon, flag, or pen in hand;   2.9.55   shì   事

when out *in public* at the crossroads, being good, doing
one's work…   2.10.56   xíng   行
    they'd be the husk of the initial protective bud
    casing but not really the true flower of 2.10.57   bù   不
    speaking out loud…   2.10.58   yán   言
        what they have, stepping on from this
        footprint,   2.10.59   zhī   之
        lessons learned the hard way, like a
        child being taught counting with

bamboo slips or divination with yarrow
stalks, tapping them lightly with a
tutoring cane.   2.10.60   jiào   教

I'm not disclosing any particular lessons here.
Not now. [Spoiler: see line 42.14 of the Dé.] But
the result of this ideal sage behavior would be…

The medicine-dancing-scorpion insect swarm of   2.11.61   wàn   萬
matter outside one's body, "cut from the cow"
by a bloodied blade,   2.11.62   wù   物
recently, exactly, immediately folded from one
straight rod into two   2.11.63   zuò   作
here, straightening things out for "nailing" that
first footstep of a journey on the back of this
yellow bird with the "dangling tail" that lives
around the Yangtze and Huai Rivers—right
here, huh!—   2.11.64   yān   焉
    yet now, bearded, you're   2.11.65   ér   而
    the husk of the initial protective bud
    casing but not really the true flower of 2.11.66   bù   不
    using a chisel (the one that marks
    slaves and criminals) to rule as a hand
    from above over a hand with a
    common bucket in a place outside the
    city;   2.11.67   cí   辭

sprouting a bud from the ground,   2.12.68   shēng   生
    yet now, bearded, you're   2.12.69   ér   而
    the husk of the initial protective bud
    casing but not really the true flower of 2.12.70   bù   不
flesh-and-meat-handling Being;   2.12.71   yǒu   有

creating something by hand, carving an
elephant likeness of good fortune and royal
power,   2.13.72   wéi   為

        yet now, bearded, you're   2.13.73   ér   而
        the husk of the initial protective bud
        casing but not really the true flower of   2.13.74   bù   不
        a mother—heart grabbed like by the
        hand of a government office or temple
        worker that was usually a eunuch in
        the old days;   2.13.75   shì   恃

and laboring with the force of a blade and the
work of one's arm or a plow   2.14.76   gōng   功
completing that final "nail" in a weapon on a
pole,   2.14.77   chéng   成
        yet now, bearded, you're   2.14.78   ér   而
        like sticks that were tied together in a
        bundle to start a fire—pfft!—and no
        longer   2.14.79   fú   弗
        staying put here, sitting over the solid
        shield of the past at this birthplace. 2.14.80   jū   居

In fact, that is to say *This Grown Man* with hairpin
and public courtesy name   2.15.81   fū   夫
—"Oh yes Ma'am," says the "short-tailed bird"—   2.15.82   wéi   唯
is like sticks that were tied together in a bundle to start
a fire—pfft!—and no longer   2.15.83   fú   弗
staying put here, sitting over the solid shield of the past
at this birthplace.   2.15.84   jū   居

        This baby footprint on bamboo-slip pages,   2.16.85   shì   是
        this is cultivating, like a plow,   2.16.86   yǐ   以

the husk of the initial protective bud casing but
not really the true flower of
leaving, a person with a cave mouth between
their legs.

2.16.87   bù   不

2.16.88   qù   去

"'This guy' was made only to get things going,
and then he ceased to exist. And if someone
doesn't exist, he can't really leave." Or so said
me, the guy walking out of the country. Yinxi
gave me another searching look.

Chapter 3: It sounded better to play small and function
as a low-ranking local official in this new, dual role
rather than to rise up through the ranks

The husk of the initial protective bud casing but not
really the true flower of
nobly assisting the emperor, dividing up and
differentiating what's faced with admiration and
echoed in there,

3.1.1   bù   不

3.1.2   shàng   尚

       as one big eye cleverly, solidly, looking down
       from atop cowry-like riches,

3.1.3   xián   賢

a low-ranking government official, his hand holding a
flag, weapon, or pen, perhaps sent as a messenger or
an envoy, putting to work, using in every way you can
think of, directing,
one of our folk, the people enslaved by blinding with a
dagger,

3.2.4   shǐ   使

3.2.5   mín   民

       is the husk of the initial protective bud casing
       but not really the true flower of

3.2.6   bù   不

competing, two hands clawing over a			
plowshare.	3.2.7	zhēng	爭
The husk of the initial protective bud casing but not			
really the true flower of	3.3.8	bù	不
held in high regard, like when two hands are wrapped			
around a person atop cowry-shell-riches,	3.3.9	guì	貴
as the solid (like that hard yellow earth with			
two little grass tufts next to River Han, where			
"short-tailed birds" find no food)	3.3.10	nán	難
"Hand-Picked Gem" (like cowry-shell-riches			
discovered along the road)	3.3.11	dé	得
and its	3.3.12	zhī	之
transformation from a right-side-up person to			
an upside-down person atop cowry-shell			
riches,	3.3.13	huò	貨
a low-ranking government official,	3.4.14	shǐ	使
one of our folk,	3.4.15	mín	民
is the husk of the initial protective bud casing			
but not really the true flower of	3.4.16	bù	不
creating something by hand, carving an			
elephant likeness of good fortune and royal			
power,	3.4.17	wéi	為
while spitting into a bowl like in an oath among			
robbers, "thick as thieves."	3.4.18	dào	盜
The husk of the initial protective bud casing but not			
really the true flower of	3.5.19	bù	不
seen by someone with one big eye for a head	3.5.20	jiàn	見
as what's lip-smackingly genuinely	3.5.21	kâ	可

missing, kneeling with a yawning mouth before			
a ravine eroded between two mountains,			
wanting, lacking,	3.5.22	yù	欲
a low-ranking government official,	3.6.23	shǐ	使
one of our folk,	3.6.24	mín	民
in their heart,	3.6.25	xīn	心
is the husk of the initial protective bud casing			
but not really the true flower of	3.6.26	bù	不
trying to govern in chaos, two people			
disentangling a roll of threads using their hands			
with the help of a comb or beater.	3.6.27	luàn	亂

*Indeed, that sounded like the safest strategy.
Competing sounded fraught with crime and chaos. But
let's consider: exactly what would be the ideal in this
situation...?*

This baby footprint on bamboo-slip pages,	3.7.28	shì	是
this is cultivating, like a plow,	3.7.29	yǐ	以
an ideal grounded sage known for his civilian petition			
to authority, standing straight, speaking, and being			
listened to,	3.7.30	shèng	聖
that person,	3.7.31	rén	人
stepping on from this footprint, would have this	3.7.32	zhī	之
"flowing the River Happy," speaking of gathering			
oneself from three sides, managing:	3.7.33	zhì	治
empty, like a tiger head upon a mound,	3.8.34	xū	虛
what it holds a basket of,	3.8.35	qí	其
their heart,	3.8.36	xīn	心

they'd be filling, like a truly rich building
crammed with jade and cowry-shells,   3.9.37   shí   實
            what it holds a basket of,   3.9.38   qí   其
            their guts, doubled back with a piece of
            meat inside;   3.9.39   fǔ   腹

in a delicate state with a pair of fragile bows,   3.10.40   ruò   弱
    what it holds a basket of,   3.10.41   qí   其
their will, stepping off from the heart's
footprint here,   3.10.42   zhì   志

they'd be revolving around themself as a
powerful bow broadening, strengthening, stiff,
hard, and compelling as a rice weevil, like a tiny
venomous snake—thwang!—   3.11.43   qiáng   強
            what it holds a basket of,   3.11.44   qí   其
            a strong framework, like bones   3.11.45   gǔ   骨

Since the ideal wise person would be fine
despite everything, why not take this step up?
Consider what might happen…

As a conventional royal administrator wearing
a men's headcloth as a skirt,   3.12.46   cháng   常
the low-ranking government official, his hand
holding a flag, weapon, or pen, perhaps sent as
a messenger or an envoy,   3.12.47   shǐ   使
one of our folk, the people enslaved by blinding
with a dagger,   3.12.48   mín   民
            would be the shamanic dancer with
            animal tails flowing from her wrists,
            Not-Having,   3.12.49   wú   無

speaking as a great big person to a
baby, distinguishing, imparting, and
administering wisdom confidently and
intimately,   3.12.50   zhī   知
and then shaman-dancing Not-Having   3.12.51   wú   無
would go missing, kneeling with a
yawning mouth before a ravine eroded
between two mountains, wanting,
lacking.   3.12.52   yù   欲

*That's a wild idea: get promoted to a royal
administrator and speak confidently, so then my Not-
Having persona is missing altogether?! As I explained in
Chapter 1, when Not-Having is missing, the powers-
that-be are on the lookout for someone with the aura
of a missing young mother. But no one suspects an
important royal advisor.*

But *a low-ranking government official,*   3.13.53   shǐ   使
in fact, that is to say *This Grown Man*, with hairpin and
public courtesy name,   3.13.54   fū   夫
*oh, so very pleasantly speaking that wise knowledge
passed on from a great big person to a baby, as if
something sweet in the mouth?!*   3.13.55   zhì   智
This is boiling sugarcane with fire as follows!   3.13.56   zhâ   者
He's the husk of the initial protective bud
casing but not really the true flower of   3.13.57   bù   不
venturing to be bold, even a little bit and ultra-
politely hunting a boar as pleasantly as if you
had something sweet in your mouth,   3.13.58   gǎn   敢
while creating something by hand, carving an
elephant likeness of fortune and royal power   3.13.59   wéi   為
—yes, that too, oh "female funnel!"   3.13.60   yâ   也

He's creating something by hand, carving an
elephant likeness of fortune and royal power   3.14.61   wéi   為
as shaman-dancing Not-Having   3.14.62   wú   無
creating something by hand, carving an
elephant likeness of good fortune and royal
power.   3.14.63   wéi   為

*Not being a royal administrator, not venturing
to be bold during the pregnancy, meant being
pregnant as a regular female nobody. And that
wasn't safe, given the situation.*

After following this sacrificial blade-and-
cauldron-like ritual regulation,   3.15.64   zé   則
shaman-dancing Not-Having   3.15.65   wú   無
is the husk of the initial protective bud casing
but not really the true flower of   3.15.66   bù   不
flowing the River Happy.   3.15.67   zhì   治

Chapter 4: This debate was interrupted by a medical emergency and help from an outside source

Walking with the footprint of the loose-haired head
buck   4.1.1   dào   道
and pouring water from the center like a stream from
the hollow drum at the base of a flagpole,   4.1.2   chōng   沖
        yet now, bearded, you're   4.1.3   ér   而
        doing truly useful work like a water bucket, by
        means of carrying-capacity,   4.1.4   yòng   用
        and, stepping on from this footprint, what that
        has is this: 4.1.5   zhī   之

in this particular enclave, defended by a
weapon on a pole   4.2.6   huò   或
it's the husk of the initial protective bud casing
but not really the true flower of   4.2.7   bù   不
full to overflowing your vessel.   4.2.8   yíng   盈

*The loose-haired buck was leaking. But the
work of pregnancy requires carrying "like a
water bucket." And a bucket shouldn't have
water coming out of it until it's full to
overflowing.*

Deep water!   4.3.9   yuān   淵
Hmmm—like wind through tree branches!   4.3.10   xī   兮

Like how a person and a turned fetus, side-by-
side, resemble one another,   4.4.11   sì   似
    the medicine-dancing-scorpion insect
    swarm of   4.4.12   wàn   萬
    matter outside one's body, "cut from
    the cow" by a bloodied blade 4.4.13   wù   物
    stepping on from this footprint, has
    this   4.4.14   zhī   之
    ancestral temple.   4.4.15   zōng   宗

The "ancestral temple" needs deep water.

But pushing down to seated on the ground   4.5.16   cuò   挫
what it holds a basket of...   4.5.17   qí   其
    a person speaking like an axe being sharpened
    on metal, pointed;   4.5.18   ruì   銳

cutting like a blade removing an ox's horn | 4.6.19 | jiâ | 解
what it holds a basket of... | 4.6.20 | qí | 其
      unravelling, a blade dividing a skein of silk into
      disorder; | 4.6.21 | fēn | 紛

and warming, wetting, and stickily kneading together,
harmonizing like breath blown into a reed-pipe mouth
organ | 4.7.22 | hé | 和
what it holds a basket of... | 4.7.23 | qí | 其
      that shining fire over the head of a kneeling
      person... | 4.7.24 | guāng | 光

then what's known as "*Fán*, one and the same," when
spoken of as ordinarily and generally as any
commonplace, | 4.8.25 | tóng | 同
what it holds a basket of... | 4.8.26 | qí | 其
      is leaving one billionth of a trace like the dust
      raised by deer running across the dirt, streaked
      with soil. | 4.8.27 | chén | 塵

Profound, clear, joy—that river as pleasant as
something sweet in the mouth tucked into the ends of
folded cloth! | 4.9.28 | zhàn | 湛
Hmmm—like wind through tree branches! | 4.9.29 | xī | 兮

      Like how a person and a turned fetus, side-by-
      side, resemble one another, | 4.10.30 | sì | 似
            in <u>this</u> particular enclave, defended by
            a weapon on a pole, | 4.10.31 | huò | 或
            it continues existing, a baby with health
            issues, maybe a large head, but still a
            seed sprouting! | 4.10.32 | cún | 存

Counting up on all five fingers, aren't I,   4.11.33   wú   吾
the husk of the initial protective bud casing but not
really the true flower of   4.11.34   bù   不
speaking as a great big person to a baby, distinguishing,
imparting, and administering wisdom confidently and
intimately,   4.11.35   zhī   知
     the one of whom "the short-tailed bird"
     speaks, who   4.11.36   shuí   誰
     stepping on from this footprint, has this   4.11.37   zhī   之
     baby with arms wide open and legs swaddled?   4.11.38   zǐ   子

Like an elephant skeleton to a living elephant,
it's bearing a likeness to something, to   4.12.39   xiàng   象
God of Heaven, as we call our emperors (the
husk of a flower's initial bud casing connecting
them to above, covering the traditional
gendered head-cloth we wrap around our hair
once we receive our adult courtesy names)...   4.12.40   dì   帝
     stepping on from this footprint, it has
     this   4.12.41   zhī   之
     leading, long before, stepping off from
     this footprint, this ancestor.   4.12.42   xiān   先

Chapter 5: Timely advice for me, along with a challenge

"If the heavenly from high above this great big person	5.1.1	tiān	天
now down here in this earthly womb	5.1.2	dì	地
is the husk of the initial false guard-petals but not really			
the true flower of	5.1.3	bù	不
a kernel of humanity—a person seated over not just			
one but two, a different 'èr'—	5.1.4	rén	仁
cultivating, like a plow,	5.2.5	yǐ	以
the medicine-dancing-scorpion insect swarm of	5.2.6	wàn	萬
matter outside one's body, 'cut from the cow,' by a			
bloodied blade,	5.2.7	wù	物
creating something by hand, carving an elephant			
likeness of good fortune and royal power,	5.2.8	wéi	為
is merely a pair of grass stalks wrapped up into	5.2.9	chú	芻
a straw dog, a symbolic sacrificial object.	5.2.10	gǒu	狗
And if an ideal grounded sage known for his civilian			
petition to authority, standing straight, speaking, and			
being listened to,	5.3.11	shèng	聖
that person,	5.3.12	rén	人
is the husk of the initial false guard-petals but not really			
the true flower of	5.3.13	bù	不
a kernel of humanity—a person seated over not just			
one but two, a different 'èr'—	5.3.14	rén	仁
cultivating, like a plow,	5.4.15	yǐ	以
the hundred	5.4.16	bǎi	百
family names that a kneeling woman sprouts from the			
ground,	5.4.17	xìng	姓

creating something by hand, carving an elephant
likeness of good fortune and royal power,   5.4.18   wéi   為
     is merely a pair of grass stalks wrapped up into   5.4.19   chú   芻
     a straw dog, a symbolic sacrificial object."   5.4.20   gǒu   狗

*If either that heavenly spirit or I didn't survive, then this
offspring and lineage I'm creating would be gone like a
straw dog burned up as part of a ritual.*

"The heavenly from high above this great big person   5.5.21   tiān   天
now down here in this earthly womb,   5.5.22   dì   地
stepping on from this footprint, it has   5.5.23   zhī   之
this interstitial, transitional space where moonlight's
peeking through the two-winged gateway: 5.5.24   jiān   間

what it holds a basket of...   5.6.25   qí   其
in the same manner as the unlikely rise of a dog
monkey to the top of the alcohol vat to become chief
of brewing, it's like   5.6.26   yóu   猶
a bellows   5.6.27   tuó   橐
flute that you blow into, made of bamboo-slips with
three mouth frets   5.6.28   yuè   籥
     —PAH, CAN YOU BE?!   5.6.29   hū   乎

     Can you be empty, disappearing as a tiger head
     upon a mound,   5.7.30   xū   虛
         yet, now you're bearded,   5.7.31   ér   而
         the husk of the initial protective bud
         casing but *not really* the true flower of   5.7.32   bù   不
         bending like one who represents the
         dead in a rite, flexing to step out of a
         cave, and   5.7.33   qū   屈

easily doing work as hard as moving a heavy
bag tied at both ends with the strong force of
an arm or plow,   5.8.34   dòng   動
    yet, now you're bearded,   5.8.35   ér   而
    a person *after an illness who gathered*
    themself together from three sides by
    moonlight over their heart after a
    blade cut off their foot as punishment,
    and now they're recovered,   5.8.36   yù   愈
    stepping out of their cave?   5.8.37   chū   出

Having more, like two pieces of meat,   5.9.38   duō   多
speaking out loud   5.9.39   yán   言
adds up (tapping lightly with a tutoring cane up
through the stack from a kneeling woman to a round
center drum with a flagpole and then a suckling
mother) to   5.9.40   shǔ   數
being thoroughly used up and destitute, your pregnant
self buried with a bow,   5.9.41   qióng   窮

the husk of the initial false guard-petals but not really
the true flower of   5.10.42   bù   不
a kneeling woman with breasts doing as told   5.10.43   rú   如
and hand-defending this building   5.10.44   shǒu   守
in the center, that drum with a flagpole placed in the
middle of a field to gather the people and detect wind."   5.10.45   zhōng   中

Who gave me this warning, you ask…?

Chapter 6: The Good News and an introduction to
A Certain Someone

In a difficult position in a ravine, in an emptied, eroded			
valley mouth between two mountains,	6.1.1	gǔ	谷
that magical god spirit lightning, the divine spark	6.1.2	shén	神
is the husk of the initial protective bud casing but not			
really the true flower of	6.1.3	bù	不
dying, a person turning to a pile of bones!	6.1.4	sǐ	死

The baby and I were alive despite its difficult position.

This baby footprint on bamboo-slip pages,	6.2.5	shì	是
by the nitty-gritty, grinding gizzard of a fowl, what			
that's called,	6.2.6	wèi	謂
this hard-to-see structure of a double-looped, figure-			
eight skein of string-dyed-black…	6.2.7	xuán	玄
the spoon of a cow or a woman's valley.	6.2.8	pìn	牝

This hard-to-see structure of a double-looped,			
figure-eight skein of string-dyed-black,	6.3.9	xuán	玄
the spoon of a cow or a woman's valley…	6.3.10	pìn	牝
stepping on from this footprint, it has this	6.3.11	zhī	之
two-winged gateway.	6.3.12	mén	門

You remember the two-winged gateway in Chapter 1.

This baby footprint on bamboo-slip pages,	6.4.13	shì	是
by the nitty-gritty, grinding gizzard of a fowl, what			
that's called,	6.4.14	wèi	謂
the heavenly from high above this great big person	6.4.15	tiān	天
now down here in this earthly womb…	6.4.16	dì	地

the root of the family tree, like an ancestor's
manhood.   6.4.17   gēn   根

Barely perceptible, like the fine, white silk
threads making up the traditional gendered
head-cloth,   6.5.18   mián   綿
barely perceptible…   6.5.19   mián   綿
A Certain Someone compliantly combing her
loose hair seems to be saying, "this is as if   6.5.20   ruò   若
it continues existing, a baby with health issues,
maybe a large head, but still a seed sprouting." 6.5.21   cún   存

*And, so, you finally meet A Certain Someone—the
person who delivered not only the medical intervention
and happy result in Chapter 4 but also the intense
advice that followed in Chapter 5. I don't like to think of
what would have happened without this amazing
midwife and friend. Here's the crux of her advice…*

"Doing truly useful work like a water bucket, by means
of carrying-capacity,   6.6.22   yòng   用
stepping on from this footprint, has this: 6.6.23   zhī   之
    the husk of the initial false guard-petals but not
    really the true flower of   6.6.24   bù   不
    exerting with force, working hard with the
    strong force of an arm, a bladed tool, or a plow
    on the soil."   6.6.25   qín   勤

*The creative-capacity kind of work needed for this
creative undertaking required that I avoid grueling
work. Spoiler: this is perhaps the main lesson I learned
from my whole experience. When applied to everything
I did, this philosophy made life easier, better, and more*

productive, even when I wasn't pregnant. I dare say it's what gave me the reputation of a wise sage. But how could a non-grueling approach be possible? She told me...

Chapter 7: "You can't create 'this place' for the heavenly spirit in your earthly womb by being 'you,'" she said.

"The heavenly from high above this great big person is lengthening as long as hair that has to be tied with a	7.1.1	tiān	天
brooch, like a loose-haired old man,	7.1.2	cháng	長
here in this earthly womb	7.1.3	dì	地
by enduring through time as a person receiving moxibustion, that mugwort treatment for cramps, turning a breech baby, or other health issues.	7.1.4	jiǔ	久
The heavenly from high above this great big person,	7.2.5	tiān	天
here in this earthly womb	7.2.6	dì	地
with 'that place' being intentionally created like any household gate hewn with an axe,	7.2.7	suǒ	所
this is cultivating, like a plow,	7.2.8	yǐ	以
using that legendary Hybrid Power of a mythical bear-like animal who has the legs of a deer for	7.2.9	néng	能
lengthening,	7.2.10	cháng	長
lasting over time like the erect manhood of a male ancestor	7.2.11	qiâ	且
enduring through time as a person receiving moxibustion	7.2.12	jiǔ	久
and—this is boiling sugarcane with fire as follows!—	7.2.13	zhâ	者

this is cultivating, like a plow,	7.3.14	yǐ	以
what it holds a basket of…	7.3.15	qí	其
the husk of the initial false guard-petals but not			
really the true flower of	7.3.16	bù	不
'yourself' personally, right on the nose,	7.3.17	zì	自
sprouting a bud from the ground.	7.3.18	shēng	生

This taps lightly with a tutoring cane and leaves			
a mark on the solid shield of the past:	7.4.19	gù	故
use the legendary Hybrid Power of a mythical			
bear-like animal who has the legs of a deer for	7.4.20	néng	能
lengthening	7.4.21	cháng	長
sprouting a bud from the ground.	7.4.22	shēng	生

This baby footprint on bamboo-slip pages,	7.5.23	shì	是
this is cultivating, like a plow,	7.5.24	yǐ	以
an ideal grounded sage known for his civilian petition			
to authority, standing straight, speaking, and being			
listened to,	7.5.25	shèng	聖
that person:	7.5.26	rén	人
walking slowly with just the left leg leading the way,			
leaving behind this tiny silk thread footprint like a knot			
in a thread, a descendant, at the end,	7.5.27	hòu	後
is what it holds a basket of,	7.5.28	qí	其
your pregnant self,	7.5.29	shēn	身

yet now you're bearded…	7.6.30	ér	而
your pregnant self	7.6.31	shēn	身
would be leading, long before, stepping off			
from this footprint, the ancestor;	7.6.32	xiān	先

'outside,' foreign as the relatives of a mother, sister,
and daughter who divine by the moon,   7.7.33   wài   外
        is what it holds a basket of,   7.7.34   qí   其
        your pregnant self,   7.7.35   shēn   身

        yet now you're bearded...   7.8.36   ér   而
        your pregnant self   7.8.37   shēn   身
        would continue existing, a baby with health
        issues, maybe a large head, but still a seed
        sprouting.   7.8.38   cún   存

Wring to backward the two wings of   7.9.39   fēi   非
cultivating, like a plow,   7.9.40   yǐ   以
        what it holds a basket of,   7.9.41   qí   其
        the shamanic dancer with animal tails flowing
        from her wrists, Not-Having,   7.9.42   wú   無
                and your personal concerns, turning
                about your own private grain supply,   7.9.43   sī   私
                as unwholesome in nature as the
                disease-causing environment around
                Elephant, Tusk Town, Lángyá.   7.9.44   yé   邪

This taps lightly with a tutoring cane and leaves a mark
on the solid shield of the past: 7.10.45   gù   故
use the legendary Hybrid Power of a mythical bear-like
animal who has the legs of a deer for   7.10.46   néng   能
completing, that final 'nail' in a weapon on a pole,   7.10.47   chéng   成
        what it holds a basket of...   7.10.48   qí   其
                your personal concerns, turning about
                your own private grain supply."   7.10.49   sī   私

This healer recommended I not stick to small private
preferences like those listed at the beginning of Chapter

Chapter 8: "You need to be one of the elite."

"On top, the traditionally virtuous, offering up a ram's head	8.1.1	shàng	上
while speaking back and forth, tongues waggling,"	8.1.2	shàn	善
A Certain Someone compliantly combing her loose hair seems to be saying, "this is as if	8.1.3	ruò	若
water flowing right in the center a river, spraying up on both sides."	8.1.4	shuǐ	水

"Water flowing right in the center a river, spraying up on both sides like	8.2.5	shuǐ	水
the traditionally virtuous,	8.2.6	shàn	善
reaps benefits (in the manner of a sharp-edged blade slicing grain):	8.2.7	lì	利
the medicine-dancing-scorpion insect swarm of	8.2.8	wàn	萬
matter (outside one's body, 'cut from the cow,' by a bloodied blade).	8.2.9	wù	物
Yet, now you're bearded,	8.3.10	ér	而
and the husk of the initial protective bud casing *but not really the true flower of*	8.3.11	bù	不
competing, two hands clawing over a *plowshare.*"	8.3.12	zhēng	爭

"Disappearing like a tiger head at home, footprint
pointed back down by a table, staying here, chaste,
rather than accepting a government position or getting
married?   8.4.13   chù   處
          The sun, shining down like an eye on the
          people, sees all this, sees   8.4.14   zhòng   眾
          that person,   8.4.15   rén   人
          stepping on from this footprint, has this: 8.4.16   zhī   之
                    'that place' being intentionally created
                    like any household gate hewn with an
                    axe   8.4.17   suǒ   所
                    is a tomb constructed over the heart.   8.4.18   è   惡

This taps lightly with a tutoring cane and leaves a mark
on the solid shield of the past: 8.5.19   gù   故
like two little silk threads separated by the sword of a
garrison guard, so, so near   8.5.20   jǐ   幾
is this place and time, oh, black, icy raven sun, to   8.5.21   yú   於
walking with the footprint of the loose-haired head
buck."   8.5.22   dào   c

The virtuous life is like a river… and a lot like when you
were living as that free, wild-haired creature, she said.

"In staying put here, sitting over the solid shield of the
past at this birthplace, where   8.6.23   jū   居
          the traditionally virtuous is   8.6.24   shàn   善
          here in this earthly womb,   8.6.25   dì   地

in their heart,   8.7.26   xīn   心
          the traditionally virtuous is   8.7.27   shàn   善
          deep water.   8.7.28   yuān   淵

In participating with someone, a 'biting tooth' lifted by
two hands onto strong shoulders, perhaps interfering
with or perhaps supporting,   8.8.29   yǔ   與
    the traditionally virtuous is   8.8.30   shàn   善
    a kernel of humanity—a person seated over
    not just one but two, a different *èr*.   8.8.31   rén   仁

In *speaking out loud,*   8.9.32   yán   言
    the traditionally virtuous is   8.9.33   shàn   善
    giving one's word to a person.   8.9.34   xìn   信

In straightening up, straightening things out for 'nailing'
that first footstep of a journey,   8.10.35   zhèng   正
    the traditionally virtuous is   8.10.36   shàn   善
    flowing the River Happy, speaking of gathering
    oneself from three sides, managing.   8.10.37   zhì   治

In their task, what they do with a weapon, flag, or pen
in hand,   8.11.38   shì   事
    the traditionally virtuous is   8.11.39   shàn   善
    using that legendary Hybrid Power of a
    mythical bear-like animal with deer legs.   8.11.40   néng   能

In easily doing work as hard as moving a heavy bag tied
at both ends with the strong force of an arm or plow,   8.12.41   dòng   動
    the traditionally virtuous is   8.12.42   shàn   善
    as seasonally timely as the sunny spot where
    you measure your pulse between the footprint
    and the hand.   8.12.43   shí   時

So, in fact, that is to say This Grown Man with hairpin
and public courtesy name,   8.13.44   fū   夫
'Oh, YES, Ma'am,' says the 'short-tailed bird,'   8.13.45   wéi   唯
the husk of the initial false guard-petals but not really
the true flower of   8.13.46   bù   不
competing, two hands clawing over a plowshare,   8.13.47   zhēng   爭

> taps lightly with a tutoring cane and leaves a
> mark on the solid shield of the past: 8.14.48   gù   故
> the shamanic dancer with animal tails flowing
> from her wrists, Not-Having,   8.14.49   wú   無
> *is like a hand with a wart: particularly strangely*
> *outstanding."*   8.14.50   yóu   尤

It had to be said. Not stepping up to the level of
"virtuous" wasn't working. In avoiding that elite role, in
trying to act like a low-level guy, I simply looked weird.

But A Certain Someone could see that I still was
hesitant, so she continued her persuasive argument...

Chapter 9: "But you don't have to, nor should you, get carried away or do this forever."

"Grasping, like a government office or temple holding
onto what comes from this footprint with the very
skillful human hand of that official (usually a eunuch in
the old days),   9.1.1   chí   持
> yet, now you're bearded,   9.1.2   ér   而
> full to overflowing your vessel,   9.1.3   yíng   盈
> what it has, stepping on from this footprint: 9.1.4   zhī   之

the husk of the initial false guard-petals but not
really the true flower of
a kneeling woman with breasts doing as told,
what it holds a basket of...
already finishing it in the womb.

Polishing a vessel by hand,
    yet, now you're bearded,
    grinding that axe between two blocks of metal
    to a sharp point,
    what it has, stepping on from this footprint:

    the husk of the initial false guard-petals but not
    really the true flower of
    lip-smackingly genuinely
    lengthening as long as hair that has to be tied
    with a brooch, like a loose-haired old man,
    safeguarding, like carrying a child on one's
    back.

Gold joined together from three sides by grinding it like
an axe between two blocks of metal
and a pure jade totem,
    like arrowheads tightly wrapped in the
    traditional gendered head-cloth to protect
    them from water, packed in
    a palace courtyard:

    like the sun sinking down in four bushes, one
    must not be—cannot be, eh?—
    using that legendary Hybrid Power of a
    mythical bear-like animal who has the legs of a
    deer for

9.2.5	bù	不
9.2.6	rú	如
9.2.7	qí	其
9.2.8	yǐ	已
9.3.9	chuǎi	揣
9.3.10	ér	而
9.3.11	zhuō	銳
9.3.12	zhī	之
9.4.13	bù	不
9.4.14	kâ	可
9.4.15	cháng	長
9.4.16	bǎo	保
9.5.17	jīn	金
9.5.18	yù	玉
9.5.19	mǎn	滿
9.5.20	táng	堂
9.6.21	mò	莫
9.6.23	néng	能

    hand-defending this building.   9.6.24   shǒu 守

Wealthy, a home full of valuable vessels with lots of
capacity,   9.7.25   fù 富
and held in high regard, like when two hands are
wrapped around a person atop cowry-shell-riches,   9.7.26   guì 貴
    yet, now you're bearded,   9.7.27   ér 而
    arrogant, a young person dangerously racing
    through the city outskirts on a tall horse with
    its mane flying: 9.7.28   jiǎo 驕

    yourself personally, right on the nose,   9.8.29   zì 自
    walking with the footprint of someone slowly
    leaving behind cowry-like riches after *dying*,
    the left leg leading the way with two hands are
    wrapped around them, dragging them off,   9.8.30   yí 遺
    what it holds a basket of,   9.8.31   qí 其
    a person following this upside-down footprint
    sees its calamity.   9.8.32   jiù 咎

But, laboring with the force of a blade and the work of
one's arm or a plow,   9.9.33   gōng 功
slowly walking with the footprint of *post-harvest* time
after dividing up the pigs, the left leg leading the way,   9.9.34   suì 遂
    your pregnant self   9.9.35   shēn 身
    withdrawing, walking with the footprint of a
    person slowly retreating from the table after
    eating, like the ending of a thread in a knot,
    their eye looking backward, the left leg leading
    the way: 9.9.36   tuì 退

the heavenly from high above this great big
person,
what it has, stepping on from this footprint,
is walking with the footprint of the loose-haired
head buck."

*This will be part of the challenge, she said: knowing it's
time to step back from the high-status life after labor is
done, after I have my "treasure." Then the heavenly
spirit can have that wild creature in their life, and that's
what it needs.*

Chapter 10: A succinct description of my task and the name we gave it

"Carrying and protecting a chariot load of sprouting
seeds and talents, guarding with a weapon on a pole
the spiritual soul, that light of a palatial womb's
crossed torches, plus
the physical soul that stays with a body after death,
that skull-white ghost with a tail,
and bundling it all up together in both arms
into
The One

while using that legendary Hybrid Power of a mythical
bear-like animal who has the legs of a deer for
the shamanic dancer with animal tails flowing from her
wrists, Not-Having,
remaining set apart (as separate as 'a short-tailed bird'
is from that infamous wild animal hunted in the forest
with webbed nets)

9.10.37	tiān	天
9.10.38	zhī	之
9.10.39	dào	道
10.1.1	zāi	載
10.1.2	yǐng	營
10.1.3	bō	魄
10.1.4	bào	抱
10.1.5	yī	一
10.2.6	néng	能
10.2.7	wú	無
10.2.8	lí	離

—PAH, CAN YOU?!

Monopolizing (like a big round spindle rolling over an
inch-sized spot as small as that spot on your forearm
where your pulse beats strong)
that vital qì energy, the breath of life, that air flow
that's like a gift of rice,
> and thoroughly delivering, exhausting, arriving
> at the extreme (like an arrow stuck in the
> ground and tapped lightly with a tutoring cane
> so as to leave a mark)
> softening to be as supple as a tree that can be
> cut with a spear

while using that legendary Hybrid Power of a mythical
bear-like animal who has the legs of a deer for
an infant, a kneeling young mother's wealth just as
surely as two cowry-like riches around her neck,
a baby son that still has an open fontanelle
—PAH, CAN YOU?!"

*"Delivering while softening" is something you'll hear a
lot about in this book (and if you ever find yourself in a
birthing class).*

"Washing and arranging things, hitting lightly, stripping,
and knotting twigs into slips to write on or a broom
in a new posting in a thatched cottage by a soil
mountain,
> and this hard-to-see structure of a double-
> looped, figure-eight skein of string-dyed-black

> overseeing everything as royalty acting on
> behalf of the emperor, commanding as 'blood'

10.2.9	hū	乎
10.3.10	zhuān	專
10.3.11	qì	氣
10.3.12	zhì	致
10.3.13	róu	柔
10.4.14	néng	能
10.4.15	yīng	嬰
10.4.16	ér	兒
10.4.17	hū	乎
10.5.18	dī	滌
10.5.19	chú	除
10.5.20	xuán	玄

family bonded by a drop of blood in a
ceremonial vessel, bent over and looking down,
perhaps in seclusion, all eyes,   10.5.21   lǎn   覽

while using that legendary Hybrid Power of a mythical
bear-like animal who has the legs of a deer for   10.6.22   néng   能
shaman-dancing Not-Having   10.6.23   wú   無
being so ill that she needs to lie on a stretcher   10.6.24   cī   疵
—PAH, CAN YOU?!   10.6.25   hū   乎

Loving, kneeling with your head turned this way and
your heart in your throat,   10.7.26   ài   愛
one of our folk, the people enslaved by blinding with a
dagger,   10.7.27   mín   民
        and flowing the River Happy, speaking of
        gathering oneself from three sides, managing   10.7.28   zhì   治
        our domestic enclave, defended by a weapon
        on a pole,   10.7.29   guó   國

while using that legendary Hybrid Power of a mythical
bear-like animal who has the legs of a deer for   10.8.30   néng   能
shaman-dancing Not-Having   10.8.31   wú   無
speaking as a great big person to a baby, distinguishing,
imparting, and administering wisdom confidently and
intimately,   10.8.32   zhī   知
—PAH, CAN YOU?!   10.8.33   hū   乎

The heavenly from high above this great big person,   10.9.34   tiān   天
this two-winged gateway   10.9.35   mén   門
coming unlatched, this two-winged gateway with a pair
of hands,   10.9.36   kāi   開

        and shutting it, this great big person with a
        cave mouth between their legs withdrawing

from within the two-winged gateway, covering
an empty chalice,   10.9.37   hé   闔

while using that legendary Hybrid Power of a mythical
bear-like animal who has the legs of a deer for   10.10.38   néng   能
creating something by hand, carving an elephant
likeness of good fortune and royal power,   10.10.39   wéi   為
female, the foot stopping a person here in the footprint
of the 'short-tailed bird'   10.10.40   cí   雌
—PAH, CAN YOU?!   10.10.41   hū   乎

As bright as dawn rising on a crescent moon,
enlightened,   10.11.42   míng   明
        and a hundred,   10.11.43   bǎi   百
        from all four directions,   10.11.44   sì   四
        arriving with the footprint of small lambs
        walking slowly on their track, the left leg
        leading the way   10.11.45   dá   達

while using that legendary Hybrid Power of a mythical
bear-like animal who has the legs of a deer for   10.12.46   néng   能
shaman-dancing Not-Having   10.12.47   wú   無
speaking as a great big person to a baby, distinguishing,
imparting, and administering wisdom confidently and
intimately,   10.12.48   zhī   知
—PAH, CAN YOU?!   10.12.49   hū   乎

Sprouting a bud from the ground,   10.13.50   shēng   生
        what it has, stepping on from this footprint,   10.13.51   zhī   之
rearing animals, feeding them from a bag tied with a
rope,   10.13.52   chù   畜
        what it has stepping on from this footprint...   10.13.53   zhī   之

sprouting a bud from the ground,
  yet, now you're bearded,
  the husk of the initial false guard-petals but not
  really the true flower of
  flesh-and-meat-handling Being;

creating something by hand, carving an elephant
likeness of good fortune and royal power,
  yet, now you're bearded,
  the husk of the initial false guard-petals but not
  really the true flower of
  a mother—heart grabbed like by the hand of a
  government office or temple worker that was
  usually a eunuch in the old days;

lengthening as long as hair that has to be tied with a
brooch, like a loose-haired old man,
  yet, now you're bearded,
  the husk of the initial false guard-petals but not
  really the true flower of
  dominating as the house of that chisel used to
  mark slaves and criminals.

This baby footprint on bamboo-slip pages,
by the nitty-gritty, grinding gizzard of a fowl, what
that's called,
this hard-to-see structure of a double-looped, figure-
eight skein of string-dyed-black,
  Dé, walking with the footprint of someone
  who's in alignment (eyes looking forward,
  directly over the heart, left leg slowly leading
  the way)."

10.14.54	shēng	生
10.14.55	ér	而
10.14.56	bù	不
10.14.57	yǒu	有
10.15.58	wéi	為
10.15.59	ér	而
10.15.60	bù	不
10.15.61	shì	恃
10.16.62	zhǎng	長
10.16.63	ér	而
10.16.64	bù	不
10.16.65	zǎi	宰
10.17.66	shì	是
10.17.67	wèi	謂
10.17.68	xuán	玄
10.17.69	dé	德

Chapter 11: *So, I embraced my task. I stepped into the Dé life—and it was lovely.*

Three	11.1.1	sān	三
tens of	11.1.2	shí	十
hem-width strips	11.1.3	fú	幅
share, like two hands holding something aloft,	11.1.4	gòng	共
The One	11.1.5	yī	一
hub of a wheel, that working part of a carriage you tend to with a hand tool:	11.1.6	gǔ	轂

equally as suburbs and fields facing one another,	11.2.7	dāng	當
what that holds a basket of	11.2.8	qí	其
is the shamanic dancer with animal tails flowing from her wrists, Not-Having,	11.2.9	wú	無
and flesh-and-meat-handling Being.	11.2.10	yǒu	有
A carriage,	11.2.11	chē	車
what it has, stepping on from this footprint,	11.2.12	zhī	之
is doing truly useful work like a water bucket, by means of carrying-capacity.	11.2.13	yòng	用

Molding clay on a potter's wheel,	11.3.14	yán	埏
clay that looks straight on, up and down,	11.3.15	zhí	埴
this is cultivating, like a plow,	11.3.16	yǐ	以
hand-making, creating, like carving an elephant likeness of good fortune and royal power,	11.3.17	wéi	為
a set of highly regarded vessels with lots of capacity, worthy of a guard dog:	11.3.18	qì	器

equally as suburbs and fields facing one another,	11.4.19	dāng	當
what it holds a basket of	11.4.20	qí	其
is shaman-dancing Not-Having	11.4.21	wú	無
and flesh-and-meat-handling Being.	11.4.22	yǒu	有

A set of highly regarded vessels,   11.4.23   qì   器
what it has, stepping on from this footprint,   11.4.24   zhī   之
is doing truly useful work like a water bucket,
by means of carrying-capacity.   11.4.25   yòng   用

Chiseling, with that tool used to mark slaves and
criminals,   11.5.26   zào   鑿
the single-gate doorway to a household,   11.5.27   hù   戶
and a window, like a boudoir window's sliver of wood
that's half of a two-winged gateway and lets the moon
shine in on the family's primordial father, ten spindles
hanging,   11.5.28   yǒu   牖
this is cultivating, like a plow,   11.5.29   yǐ   以
hand-making, creating, like carving an elephant likeness
of good fortune and royal power,   11.5.30   wéi   為
a living space where a wife comes to live: 11.5.31   shì   室

equally as suburbs and fields facing one another   11.6.32   dāng   當
what it holds a basket of   11.6.33   qí   其
is shaman-dancing Not-Having   11.6.34   wú   無
and flesh-and-meat-handling Being.   11.6.35   yǒu   有
          Such a living space (where a wife comes to
          live),   11.6.36   shǐ   室
     what it has, stepping on from this footprint,   11.6.37   zhī   之
     is doing truly useful work like a water bucket,
     by means of carrying-capacity.   11.6.38   yòng   用

This tapped lightly with a tutoring cane and left a mark
on the solid shield of the past: 11.7.38   gù   故
flesh-and-meat-handling Being,   11.7.39   yǒu   有
what it has, stepping on from this footprint,   11.7.40   zhī   之
cultivates, like a plow,   11.7.41   yǐ   以

creating something by hand, carving an elephant
likeness of good fortune and royal power   11.7.42   wéi   為
       by reaping benefits in the manner of a sharp-
       edged blade slicing grain;   11.7.43   lì   利

shaman-dancing Not-Having,   11.8.45   wú   無
what it has, stepping on from this footprint,   11.8.46   zhī   之
cultivates, like a plow,   11.8.47   yǐ   以
creating something by hand, carving an elephant
likeness of good fortune and royal power   11.8.48   wéi   為
       by doing truly useful work like a water bucket,
       by means of carrying-capacity.   11.8.49   yòng   用

And that, my friends, felt like living the dream.

Chapter 12: I was reminded not to get carried away in my role as "The Hand-Picked Gem."

"If five times   12.1.1   wǔ   五
the coloring (hand-clawing a kneeling person and
tinting their complexion as a feminine charm albeit
sometimes to a perverted countenance)   12.1.2   sè   色
is controlling, joining together from three sides over a
kneeling person and ordering an action or perhaps
sending off to somewhere,   12.1.3   lìng   令
that person,   12.1.4   rén   人
       then where the eye sees   12.1.5   mù   目
       and what their eye sees, is lost, blind.   12.1.6   máng   盲

If five times   12.2.7   wǔ   五
singing one tone from their mouth   12.2.8   yīn   音
is controlling   12.2.9   lìng   令

that person,
      then their ear ('*Âr*')
      is deaf as a dragon with an ice-cold wing ear.

	12.2.10	rén	人
	12.2.11	âr	耳
	12.2.12	lóng	聾

If five times
the tasting, reflecting on a flavor in the mouth which is
still forming like a tree whose top branches are not yet
fully grown,
is controlling
that person,
      then the words from their mouth
      are invigoratingly clear and broken, possibly
      angry as this great big person with a pair of
      hatch-marks cut on each side of the chest in
      the style of that ancient women's chest tattoo.

	12.3.13	wǔ	五
	12.3.14	wèi	味
	12.3.15	lìng	令
	12.3.16	rén	人
	12.3.17	kǒu	口
	12.3.18	shuǎng	爽

If galloping—'Oh yeah, female funnel!'—
like a horse given free rein by a chivalrous martial
warrior, that knight with a pair of helmets and a sharp
exhalation, galloping all over,
tilling a field, hitting it lightly, marking it up like a tattoo
with a bristly dog beating the game toward you for the
hunt, a witch hunt,
is controlling
that person,
      then their heart,
      as if shot by a bow launching—'thwang!'—and
      leveling grass underfoot as effectively as if by
      hand with a halberd,
      is like a mad dog roaring as insanely,
      unrestrainedly as a king.

	12.4.19	chí	馳
	12.4.20	chǎng	騁
	12.4.21	tián	畋
	12.4.22	liè	獵
	12.5.23	lìng	令
	12.5.24	rén	人
	12.5.25	xīn	心
	12.5.26	fā	發
	12.5.27	kuáng	狂

If the solid (like that hard yellow earth with two little
grass tufts next to River Han, where "short-tailed birds"
find no food)   12.6.28   nán   難
'Hand-Picked Gem,' like cowry-shell-riches discovered
along the road   12.6.29   dé   得
and its   12.6.30   zhī   之
transformation from a right-side-up person to an
upside-down person atop cowry-shell riches   12.6.31   huò   貨

is controlling   12.7.32   lìng   令
that person,   12.7.33   rén   人
     then out in public at the crossroads being good,
     doing one's work,   12.7.34   xíng   行
     they're oppositional, holding the tip of a sword
     over a kneeling woman.   12.7.35   fāng   妨

This baby footprint on bamboo-slip pages,   12.8.36   shì   是
this is cultivating, like a plow,   12.8.37   yǐ   以
an ideal grounded sage known for his civilian petition
to authority, standing straight, speaking, and being
listened to: 12.8.38   shèng   聖
that person   12.8.39   rén   人

would be creating something by hand, carving an
elephant likeness of good fortune and royal power   12.9.40   wéi   為
in their gut, doubled back with a piece of meat inside… 12.9.41   fǔ   腹
     the husk of the initial false guard-petals *but not
     really* the true flower of   12.9.42   bù   不
     creating something by hand, carving an
     elephant likeness of good fortune and royal
     power,   12.9.43   wéi   為
     where the eye sees.   12.9.44   mù   目

This tapped lightly with a tutoring cane and left a mark
on the solid shield of the past:
leave, like a person with a cave mouth between their
legs,
     that—that fur stripped by hand from its pelt on
     the road where they stepped slowly, the left
     leg leading the way;
and get hold of, grab the ear of, 'marry'
     this here—the foot stops a person here on this
     footprint!"

12.10.45	gù	故
12.10.46	qù	去
12.10.47	bǐ	彼
12.10.48	qù	取
12.10.49	cǐ	此

***Chapter 13: My new life was interrupted by the shock
of being sick… and sick with worry. I'd somehow
thought the high life would prevent that.***

Pampered as a favorite concubine in the home of an
emperor dragon crowned with the chisel used to mark
slaves or criminals
AND hanging from a cliff above a hand underneath,
shaking, humiliated?!
     A Certain Someone compliantly combing her
     loose hair seems to be saying "this is as if
     startling, making you jump like a horse spooked
     by the sound of someone tapping a dog lightly
     with a tutoring cane?"

13.1.1	chǒng	寵
13.1.2	rǔ	辱
13.1.3	ruò	若
13.1.4	jīng	驚

Held in high regard, like when two hands are wrapped
around a person atop cowry-shell-riches,
this great big person,
AND sick with worry (or worrisomely sick), two objects
strung together over the heart?

13.2.5	guì	貴
13.2.6	dà	大
13.2.7	huàn	患

A Certain Someone compliantly combing her
loose hair seems to be saying "this is as if
your pregnant self."

    13.2.8   ruò   若
    13.2.9   shēn   身

That one—that very one shouldering a weapon—
by the nitty-gritty, grinding gizzard of a fowl, what does
that mean to say
    13.3.10   hé   何
    13.3.11   wèi   謂

    "pampered as a favorite concubine in the home
    of an emperor dragon crowned with the chisel
    used to mark slaves or criminals AND
    hanging from a cliff above a hand underneath,
    shaking, humiliated:
    A Certain Someone compliantly combing her
    loose hair seems to be saying 'this is as if
    startling, making you jump like a horse spooked
    by the sound of someone tapping a dog lightly
    with a tutoring cane?'"

    13.3.12   chǒng   寵
    13.3.13   rǔ   辱
    13.3.14   ruò   若
    13.3.15   jīng   驚

    Pampered as a favorite concubine in the home
    of an emperor dragon crowned with the chisel
    used to mark slaves or criminals
    and creating something by hand, carving an
    elephant likeness of good fortune and royal
    power,
    now here down below:

    13.4.16   chǒng   寵
    13.4.17   wéi   為
    13.4.18   xià   下

    when you're The Hand-Picked Gem, like cowry-
    shell-riches discovered along the road,
    what it has, stepping on from this footprint,
    A Certain Someone compliantly combing her
    loose hair seems to be saying "this IS as if

    13.5.19   dé   得
    13.5.20   zhī   之
    13.5.21   ruò   若

startling, making you jump like a horse spooked
by the sound of someone tapping a dog lightly
with a tutoring cane;"   13.5.22   jīng   驚

when you're dropped from a hand,   13.6.23   shī   失
what it has, stepping on from this footprint,   13.6.24   zhī   之
A Certain Someone compliantly combing her
loose hair seems to be saying, "this ALSO is as if   13.6.25   ruò   若
startling, making you jump like a horse spooked
by the sound of someone tapping a dog lightly
with a tutoring cane."   13.6.26   jīng   驚

This baby footprint on bamboo-slip pages,   13.7.27   shì   是
by the nitty-gritty, grinding gizzard of a fowl,
that's what it means to say   13.7.28   wèi   謂
"pampered as a favorite concubine in the home
of an emperor dragon crowned with the chisel
used to mark slaves or criminals   13.7.29   chǒng 寵
AND hanging from a cliff above a hand
underneath, shaking, humiliated?   13.7.30   rǔ   辱
A Certain Someone compliantly combing her
loose hair seems to be saying 'this is as if   13.7.31   ruò   若
startling, making you jump like a horse spooked
by the sound of someone tapping a dog lightly
with a tutoring cane.'"   13.7.32   jīng   驚

It doesn't matter if you're the chosen one or you've
been dropped—pregnancy is always startling.

That one—that very one shouldering a weapon—   13.8.33   hé   何
by the nitty-gritty, grinding gizzard of a fowl, what does
that mean to say   13.8.34   wèi   謂

"held in high regard, like when two hands are
wrapped around a person atop cowry-shell-
riches,   13.8.35   guì   貴
this great big person   13.8.36   dà   大
and sick with worry (or worrisomely sick... or
both!), two objects strung together over the
heart,   13.8.37   huàn   患
A Certain Someone compliantly combing her
loose hair seems to be saying 'this is as if   13.8.38   ruò   若
your pregnant self?'"   13.8.39   shēn   身

Counting up on all five fingers, aren't I,   13.9.40   wú   吾
"that place" being intentionally created like any
household gate hewn with an axe,   13.9.41   suǒ   所
cultivating, like a plow,   13.9.42   yǐ   以
        flesh-and-meat-handling Being,   13.9.43   yǒu   有
        this great big person,   13.9.44   dà   大
        sick with worry (or worrisomely sick...
        or both!), two objects strung together
        over the heart?   13.9.45   huàn   患
        This is boiling sugarcane with fire as
        follows!   13.9.46   zhâ   者

While *creating something by hand, carving an
elephant likeness of good fortune and royal
power*,   13.10.47   wéi   為
counting up on all five fingers, aren't I   13.10.48   wú   吾
        flesh-and-meat-handling Being   13.10.49   yǒu   有
        "your pregnant self?"   13.10.50   shēn   身

While *finally reaching, hand-grabbing and
holding onto a person*,   13.11.51   jí   及
counting up on all five fingers, aren't I   13.11.52   wú   吾

the shamanic dancer with animal tails
flowing from her wrists, Not-Having,   13.11.53   wú   無
"your pregnant self?"   13.11.54   shēn   身

Counting up on all five fingers, aren't I   13.11.55   wú   吾
flesh-and-meat-handling Being,   13.11.56   yǒu   有
that one—that very one shouldering a
weapon—   13.11.57   hé   何
sick with worry (or worrisomely sick…
or both!), two objects strung together
over the heart?   13.11.58   huàn   患

*It all just goes with the territory of pregnancy. Whether
gestating as that meat-handling guy or delivering the
baby as that shaman-dancing person woman, you're
sick and worried sick, even when you're a higher-up.*

Anciently, for ten generations, this tapped lightly with a
tutoring cane and left a mark of reason…   13.12.59   yǐ   故
*"when held in high regard, like when two hands are
wrapped* around a person atop cowry-shell-riches,   13.12.60   guì   貴
cultivating, like a plow,   13.12.61   yǐ   以
your pregnant self   13.12.62   shēn   身
creating something by hand, carving an elephant
likeness of good fortune and royal power,   13.12.63   wéi   為
the heavenly from high above this great big person   13.12.64   tiān   天
now here down below,"   13.12.65   xià   下

A Certain Someone compliantly combing her
loose hair seems to be saying "this is as if,   13.13.66   ruò   若
lip-smackingly genuinely   13.13.67   kâ   可

a *strange* great big person exiled to a house in
the east as punishment *but still counted on* to
translate there, *you're trusted with*   13.13.68   jì   寄
    the heavenly from high above this
    great big person   13.13.69   tiān   天
    now here down below."   13.13.70   xià   下

"And when loving, kneeling with your head turned this
way and your heart in your throat,   13.14.71   ài   愛
cultivating, like a plow,   13.14.72   yǐ   以
your pregnant self   13.14.73   shēn   身
creating something by hand, carving an elephant
likeness of good fortune and royal power,   13.14.74   wéi   為
the heavenly from high above this great big person   13.14.75   tiān   天
now here down below,"   13.14.76   xià   下

A Certain Someone compliantly combing her
loose hair seems to be saying "this is as if,   13.15.77   ruò   若
lip-smackingly genuinely   13.15.78   kâ   可
caring for something like a blade of grass with
words from your mouth, *you're trusted with*   13.15.79   tuō   託
    the heavenly from high above this
    great big person   13.15.80   tiān   天
    now here down below."   13.15.81   xià   下

I was both a highly regarded person living in luxury AND
an emotionally vulnerable, deeply caring person, and
she told me that was okay because both made me
worth trusting with this new little spirit once it's born
down below here. Like all pregnant women, I was
grateful for that reassurance.

Chapter 14: I carried on through all of it, and I made it to the critical point. I did the thing. And, then I went a little crazy.

Regarded as by one big eye for a head, kneeling at an altar,

14.1.1   shì   視

what it has, stepping on from this footprint,

14.1.2   zhī   之

    the husk of the initial protective bud casing but not really the true flower of

14.1.3   bù   不

    seen by someone with one big eye for a head…

14.1.4   jiàn   見

    that personal name given in childhood and still whispered by moonlight,

14.2.5   míng   名

    what that's called when issued on a breath from the mouth is

14.2.6   yuē   曰

        "foreign," part of the great barbarian tribe of the east carrying bows, leveling and razing.

14.2.7   yí   夷

Hearing, an ear listening to voices, perhaps heeding, allowing, or handling matters of state,

14.3.8   tīng   聽

what it has, stepping on from this footprint,

14.3.9   zhī   之

    the husk of the initial protective bud casing but not really the true flower of

14.3.10   bù   不

    heard at the two-winged gateway and famously reported on…

14.3.11   wén   聞

    that personal name given in childhood and still whispered by moonlight,

14.4.12   míng   名

    what that's called when issued on a breath from the mouth is

14.4.13   yuē   曰

        "barely there," as sparse as the few interconnecting threads in the

14.4.14   xī   希

gendered head-cloth we wear after
reaching adulthood, rarely seen or
heard.

Rolled around by hand, modeled or monopolized (like a
hand turning a big round spindle over an inch-sized
spot that's as small as that spot on your forearm where
your pulse beats strong),   14.5.15   bó   搏
what it has, stepping on from this footprint,   14.5.16   zhī   之
    the husk of the initial protective bud casing but
    not really the true flower of   14.5.17   bù   不
    The Hand-Picked Gem, like cowry-shell-riches
    discovered along the road...   14.5.18   dé   得

    that personal name given in childhood and still
    whispered by moonlight,   14.6.19   míng   名
    what that's called when issued on a breath
    from the mouth is   14.6.20   yuē   曰
        "trifling," a slight thing, this admired
        beauty wearing a ram's horn headdress
        and stepping slowly with only the left
        leg leading, a tutoring cane lightly
        tapping their hair, combing out or
        "splitting hairs," not having much.   14.6.21   wēi   微

This here—the foot stops a person here on this
footprint!   14.7.22   cǐ   此
These three   14.7.23   sān   三
—this is boiling sugarcane with fire as follows!—   14.7.24   zhâ   者
are the husk of the initial protective bud casing but not
really the true flower of   14.7.25   bù   不
lip-smackingly genuinely   14.7.26   kâ   可

thoroughly delivering, exhausting, arriving at the
extreme (like an arrow stuck in the ground and tapped
lightly with a tutoring cane so as to leave a mark) 14.7.27 zhì 致
     with someone questioning or interrogating the
     empty, quiet, lucky mouth with a soldier's axe
     above it. 14.7.28 jié 詰

Towing the line kept me invisible, so I could reach
delivery without interrogation.

This tapped lightly with a tutoring cane and left a mark
on the solid shield of the past: 14.8.29 gù 故
turbulently blending torrential waters like a river of
insects, muddling along and maybe even stirring up
trouble, joking, 14.8.30 hùn 混
     yet, now you're bearded, 14.8.31 ér 而
     creating something by hand, carving an
     elephant likeness of good fortune and royal
     power, 14.8.32 wéi 為
     The One, 14.8.33 yī 一

what it holds a basket of 14.9.34 qí 其
on top 14.9.35 shàng 上
is the husk of the initial protective bud casing but not
really the true flower of 14.9.36 bù 不
     bright as a blank white acorn stirred like that
     musical instrument resembling an acorn atop
     the wide, parallel side of a tipped blade, lightly
     plucked or hit by hand; 14.9.37 jiǎo 皦

what it holds a basket of 14.10.38 qí 其
now here down below 14.10.39 xià 下

is the husk of the initial protective bud casing but not
really the true flower of
        dark as "the eight earthly branches" phase of
        the waxing moon before it's full (like a tree
        that's upper branches aren't fully grown, not
        yet mature but venturing out, perhaps
        violating, coveting).

*My strategy was to be not too glowy and guitar-shaped
on the surface nor too dim and chubby below. Maybe it
was the best of both worlds; maybe it was the worst.
Probably it was both. But, one thing was for sure, I was
bound by this life that wasn't the real me...*

A skein of silk around a striving toad!
A skein of silk around a striving toad,
the husk of the initial protective bud casing but not
really the true flower of
lip-smackingly genuinely
that personal name given in childhood and still
whispered by moonlight.

*And that was the point. I was able to remain unseen
even under some of the hardest circumstances a human
being can face: war. It wasn't until returning, with
delivery imminent, that I lost the ability to hide my real
identity...*

Walking with a footprint of slowly returning with the
left leg leading the way, doubling back (like the gut) on
one's footprint,
coming back after sweeping troops out of the soil
mound hills

14.10.40	bù	不
14.10.41	mèi	昧
14.11.42	shéng	繩
14.11.43	shéng	繩
14.11.44	bù	不
14.11.45	kâ	可
14.11.46	míng	名
14.12.47	fù	復
14.12.48	guī	歸

to this place and time, oh, black, icy raven sun, | 14.12.49 | yú | 於
the shamanic dancer with animal tails flowing from her | | |
wrists, Not-Having, | 14.12.50 | wú | 無
matter (outside one's body, "cut from the cow" by a | | |
bloodied blade)… | 14.12.51 | wù | 物

    this baby footprint on bamboo-slip pages, — 14.13.52 — shì — 是
    by the nitty-gritty, grinding gizzard of a fowl,
    that was called, — 14.13.53 — wèi — 謂
        "shaman-dancing Not-Having — 14.13.54 — wú — 無
        in this distinctive shape (differently
        formed like the way a piece of chopped
        wood can be sculpted in the shape of a
        dog), — 14.13.55 — zhuàng — 狀
        what it has, stepping on from this
        footprint, it has this, — 14.13.56 — zhī — 之
        this distinctive shape (differently
        formed like the way a piece of chopped
        wood can be sculpted in the shape of a
        dog)." — 14.13.57 — zhuàng — 狀

Shaman-dancing Not-Having — 14.14.58 — wú — 無
matter (outside one's body, "cut from the cow" by a
bloodied blade)… — 14.14.59 — wù — 物
what it has, stepping on from this footprint, — 14.14.60 — zhī — 之
is like an elephant skeleton to a living elephant, bearing
a likeness to something… — 14.14.61 — xiàng — 象

    this baby footprint on bamboo-slip pages, — 14.15.62 — shì — 是
    by the nitty-gritty, grinding gizzard of a fowl,
    that was called, — 14.15.63 — wèi — 謂
        "a heart cut by a heart, elusive and
        difficult to understand, — 14.15.64 — hū — 惚

the heart of a person kneeling with
shining fire over their head, brilliant yet
incomprehensible."   14.15.65   huǎng   恍

*When I came home from war in my advanced condition,
people wondered, "What's up with that guy? He's
shaped like… like, something." Like what, they couldn't
really say. Before I'd avoided being both too bright and
too dim, but now I was both glowing and unreachably
raw.*

In welcoming, a real hero's parade, slowly walking with
the footprint of an admired one, the left leg leading the
way,   14.16.66   yíng   迎
what it had, stepping on from this footprint,   14.16.67   zhī   之
    *was the husk of the initial protective bud casing
    but not really the true flower of*   14.16.68   bù   不
    seen by someone with one big eye for a head,   14.16.69   jiàn   見
        what it holds a basket of,   14.16.70   qí   其
        the face of the loose-haired head buck.   14.16.71   shǒu   首

But "the eye" still didn't recognize the real me.

Accompanying one another single file near soil
mountains, slowly walking with the footprint of a flesh-
and-meat-handling Being, the left leg leading the way,   14.17.72   suí   隨
    what it has, stepping on from this footprint,   14.17.73   zhī   之
    *was the husk of the initial protective bud casing
    but not really the true flower of*   14.17.74   bù   不
    seen by someone with one big eye for a head,   14.17.75   jiàn   見
    what it holds a basket of...   14.17.76   qí   其

    walking slowly with just the left leg
    leading the way, leaving behind this

tiny silk thread footprint like a knot in a
thread, a descendant, at the end.   14.17.77   hòu   後

*Just as when we were walking together, he didn't
notice me even though I was carrying an heir. And the
thing is: he should have. For we had a past…*

A kneeling person, arrested and held, arms
outstretched in handcuffs: 14.18.78   zhí   執
    speaking of the solid shield of the *past*,   14.18.79   gǔ   古
    what it had, stepping on from this footprint,   14.18.80   zhī   之
        was walking with the footprint of the
        loose-haired head buck;   14.18.81   dào   道

this cultivated, like a plow,   14.19.82   yǐ   以
"you, royal sir," with a person kneeling before a pestle
in welcome, managing: 14.19.83   yù   御
    gathering from three sides over this *now*, in
    current times,   14.19.84   jīn   今
    what it has, stepping on from this footprint,   14.19.85   zhī   之
        is flesh-and-meat-handling Being.   14.19.86   yǒu   有

*When I was that wandering head-buck creature, I'd
been arrested.*

*Later, of course I hid out in a cave and emerged with my
Being persona hiding my pregnant self, as I described in
Chapter 1, and that's the secret duality I'd maintained
for months and turned into a very important position
for myself.*

*But now? Well, I was so confident in my higher-up self
and also so exhausted by all these intense events taking*

*place concurrently that perhaps you can understand
what I did next...*

Using that legendary Hybrid Power of a mythical bear-
like animal who has the legs of a deer for
speaking as a great big person to a baby, distinguishing,
imparting, and administering wisdom confidently and
intimately,
  speaking of the solid shield of the *past
  conceiving*, a woman kneeling, happy, speaking
  of gathering herself from three sides,

this baby footprint on bamboo-slip pages,
by the nitty-gritty, grinding gizzard of a fowl, what
that's called,
  is walking with the footprint of the loose-haired
  head buck,
  binding itself with fine silk thread, a particular
  written story or rule.

14.20.87	néng	能
14.20.88	zhī	知
14.20.89	gǔ	古
14.20.90	shǐ	始
14.21.91	shì	是
14.21.92	wèi	謂
14.21.93	dào	道
14.21.94	jì	紀

*I told the king. I did. I told him who I was; I told him
about the pregnancy; I told him everything. And in
doing so, I bound myself in a whole new way by the
truth.*

Chapter 15: My famously calm manner, the truth behind it, and how it helped me achieve my goal

Speaking of the solid shield of the past,
stepping on from this footprint, it had this
traditionally virtuous, offering up a ram's head while
speaking back and forth, tongues waggling,

15.1.1	gǔ	古
15.1.2	zhī	之
15.1.3	shàn	善

creating something by hand, carving an elephant
likeness of good fortune and royal power, 15.1.4 wéi 為
ax-wielding bachelor-soldier-scholar-official appointed
by the emperor 15.1.5 shì 士
—this is boiling sugarcane with fire as follows! 15.1.6 zhâ 者

That "trifling," a slight thing, this admired beauty
wearing a ram's horn headdress and stepping slowly
with only the left leg leading, a tutoring cane lightly
tapping their hair, combing out or "splitting hairs," not
having much, 15.2.7 wēi 微
  was like a young woman kneeling with four tiny
  drops belittled as a rich young master—that
  subtle, ingenious, exquisite aura 15.2.8 miào 妙
  with this hard-to-see structure of a double-
  looped, figure-eight skein of string-dyed-black 15.2.9 xuán 玄
  walking right between two walls, patiently,
  slowly, the left leg leading the way; 15.2.10 tōng 通

that "deep as far water" 15.3.11 shēn 深
  was like the husk of the initial protective bud
  casing but not really the true flower of 15.3.12 bù 不
  lip-smackingly genuinely 15.3.13 kâ 可
  intimately known, speaking of what's gathered
  with a tone from the mouth by a dagger-ax,
  marked and remembered. 15.3.14 shí 識

*I was the emperor's famously virtuous favorite right-
hand-man, humble and deep in appearance, but no one
knew the real me or that my manner was a direct result
of my delicate internal situation... no one except of
course A Certain Someone.*

In fact, that is to say This Grown Man with hairpin and
public courtesy name,   15.4.15   fū   夫
"Oh, YES, Ma'am," says the "short-tailed bird,"   15.4.16   wéi   唯
was the husk of the initial protective bud casing but not
really the true flower of   15.4.17   bù   不
lip-smackingly genuinely   15.4.18   kâ   可
intimately known, and   15.4.19   shí   識

this tapped lightly with a tutoring cane and left a mark
on the solid shield of the past...   15.5.20   gù   故
revolving around themself as a powerful bow
broadening, strengthening, stiff, hard, and compelling
as a rice weevil, like a tiny venomous snake—
thwang!—   15.5.21   qiáng   強
in creating something by hand, carving an elephant
likeness of good fortune and royal power,   15.5.22   wéi   為
          stepping on from this footprint, it had   15.5.23   zhī   之
          an outward public container of private parts,
          like a building housing an important, older man
          who's "got balls," a duke: 15.5.24   róng   容

A content countenance, two hands trading something
for an elephant?   15.6.25   yù   豫
Hmmm—like wind through tree branches!   15.6.26   xī   兮
          A Certain Someone compliantly combing her
          loose hair seems to be saying this is as if   15.6.27   ruò   若
          at the end of the year when things ice up,
          coming at the end like the knot at the end of a
          cord,   15.6.28   dōng   冬
          wading, one foot in front of the other, through
          a watery   15.6.29   shè   涉
          stream.   15.6.30   chuān   川

In the same manner as the unlikely rise of a dog
monkey to the top of the alcohol vat to become chief
of brewing?
Hmmm—like wind through tree branches!
    A Certain Someone compliantly combing her
    loose hair seems to be saying this is as if
    scared—like of a ghost with a stick—of,
    in all four directions,
    the neighboring countries, appealing as the will
    o' wisp light emanating from a corpse
    attracting a kneeling person to a grave.

Respectful, making oneself listen even when someone's
too chatty?
Hmmm—like wind through tree branches!
    What it holds a basket of...
    A Certain Someone compliantly combing her
    loose hair seems to be saying this is as if
    entering a house as a guest like you're the last
    one, sticking out like the knot at the end of a
    cord.

Dissolving, dispersing like water in the city outskirts
where there are so many people?
Hmmm—like wind through tree branches!
    A Certain Someone compliantly combing her
    loose hair seems to be saying this is as if
    freezing stream water,
    what it has, stepping on from this footprint,
    assured, as if by hand-offering a meat tribute at
    an altar, a certain future of

    distinguishing the sight of the opposite, of the
    upside-down version of a running man who will

15.7.31	yóu	猶
15.7.32	xī	兮
15.7.33	ruò	若
15.7.34	wèi	畏
15.7.35	sì	四
15.7.36	lín	鄰
15.8.37	yǎn	儼
15.8.38	xī	兮
15.8.39	qí	其
15.8.40	ruò	若
15.8.41	kè	客
15.9.42	huàn	渙
15.9.43	xī	兮
15.9.44	ruò	若
15.9.45	bīng	冰
15.9.46	zhī	之
15.9.47	jiāng	將

die young, spying on good luck or an emperor's
personal favor—that is, melting.

15.9.48   shì   釋

Plentiful and esteemed as a ram's head at the ancestral
shrine or that thick globe-shaped alloy grain vessel
studded with three sculptural legs and two handles
protruding top and bottom, on each hemisphere, so
they could be taken apart and used as bowls?

15.10.49   dūn   敦

Hmmm—like wind through tree branches!

15.10.50   xī   兮

    What it holds a basket of...

15.10.51   qí   其

    A Certain Someone compliantly combing her
    loose hair seems to be saying this is as if

15.10.52   ruò   若

    that "piece of wood" in the dense, unpolished,
    sticking, natural state of a thicket of oak trees.

15.10.53   pǔ   樸

*I did look abundant, versatile, and ready for
anything in that phase when the cervix was
thick.*

Bright, clear, carefree, and spacious as a yellow sun
shining on a habitable cave in a cliff holding this great
big person with a large belly?

15.11.54   kuàng   曠

Hmmm—like wind through tree branches!

15.11.55   xī   兮

    What it holds a basket of...

15.11.56   qí   其

    A Certain Someone compliantly combing her
    loose hair seems to be saying this is as if

15.11.57   ruò   若

    in a difficult position in a ravine, in an emptied,
    eroded valley mouth between two mountains.

15.11.58   gǔ   谷

*I kept a sunny outlook even though it was a
tenuous time.*

Turbulently blending torrential waters, like a river of
insects, muddling along and maybe even stirring up
trouble, joking?   15.12.59   hùn   混

Hmmm—like wind through tree branches!   15.12.60   xī   兮

      What it holds a basket of...   15.12.61   qí   其

      A Certain Someone compliantly combing her
      loose hair seems to be saying this is as if   15.12.62   ruò   若
      yellow water, like that of the far western sub-
      state *Shū* whose name means "a silkworm
      caterpillar on a hollyhock leaf," that all-seeing
      eye above a wiggly body.   15.12.63   zhuó   濁

*The meconium-tinged water was scary. But I
managed it too.*

Whichever kneeling person using both arms for paying
tribute to an ancestral shrine is fully processing   15.13.64   shú   孰
using that legendary Hybrid Power of a mythical bear-
like animal who has the legs of a deer for   15.13.65   néng   能
yellow water   15.13.66   zhuó   濁
cultivating, like a plow,   15.13.67   yǐ   以
calm peace, the clear blue-green growth of the
sedative cinnabar plant quieting a dispute between two
hands on a plowshare...   15.13.68   jìng   靜

      stepping on from this footprint, they have   15.13.69   zhī   之
      the quiet composure of the left side of the
      royal "I" used by the Shang Dynasty kings,   15.13.70   xú   徐
      the clarity of still bright blue-green water, the
      color resembling the growth of that sedative
      cinnabar plant.   15.13.71   qīng   清

Whichever kneeling person using both arms for paying
tribute to an ancestral shrine is fully processing   15.14.72   shú   孰

using that legendary Hybrid Power of a mythical bear-
like animal who has the legs of a deer for   15.14.73   néng   能
staying calm as a woman sitting on her heels at home   15.14.74   ān   安
cultivating, like a plow,   15.14.75   yǐ   以
enduring through time as a person receiving
moxibustion, that mugwort treatment for cramps,
turning a breech baby, or other health issues,   15.14.76   jiǔ   久
and easily doing work as hard as moving a heavy bag
tied at both ends with the strong force of an arm or
plow...   15.14.77   dòng   動
    stepping on from this footprint, they have   15.14.78   zhī   之
    the quiet composure of the left side of the
    royal "I" used by the Shang Dynasty kings   15.14.79   xú   徐
    sprouting a bud from the ground.   15.14.80   shēng   生

*I stayed calm all the way through labor and, yes, the
birth. I did it!*

*But then, of course, I discovered that the challenge was
only beginning.*

Safeguarding, like carrying a child on one's back   15.15.81   bǎo   保
this here—the foot stops a person here on this
footprint!—   15.15.82   cǐ   此
when walking with the footprint of the loose-haired
head buck?   15.15.83   dào   道
This is boiling sugarcane with fire as follows!   15.15.84   zhâ   者
    It's the husk of the initial protective bud casing
    but not really the true flower of   15.15.85   bù   不
    missing, kneeling with a yawning mouth before
    a ravine eroded between two mountains,
    wanting, lacking,   15.15.86   yù   欲
        full to overflowing your vessel...   15.15.87   yíng   盈

In fact, that is to say This Grown Man with
hairpin and public courtesy name,   15.16.88   fū   夫
"Oh, YES, Ma'am," says the "short-tailed bird,"   15.16.89   wéi   唯
       is the husk of the initial protective bud
       casing but not really the true flower of   15.16.90   bù   不
       full to overflowing your vessel.   15.16.91   yíng   盈

How could I protect the little one when I hadn't really
left before having the baby? How could I be "this guy"
when I was no longer pregnant?

This tapped lightly with a tutoring cane and left a mark
on the solid shield of the past: 15.17.92   gù   故
use that legendary Hybrid Power of a mythical bear-like
animal who has the legs of a deer for   15.17.93   néng   能
grassing over, like fatigued raggedy clothing cut into
rags by tapping lightly with a tutoring cane hiding
under a pair of horizontal grass sprouts,   15.17.94   bì   蔽
       the husk of the initial protective bud casing but
       not really the true flower of   15.17.95   bù   不
       having the look of a freshly chopped hazelnut
       tree axed by that chisel used to mark slaves
       and criminals, like someone newly married,
       recently   15.17.96   xīn   新
       completing, that final "nail" in a weapon on a
       pole.   15.17.97   chéng   成

I used my dual identity and its power to hide what had
happened. The public had to be kept in the dark.

Chapter 16: Post-partum, it all seemed like destiny.
At least I kept telling myself that…

Thoroughly delivering, exhausting, arriving at the
extreme (like an arrow stuck in the ground and tapped
lightly with a tutoring cane so as to leave a mark)   16.1.1   zhì   致
empty, like a tiger head upon a mound,   16.1.2   xū   虛
in the utmost position, a person pressing urgently
against a double-beamed wooden ridgepole that's high
as a tree;   16.1.3   jí   極

hand-defending this building   16.2.4   shǒu   守
with calm peace, the clear blue-green growth of the
sedative cinnabar plant quieting a dispute between two
hands on a plowshare,   16.2.5   jìng   靜
honestly and sincerely as a horse under two bamboo
stalks;   16.2.6   dǔ   篤

and the medicine-dancing-scorpion insect swarm of   16.3.7   wàn   萬
matter (outside one's body, "cut from the cow" by a
bloodied blade)   16.3.8   wù   物
side by side as two arrows on the ground pointing up,   16.3.9   bìng   並
recently, exactly, having immediately folded from one
straight rod into two…   16.3.10   zuò   作

counting up on all five fingers, aren't I   16.4.11   wú   吾
cultivating, like a plow,   16.4.12   yǐ   以
someone with one big eye for a head kneeling on a
stork-like temple or watchtower, keeping lookout for   16.4.13   guān   觀
someone walking with a footprint of slowly *returning*
with the left leg leading the way, doubling back (like
the gut) on one's footprint to   16.4.14   fù   復

the heavenly from high above this great big person
matter (outside one's body, "cut from the cow" by a
bloodied blade)
quick-growing, voluminous and numerous as a pair of
rapeseed plant sprouts ("cloud-grass," that source of
the personal lubricant canola oil),
quick-growing, voluminous and numerous...

a particular one, unusual as the knot coming at the end
of a cord sticking out from a mouth,
walking with a footprint of slowly returning with the
left leg leading the way, doubling back (like the gut) on
one's footprint,
coming back after sweeping troops out of the soil
mound hills to this,
what it holds a basket of,
       the root of the family tree, like an ancestor's
       manhood?

I returned to it all. I went back out with the troops, and
the emperor watched for my return. How did he know
I'd return? Well, he had my little one, who was growing
like a weed.

Coming back after sweeping troops out of the soil
mound hills to this,
the root of the family tree, like an ancestor's manhood,
what that was called when issued on a breath from the
mouth...
       calm peace, the clear blue-green growth of the
       sedative cinnabar plant quieting a dispute
       between two hands on a plowshare.

16.5.15	tiān	天
16.5.16	wù	物
16.5.17	yún	芸
16.5.18	yún	芸
16.6.19	gè	各
16.6.20	fù	復
16.6.21	guī	歸
16.6.22	qí	其
16.6.23	gēn	根
16.7.24	guī	歸
16.7.25	gēn	根
16.7.26	yuē	曰
16.7.27	jìng	靜

This baby footprint on bamboo-slip pages,
by the nitty-gritty, grinding gizzard of a fowl, what that
was called,
someone walking with a footprint of slowly returning
with the left leg leading the way, doubling back (like
the gut) on one's footprint,
       what has to be, destiny like a command from a
       magistrate speaking, joining from three sides
       over a kneeling person.

*It was meant to be. That's what he said, anyway, and
what I agreed to.*

Someone walking with a footprint of slowly returning
with the left leg leading the way, doubling back (like
the gut) on one's footprint to
what has to be, to destiny,
what that's called when issued on a breath from the
mouth...
       the conventional royal administrator wearing a
       men's headcloth as his skirt.

Speaking as a great big person to a baby, distinguishing,
imparting, and administering wisdom confidently and
intimately,
as the conventional royal administrator wearing a
men's headcloth as his skirt,
what that's called when issued on a breath from the
mouth...
       as bright as dawn rising on a crescent moon,
       enlightened.

16.8.28	shì	是
16.8.29	wèi	謂
16.8.30	fù	復
16.8.31	mìng	命
16.9.32	fù	復
16.9.33	mìng	命
16.9.34	yuē	曰
16.9.35	cháng	常
16.10.36	zhī	知
16.10.37	cháng	常
16.10.38	yuē	曰
16.10.39	míng	明

The husk of the initial protective bud casing but
not really the true flower of   16.11.40   bù   不
speaking as a great big person to a baby,
distinguishing, imparting, and administering
wisdom confidently and intimately,   16.11.41   zhī   知
as the conventional royal administrator
wearing a men's headcloth as his skirt...   16.11.42   cháng   常

    improper and willful, reckless, a
    kneeling woman fleeing,   16.12.43   wáng   妄
    recently, exactly, having immediately
    folded from one straight rod into two...   16.12.44   zuò   作
        unlucky as a hole in the ground
        with rock, mud, or bamboo in
        the bottom.   16.12.45   xiōng   凶

*The alternative was horrible: a pit-trap of bad
luck. My thinking was that my return to the
enlightened advisor role would lead to safety.
And I had a plan for what could come next...*

Speaking as a great big person to a baby, distinguishing,
imparting, and administering wisdom confidently and
intimately   16.13.46   zhī   知
as the conventional royal administrator wearing a
men's headcloth as his skirt   16.13.47   cháng   常
    is an outward public container of private parts,
    like a building housing an important, older man
    who's 'got balls,' a duke.   16.13.48   róng   容

An outward public container of private parts, like a
building housing an important, older man who's "got
balls," a duke...   16.14.49   róng   容

only then do you get | 16.14.50 | năi | 乃
    a duke, someone as publicly fair and impartial
    as a high-ranking older man who's "got balls;" | 16.14.51 | gōng | 公

a duke, someone as publicly fair and impartial as a
high-ranking older man who's "got balls…" | 16.15.52 | gōng | 公
only then do you get | 16.15.53 | năi | 乃
    the king with his ceremonial jade axe or crown
    connecting the three levels of heaven, man,
    and earth; | 16.15.54 | wáng | 王

the king with his ceremonial jade axe or crown
connecting the three levels of heaven, man, and earth… | 16.16.55 | wáng | 王
only then do you get | 16.16.56 | năi | 乃
    the heavenly, from high above this great big
    person; | 16.16.57 | tiān | 天

the heavenly, from high above this great big person… | 16.17.58 | tiān | 天
only then do you get | 16.17.59 | năi | 乃
    walking with the footprint of the loose-haired
    head buck. | 16.17.60 | dào | 道

*I needed my little one back before I could head out on
my own again.*

Walking with the footprint of the loose-haired head
buck… | 16.18.61 | dào | 道
only then do you get | 16.18.62 | năi | 乃
    enduring through time as a person receiving
    moxibustion, that mugwort treatment for
    cramps, turning a breech baby, or other health
    issues, | 16.18.63 | jiŭ | 久

and no longer, as if diving into the water, knife in hand,
it's gone,
your pregnant self...
  you're the husk of the initial protective bud
  casing but not really the true flower of
  endangered as human remains, spoken of
  privately, revolving around yourself.

*My thinking was that this role would get me full access
to the king and therefore my little heavenly one. And
only then could I go out again as a wild free thing and
survive.*

Chapter 17: But my real progression was different. It went in phases...

The quite greatest biggest person—period!—
on top:
  now here down below
  speaking as a great big person to a baby,
  distinguishing, imparting, and administering
  wisdom confidently and intimately...
    flesh-and-meat-handling Being,
    stepping on from this footprint, it had
    this.

What it held a basket of
next (a little more deficient and lacking, like the second
yawn):
  an intimate one, a beloved whose suffering,
  like from that chisel used to mark slaves and

16.19.64	mò	沒
16.19.65	shēn	身
16.19.66	bù	不
16.19.67	dài	殆
17.1.1	tài	太
17.1.2	shàng	上
17.1.3	xià	下
17.1.4	zhī	知
17.1.5	yǒu	有
17.1.6	zhī	之
17.2.7	qí	其
17.2.8	cì	次
17.2.9	qīn	親

criminals, you see up close, with one big eye
for a head…

      yet, now you're bearded,   17.2.10   ér   而
      receiving praise, famously spoken of as
      participating with someone, a "biting
      tooth" lifted by two hands onto strong
      shoulders, perhaps interfering with or
      perhaps supporting,   17.2.11   yù   譽
      stepping on from this footprint, it had
      this.   17.2.12   zhī   之

What it held a basket of   17.3.13   qí   其
next: 17.3.14   cì   次
      scared—like of a ghost with a stick—   17.3.15   wèi   畏
      stepping on from this footprint, it had this.   17.3.16   zhī   之

What it held a basket of   17.4.17   qí   其
next: 17.4.18   cì   次
      ridiculed and disgraced as a person whose lush
      flourishing sprouts out of a kneeling, suckling
      woman,   17.4.19   wǔ   侮
      stepping on from this footprint, it had this.   17.4.20   zhī   之

*On top, I simply was known as the admired, competent
logistics-handling guy. Then, having revealed
everything to the king, we became intimate, and he
lavished me with adoration! But then it got scary. In the
end, he humiliated me. What was I to do? Here's the
lesson I learned:*

If giving one's word to a person…   17.5.21   xìn   信
the husk of the initial protective bud casing but not
really the true flower of   17.5.22   bù   不

fully enough, like the entire leg as well as the footprint?

Hmmm—like wind through tree branches!
    Then flesh-and-meat-handling Being…
    the husk of the initial protective bud casing but
    not really the true flower of
    giving one's word to a person.
    Hmmm—like wind through tree branches!

Distant and leisurely, like a person having water gently
poured over their back, purifying their heart?
Hmmm—like wind through tree branches!
    Then what it holds a basket of…
    held in high regard (as two hands are wrapped
    around a person atop cowry-shell-riches)
    speaking out loud.

Sometimes the truth doesn't work. Sometimes, the less
known, less intimate, and more relaxed person's words
are more respected. And safer. And then…

Laboring with the force of a blade and the work of
one's arm or a plow
completed, that final "nail" in a weapon on a pole,
    one's task, what one does with a weapon, flag,
    or pen in hand,
    is fulfilled, slowly walking with the footprint of
    post-harvest time after dividing up the pigs, the
    left leg leading the way.

Then I could finish my work. And…

Regarding a hundred

17.5.23	zú	足
17.5.24	xī	兮
17.5.25	yǒu	有
17.5.26	bù	不
17.5.27	xìn	信
17.5.28	xī	兮
17.6.29	yōu	悠
17.6.30	xī	兮
17.6.31	qí	其
17.6.32	guì	貴
17.6.33	yán	言
17.7.34	gōng	功
17.7.35	chéng	成
17.7.36	shì	事
17.7.37	suì	遂
17.8.38	bǎi	百

family names that a kneeling woman sprouts from the
ground,   17.8.39   xìng   姓
what gossip says, comparing two people like there was
something oh so sweet in their mouth...   17.8.40   jiē   皆
        by the nitty-gritty, grinding gizzard of a fowl,
        what that's called is: 17.8.41   wèi   謂
        I, holding a rake-like weapon to defend myself
        and my opinion,   17.8.42   wǒ   我
        myself personally, right on the nose   17.8.43   zì   自
        accomplishing this thus, as naturally as dog
        meat over a fire.   17.8.44   rán   然

*You remember gossip: it had some things to say about
the baby before he was even born, back in Chapter 2,
sparking this whole journey that I just completed. As far
as what everyone says now about this lineage? I myself,
as myself, accomplished that.*

Chapter 18: A review of the slippery slope I'd travelled

When this great big person   18.1.1   dà   大
walking with the footprint of the loose-haired head
buck   18.1.2   dào   道
collapsed like a house shot by a bow launching—
thwang!—leveling a pair of grass sprouts with one's
feet as effectively as if by hand with a halberd,   18.1.3   fèi   廢
        flesh-and-meat-handling Being   18.1.4   yǒu   有
        was a kernel of humanity—a person seated
        over not just one but two, a different *èr*—   18.1.5   rén   仁
        sacrificing a ram with that rake-like weapon we
        use to defend ourselves and our opinions,
        righteous.   18.1.6   yì   義

When bright, intelligent wisdom, having hand-swept
one's heart with a broom of two bamboo sprouts,   18.2.7   huì   慧
oh, so very pleasantly speaking with that wise
knowledge passed on from a great big person to a
baby, as if something sweet in the mouth,   18.2.8   zhì   智
stepped out of their cave,   18.2.9   chū   出
  flesh-and-meat-handling Being   18.2.10   yǒu   有
  was this great big person   18.2.11   dà   大
  fronting the hand-making of an elephant—the
  creating happening right behind them, out of
  sight.   18.2.12   wâi   僞

When six   18.3.13   liù   六
intimate ones, beloveds whose suffering, like from that
chisel used to mark slaves and criminals, you see up
close with one big eye for a head,   18.3.14   qīn   親
were the husk of the initial protective bud casing but
not really the true flower of   18.3.15   bù   不
warming, wetting, and stickily kneading together,
harmonizing like breath blown into a reed-pipe mouth
organ,   18.3.16   hé   和
  flesh-and-meat-handling Being   18.3.17   yǒu   有
  did their filial duty as a loose-haired elder
  leaning over a baby, filled with piety or, at
  times, mourning,   18.3.18   xiào   孝
  benevolent as a mother, two loops of string-
  dyed-black over the heart.   18.3.19   cí   慈

When our domestic enclave, defended by a weapon on
a pole,   18.4.20   guó   國
this home, complete with a pig under the roof,   18.4.21   jiā   家
darkened as the sun bowing down to the ground,   18.4.22   hūn   昏

trying to govern in chaos, two people disentangling a
roll of threads using their hands with the help of a
comb or beater,

    flesh-and-meat-handling Being
    was a centered heart, like that drum with a
    flagpole placed in the middle of a field to
    gather the people,
    casting their eye down, humble, subjecting like
    a slave, vassal, or servile government official.

comb or beater,	18.4.23	luàn	亂
flesh-and-meat-handling Being	18.4.24	yǒu	有
gather the people,	18.4.25	zhōng	忠
a slave, vassal, or servile government official.	18.4.26	chén	臣

*At every step, I used my Being identity to do everything
I could, and I ended up a servile vassal.*

Chapter 19: Now what?

After slicing apart, like a blade halving each strand of a
pair of silk threads,

    the ideal grounded sage known for his civilian
    petition to authority, standing straight,
    speaking, and being listened to,
and tossing out, two hands throwing a baby from a
basket,

    oh, so very pleasantly speaking with that wise
    knowledge passed on from a great big person
    to a baby, as if something sweet in the mouth...

    one of our folk, the people enslaved by blinding
    with a dagger,
    reaped benefits in the manner of a sharp-
    edged blade slicing grain
        a hundred

pair of silk threads,	19.1.1	jué	絕
speaking, and being listened to,	19.1.2	shèng	聖
basket,	19.1.3	qì	棄
to a baby, as if something sweet in the mouth...	19.1.4	zhì	智
with a dagger,	19.2.5	mín	民
edged blade slicing grain	19.2.6	lì	利
a hundred	19.2.7	bǎi	百

fold, again and again, turning one's
back on another as in betrayal, spitting
out the words, "just the husk, not really
the inner flower!"   19.2.8   bèi   倍

After slicing apart   19.3.9   jué   絕
    a kernel of humanity—a person seated over
    not just one but two, a different *èr*—   19.3.10   rén   仁
and tossing out   19.3.11   qì   棄
    sacrificing a ram with that rake-like weapon we
    use to defend ourselves and our opinions,
    righteous...   19.3.12   yì   義

    one of our folk, the people enslaved by blinding
    with a dagger,   19.4.13   mín   民
    was someone walking with a footprint of slowly
    returning with the left leg leading the way,
    doubling back (like the gut) on one's footprint
    to   19.4.14   fù   復
        doing their filial duty as a loose-haired
        elder leaning over a baby, filled with
        piety or, at times, mourning,   19.4.15   xiào   孝
        benevolent as a mother, two loops of
        string-dyed-black over the heart!   19.4.16   cí   慈

        *Like in that slippery slope I described
        last chapter.*

After slicing apart   19.5.17   jué   絕
    the craftiness of a bladed tool on exhaled air   19.5.18   qiǎo   巧
and tossing out   19.5.19   qì   棄
    reaping benefits in the manner of a sharp-
    edged blade slicing grain...   19.5.20   lì   利

spitting into a bowl like in an oath among
robbers, "thick as thieves,"   19.6.21   dào   盗
used a weapon on a pole to harm that
sacrificial blade-and-cauldron-like ritual
regulation, like an insect that eats at the joints
and roots of a plant, destroying   19.6.22   zéi   賊
    the shamanic dancer with animal tails
    flowing from her wrists, Not-Having,   19.6.23   wú   無
    and flesh-and-meat-handling Being!   19.6.24   yǒu   有

This here—the foot stops a person here on this
footprint—these   19.7.25   cǐ   此
three?   19.7.26   sān   三
This is boiling sugarcane with fire as follows!   19.7.27   zhâ   者
Cultivating, like a plow,   19.7.28   yǐ   以
creating something by hand, carving an elephant
likeness of good fortune and royal power   19.7.29   wéi   為
while covering with this pattern, like a tattoo on the
chest of a great big man,   19.7.30   wén   文
    is the husk of the initial protective bud casing
    but not really the true flower of   19.7.31   bù   不
    fully enough, like the whole leg as well as the
    footprint.   19.7.32   zú   足

This tapped lightly with a tutoring cane and left a mark
on the solid shield of the past: 19.8.33   gù   故
when someone is controlling, joining together from
three sides over a kneeling person and ordering an
action or perhaps sending off to somewhere,   19.8.34   lìng   令
flesh-and-meat-handling Being,   19.8.35   yǒu   有
    and "that place" being intentionally created,
    like any household gate hewn with an axe,   19.8.36   suǒ   所

is joining and submitting to the category to
which they were born (the most recent or "tail-
end" person, "a silkworm caterpillar on a
hollyhock leaf," as we call the *Shǔ* province);   19.8.37   shǔ   屬

when someone with one big eye for a head is seeing   19.9.38   jiàn   見
plain, unprocessed white silk being braided by two
hands,   19.9.39   sù   素
    and it's being bundled all up together in both
    arms into   19.9.40   bào   抱
    that "piece of wood" in the dense, unpolished,
    sticking, natural state of a thicket of oak trees;   19.9.41   pǔ   樸

then someone is belittling, considering to be
insignificant as four tiny dots like a young master's
youthful period   19.10.42   shǎo   少
your personal concerns, turning about your own
private grain supply,   19.10.43   sī   私
    and the loose-haired head buck who
    differentiates right from wrong is kneeling in a
    house like a widow, *alone,*   19.10.44   guǎ   寡
    and goes missing, kneeling with a yawning
    mouth before a ravine eroded between two
    mountains, wanting, lacking.   19.10.45   yù   欲

*I was already missing, you could say. I needed
to leave, you could say.*

Chapter 20: In which I contemplate leaving my home life and the two most important people to me, and I get very sad

After slicing apart, like a blade halving each strand of a
pair of silk threads,   20.1.1   jué   絕
learning and understanding with divination or tally
marks held between one's hands and a child safe
beneath a roof,   20.1.2   xué   學
> the shamanic dancer with animal tails flowing
> from her wrists, Not-Having,   20.1.3   wú   無
> is grieving, their heart under the moon inside
> the backward footprint of returning.   20.1.4   yōu   憂

"Oh YES, Ma'am," says the "short-tailed bird,"   20.2.5   wéi   唯
what it has, stepping on from this footprint,   20.2.6   zhī   之
is participating with (a "biting tooth" lifted by a pair of
hands onto strong shoulders, perhaps interfering with
or perhaps supporting)   20.2.7   yǔ   與
"Oh NO... that familiar one, that big soil mountain that
tastes lip-smackingly genuinely of the big soil mound I
know,"   20.2.8   ē   阿

and like a seen tree and the eye seeing it (or like a well-
tended lord and his attentive attendant), when taken
together, they create this singular phenomenon...   20.3.9   xiāng   相
> leaving, a person with a cave mouth between
> their legs,   20.3.10   qù   去
> two little silk threads separated by the sword of
> a garrison guard, so, so near...   20.3.11   jǐ   幾
> > that very one shouldering a weapon.   20.3.12   hé   何

The traditionally *virtuous*, offering up a ram's head
while speaking back and forth, tongues waggling,   20.4.13 shàn 善
what it has, stepping on from this footprint,   20.4.14 zhī   之
is participating with (a "biting tooth" lifted by a pair of
hands onto strong shoulders, perhaps interfering with
or perhaps supporting)   20.4.15 yǔ   與
a *tomb constructed over the heart*,   20.4.16 è   惡

and together they create this singular phenomenon...   20.5.17 xiāng 相
    leaving   20.5.18 qù   去
    A Certain Someone compliantly combing her
    loose hair who seems to be saying "this is as
    if..."   20.5.19 ruò   若
        that very one shouldering a weapon.   20.5.20 hé   何

That person,   20.6.21 rén   人
what it has, stepping on from this footprint, it has this: 20.6.22 zhī   之
"that place" being intentionally created like any
household gate hewn with an axe   20.6.23 suǒ   所
is scared—like of a ghost with a stick.   20.6.24 wèi   畏

Who could blame me...

It is the husk of the initial protective bud casing but not
really the true flower of   20.7.25 bù   不
lip-smackingly genuinely   20.7.26 kâ   可
the husk of the initial protective bud casing but not
really the true flower of   20.7.27 bù   不
scared—like of a ghost with a stick.   20.7.28 wèi   畏

The choice left me terrified deep in my womb.

*Meanwhile A Certain Someone was observing me and
what I said (my words are in quotation marks below)
and had her own explanation of my underlying
situation, behavior, and emotions.*

"A desolate wasteland under a pair of grass sprouts
atop the watery uncultivated land of the lost dead."   20.8.29   huāng   荒
    Hmmm—like wind through tree branches!   20.8.30   xī   兮
    What it holds a basket of   20.8.31   qí   其
    is like a tree whose top branches aren't yet
    fully grown, not yet   20.8.32   wèi   未
    really in the middle of it like a person with a
    pole over their shoulders, one thing on either
    end, their head in the center.   20.8.33   yāng   央
        I say, "Oh, indeed, that hurts, a weapon
        on a pole wounding sprouting seeds
        and talents."   20.8.34   zāi   哉

       She could be so cutting!

The sun, shining down like an eye on the people, sees
all this, sees   20.9.35   zhòng   眾
that person,   20.9.36   rén   人
bright as the flame of a healthy fetus, nourished like a
beautiful broad chin...   20.9.37   xí   熙
bright   20.9.38   xí   熙

as if you're a woman doing as told, like   20.10.39   rú   如
enjoying a tribute offering at the ancestral shrine, a
baby, a mouth, a cap on it...   20.10.40   xiang   享
    "the quite greatest biggest person—period!—   20.10.41   tài   太
    a sacrificial animal in a pen;"   20.10.42   láo   牢

as if you're a woman doing as told,
vital and alive as a pair of grass sprouts sprouting at
camp in the spring sunshine…
        "ascending as one succeeding in imperial
        exams, left and right feet reversed, stepping up
        on a bean-shaped food container,
        a lookout tower from which a person can shoot
        an arrow."

"I, holding a rake-like weapon to defend myself and my
opinion,
am alone as a dog, the last one, a 'silkworm caterpillar
on a hollyhock leaf,' as we call the *Shǔ* province,
mooring in tranquil water, clear and blank as a little
white acorn."
        Hmmm—like wind through tree branches!
        What it holds a basket of
        is like a tree whose top branches aren't yet
        fully grown, not yet
        an omen, the cracks on a divination shell…

        a kneeling woman with breasts doing as told
        and an infant, a kneeling young mother's
        wealth just as surely as two cowry-like riches
        around her neck,
        a baby son that still has an open fontanelle,
        what it has, stepping on from this footprint, it
        has this:
        like a tree whose top branches aren't yet fully
        grown, not yet
        a baby animal, giggling.

20.11.43	rú	如
20.11.44	chūn	春
20.11.45	dēng	登
20.11.46	tái	臺
20.12.47	wǒ	我
20.12.48	dú	獨
20.12.49	bó	泊
20.12.50	xī	兮
20.12.51	qí	其
20.12.52	wèi	未
20.12.53	zhǎo	兆
20.13.54	rú	如
20.13.55	yīng	嬰
20.13.56	ér	兒
20.13.57	zhī	之
20.13.58	wèi	未
20.13.59	hái	孩

"That sounds like any young woman with a small infant younger than, say three or four months," she said.

"A worn out person, backed by a figure-eight skein of
silk-dyed-black and the soil margin between three
croplands, lazy or perhaps fatigued, maybe bound
despite being innocent... 20.14.60 lèi 儽
a worn out person." 20.14.61 lèi 儽
Hmmm—like wind through tree branches! 20.14.62 xī 兮
A Certain Someone compliantly combing her
loose hair seems to be saying this is as if 20.14.63 ruò 若
the shaman-dancing Not-Having 20.14.64 wú 無
"place" being intentionally created like any
household gate hewn with an axe, 20.14.65 suǒ 所
coming back after sweeping troops out of the
soil mound hills. 20.14.66 guī 歸

She noted my level of fatigue was like that time when I'd been returning from war in Chapter 14, very pregnant.

The sun, shining down like an eye on the people, sees
all this, sees 20.15.67 zhòng 眾
regarding that person: 20.15.68 rén 人
gossip, comparing two people like there was something
oh so sweet in their mouth, said... 20.15.69 jiē 皆
flesh-and-meat-handling Being 20.15.70 yǒu 有
has leftover excess food remains in their house, 20.15.71 yú 餘

yet now you're bearded... 20.16.72 ér 而
"I, holding a rake-like weapon to defend myself and my
opinion, 20.16.73 wǒ 我

am alone as a dog!"
    A Certain Someone compliantly combing her
loose hair seems to be saying this is as if
walking with the footprint of someone slowly
leaving behind cowry-like riches after *dying*,
the left leg leading the way with two hands are
wrapped around them, dragging them off.

Despite have more than enough, I was whining.
I sounded like I was dying, she noted.

"I, holding a rake-like weapon to defend myself and my
opinion,
have a heart like that trampling monkey with the head
of a ghost!"
    That person,
    stepping on from this footprint, has this
    heart
    —yes, that too, oh female funnel!
        I say, "Oh, indeed, that hurts, a weapon
        on a pole wounding sprouting seeds
        and talents."

"Muddled and murky as water made turbid in the camp
or village...
muddled and murky!"
    Hmmm—like wind through tree branches!

In the common practices of the people from
that difficult position in the valley between two
mountains,
    that person,

20.16.74	dú	獨
20.16.75	ruò	若
20.16.76	yí	遺
20.17.77	wǒ	我
20.17.78	yú	愚
20.17.79	rén	人
20.17.80	zhī	之
20.17.81	xīn	心
20.17.82	yâ	也
20.17.83	zāi	哉
20.18.84	dùn	沌
20.18.85	dùn	沌
20.18.86	xī	兮
20.19.87	sú	俗
20.19.88	rén	人

is bright, bright as a blade-like imperial
summons...   20.19.89   zhāo   昭
bright.   20.19.90   zhāo   昭

"I, holding a rake-like weapon to defend myself and my
opinion,
                                                 20.20.91   wǒ   我
alone as a dog,   20.20.92   dú   獨
am darkening as the sun bowing down to the ground...   20.20.93   hūn   昏
darkening!"   20.20.94   hūn   昏

In the common practices of the people from
that difficult position in the valley between two
mountains,   20.21.95   sú   俗
that person,   20.21.96   rén   人
is carefully discerning, studying at home,
making a meat offering by hand at an altar...   20.21.97   chá   察
carefully discerning.   20.21.98   chá   察

"I, holding a rake-like weapon to defend myself and my
opinion,
                                                 20.22.99   wǒ   我
alone as a dog,   20.22.100   dú   獨
have my heart right in the middle of the two-winged
gateway, dark and melancholy...   20.22.101   mèn   悶
dark and melancholy!"   20.22.102   mèn   悶

A person talking and talking, looking upward at
a person atop a cliff with a habitable cave by
the rippling water, calmly indifferent to fame
and fortune...   20.23.103   dàn   澹
Hmmm—like wind through tree branches!   20.23.104   xī   兮
What it holds a basket of,   20.23.105   qí   其
A Certain Someone compliantly combing her
loose hair seems to be saying, is as if   20.23.106   ruò   若

a lushness like that of a river of new life
sprouting from a nursing mother, like the
ocean.   20.23.107   hǎi   海

*A Certain Someone made a diagnosis: I was
pregnant. Again. While I still was nursing my
firstborn.*

Wafting with the wind in a high place, drifting
like three insects blowing below a
commonplace bucket between two aligned
wings and a couple people with two strands of
hair hanging down in front...   20.24.108   liáo   飂
Hmmm—like wind through tree branches!   20.24.109   xī   兮
    A Certain Someone compliantly
    combing her loose hair seems to be
    saying this is as if   20.24.110   ruò   若
    shaman-dancing Not-Having   20.24.111   wú   無
    is halting right here in this footprint.   20.24.112   zhǐ   止

The sun, shining down like an eye on the people, sees
all this, sees   20.25.113   zhòng   眾
regarding that person: 20.25.114   rén   人
gossip, comparing two people like there was something
oh so sweet in their mouth, said...   20.25.115   jiē   皆
    flesh-and-meat-handling Being,   20.25.116   yǒu   有
    this is what it's cultivating, like a plow,   20.25.117   yǐ   以

    yet now you're bearded...   20.26.118   ér   而
    "I, holding a rake-like weapon to defend myself
    and my opinion,   20.26.119   wǒ   我
    alone as a dog..."   20.26.120   dú   獨

obstinate as a head above the kneeling
loose-haired wild head buck...   20.26.121   wán   頑
like how a person and a turned fetus,
side-by-side, resemble one another,
like   20.26.122   sì   似
a lowly country person, kneeling,
receiving from the granary, corralled
on all sides;   20.26.123   bǐ   鄙

"I, holding a rake-like weapon to defend myself
and my opinion,   20.27.124   wǒ   我
alone as a dog..."   20.27.125   dú   獨
        a person wearing a mask, hiding   20.27.126   yì   異
        in this place and time, oh, black, icy
        raven sun: 20.27.127   yú   於
        that person;   20.27.128   rén   人

yet now you're bearded...   20.28.129   ér   而
held in high regard, like when two hands are
wrapped around a person atop cowry-shell-
riches   20.28.130   guì   貴
eating, mouth over a bowl of rice on a stand   20.28.131   shí   食
suckling, a woman kneeling with breasts full of
milk.   20.28.132   mǔ   母

So, there I was, moping, feeling alone, but still
in my fancy position, nursing my little one.

Chapter 21: Here's what staying did to me. Again

A profound unimpeded fontanelle-type opening, "Cave	21.1.1	kǒng	孔
Dé," walking with the footprint of someone who's in			
alignment (eyes looking forward, directly over the heart,			
left leg slowly leading the way),	21.1.2	dé	德
stepping on from this footprint, it had	21.1.3	zhī	之
an outward public container of private parts, like a			
building housing an important, older man who's "got			
balls," a duke,	21.1.4	róng	容
and "oh, YES, Ma'am," says the "short-tailed bird,"	21.2.5	wéi	唯
walking with the footprint of the loose-haired head			
buck...	21.2.6	dào	道
this baby footprint on bamboo-slip pages,	21.2.7	shì	是
it was *following*, slowly walking directly after			
another person in that footprint, the left leg			
leading the way, straightening up, straightening			
things out for "nailing" that first footstep of a			
journey or campaign.	21.2.8	cóng	從

*Remember at the end of Chapter 10, we named the
daily logistics of my complex double life, "Dé." You
could say that it became my opening, my hidden home
with the outside appearance of royalty. But don't forget
that, originally, it followed the Dào, the free, wandering
buck phase of my life.*

Walking with the footprint of the loose-haired head			
buck,	21.3.9	dào	道
stepping on from this footprint, had this	21.3.10.	zhī	之
creating something by hand, carving an elephant			
likeness of good fortune and royal power,	21.3.11	wéi	為

matter (outside one's body, "cut from the cow" by a
bloodied blade)...   21.3.12   wù   物

    "Oh, YES, Ma'am," says the "short-tailed bird,"   21.4.13   wéi   唯
    the heart of a person kneeling with shining fire
    over their head, brilliant yet incomprehensible;   21.4.14   huǎng   恍
    "Oh, YES, Ma'am," says the "short-tailed bird,"   21.4.15   wéi   唯
    a heart cut by a heart, elusive and difficult to
    understand.   21.4.16   hū   惚

A heart cut by a heart, elusive and difficult to
understand?   21.5.17   hū   惚
Hmmm—like wind through tree branches!   21.5.18   xī   兮
    The heart of a person kneeling with shining fire
    over their head, brilliant yet incomprehensible?   21.5.19   huǎng   恍
    Hmmm—like wind through tree branches!   21.5.20   xī   兮

    What that held a basket of   21.6.21   qí   其
    in the center, that drum with a flagpole placed
    in the middle of a field to gather the people
    and detect wind,   21.6.22   zhōng   中
    flesh-and-meat-handling Being: 21.6.23   yǒu   有
        like an elephant skeleton to a living
        elephant, bearing a likeness to
        something.   21.6.24   xiàng   象

The heart of a person kneeling with shining fire over
their head, brilliant yet incomprehensible?   21.7.25   huǎng   恍
Hmmm—like wind through tree branches!   21.7.26   xī   兮
    A heart cut by a heart, elusive and difficult to
    understand?   21.7.27   hū   惚
    Hmmm—like wind through tree branches!   21.7.28   xī   兮

What that held a basket of   21.8.29   qí   其
in the center,   21.8.30   zhōng   中
flesh-and-meat-handling Being: 21.8.31   yǒu   有
        matter (outside one's body, "cut from
        the cow" by a bloodied blade).   21.8.32   wù   物

Profoundly secluded behind the two-winged flap
covering a cave, harboring the strength of an arm, a
bladed tool, or a plow, caring for an infant as fragile as
one fine silk thread, hard to see, dim and quiet?   21.9.33   yǎo   窈
Hmmm—like wind through tree branches!   21.9.34   xī   兮
        A cover over the sun and two hands below,
        darkly profound?   21.9.35   míng   冥
        Hmmm—like wind through tree branches!   21.9.36   xī   兮

What that held a basket of   21.10.37   qí   其
in the center,   21.10.38   zhōng   中
flesh-and-meat-handling Being: 21.10.39   yǒu   有
        a strong essence or soul, like polished
        raw rice, seminal fluid, or spring's blue-
        green lush ripening of the sedative
        cinnabar plant.   21.10.40   jīng   精

        What that held a basket of,   21.11.41   qí   其
        a strong essence or soul, like polished
        raw rice, seminal fluid, or spring's blue-
        green lush ripening of the sedative
        cinnabar plant: 21.11.42   jīng   精
                pairing like one-half of a
                double-yoked harness as
                pleasant as something sweet in
                the mouth and therefore extra   21.11.43   shèn   甚

genuinely getting into it, like
using a fork to get food right
from the cauldron.   21.11.44   zhēn   真

What that held a basket of   21.12.45   qí   其
in the center,   21.12.46   zhōng   中
flesh-and-meat-handling Being: 21.12.47   yǒu   有
giving one's word to a person.   21.12.48   xìn   信

*But telling the truth was exactly what I determined to
be unwise, back in Chapter 17.*

Myself personally, right on the nose,   21.13.49   zì   自
speaking of the solid shield of the <u>past</u>   21.13.50   gǔ   古
finally reaching, hand-grabbing, and holding
onto a person,   21.13.51   jí   及
gathering from three sides over this <u>now</u>, in
current times...   21.13.52   jīn   今

what that held a basket of,   21.14.53   qí   其
that personal name, given in childhood and still
whispered by moonlight: 21.14.54   míng   名
the husk of the initial protective bud
casing but not really the true flower of   21.14.55   bù   不
leaving, a person with a cave mouth
between their legs.   21.14.56   qù   去

*When I finally got a hold of what I'd wanted, the real
me couldn't seem to leave.*

This cultivated, like a plow,   21.15.57   yǐ   以
a person smiling, exhaling, exchanging through the
two-winged gateway, experiencing and reviewing.   21.15.58   yuè   閱

The sun, shining down like an eye on the
people, saw all this, saw
a "Respected Father," a hand holding a working
stone blade axe.   21.15.59 zhòng 眾

   21.15.60 fù 父

Counting up on all five fingers, aren't I 21.16.61 wú 吾
that one, that very one shouldering a weapon, 21.16.62 hé 何
cultivating, like a plow, 21.16.63 yǐ 以
speaking as a great big person to a baby, distinguishing,
imparting, and administering wisdom confidently and
intimately? 21.16.64 zhī 知
The sun, shining down like an eye on the
people, sees all this, sees 21.16.65 zhòng 眾
a "Respected Father," a hand holding a working
stone blade axe, 21.16.66 fù 父
stepping on from this footprint, had this, 21.16.67 zhī 之
distinctive shape (differently formed
like the way a piece of chopped wood
can be sculpted in the shape of a dog). 21.16.68 zhuàng 狀
I say, "Oh, indeed, that hurts, a weapon
on a pole wounding sprouting seeds
and talents." 21.16.69 zāi 哉

This is cultivating, like a plow, 21.17.70 yǐ 以
this here—the foot stops a person here on this
footprint! 21.17.71 cǐ 此

*That's what intimate truth-telling got me: that
"distinctive shape," which you remember from Chapter
14 when I came home from war about to deliver. Yes,
again.*

**Chapter 24: But this time around, staying
can't serve me the same way it did before,
because this time I am known.**

*[In the oldest known versions, what's now called
Chapter 24 was here, after Chapter 21.]*

A person on tiptoes	24.1.1	qǐ	企
—this is boiling sugarcane with fire as follows!—	24.1.2	zhâ	者
is the husk of the initial false guard-petals but			
not really the true flower of	24.1.3	bù	不
a person standing straight up on the ground;	24.1.4	lì	立

overstepping, straddling, like the full leg-cut of an			
animal, fully enough, this great big person on exhaled			
air, extravagantly good-looking	24.2.5	kuà	跨
—this is boiling sugarcane with fire as follows!—	24.2.6	zhâ	者
is the husk of the initial false guard-petals but			
not really the true flower of	24.2.7	bù	不
being out in public at the crossroads, being			
good, doing one's work.	24.2.8	xíng	行

As myself personally, right on the nose,	24.3.9	zì	自
seen by someone with one big eye for a head	24.3.10	jiàn	見
—this is boiling sugarcane with fire as follows!—	24.3.11	zhâ	者
I'm the husk of the initial false guard-petals but			
not really the true flower of	24.3.12	bù	不
as bright as dawn rising on a crescent moon,			
enlightened;	24.3.13	míng	明

as myself personally, right on the nose,	24.4.14	zì	自
this baby footprint on bamboo-slip pages,	24.4.15	shì	是
—this is boiling sugarcane with fire as follows!—	24.4.16	zhâ	者

I'm the husk of the initial false guard-petals but
not really the true flower of   24.4.17   bù   不
shining forth as obviously clear and
"enlightened" as the hair on a person standing
on the ground in the early morning sun over
the thorny jujube plant that's used for
insomnia and contraception and causes
midterm miscarriages;   24.4.18   zhāng   彰

as myself personally, right on the nose,   24.5.19   zì   自
beheading a person with a weapon on a pole   24.5.20   fá   伐
—this is boiling sugarcane with fire as follows!—   24.5.21   zhâ   者
    I'm the shamanic dancer with animal tails
    flowing from her wrists, Not-Having,   24.5.22   wú   無
    laboring with the force of a blade and the work
    of one's arm or a plow;   24.5.23   gōng   功

and as myself personally, right on the nose,   24.6.24   zì   自
gathering together from three sides over a kneeling
person with a spear as a magistrate, commanding   24.6.25   jīn   矜
—this is boiling sugarcane with fire as follows!—   24.6.26   zhâ   者
    I'm the husk of the initial false guard-petals but
    not really the true flower of   24.6.27   bù   不
    lengthening as long as hair that has to be tied
    with a brooch, like a loose-haired old man.   24.6.28   zhǎng   長

What it holds a basket of,   24.7.29   qí   其
the existing sprouting of seedlings and talents, here on
earth, of   24.7.30   zài   在
walking with the footprint of the loose-haired head
buck   24.7.31   dào   道
—yes, that too, oh "female funnel!"—   24.7.32   yâ   也

what that's called when issued on a breath from the
mouth: 24.7.33   yuē   曰

having leftover excess food in the house,   24.8.34   yú   餘
but eating (mouth over a bowl of rice on a stand); or   24.8.35   shí   食
        marrying a woman for their family riches and
        living there (playing around, tapping lightly
        with a tutoring cane a feathered headdress
        who died before taking the throne and
        therefore had no posthumous name, with
        superfluous cowry-like riches)   24.8.36   zhuì   贅
        but shaping as finely and level as two shields
        side by side with measuring lines of three hairs'
        breadth.   24.8.37   xíng   形

*Trying to pull off what I did the first time I was pregnant
but while also having the first baby already here was
like "having leftovers but eating more," or "marrying
rich but penny pinching..."*

Matter (outside one's body, "cut from the cow" by a
bloodied blade)   24.9.38   wù   物
in this particular enclave that's defended by a weapon
on a pole: 24.9.39   huò   或
        a tomb built over the heart   24.9.40   wù   惡
        is what it has, stepping on from this footprint.   24.9.41   zhī   之

This tapped lightly with a tutoring cane and left a mark
on the solid shield of the past: 24.10.42   gù   故
flesh-and-meat-handling Being   24.10.43   yǒu   有
*walking with the footprint of the loose-haired head
buck*   24.10.44   dào   道
—this is boiling sugarcane with fire as follows!—   24.10.45   zhâ   者

is the husk of the initial false guard-petals but
not really the true flower of   24.10.46   bù   不
disappearing like a tiger head at home,
footprint pointed back down by a table, staying
here, chaste, rather than accepting a
government position or getting married.   24.10.47   chù   處

My Not-Having self could be hidden at home the first
time around, and that had been vital to my survival. But
it was impossible in this new situation since the
emperor knew my Being persona to be that wild-haired
head buck.

Chapter 22: It worked in the past

Bent and segmented like a river or a song,   22.1.1   qū   曲
after following this sacrificial blade-and-cauldron-like
ritual regulation, became   22.1.2   zé   則
    whole like a piece of pure jade, entire as it
    arrived.   22.1.3   quán   全

Bending like a tree king connecting heaven, man, and
earth,   22.2.4   wǎng   枉
after following this sacrificial blade-and-cauldron-like
ritual regulation, became   22.2.5   zé   則
    looking straight on, forward.   22.2.6   zhí   直

Hollow as a watery sinkhole (as a Royal Jade River or
"River *Guī*") behind a two-winged flap covering a cave,   22.3.7   wā   窪
after following this sacrificial blade-and-cauldron-like
ritual regulation, became   22.3.8   zé   則
    full to overflowing its vessel.   22.3.9   yíng   盈

Tattered as one of our traditional gendered head-cloths
that's been cut into rags, tapped lightly with a tutoring
cane by hand,   22.4.10   bì   敝
after following this sacrificial blade-and-cauldron-like
ritual regulation, became   22.4.11   zé   則
        having the look of a freshly chopped hazelnut
        tree axed by that chisel used to mark slaves
        and criminals, like someone newly married,
        recently.   22.4.12   xīn   新

Belittled, considered to be insignificant as four tiny dots
like a young master's youthful period,   22.5.13   shǎo 少
after following this sacrificial blade-and-cauldron-like
ritual regulation, became   22.5.14   zé   則
        The Hand-Picked Gem, like cowry-shell-riches
        discovered along the road.   22.5.15   dé   得

But now, doing this with a second child...

Having more, like two pieces of meat,   22.6.16   duō   多
after following this sacrificial blade-and-cauldron-like
ritual regulation, becomes   22.6.17   zé   則
        confused as a heart under this particular
        enclave defended by a weapon on a pole,
        infatuated.   22.6.18   huò   惑

My old ideal sage model worked when I was <u>not seen</u>—
it was the exact opposite of what I described in the
previous chapter...

This baby footprint on bamboo-slip pages,   22.7.19   shì   是
this is cultivating, like a plow,   22.7.20   yǐ   以

an ideal grounded sage known for his civilian petition
to authority, standing straight, speaking, and being
listened to,   22.7.21   shèng   聖
that person,   22.7.22   rén   人
bundling it all up together in both arms into   22.7.23   bào   抱
The One,   22.7.24   yī   一

creating something by hand, carving an elephant
likeness of good fortune and royal power,   22.8.25   wéi   為
the heavenly from high above this great big person   22.8.26   tiān   天
now here down below,   22.8.27   xià   下
a model example, like a bladed tool and a retrievable
arrow attached to a string for effective shooting and
catching, would be: 22.8.28   shì   式

the husk of the initial false *guard-petals but not really*
the true flower of   22.9.29   bù   不
as oneself personally, right on the nose,   22.9.30   zì   自
seen by someone with one big eye for a head...   22.9.31   jiàn   見

 this taps lightly with a tutoring cane and leaves
 a mark on the solid shield of the past...   22.10.32   gù   故
 as bright as dawn rising on a crescent moon,
 enlightened;   22.10.33   míng   明

the husk of the initial false guard-petals but not really
the true flower of   22.11.34   bù   不
as oneself personally, right on the nose,   22.11.35   zì   自
this baby footprint on bamboo-slip pages...   22.11.36   shì   是

 this taps lightly with a tutoring cane and leaves
 a mark on the solid shield of the past...   22.12.37   gù   故

shining forth as obviously clear and
"enlightened" as the hair on a person standing
on the ground in the early morning sun over
the thorny jujube plant that's used for
insomnia and contraception and causes
midterm miscarriages;   22.12.38   zhāng   彰

the husk of the initial false guard-petals but not really
the true flower of   22.13.39   bù   不
as oneself personally, right on the nose,   22.13.40   zì   自
beheading with a weapon on a pole...   22.13.41   fá   伐

this taps lightly with a tutoring cane and leaves
a mark on the solid shield of the past...   22.14.42   gù   故
flesh-and-meat-handling Being   22.14.43   yǒu   有
laboring with the force of a blade and the work
of one's arm or a plow;"   22.14.44   gōng   功

*[Rather than "Not-Having laboring," like in the previous
chapter.]*

"the husk of the initial false guard-petals but not really
the true flower of   22.15.45   bù   不
as oneself personally, right on the nose,   22.15.46   zì   自
gathering together from three sides over a kneeling
person with a spear as a magistrate, commanding...   22.15.47   jīn   矜

this taps lightly with a tutoring cane and leaves
a mark on the solid shield of the past...   22.16.48   gù   故
lengthening as long as hair that has to be tied
with a brooch, like a loose-haired old man."   22.16.49   zhǎng   長

"In fact, that is to say This Grown Man with hairpin and
public courtesy name,   22.17.50   fū   夫
'Oh, YES, Ma'am,' says the 'short-tailed bird,'   22.17.51   wéi   唯
the husk of the initial protective bud casing but not
really the true flower of   22.17.52   bù   不
competing, two hands clawing over a plowshare...   22.17.53   zhēng   爭

this taps lightly with a tutoring cane and leaves a mark
on the solid shield of the past...   22.18.54   gù   故
the heavenly from high above this great big person   22.18.55   tiān   天
now here down below...   22.18.56   xià   下
    like the sun sinking down in four bushes, one
    must not be—cannot be, eh?—   22.18.57   mò   莫
    using that legendary Hybrid Power of a
    mythical bear-like animal who has the legs of a
    deer for   22.18.58   néng   能
    participating with (a "biting tooth" lifted by a
    pair of hands onto strong shoulders, perhaps
    interfering with or perhaps supporting)   22.18.59   yǔ   與
    what it has, stepping on from this footprint,   22.18.60   zhī   之
        competing, two hands clawing over a
        plowshare.   22.18.61   zhēng   爭

With this first little heavenly one now here, competing
isn't going to work.

"But, but, but..." I tried to argue with myself...

Speaking of the solid shield of the past,   22.19.62   gǔ   古
what it had, stepping on from this footprint,   22.19.63   zhī   之
"that place" being intentionally created like any
household gate hewn with an axe,   22.19.64   suǒ   所

by the nitty-gritty, grinding gizzard of a fowl, what
that's called,   22.19.65   wèi   謂

       bent and segmented like a river or a song,   22.19.66   qū   曲
       after following this sacrificial blade-and-
       cauldron-like ritual regulation: 22.19.67   zé   則
       whole like a piece of pure jade, entire as it
       arrived   22.19.68   quán   全
       —this is boiling sugarcane with fire as follows!   22.19.69   zhâ   者

What? How? Is this "mountains from beans?"   22.20.70   qí   豈
Empty, like a tiger head upon a mound,   22.20.71   xū   虛
speaking out loud?"   22.20.72   yán   言
I say, Oh, indeed, that hurts, a weapon on a
pole wounding sprouting seeds and talents.   22.20.73   zāi   哉

Speaking completely and truly of putting that
final nail in a weapon on the pole: 22.21.74   chéng   誠
whole like a piece of pure jade, entire as it
arrived,   22.21.75   quán   全
       yet now, bearded, you were   22.21.76   ér   而
       coming back after sweeping troops out
       of the soil mound hills to this...   22.21.77   guī   歸
       what it had, stepping on from this
       footprint.   22.21.78   zhī   之

It's not empty words. It did work in the past!

Chapter 23: It worked when I knew I was myself, no matter what, and therefore could play whatever role was needed and do it happily.

"Barely there," as sparse as the few interconnecting
threads in the gendered head-cloth we wear after
reaching adulthood, rarely seen or heard,   23.1.1   xī   希
speaking out loud: 23.1.2   yán   言
      as myself personally, right on the nose,   23.1.3   zì   自
      I am accomplishing this thus, as naturally as
      dog meat over a fire.   23.1.4   rán   然

I always have been fully capable of saying very little.

This tapped lightly with a tutoring cane and left a mark
on the solid shield of the past: 23.2.5   gù   故
two hands placing a cover on an altar, making a swift
mark, doing some kind of business that's blowing wind
as a male, majestic, legendary bird, fluttering animals
and insects adrift like a whirlwind,   23.2.6   piāo 飄
blowing as a male majestic legendary bird with three
strands of hair or feathers hanging now here down
below and a common, earthly bucket above, fluttering
insects and animals in the wind,   23.2.7   fēng 風
      were the husk of the initial false guard-petals
      but not really the true flower of   23.2.8   bù   不
      ending (like the knot at the end of a thick silk
      skein, like winter)   23.2.9   zhōng 終
      the beginning of morning when the sun's just
      rising out of the grass alongside a river,
      perhaps paying a visit to the emperor.   23.2.10   cháo 朝

Sudden as your horse moving sharply when you're
gathering and carrying in your hand the ear of an
enemy people, quick   23.3.11   zhòu   驟
cloudbursts of rain,   23.3.12   yǔ   雨
     were the husk of the initial false guard-petals
     but not really the true flower of   23.3.13   bù   不
     ending   23.3.14   zhōng   終
     the entire day—the full sun.   23.3.15   rì   日

Which kneeling person using both arms for paying
tribute to an ancestral shrine is fully processing   23.4.16   shú   孰
creating something by hand, carving an elephant
likeness of good fortune and royal power,   23.4.17   wéi   為
this here, the foot stops a person here on this footprint   23.4.18   cǐ   此
—this is boiling sugarcane with fire as follows!—   23.4.19   zhâ   者

with the heavenly from high above this great big
person   23.5.20   tiān   天
now down here in this earthly womb?   23.5.21   dì   地

But who can do this with the heavenly now down here?

The heavenly from high above this great big person   23.6.22   tiān   天
now down here in this earthly womb   23.6.23   dì   地
<u>*and*</u> *nobly assisting the emperor*, dividing up and
differentiating what's faced with admiration and
echoed in there,   23.6.24   shàng   尚
     is the husk of the initial false guard petals, not
     really the true flower of   23.6.25   bù   不
     using that legendary Hybrid Power of a
     mythical bear-like animal who has the legs of a
     deer for   23.6.26   néng   能

enduring through time as a person receiving
moxibustion, that mugwort treatment for
cramps, turning a breech baby, or other health
issues... 23.6.27 jiǔ 久

yet, now you're bearded, 23.7.28 ér 而
and in this river you find yourself, brother, 23.7.29 kuàng 況
in this place and time, oh, black, icy raven sun... 23.7.30 yú 於
that person, 23.7.31 rén 人
—PAH, CAN YOU?! 23.7.32 hū 乎

It couldn't work with the heavenly down here and me
assisting the emperor, yet here I was.

So, why did it work in the past? What were the keys to
its success?

This tapped lightly with a tutoring cane and left a mark
on the solid shield of the past: 23.8.33 gù 故
When I was *following*, slowly walking directly after
another person in that footprint, the left leg leading the
way, straightening up, straightening things out for
"nailing" that first footstep of a journey or campaign, 23.8.34 cóng 從
my personal task, what it is one does with a weapon,
flag, or pen in hand, 23.8.35 shì 事
in this place and time, oh, black, icy raven sun, 23.8.36 yú 於
walking with the footprint of the loose-haired head
buck? 23.8.37 dào 道
This is boiling sugarcane with fire as follows! 23.8.38 zhâ 者

Walking with the footprint of the loose-haired
head buck— 23.9.39 dào 道
this is boiling sugarcane with fire as follows!— 23.9.40 zhâ 者

what's known as "Fán, one and the
same," when spoken of as ordinarily
and generally as any commonplace
bucket,   23.9.41   tóng   同
in this place and time, oh, black, icy
raven sun,   23.9.42   yú   於
was walking with the footprint of the
loose-haired head buck;   23.9.43   dào   道

walking with the footprint of someone who's in
alignment (eyes looking forward, directly over
the heart, left leg slowly leading the way)—   23.10.44 dé   德
this is boiling sugarcane with fire as follows!—   23.10.45 zhâ   者
    what's known as "*Fán*, one and the
    same," when spoken of as ordinarily
    and generally as any commonplace
    bucket,   23.10.46 tóng   同
    in this place and time, oh, black, icy
    raven sun,   23.10.47 yú   於
    was walking with the footprint of
    someone who's in alignment (eyes
    looking forward, directly over the heart,
    left leg slowly leading the way);   23.10.48 dé   德

dropped from a hand—   23.11.49 shī   失
this is boiling sugarcane with fire as follows!—   23.11.50 zhâ   者
    what's known as "*Fán*, one and the
    same," when spoken of as ordinarily
    and generally as any commonplace
    bucket,   23.11.51 tóng   同
    in this place and time, oh, black, icy
    raven sun,   23.11.52 yú   於
    was dropped from a hand.   23.11.53 shī   失

Simply put, when my only personal role was following the Dào ("walking the way of the head buck"), my true self (the real me, "on and the same," from before I stepped out of that cave back in Chapter 1) could and did go along with whatever role I was taking at the time be it the head buck, the daily ethical system of my hybrid life, or even being completely dropped.

And what's known as "*Fán*, one and the same," when spoken of as ordinarily and generally as any commonplace bucket,
in this place and time, oh, black, icy raven sun,
walking with the footprint of the loose-haired head buck?
This is boiling sugarcane with fire as follows!

> Walking with the footprint of the loose-haired head buck
> —this is boiling sugarcane with fire as follows!—
>> pleasurably playing, as glad music upon a wooden instrument's two silk strings, The Hand-Picked Gem, like cowry-shell-riches discovered along the road, was what it had, stepping on from this footprint.

What's known as "*Fán*, one and the same," when spoken of as ordinarily and generally as any commonplace bucket,
in this place and time, oh, black, icy raven sun,

23.12.54	tóng	同
23.12.55	yú	於
23.12.56	dào	道
23.12.57	zhâ	者
23.13.58	dào	道
23.13.59	yì	亦
23.13.60	lè	樂
23.13.61	dé	得
23.13.62	zhī	之
23.14.63	tóng	同
23.14.64	yú	於

walking with the footprint of someone who's in
alignment (eyes looking forward, directly over the heart,
left leg slowly leading the way)?   23.14.65   dé   德
This is boiling sugarcane with fire as follows!   23.14.66   zhâ   者

    Walking with the footprint of someone who's in
    alignment, whose eyes are looking forward,
    directly aligned over the heart, the left leg
    slowly leading the way —   23.15.67   dé   德
    this is boiling sugarcane with fire as follows!—   23.15.68   yì   亦
        pleasurably playing   23.15.69   lè   樂
        The Hand-Picked Gem, like cowry-shell-
        riches discovered along the road,   23.15.70   dé   得
        was what it had, stepping on from this
        footprint.   23.15.71   zhī   之

What's known as "*Fán*, one and the same," when
spoken of as ordinarily and generally as any
commonplace bucket,   23.16.72   tóng   同
in this place and time, oh, black, icy raven sun,   23.16.73   yú   於
dropped from a hand?   23.16.74   shī   失
This is boiling sugarcane with fire as follows!   23.16.75   zhâ   者

    Dropped from a hand—   23.17.76   shī   失
    this is boiling sugarcane with fire as follows!—   23.17.77   yì   亦
        pleasurably playing   23.17.78   lè   樂
        The Hand-Picked Gem, like cowry-shell-
        riches discovered along the road,   23.17.79   dé   得
        was what it had, stepping on from this
        footprint.   23.17.80   zhī   之

In fact, no matter whether my true self was walking the Dào, walking the Dé, or dropped, I happily played The Hand-Picked Gem role.

If giving one's word to a person...   23.18.81   xìn   信
the husk of the initial protective bud casing but not really the true flower of   23.18.82   bù   不
fully enough, like the whole leg as well as the footprint?   23.18.83   zú   足
Hmmm—like wind through tree branches!   23.18.84   xī   兮
 Then flesh-and-meat-handling Being...   23.18.85   yǒu   有
 the husk of the initial protective bud casing but not really the true flower of   23.18.86   bù   不
 giving one's word to a person.   23.18.87   xìn   信
 Hmmm—like wind through tree branches!   23.18.88   xī   兮

You remember this adage from Chapter 17. Now, perhaps, you see even more clearly how important it was and why. I couldn't have succeeded the first time with the complete truth.

Chapter 25: What I did as Being the first time around

[Remember, Chapter 24 was located behind Chapter 21 in the oldest known versions.]

Flesh-and-meat-handling Being,   25.1.1   yǒu   有
 matter (outside one's body, "cut from the cow" by a bloodied blade)   25.1.2   wù   物
 turbulently blending torrential waters like a river of insects, muddling along and maybe even stirring up trouble, joking,   25.1.3   hùn   混

and completing that final "nail" in a
weapon on a pole,   25.1.4   chéng   成

was leading long before, stepping off from this
footprint, an ancestor of   25.2.5   xiān   先
    the heavenly from high above this great big
    person   25.2.6   tiān   天
    now down here in this earthly womb,   25.2.7   dì   地
      and sprouting a bud from the ground.   25.2.8   shēng   生

Quiet as hand-husking peas at home—   25.3.9   jì   寂
hmmm—like wind through tree branches!   25.3.10   xī   兮
Deserted as a house through which blows the wind like
two wings with two strands of hair hanging down in
front—   25.3.11   liáo   寥
hmmm—like wind through tree branches!   25.3.12   xī   兮
    Alone as a dog, the last one, a "silkworm
    caterpillar on a hollyhock leaf," as we call the
    Shǔ province,   25.3.13   dú   獨
    a person standing straight up on the ground,   25.3.14   lì   立
      the husk of the initial protective bud
      casing but not really the true flower of   25.3.15   bù   不
      transforming something like a fetus by
      cracking lightly by hand or binding with
      a silk rope;   25.3.16   gǎi   改

    meticulously organizing something into
    compartments (like space into circuits, time
    into weekly structure, or money into
    allotments that can be distributed to help
    people... "*Zhōu*" as our dynasty is called)   25.4.17   zhōu   周
    out in public at the crossroads, being good,
    doing one's work,   25.4.18   xíng   行

yet, now you're bearded,	25.4.19	ér 而
the husk of the initial protective bud		
casing but not really the true flower of	25.4.20	bù 不
endangered as human remains, spoken		
of privately, revolving around		
yourself...	25.4.21	dài 殆

[My strategy was to be quiet, alone, and hard-working,
and, with that beard, it kept me free and safe.]

...lip-smackingly genuinely	25.5.22	kâ 可
this cultivated, like a plow,	25.5.23	yǐ 以
creating something by hand, carving an elephant		
likeness of good fortune and royal power,	25.5.24	wéi 為
with the heavenly	25.5.25	tiān 天
now here down below,	25.5.26	xià 下
suckling, a woman kneeling with breasts full of milk.	25.5.27	mǔ 母

But that strategy also got me to this situation: pregnant
while still nursing the first baby.

Remember, looking back even further, that I was known
by different names in all the different phases of this
journey.

Counting up on all five fingers, aren't I,	25.6.28	wú 吾
the husk of the initial protective bud casing but not		
really the true flower of	25.6.29	bù 不
speaking as a great big person to a baby, distinguishing,		
imparting, and administering wisdom confidently and		
intimately,	25.6.30	zhī 知
what it holds a basket of,	25.6.31	qí 其

that personal name given in childhood and still
whispered by moonlight?   25.6.32   míng   名

"Zì," that public courtesy name, received as a baby
under the family roof from their parents or first tutor
but not used until a man reaches age 20 or a woman is
married,   25.7.33   zì   字
what it has, stepping on from this footprint,   25.7.34   zhī   之
    what that's called when issued on a breath
    from the mouth   25.7.35   yuē   曰
    is "walking with the footprint of the loose-
    haired head buck."   25.7.36   dào   道

Revolving around myself as a powerful bow
broadening, strengthening, stiff, hard, and compelling
as a rice weevil, like a tiny venomous snake—
thwang!—   25.8.37   qiáng   強
while creating something by hand, carving an elephant
likeness of good fortune and royal power,   25.8.38   wéi   為
what it has, stepping on from this footprint,   25.8.39   zhī   之
that personal name given in childhood and still
whispered by moonlight,   25.8.40   míng   名
    what that's called when issued on a breath
    from the mouth   25.8.41   yuē   曰
    is *this great big person.*   25.8.42   dà   大

But also, no one thought I'd survived.

This great big person,   25.9.43   dà   大
    what that's called when issued on a breath
    from the mouth   25.9.44   yuē   曰

is "passing on, slowly walking with the footprint of a hand axe *severing life early*, the left leg leading the way;" — 25.9.45 — shì 逝

passing on, slowly walking with the footprint of a hand axe severing life early, the left leg leading the way, — 25.10.46 — shì 逝
what that's called when issued on a breath from the mouth — 25.10.47 — yuē 曰
is "the much *distant*, not intimate or near but profound way of slowly walking with the footprint of a big round spindle with a long robe hanging like the afterbirth from a *postpartum* woman, the left leg leading the way;" — 25.10.48 — yuǎn 遠

the much distant, not intimate or near but profound way of slowly walking with the footprint of a big round spindle with a long robe hanging like the afterbirth from a postpartum woman, the left leg leading the way, — 25.11.49 — yuǎn 遠
what that's called when issued on a breath from the mouth — 25.11.50 — yuē 曰
is "a different-sounding Fǎn, *turning your palm over in a habitable cave in a cliff, reversing, returning, reflecting, maybe countering with the opposite*." — 25.11.51 — fǎn 反

People said I seemed to be dying, fading post-partum, and that sentiment allowed me the freedom to return to "Fǎn," the cave.

This tapped lightly with a tutoring cane and left a mark on the solid shield of the past: — 25.12.52 — gù 故

Walking with the footprint of the loose-haired head
buck: 25.12.53   dào   道
     this great big person.   25.12.54   dà   大
The heavenly, from high above this great big person: 25.12.55   tiān   天
     this great big person.   25.12.56   dà   大
Here in this earthly womb: 25.12.57   dì   地
     this great big person.   25.12.58   dà   大
The king with his ceremonial jade axe or crown
connecting the three levels of heaven, man, and earth   25.12.59   wáng   王
—both armpits sweat this too: 25.12.60   yì   亦
     this great big person.   25.12.61   dà   大

Everything tied back to being the big pregnant person.

The soil of this particular territory, this enclave
defended by a weapon on a pole,   25.13.62   yù   域
in the center, that drum with a flagpole placed in the
middle of a field to gather the people and detect wind,   25.13.63   zhōng   中
flesh-and-meat-handling Being   25.13.64   yǒu   有
     in all four directions   25.13.65   sì   四
     is this great big person,   25.13.66   dà   大
yet, now you're bearded,   25.13.67   ér   而
the king with his ceremonial jade axe or crown
connecting the three levels of heaven, man, and earth,   25.13.68   wáng   王
is staying put here, sitting over the solid shield of the
past at this birthplace, where   25.13.69   jū   居
what it holds a basket of   25.13.70   qí   其
     is The One,   25.13.71   yī   一
     here, straightening things out for "nailing" that
     first footstep of a journey on the back of this
     yellow bird with the "dangling tail" that lives
     around the Yangtze and Huai Rivers—right
     here, huh!   25.13.72   yān   焉

That person,
like the mythical head buck who distinguishes right and
wrong kneeling at the river flowing by a person with a
mouth or cave between their legs, leaving, *comes from
and emulates the standards or even magic of*
    here in this earthly womb.

Here in this earthly womb,
like the mythical head buck who distinguishes right and
wrong kneeling at the river flowing by a person with a
mouth or cave between their legs, leaving, comes from
and emulates the standards or even magic of
    the heavenly from high above this great big
    person.

The heavenly from high above this great big person
like the mythical head buck who distinguishes right and
wrong kneeling at the river flowing by a person with a
mouth or cave between their legs, leaving, comes from
and emulates the standards or even magic of
    walking with the footprint of the loose-haired
    head buck.

Walking with the footprint of the loose-haired head
buck,
like the mythical head buck who distinguishes right and
wrong kneeling at the river flowing by a person with a
mouth or cave between their legs, leaving, comes from
and emulates the standards or even magic of
    myself personally, right on the nose,
    accomplishing this thus, as naturally as dog
    meat over a fire.

25.14.73	rén	人
25.14.74	fǎ	法
25.14.75	dì	地
25.15.76	dì	地
25.15.77	fǎ	法
25.15.78	tiān	天
25.16.79	tiān	天
25.16.80	fǎ	法
25.16.81	dào	道
25.17.82	dào	道
25.17.83	fǎ	法
25.17.84	zì	自
25.17.85	rán	然

It all came from me, being myself.

The question is, could I do that again?

Chapter 26: This delicate pregnancy makes certain activities tricky.

What about the seriously heavy (like a bag tied at both
ends, so weighty that a man has to kneel to put it on
his back)   26.1.1   zhòng   重
when creating something by hand, carving an elephant
likeness of good fortune and royal power,   26.1.2   wéi   為
      a lightweight (like a light carriage, portable,
      running through the whole like a lengthwise
      warp thread of something woven, like menses,
      like a classic text)   26.1.3   qīng   輕
      root of the family tree, like an ancestor's
      manhood,   26.1.4   gēn   根

or calm peace, the clear blue-green growth of the
sedative cinnabar plant quieting a dispute between two
hands on a plowshare,   26.2.5   jìng   靜
when creating something by hand, carving an elephant
likeness of good fortune and royal power,   26.2.6   wéi   為
      a fidgety, impetuous as the footprint of three
      birds chirping in a tree,   26.2.7   zào   躁
      lord prince, his hand holding a rod over a
      mouth?   26.2.8   jūn   君

This baby footprint on bamboo-slip pages,   26.3.9   shì   是
this is cultivating, like a plow,   26.3.10   yǐ   以

an ideal grounded sage known for his civilian petition
to authority, standing straight, speaking, and being
listened to,   26.3.11   shèng   聖
that person would be: 26.3.12   rén   人
ending, like the knot at the end of a thick silk skein, like
winter,   26.3.13   zhōng   終
the entire day—the full sun—   26.3.14   rì   日
out in public at the crossroads, being good, doing one's
work...   26.3.15   xíng   行

    the husk of the initial protective bud casing but
    not really the true flower of   26.4.16   bù   不
    remaining set apart from (as "a short-tailed
    bird" from that infamous wild animal hunted in
    the forest with webbed nets)   26.4.17   lí   離
    a curtained carriage carrying items over field
    and stream, like for military supply,   26.4.18   zī   輜
    of the seriously heavy (like a bag tied at both
    ends, so weighty that a man has to kneel to put
    it on his back);   26.4.19   zhòng   重

if he's immediately adjacent (like a venomous snake
with "a short-tailed bird," right next to it),   26.5.20   suī   雖
flesh-and-meat-handling Being   26.5.21   yǒu   有
brilliant flourishing—like two torches atop a tree,   26.5.22   róng   榮
to someone with one big eye for a head kneeling on a
stork-like temple or watchtower, keeping lookout...   26.5.23   guān   觀

    he'd be calmly (as the swallow for whom the
    kingdom *Yàn* is named)   26.6.24   yàn   燕
    disappearing like a tiger head at home,
    footprint pointed back down by a table, staying   26.6.25   chù   處

here, chaste, rather than accepting a
government position or getting married,
crossing over the far distance via a young man
running on foot with a blade from the mouth,
carrying an imperious decree,   26.6.26   chāo   超
accomplishing this thus, as naturally as dog
meat over a fire.   26.6.27   rán   然

*I developed those tricks. But for some things, there was
no solution…*

But how, how, indeed would he bear it, this great big
person on an altar,   26.7.28   nài   奈
that one, that very one shouldering a weapon   26.7.29   hé   何
        with the medicine-dancing-scorpion insect
        swarm of   26.7.30   wàn   萬
        four-horse military carriages   26.7.31   shèng   乘
        stepping on from this footprint, having   26.7.32   zhī   之
        you, as "oh, honored senior official master,"
        owner, and host of the flame,   26.7.33   zhǔ   主

yet, now you're bearded,   26.8.34   ér   而
cultivating, like a plow,   26.8.35   yǐ   以
your pregnant self,   26.8.36   shēn   身
        a lightweight (like a light carriage, portable,
        running through the whole like a lengthwise
        warp thread of something woven, like menses,
        like a classic text),   26.8.37   qīng   輕
        with the heavenly from high above this great
        big person   26.8.38   tiān   天
        now here down below?   26.8.39   xià   下

A lightweight (like a light carriage, portable,
running through the whole like a lengthwise
warp thread of something woven, like menses,
like a classic text),   26.9.40   qīng   輕
after following this sacrificial blade-and-
cauldron-like ritual regulation,   26.9.41   zé   則
it's dropped from a hand,   26.9.42   shī   失
        the root of the family tree, like an
        ancestor's manhood.   26.9.43   gēn   根

The fidgety, impetuous as the footprint of
three birds chirping in a tree,   26.10.44   zào   躁
after following this sacrificial blade-and-
cauldron-like ritual regulation   26.10.45   zé   則
it's dropped from a hand,   26.10.46   shī   失
        the lord prince, his hand holding a rod
        over a mouth.   26.10.47   jūn   君

Chapter 27: Our inherited pattern for "enlightenment"
doesn't work well.

The traditionally virtuous, offering up a ram's head,
speaking back and forth, tongues waggling,   27.1.1   shàn   善
out in public at the crossroads, being good, doing one's
work,   27.1.2   xíng   行
        this shamanic dancer with animal tails flowing
        from her wrists, Not-Having   27.1.3   wú   無
        —this is boiling sugarcane with fire as
        follows!—   27.1.4   zhâ   者
        is leaving tracks with the full leg of the animal,
        both armpits sweating this too.   27.1.5   jì   跡

The traditionally virtuous
speaking out loud,
    this shaman-dancing Not-Having
    is like a king who borrowed or forged a gem, a
    flaw,
    speaking of the base stem of the stalk, exiling a
    high-ranking person to a lowly outlying post.

The traditionally virtuous
adding up (tapping lightly with a tutoring cane up
through the stack... from a kneeling woman to a round
center drum with a flagpole and then a suckling
mother)
    is the husk of the initial false guard-petals but
    not really the true flower of
    doing truly useful work like a water bucket, by
    means of carrying-capacity,
    tallying as an old man, scheming, measuring
    the inches aloud with multiple mouths inside,
    bamboo-slips pierced by thorns, strung
    together and written on.

The traditionally virtuous
obstructing the two-winged gateway with sprouting
seeds, blocking entry,
    this shaman-dancing Not-Having
    is locking, weaving a pair of the tiniest silk
    thread youngsters, hair still in two tufts,
    through the two-winged gateway,
    a bar, a door bolt, hand-built from a tree by a
    striding person skillful with a bamboo brush,

27.2.6	shàn	善
27.2.7	yán	言
27.2.8	wú	無
27.2.9	xiá	瑕
27.2.10	zhé	謫
27.3.11	shàn	善
27.3.12	shǔ	數
27.3.13	bù	不
27.3.14	yòng	用
27.3.15	chóu	籌
27.3.16	cè	策
27.4.17	shàn	善
27.4.18	bì	閉
27.4.19	wú	無
27.4.20	guān	關
27.4.21	jiàn	楗

yet, now you're bearded, 27.5.22 ér 而
the husk of the initial false guard-petals but not
really the true flower of 27.5.23 bù 不
lip-smackingly genuinely 27.5.24 kâ 可
unlatching that two-winged gateway with a pair
of hands. 27.5.25 kāi 開

The traditionally virtuous 27.6.26 shàn 善
tying up, joining with an emotional knot, a skein of silk
with the auspicious empty mouth of a bachelor soldier-
scholar-official appointed by the emperor, 27.6.27 jié 結
    this shaman-dancing Not-Having 27.6.28 wú 無
    has a skein of silk around a striving toad 27.6.29 shéng 繩
    binding it like a skein of silk keeping something
    in the ladle, 27.6.30 yuē 約

    yet, now you're bearded, 27.7.31 ér 而
    the husk of the initial false guard-petals but not
    really the true flower of 27.7.32 bù 不
    lip-smackingly genuinely 27.7.33 kâ 可
    cutting it, like a blade removing an ox's horn. 27.7.34 jiâ 解

This baby footprint on bamboo-slip pages, 27.8.35 shì 是
this is cultivating, like a plow, 27.8.36 yǐ 以
an ideal grounded sage known for his civilian petition to
authority, standing straight, speaking, and being
listened to, 27.8.37 shèng 聖
that person: 27.8.38 rén 人

as the conventional royal administrator wearing a
men's headcloth as his skirt, 27.9.39 cháng 常
the traditionally virtuous 27.9.40 shàn 善

         is tapping lightly with a tutoring cane a fur coat,
         saving by forbidding   27.9.41   jiù   救
         that person,   27.9.42   rén   人

and this taps lightly with a tutoring cane and leaves a
mark on the solid shield of the past...   27.10.43   gù   故
shaman-dancing Not-Having   27.10.44   wú   無
         tosses out, two hands throwing a baby from a
         basket,   27.10.45   qì   棄
         that person.   27.10.46   rén   人

As the conventional royal administrator wearing a
men's headcloth as his skirt,   27.11.47   cháng   常
the traditionally virtuous   27.11.48   shàn   善
         is tapping lightly with a tutoring cane a fur coat,
         saving by forbidding   27.11.49   jiù   救
         matter (outside one's body, 'cut from the cow,'
         by a bloodied blade),   27.11.50   wù   物

and this taps lightly with a tutoring cane and leaves a
mark on the solid shield of the past...   27.12.51   gù   故
shaman-dancing Not-Having   27.12.52   wú   無
         tosses out, two hands throwing a baby from a
         basket,   27.12.53   qì   棄
         matter (outside one's body, "cut from the cow"
         by a bloodied blade).   27.12.54   wù   物

This baby footprint on bamboo-slip pages,   27.13.55   shì   是
by the nitty-gritty, grinding gizzard of a fowl, what
that's called: 27.13.56   wèi   謂
         an inherited, raiding pattern (superimposed
         atop, like something received from the clothing
         or placenta of a flying dragon) for 27.13.57   xí   襲

being bright as dawn rising on a crescent moon,
enlightened.   27.13.58   míng   明

This taps lightly with a tutoring cane and leaves a mark
on the solid shield of the past...   27.14.59   gù   故
the traditionally virtuous,   27.14.60   shàn   善
that person?   27.14.61   rén   人
This is boiling sugarcane with fire as follows!   27.14.62   zhâ   者
The husk of the initial false guard-petals and not really
true flower of   27.14.63   bù   不
the traditionally virtuous,   27.14.64   shàn   善
that person,   27.14.65   rén   人
    what it has, stepping on from this footprint, it
    has this   27.14.66   zhī   之
    army of 2,500 soldiers stationed on a soil
    mound hill.   27.14.67   shī   師

And the husk of the initial false guard-petals and not
really true flower of   27.15.68   bù   不
the traditionally virtuous,   27.15.69   shàn   善
that person?   27.15.70   rén   人
This is boiling sugarcane with fire as follows!   27.15.71   zhâ   者
The traditionally virtuous,   27.15.72   shàn   善
that person,   27.15.73   rén   人
    what it has, stepping on from this footprint, it
    has this   27.15.74   zhī   之
    supporting material, second-tier cowry-like
    riches.   27.15.75   zī   資

When the husk of the initial false guard-petals but not
really the true flower of   27.16.76   bù   不
being held in high regard, like when two hands are
wrapped around a person atop cowry-shell-riches,   27.16.77   guì   貴

what it holds a basket of,
    an army of 2,500 soldiers stationed on a soil
      mound hill,
and the husk of the initial false guard-petals but not
really the true flower of
loving, kneeling with your head turned this way and
your heart in your throat,
    what it holds a basket of,
      supporting material, second-tier cowry-like
      riches,

then even immediately adjacent (like a venomous
snake with "a short-tailed bird," right next to it) to
oh, so very pleasantly speaking with that wise
knowledge passed on from a great big person to a
baby, as if something sweet in the mouth,
    this great big person
    is getting lost, slowly walking with the footprint
    of raw rice scattered on the footprint, the left
    leg leading the way, bewitched, infatuated.

This baby footprint on bamboo-slip pages,
by the nitty-gritty, grinding gizzard of a fowl, what
that's called
is demanding something vital as a woman with both
hands pointing to her waist,
a young woman kneeling with four tiny drops belittled
as a rich young master—that subtle, ingenious,
exquisite aura.

Something else was required by the most essential part
of me.

27.16.78	qí	其
27.16.79	shī	師
27.16.80	bù	不
27.16.81	ài	愛
27.16.82	qí	其
27.16.83	zī	資
27.17.84	suī	雖
27.17.85	zhì	智
27.17.86	dà	大
27.17.87	mí	迷
27.18.88	shì	是
27.18.89	wèi	謂
27.18.90	yào	要
27.18.91	miào	妙

Chapter 28: But I kept walking that path of "good" behavior, and of course nothing changed.

Speaking as a great big person to a baby, distinguishing,
imparting, and administering wisdom confidently and
intimately,   28.1.1   zhī   知
       what it holds a basket of,   28.1.2   qí   其
       maleness, "a short-tailed bird" with the left
       hand flipped, revolving around oneself,   28.1.3   xióng   雄

and hand-defending this building,   28.2.4   shǒu   守
       what it holds a basket of,   28.2.5   qí   其
       the female, the foot stopping a person here in
       the footprint of the "short-tailed bird,"   28.2.6   cí   雌

is creating something by hand, carving an elephant
likeness of good fortune and royal power,   28.3.7   wéi   為
the heavenly from high above this great big person   28.3.8   tiān   天
now here down below   28.3.9   xià   下
       in a valley mouth between two mountains with
       the tiniest little silk string of a child between a
       claw-like hand grabbing from above and this
       great big person below.   28.3.10   xī   谿

And "creating something by hand, carving an elephant
likeness of good fortune and royal power,   28.4.11   wéi   為
the heavenly   28.4.12   tiān   天
now here down below   28.4.13   xià   下
in a valley mouth between two mountains with the
tiniest little silk string of a child between a claw-like
hand grabbing from above and this great big person
below,"   28.4.14   xī   谿

as the conventional royal administrator wearing a
men's headcloth as his skirt,   28.5.15   cháng   常
walking with the footprint of someone who's in
alignment (eyes looking forward, directly over the heart,
left leg slowly leading the way),   28.5.16   dé   德
    is the husk of the initial false guard-petals but
    not really the true flower of   28.5.17   bù   不
    remaining *set apart* (as "a short-tailed bird"
    from that infamous wild animal hunted in the
    forest with webbed nets) *from*   28.5.18   lí   離

    someone walking with a footprint of slowly
    returning with the left leg leading the way,
    doubling back (like the gut) on one's footprint,   28.6.19   fù   復
    coming back after sweeping troops out of the
    soil mound hills to this,   28.6.20   guī   歸
    in this place and time, oh, black, icy raven sun: 28.6.21   yú   於
        an infant, a kneeling young mother's
        wealth just as surely as two cowry-like
        riches around her neck,   28.6.22   yīng   嬰
        a baby son that still has an open
        fontanelle.   28.6.23   ér   兒

Speaking as a great big person to a baby, distinguishing,
imparting, and administering wisdom confidently and
intimately,   28.7.24   zhī   知
    what it holds a basket of...   28.7.25   qí   其
    a little white, blank acorn, pure, gratuitous,   28.7.26   bái   白

and hand-defending this building,   28.8.27   shǒu   守
    what it holds a basket of...   28.8.28   qí   其
    a dark criminal face-tattoo, shady,   28.8.29   hèi   黑

is creating something by hand, carving an elephant
likeness of good fortune and royal power,   28.9.30   wéi   為
the heavenly   28.9.31   tiān   天
now here down below   28.9.32   xià   下
    a model example, like a bladed tool and a
    retrievable arrow attached to a string for
    effective shooting and catching.   28.9.33   shì   式

And "creating something by hand, carving an elephant
likeness of good fortune and royal power,   28.10.34   wéi   為
the heavenly   28.10.35   tiān   天
now here down below   28.10.36   xià   下
a model example, like a bladed tool and a retrievable
arrow attached to a string for effective shooting and
catching,"   28.10.37   shì   式

as the conventional royal administrator, wearing the
gendered head-cloth wrapped around his waist,   28.11.38   cháng   常
walking with the footprint of someone who's in
alignment (eyes looking forward, directly over the heart,
left leg slowly leading the way),   28.11.39   dé   德
    is the husk of the initial false guard-petals but
    not really the true flower of   28.11.40   bù   不
    shooting a retrievable arrow attached to a
    string in the heart, catching and *changing*   28.11.41   tài   忕

    someone walking with a footprint of slowly
    returning with the left leg leading the way,
    doubling back (like the gut) on one's footprint   28.12.42   fù   復
    coming back after sweeping troops out of the
    soil mound hills to this,   28.12.43   guī   歸
    in this place and time, oh, black, icy raven sun: 28.12.44   yú   於

the shamanic dancer with animal tails
flowing from her wrists, Not-Having,   28.12.45   wú   無
in the utmost position, a person
pressing urgently against a double-
beamed wooden ridgepole that's high
as a tree.   28.12.46   jí   極

Speaking as a great big person to a baby, distinguishing,
imparting, and administering wisdom confidently and
intimately,   28.13.47   zhī   知
      what it holds a basket of...   28.13.48   qí   其
      an outward public container of private parts,
      like a building housing an important, older man
      who's "got balls," a duke,   28.13.49   róng   容

and hand-defending this building,   28.14.50   shǒu   守
      what it holds a basket of...   28.14.51   qí   其
      hanging from a cliff above a hand underneath,
      shaking, humiliated,   28.14.52   rǔ   辱

is creating something by hand, carving an elephant
likeness of good fortune and royal power,   28.15.53   wéi   為
the heavenly   28.15.54   tiān   天
now here down below   28.15.55   xià   下
      in a difficult position in a ravine, in an emptied,
      eroded valley mouth between two mountains.   28.15.56   gǔ   谷

And "creating something by hand, carving an elephant
likeness of good fortune and royal power,   28.16.57   wéi   為
the heavenly   28.16.58   tiān   天
now here down below   28.16.59   xià   下
in a difficult position in a ravine, in an emptied, eroded
valley mouth between two mountains..."   28.16.60   gǔ   谷

the conventional royal administrator, wearing the
gendered head-cloth wrapped around his waist,   28.17.61   cháng   常
walking with the footprint of someone who's in
alignment (eyes looking forward, directly over the
heart, left leg slowly leading the way),   28.17.62   dé   德
       only then do you get   28.17.63   nǎi   乃
       fully enough, like the whole leg as well as the
       footprint,   28.17.64   zú   足

       someone walking with a footprint of slowly
       returning with the left leg leading the way,
       doubling back (like the gut) on one's footprint,   28.18.65   fù   復
       coming back *after sweeping troops* out of the
       soil mound hills *to this*,   28.18.66   guī   歸
       in this place and time, oh, black, icy raven sun: 28.18.67   yú   於
           that "piece of wood" in the dense,
           unpolished, sticking, natural state of a
           thicket of oak trees.   28.18.68   pǔ   樸

The only way to get to "fully enough" returning home
from war in this thickened state is as the imperial
administrator living the Dé life.

This is the last you'll hear of Dé *in this book of* Dào, *but*
my entire second book, which begins with Chapter 38, is
devoted to it.

"That *piece of wood* in the dense, unpolished, sticking,
natural state of a thicket of oak trees"   28.19.69   pǔ   樸
scattered like a pair of bamboo stalks atop the crescent
moon, tapped lightly with a tutoring cane,   28.19.70   sàn   散
       after following this sacrificial blade-and-
       cauldron-like ritual regulation,   28.19.71   zé   則

is creating something by hand, carving an
elephant likeness of good fortune and royal
power,   28.19.72   wéi   為
    a set of highly regarded vessels with
    lots of capacity, worthy of a guard dog.   28.19.73   qì   器

An ideal grounded sage known for his civilian petition
to authority, standing straight, speaking, and being
listened to,   28.20.75   shèng   聖
that person   28.20.75   rén   人
doing truly useful work like a water bucket, by means
of carrying-capacity,   28.20.76   yòng   用
what it has, stepping on from this footprint,   28.20.77   zhī   之

    after following this sacrificial blade-and-
    cauldron-like ritual regulation,   28.21.78   zé   則
    would be creating something by hand, carving
    an elephant likeness of good fortune and royal
    power,   28.21.79   wéi   為
        working in a government building with
        many rooms under one roof as an
        official,   28.21.80   guān   官
        lengthening as long as hair that has to
        be tied with a brooch, like a loose-
        haired old man.   28.21.81   zháng   長

This taps lightly with a tutoring cane and leaves a mark
on the solid shield of the past: 28.22.82   gù   故
this great big person,   28.22.83   dà   大
and those ruler edicts (like saying, "cut that tree!" as
was done for parent-mourning rituals)   28.22.84   zhì   制
    are the husk of the initial false guard-petals but
    not really the true flower of   28.22.85   bù   不

cutting apart a harmful house in which lush,
abundant plant growth is spoken of.   28.22.86   gē   割

*I was following what was expected of me, and the
result wasn't great: I was working like an old man in a
government job. It rendered me ineffective in righting
the wrongs in my own home.*

Chapter 29: I needed to leave.

Assured, as if by hand-offering a meat tribute at an
altar, a certain future of   29.1.1   jiāng   將
missing, kneeling with a yawning mouth before a ravine
eroded between two mountains, wanting, lacking,   29.1.2   yù   欲
and getting hold of, grabbing the ear of   29.1.3   qù   取
the heavenly from high above this great big person   29.1.4   tiān   天
now here down below,   29.1.5   xià   下
    yet, now you're bearded,   29.1.6   ér   而
    creating something by hand, carving an
    elephant likeness of good fortune and royal
    power,   29.1.7   wéi   為
    what it has, stepping on from this footprint.   29.1.8   zhī   之

Yet, now you're bearded,   29.2.6   ér   而
counting up on all five fingers, aren't I   29.2.9   wú   吾
seen by someone with one big eye for a head?   29.2.10   jiàn   見
    What it holds a basket of   29.2.11   qí   其
    is the husk of the initial false guard-
    petals but not really the true flower of   29.2.12   bù   不
    The Hand-Picked Gem, like cowry-shell-
    riches discovered along the road,   29.2.13   dé   得
    already finishing it in the womb.   29.2.14   yǐ   已

*I wanted to be gone and take my little one with me. But
ever since my secret was out, I was no longer The Hand-
Picked Gem with all the those privileges.*

With the heavenly	29.3.15	tiān	天
now here down below,	29.3.16	xià	下
that magical god spirit lightning, the divine			
spark	29.3.17	shén	神
a set of highly regarded vessels with lots of			
capacity, worthy of a guard dog,	29.3.18	qì	器
is the husk of the initial false guard-petals but			
not really the true flower of	29.4.19	bù	不
lip-smackingly genuinely	29.4.20	kâ	可
creating something by hand, carving an			
elephant likeness of good fortune and royal			
power,	29.4.21	wéi	為
—yes, that too, oh "female funnel!"	29.4.22	yâ	也
Creating something by hand, carving an			
elephant likeness of good fortune and royal			
power?	29.5.23	wéi	為
This is boiling sugarcane with fire as follows!	29.5.24	zhâ	者
Defeat, riches hit lightly by hand, failing,			
decaying,	29.5.25	bài	敗
is what it has, stepping on from this footprint.	29.5.26	zhī	之
A kneeling person, arrested and held, arms			
outstretched in handcuffs?	29.6.27	zhí	執
This is boiling sugarcane with fire as follows!	29.6.28	zhâ	者
Dropped from a hand	29.6.29	shī	失
is what it has, stepping on from this footprint.	29.6.30	zhī	之

It was a wholly different scenario than before...

This taps lightly with a tutoring cane and leaves a mark
on the solid shield of the past: 29.7.31   gù   故
matter (outside one's body, "cut from the cow" by a
bloodied blade)   29.7.32   wù   物
in this particular enclave that's defended by a weapon
on a pole   29.7.33   huò   或
      is out in public at the crossroads, being good,
      doing one's work;   29.7.34   xíng   行
but in this particular enclave that's defended by a
weapon on a pole,   29.7.35   huò   或
      it's accompanying one another single file near
      soil mountains, slowly walking with the
      footprint of flesh-and-meat-handling Being, the
      left leg leading the way.   29.7.36   suí   隨

In this particular enclave that's defended by a weapon
on a pole,   29.8.37   huò   或
      it's snorting through the nose at nothing like a
      person with their mouth yawning and empty
      kneeling before a tiger head on a hill with grass
      coming through the bottom;   29.8.38   xū   歔
but in this particular enclave that's defended by a
weapon on a pole,   29.8.39   huò   或
      it's blowing as hard as wind like a person with
      their mouth open kneeling at another mouth.   29.8.40   chuī   吹

In this particular enclave that's defended by a weapon
on a pole,   29.9.41   huò   或
      it's revolving around oneself as a powerful bow
      broadening, strengthening, stiff, hard, and   29.9.42   qiáng   強

compelling as a rice weevil, like a tiny
venomous snake—thwang!—
but in this particular enclave that's defended by a
weapon on a pole,
       it's fleeing by moonlight with one's cowry-shell-
       riches and dishes.

In this particular enclave that's defended by a weapon
on a pole,
       it's pushing down to seated on the ground;
but in this particular enclave that's defended by a
weapon on a pole,
       it's getting destroyed around the soil mountain,
       a left hand by moonlight over one's heart.

This baby footprint on bamboo-slip pages,
this is cultivating, like a plow:
an ideal grounded sage known for his civilian petition to
authority, standing straight, speaking, and being
listened to,
that person,
would be leaving, a person with a cave mouth between
their legs,
       pairing like one-half of a double-yoked harness
       as pleasant as something sweet in the mouth
       and therefore extra;

would be leaving
a gluttonous great big person stewing noodles or sugar
cane;

would be leaving

29.9.43	huò	或
29.9.44	léi	贏
29.10.45	huò	或
29.10.46	cuò	挫
29.10.47	huò	或
29.10.48	huī	隳
29.11.49	shì	是
29.11.50	yǐ	以
29.11.51	shèng	聖
29.11.52	rén	人
29.11.53	qù	去
29.11.54	shèn	甚
29.12.55	qù	去
29.12.56	shē	奢
29.13.57	qù	去

the excessively extravagant (this great big person trying
to clasp both arms around a flowing stream).

29.13.58   tài   泰

Chapter 30: It was crazy to continue in this job and especially crazy to go to combat in my condition.

Cultivating, like a plow,
walking with the footprint of the loose-haired head
buck
in an inferior aide position, providing left-handed help
with work as with a bladed tool, assisting,
that person,
you, "oh, honored senior official master," owner, and
host of the flame?
This is boiling sugarcane with fire as follows!

30.1.1   yǐ   以
30.1.2   dào   道
30.1.3   zuǒ   佐
30.1.4   rén   人
30.1.5   zhǔ   主
30.1.6   zhâ   者

    It's the husk of the initial false guard-petals but
    not really the true flower of
    cultivating, like a plow,
    carrying a short ax with two hands like a soldier
    or pawn
    while revolving around yourself as a powerful
    bow broadening, strengthening, stiff, hard, and
    compelling as a rice weevil, like a tiny
    venomous snake—thwang!—
    and the heavenly from high above this great big
    person
    now here down below

30.2.7   bù   不
30.2.8   yǐ   以
30.2.9   bīng   兵
30.2.10   qiáng   強
30.2.11   tiān   天
30.2.12   xià   下

    because what that holds a basket of,
    that task, what they do with a weapon, flag, or
    pen in hand,

30.3.13   qí   其
30.3.14   shì   事

is as good as a woman with a child   30.3.15   hǎo   好
giving something the eye, frightened,
while slowly walking with the footprint
of a robe hanging like placental
afterbirth from a recently pregnant
woman, long like a spindle, the left leg
leading the way, and then *doing or*
giving something or going somewhere
"in return."   30.3.16   huán   還

An army of 2,500 soldiers stationed on a soil
mound hill   30.4.17   shī   師
stepping on from this footprint, has this   30.4.18   zhī   之
"place" being intentionally created like any
household gate hewn with an axe,   30.4.19   suǒ   所
disappearing like a tiger head at home,
footprint pointed back down by a table, staying
here, chaste, rather than accepting a
government position or getting married: 30.4.20   chù   處
    the thorny 'chaste tree' whose fruit
    makes you not want sex and whose
    canes are used to flog wives, like the
    punishment of a knife by a square well
    under two sprouts of grass,   30.4.21   jīng   荆
    and the double thorny jujube, the red
    date plant, the fruit of which can be
    used as contraception and causes
    midterm miscarriages.   30.4.22   jí   棘
are sprouting a bud from the ground.   30.4.23   shēng 生
Hmmm—like wind through tree
branches!   30.4.24   xī   兮

This great big person   30.5.25   dà   大
in an army of surrounding carts   30.5.26   jūn   軍
stepping on from this footprint, has this   30.5.27   zhī   之
walking slowly with just the left leg leading the
way, leaving behind this tiny silk thread
footprint like a knot in a thread, a *descendant*,
at the end: 30.5.28   hòu   後
    hands over heart, analytically,   30.5.29   bì   必
    flesh-and-meat-handling Being,   30.5.30   yǒu   有
    will be as unlucky as a hole in the
    ground with rock, mud, or bamboo in
    the bottom,   30.5.31   xiōng   凶
    with years of carrying wheat upon
    one's back.   30.5.32   nián   年

The traditionally virtuous, offering up a ram's head
while speaking back and forth, tongues waggling,   30.6.33   shàn   善
flesh-and-meat-handling Being,   30.6.34   yǒu   有
ripened like fruit on the tree by the sun,   30.6.35   guǒ   果
yet now, bearded, you're   30.6.36   ér   而
already finishing it in the womb,   30.6.37   yǐ   已

    the husk of the initial false guard-petals but not
    really the true flower of   30.7.38   bù   不
    venturing to be bold, even a little bit and ultra-
    politely hunting a boar as pleasantly as if you
    had something sweet in your mouth   30.7.39   gǎn   敢
    in cultivating, like a plow,   30.7.40   yǐ   以
    getting hold of, grabbing the ear of   30.7.41   qù   取
    revolving around yourself as a powerful bow
    broadening, strengthening, stiff, hard, and
    compelling as a rice weevil, like a tiny
    venomous snake—thwang!   30.7.42   qiáng   強

Ripened like fruit on the tree by the sun,	30.8.43	guǒ	果
yet, now you're bearded,	30.8.44	ér	而
do not—seriously as a bloodied blade, don't be	30.8.45	wù	勿
gathering together from three sides over a			
kneeling person with a spear as a magistrate,			
commanding;	30.8.46	jīn	矜
ripened like fruit on the tree by the sun,	30.9.47	guǒ	果
yet, now you're bearded,	30.9.48	ér	而
do not—seriously as a bloodied blade, don't be	30.9.49	wù	勿
beheading with a weapon on a pole;	30.9.50	fá	伐
ripened like fruit on the tree by the sun,	30.10.51	guǒ	果
yet, now you're bearded,	30.10.52	ér	而
do not—seriously as a bloodied blade, don't be	30.10.53	wù	勿
arrogant, a young person dangerously racing			
through the city outskirts on a tall horse with			
its mane flying.	30.10.54	jiǎo	驕
Ripened like fruit on the tree by the sun,	30.11.55	guǒ	果
yet, now you're bearded,	30.11.56	ér	而
the husk of the initial false guard-petals but not			
really the true flower of	30.11.57	bù	不
The Hand-Picked Gem, like cowry-shell-riches			
discovered along the road,	30.11.58	dé	得
already finishing it in the womb;	30.11.59	yǐ	已
ripened like fruit on the tree by the sun,	30.12.60	guǒ	果
yet, now you're bearded,	30.12.61	ér	而
do not—seriously as a bloodied blade, don't be	30.12.62	wù	勿
revolving around yourself as a powerful bow			
broadening, strengthening, stiff, hard, and			

compelling as a rice weevil, like a tiny
venomous snake—thwang!

30.12.63   qiáng   強

Matter (outside one's body, "cut from the cow" by a
bloodied blade),

30.13.64   wù   物

in this distinctive shape (differently formed like the way
a piece of chopped wood can be sculpted in the shape
of a dog),

30.13.65   zhuàng   狀

after following this sacrificial blade-and-cauldron-like
ritual regulation,

30.13.66   zé   則

     is an honorable loose-haired elder, "*Lǎo*," bent
     over an arrow as a cane.

30.13.67   lǎo   老

This baby footprint on bamboo-slip pages,

30.14.68   shì   是

by the nitty-gritty, grinding gizzard of a fowl, what
that's called

30.14.69   wèi   謂

     is the husk of the initial false guard-petals but
     not really the true flower of

30.14.70   bù   不

     walking with the footprint of the loose-haired
     head buck.

30.14.71   dào   道

And "the husk of the initial false guard-petals
but not really the true flower of

30.15.72   bù   不

walking with the footprint of the loose-haired
head buck"

30.15.73   dào   道

     is early, premature as sunrise above an
     acorn on the jujube, that thorny plant
     that's used for insomnia and
     contraception and causes midterm
     miscarriages,

30.15.74   zǎo   早

     already finishing it in the womb.

30.15.75   yǐ   已

Chapter 31: War

In fact, that is to say This Grown Man with hairpin and
public courtesy name   31.1.1   fū   夫
addressing the emperor using a beautiful, stacked pair
of pointed jade tablets, so very excellent,   31.1.2   jiā   佳
and carrying a short ax with two hands like a soldier or
pawn   31.1.3   bīng   兵
—this is boiling sugarcane with fire as follows!   31.1.4   zhâ   者
    is the husk of the initial false guard-petals but
    not really the true flower of   31.1.5   bù   不
    a good omen, like a ram's head at an altar, 31.1.6   xiáng   祥
    stepping on from this footprint, for   31.1.7   zhī   之
    a set of highly regarded vessels with lots of
    capacity, worthy of a guard dog.   31.1.8   qì   器

Matter (outside one's body, "cut from the cow"
by a bloodied blade),   31.2.9   wù   物
in this particular enclave that's defended by a
weapon on a pole,   31.2.10   huò   或
    is like a tomb built over the heart,   31.2.11   wù   惡
    what it has, stepping on from this
    footprint.   31.2.12   zhī   之

"This taps lightly with a tutoring cane and
leaves a mark on the solid shield of the past: 31.3.13   gù   故
flesh-and-meat-handling Being,   31.3.14   yǒu   有
walking with the footprint of the loose-haired
head buck   31.3.15   dào   道
—this is boiling sugarcane with fire as follows!   31.3.16   zhā   者
    is the husk of the initial false guard-
    petals but not really the true flower of   31.3.17   bù   不

disappearing like a tiger head at home,
footprint pointed back down by a table,
staying here, chaste, rather than
accepting a government position or
getting married."   31.3.18   chù   處

As I said way back at the end of Chapter 24. (But it took
me a long time to process this and really get it!)

The lord prince, his hand holding a rod over a mouth,   31.4.19   jūn   君
is a baby with arms wide open and legs swaddled, 'Zǐ,'   31.4.20   zǐ   子
and you're staying put here, sitting over the solid shield
of the past at this birthplace, where: 31.4.21   jū   居
    after following this sacrificial blade-and-
    cauldron-like ritual regulation,   31.4.22   zé   則
    you're held in high regard, like when two hands
    are wrapped around a person atop cowry-shell-
    riches   31.4.23   guì   貴
    in an inferior aide position, doing left-handed
    work as with a bladed tool;   31.4.24   zuǒ   左

but doing truly useful work like a water bucket, by
means of carrying-capacity,   31.5.25   yòng   用
<u>*and*</u> *carrying a short ax with two hands like a soldier or*
pawn: 31.5.26   bīng   兵
    after following this sacrificial blade-and-
    cauldron-like ritual regulation,   31.5.27   zé   則
    you're held in high regard, like when two hands
    are wrapped around a person atop cowry-shell-
    riches   31.5.28   guì   貴
    in a priority position, right hand over mouth.   31.5.29   yòu   右

*And, paradoxically, the "priority position" is not the best
position, as we will see more clearly in a moment.*

Carrying a short ax with two hands like a soldier or
pawn   31.6.30   bīng   兵
—this is boiling sugarcane with fire as follows!—   31.6.31   zhâ   者
    is the husk of the initial false guard-petals but
    not really the true flower of   31.6.32   bù   不
    a good omen, like a ram's head at an altar,   31.6.33   xiáng   祥
    stepping on from this footprint, for   31.6.34   zhī   之
    a set of highly regarded vessels with lots of
    capacity, worthy of a guard dog;   31.6.35   qì   器

    it wrings to backward the two wings of   31.7.36   fēi   非
    the lord prince, his hand holding a rod over a
    mouth,   31.7.37   jūn   君
    a baby with arms wide open and legs swaddled,
    "Zǐ,"   31.7.38   zǐ   子
    stepping on from this footprint, having   31.7.39   zhī   之
    a set of highly regarded vessels with lots of
    capacity, worthy of a guard dog.   31.7.40   qì   器

The husk of the initial false guard-petals but not really
the true flower of   31.8.41   bù   不
The Hand-Picked Gem, like cowry-shell-riches
discovered along the road…   31.8.42   dé   得
already finishing it in the womb,   31.8.43   yǐ   已
    yet now you're bearded   31.8.44   ér   而
    and doing truly useful work like a water bucket,
    by means of carrying-capacity,   31.8.45   yòng   用
        what it has, stepping on from this
        footprint   31.8.46   zhī   之

is quietly, a heart licked by a forked
tongue emerging upward from a mouth   31.8.47   tián   恬
bland as a pair of flames doused by a
river of water   31.8.48   dàn   淡
creating something by hand, carving an
elephant likeness of good fortune and
royal power   31.8.49   wéi   為
on top;   31.8.50   shàng   上

able to withstand entirely, to be victorious as a
splendid piece of jewelry, an omen or the royal 'We'
mending something on a boat with two hands by the
strength of an arm, bladed tool, or a plow,   31.9.51   shèng   勝
    yet, now you're bearded,   31.9.52   ér   而
        the husk of the initial false guard-petals
        but not really the true flower of   31.9.53   bù   不
        an admired beauty, a person wearing a
        ram's horn headdress.   31.9.54   mâi   美

No longer the Handpicked Gem, the way for me to be
successful in pregnancy was to be bland and not grab
attention as anyone's beauty. But I was going with the
wrong approach…

Yet, now you're bearded,   31.10.55   ér   而
an admired beauty,   31.10.56   mâi   美
stepping on from this footprint, it has this   31.10.57   zhī   之
—this is boiling sugarcane with fire as follows!—   31.10.58   zhâ   者
        this baby footprint on bamboo-slip pages   31.10.59   shì   是
        pleasurably playing, as glad music upon a
        wooden instrument's two silk strings,   31.10.60   lè   樂
        killing, like impaling a boar by hand,   31.10.61   shā   殺
        that person.   31.10.62   rén   人

In fact, that is to say This Grown Man with hairpin and
public courtesy name   31.11.63   fū   夫
pleasurably playing, as glad music upon a wooden
instrument's two silk strings,   31.11.64   lè   樂
killing, like impaling a boar by hand,   31.11.65   shā   殺
that person   31.11.66   rén   人
—this is boiling sugarcane with fire as follows!—   31.11.67   zhâ   者
    after following this sacrificial blade-and-
    cauldron-like ritual regulation   31.11.68   zé   則
    is the husk of the initial false guard-petals but
    not really the true flower of   31.11.69   bù   不
    lip-smackingly genuinely   31.11.70   kâ   可
    cultivating, like a plow,   31.11.71   yǐ   以
    The Hand-Picked Gem,   31.11.72   dé   得
    their will, stepping off from the heart's
    footprint here,   31.11.73   zhì   志
    in this place and time, oh, black, icy raven sun, 31.11.74   yú   於
        the heavenly from high above this great
        big person   31.11.75   tiān   天
        now here down below   31.11.76   xià   下
    —I swear on an arrow revolving around
    oneself, that's it!   31.11.77   yǐ   矣

Lucky as an empty and quiet mouth with a soldier's axe
above it,   31.12.78   jí   吉
is their task, what they do with a weapon, flag, or pen
in hand   31.12.79   shì   事
when nobly assisting the emperor, dividing up and
differentiating what's faced with admiration and
echoed in there   31.12.80   shàng   尚
    in an *inferior* aide position, doing left-handed
    work as with a bladed tool;   31.12.81   zuǒ   左

unlucky as a hole in the ground with rock, mud, or
bamboo in the bottom,

is their task, what they do with a weapon, flag, or pen
in hand

when nobly assisting the emperor, dividing up and
differentiating what's faced with admiration and
echoed in there

      in a *priority* position, right hand over mouth.

An assistant, a person just inscribing on the door, flat,
like bamboo tablets,

is assured, as if by hand-offering a meat tribute at an
altar, a certain future with

the army of surrounding carts

      staying put here, sitting over the solid shield of
      the past at this birthplace, where
      they're in an inferior aide position, doing left-
      handed work as with a bladed tool.

On top

one is assured, as if by hand-offering a meat tribute at
an altar, a certain future with

the army of surrounding carts

      staying put here, sitting over the solid shield of
      the past at this birthplace, where
      they're in a priority position, right hand over
      mouth.

Here's what that looks like...

Speaking out loud,
this is cultivating, like a plow,

31.13.82	xiōng	凶
31.13.83	shì	事
31.13.84	shàng	尚
31.13.85	yòu	右
31.14.86	piān	偏
31.14.87	jiāng	將
31.14.88	jūn	軍
31.14.89	jū	居
31.14.90	zuǒ	左
31.15.91	shàng	上
31.15.92	jiāng	將
31.15.93	jūn	軍
31.15.94	jū	居
31.15.95	yòu	右
31.16.96	yán	言
31.16.97	yǐ	以

many mouths clamoring on a mulberry tree,
grieving the dead,   31.16.98   sāng   喪
making ritual offerings of honor at an altar with
two strings of jade and a feathered drum in the
lap of luxury.   31.16.99   lǐ   禮
Disappearing like a tiger head at home,
footprint pointed back down by a table, staying
here, chaste, rather than accepting a
government position or getting married,   31.16.100   chù   處
stepping on from this footprint, they have this.   31.16.101   zhī   之

Killing, like impaling a boar by hand,   31.17.102   shā   殺
that person,   31.17.103   rén   人
stepping on from this footprint, they have this,   31.17.104   zhī   之
and the sun, shining down like an eye on the people,
sees all this, sees   31.17.105   zhòng   眾
this is cultivating, like a plow,   31.17.106   yǐ   以
lamenting from the chest, under one's roof,   31.17.107   āi   哀
breaking the two baby wings off one's heart.   31.17.108   bēi   悲"
Sobbing a river,   31.17.109   qì   泣
stepping on from this footprint, they have this.   31.17.110   zhī   之

Battling, using a net for catching animals against a
weapon on a pole,   31.18.111   zhàn   戰
able to withstand entirely, to be victorious as a
splendid piece of jewelry, an omen or the royal 'We'
mending something on a boat with two hands by the
strength of an arm, bladed tool, or a plow,   31.18.112   shèng   勝
this is cultivating, like a plow,   31.18.113   yǐ   以
many mouths clamoring on a mulberry tree,
grieving the dead,   31.18.114   sāng   喪

making ritual offerings of honor at an altar with
two strings of jade and a feathered drum in the
lap of luxury.   31.18.115   lǐ   禮
Disappearing like a tiger head at home,
footprint pointed back down by a table, staying
here, chaste, rather than accepting a
government position or getting married,   31.18.116   chù   處
stepping on from this footprint, they have this.   31.18.117   zhī   之

All was lost in my quest to be some invincible warrior.

Chapter 32: A Certain Someone suggested a third way.

"Walking with the footprint of the loose-haired head
buck,   32.1.1   dào   道
the conventional royal administrator wearing a men's
headcloth as his skirt,   32.1.2   cháng   常
the shamanic dancer with animal tails flowing
from her wrists, Not-Having   32.1.3   wú   無
personal name given in childhood and still
whispered by moonlight,   32.1.4   míng   名

and that 'piece of wood' in the dense, unpolished,
sticking, natural state of a thicket of oak trees,   32.2.5   pǔ   樸
immediately adjacent (like a venomous snake with 'a
short-tailed bird,' right next to it) to   32.2.6   suī   雖
our tiny dear little one, like three grains of sand,   32.2.7   xiǎo   小
the heavenly from high above this great big person   32.2.8   tiān   天
now here down below,   32.2.9   xià   下
like the sun sinking down in four bushes, you
must not be—cannot be, eh?—   32.2.10   mò   莫

using that legendary Hybrid Power of a
mythical bear-like animal who has the legs of a
deer for   32.2.11   néng   能

casting your eye down, humble, subjecting like
a slave, vassal, or servile government official   32.2.12   chén   臣
—yes, that too, oh 'female funnel!'   32.2.13   yâ   也

But *a marquis, 'arrow in the cave'*   32.3.14   hóu   侯
king, with his ceremonial jade axe or crown, connecting
the three levels of heaven, man, and earth?!"   32.3.15   wáng   王
         A Certain Someone compliantly combing her
         loose hair seems to be saying, "this is as if   32.3.16   ruò   若
         using that legendary Hybrid Power of a
         mythical bear-like animal who has the legs of a
         deer for   32.3.17   néng   能
         hand-defending this building,   32.3.18   shǒu   守
         what it has, stepping on from this footprint. 32.3.19   zhī   之

*[A hóu was someone appointed by the emperor to
govern a small remote area.]*

The medicine-dancing-scorpion insect swarm of   32.4.20   wàn   萬
matter (outside one's body, 'cut from the cow,' by a
bloodied blade),   32.4.21   wù   物
         would be assured, as if by hand-offering a meat
         tribute at an altar, a certain future of   32.4.22   jiāng   將
         oneself personally, right on the nose,   32.4.23   zì   自
         receiving as a guest, like a lady of the court, 32.4.24   bīn   賓

and the heavenly   32.5.25   tiān   天
now down here in this earthly womb,   32.5.26   dì   地
         would be like a seen tree and the eye seeing it
         (or like a well-tended lord and his attentive 32.5.27   xiāng   相

attendant) that, when taken together, create
the singular phenomenon of
joining together from three sides over a mouth,
like having sex,   32.5.28   hé   合
cultivating, like a plow,   32.5.29   yǐ   以
    two upside down feet falling down the
    soil mountain being birthed,
    descending   32.5.30   jiàng   降
    with pleasant, sweet-tasting in the
    mouth   32.5.31   gān   甘
    dew (like rain falling in two pairs of
    misty little drops onto the full leg of an
    animal, enough, each foot and mouth);   32.5.32   lù   露

one of our folk, the people enslaved by blinding with a
dagger,   32.6.33   mín   民
    like the sun sinking down in four bushes, you
    would not be—could not be, eh?—   32.6.34   mò   莫
    what it has, stepping on from this footprint, 32.6.35 zhī   之
    controlling, joining together from three sides
    over a kneeling person and ordering an action
    or perhaps sending off to somewhere,   32.6.36   lìng   令
        yet now, bearded, you   32.6.37   ér   而
        yourself personally, right on the nose,   32.6.38   zì   自
        would be evened out like soil that's
        been wrapped up in two parallel lines.   32.6.39   jūn   均

Conceiving, like a woman kneeling, happy, speaking of
gathering herself from three sides,   32.7.40   shǐ   始
those ruler edicts, like saying, 'cut that tree!' as was
done for parent-mourning rituals,   32.7.41   zhì   制
    with the flesh-and-meat-handling Being   32.7.42   yǒu   有

personal name given in childhood and still
whispered by moonlight,   32.7.43   míng   名

that personal name given in childhood and still
whispered by moonlight   32.8.44   míng   名
—both armpits sweat this too!—   32.8.45   yì   亦
    would be 'done'—as de facto as a kneeling
    person turning away after eating a bowl of
    rice—done with   32.8.46   jì   既
    flesh-and-meat-handling Being.   32.8.47   yǒu   有

In fact, that is to say This Grown Man with hairpin and
public courtesy name   32.9.48   fū   夫
—both armpits sweat this too!—   32.9.49   yì   亦
    would be assured, as if by hand-offering a meat
    tribute at an altar, a certain future of   32.9.50   jiāng   將
    speaking as a great big person to a baby,
    distinguishing, imparting, and administering
    wisdom confidently and intimately,   32.9.51   zhī   知
    halting right here in this footprint.   32.9.52   zhǐ   止

I'd be able to stop being Being but also be settled, once
and for all, in this role of wise speaker.

'Speaking as a great big person to a baby,
distinguishing, imparting, and administering wisdom
confidently and intimately,   32.10.53   zhī   知
halting right here in this footprint,'   32.10.54   zhǐ   止
lip-smackingly *genuinely*   32.10.55   kâ   可
would cultivate, like a plow,   32.10.56   yǐ   以
    being the husk of the initial protective bud
    casing but not really the true flower of   32.10.57   bù   不

endangered as human remains, spoken of
privately, revolving around yourself.   32.10.58   dài   殆

Metaphorically speaking, ruling over the words coming
out of your mouth like a ruler with that chisel used to
mark slaves and criminals, making them do what you
want: 32.11.59   pì   譬
     walking with the footprint of the loose-haired
     head buck,   32.11.60   dào   道
     what it has, stepping on from this footprint,   32.11.61   zhī   之
     in its existing sprouting of seedlings and talents,
     here on earth,   32.11.62   zài   在
         with the heavenly   32.11.63   tiān   天
         now here down below   32.11.64   xià   下

in the same manner as the unlikely rise of a dog
monkey to the top of the alcohol vat to become chief of
brewing, is like   32.12.65   yóu   猶
     a stream   32.12.66   chuān   川
     in a difficult position in a ravine, in an emptied,
     eroded valley mouth between two mountains,   32.12.67   gǔ   谷
     what it has, stepping on from this footprint,   32.12.68   zhī   之
     in this place and time, oh, black, icy raven sun,   32.12.69   yú   於
         the Yangtze River (the river that works
         like a stone axe) flowing into   32.12.70   jiāng   江
         a lushness like that of a river of new life
         sprouting from a nursing mother, like
         the ocean."   32.12.71   hǎi   海

Become a Marquis, and Dào's *current earthly gift of
sprouting with a heavenly spirit already down here on
earth will be like a stream in a dangerous ravine*

suddenly flowing as the Yangtze River into the ocean—
lush with life!

But how exactly could I stop being Being AND settle into
the role of speaking wisely? My friend explained it...

Chapter 33: A new plan in which I could be myself and still be a leader.

"Speaking as a great big person to a baby,
distinguishing, imparting, and administering wisdom
confidently and intimately,

33.1.1	zhī	知

as 'that person'

| 33.1.2 | rén | 人 |

—this is boiling sugarcane with fire as follows!—

| 33.1.3 | zhâ | 者 |

it's oh, so very pleasantly speaking with that
wise knowledge passed on from a great big
person to a baby, as if something sweet in the
mouth.

| 33.1.4 | zhì | 智 |

But, as oneself *personally, right on the nose,*

| 33.2.5 | zì | 自 |

speaking as a great big person to a baby,
distinguishing, imparting, and administering
wisdom confidently and intimately,

| 33.2.6 | zhī | 知 |

—this is boiling sugarcane with fire as
follows!—

| 33.2.7 | zhâ | 者 |

it's bright as dawn rising on a crescent moon,
enlightened.

| 33.2.8 | míng | 明 |

Able to withstand entirely, to be victorious as a
splendid piece of jewelry, an omen or the royal 'We'
mending something on a boat with two hands by the
strength of an arm, bladed tool, or a plow,

| 33.3.9 | shèng | 勝 |

as that person
—this is boiling sugarcane with fire as follows!—
  it's flesh-and-meat-handling Being
  being forceful as with the strength of an arm, a
  bladed tool, or a plow.

  But as oneself personally, right on the nose,
  able to withstand entirely, to be victorious as a
  splendid piece of jewelry, an omen or the royal
  'We' mending something on a boat with two
  hands by the strength of an arm, bladed tool,
  or a plow
  —this is boiling sugarcane with fire as
follows!—
    it's revolving around oneself as a
    powerful bow broadening,
    strengthening, stiff, hard, and
    compelling as a rice weevil, like a tiny
    venomous snake—thwang!

  True invincibility, as myself, was dealing
  with very late pregnancy, with Braxton-
  Hicks contractions, readying myself for
  delivery.

Speaking as a great big person to a baby, distinguishing,
imparting, and administering wisdom confidently and
intimately,
fully enough, like the whole leg as well as the footprint
—this is boiling sugarcane with fire as follows!—
  it's wealth, a home full of valuable vessels with
  lots of capacity.

33.3.10	rén	人
33.3.11	zhâ	者
33.3.12	yǒu	有
33.3.13	lì	力
33.4.14	zì	自
33.4.15	shèng	勝
33.4.16	zhâ	者
33.4.17	qiáng	強
33.5.18	zhī	知
33.5.19	zú	足
33.5.20	zhâ	者
33.5.21	fù	富

Speaking confidently as myself: that's the ticket.

Revolving around oneself as a powerful bow
broadening, strengthening, stiff, hard, and compelling
as a rice weevil, like a tiny venomous snake—
thwang!—   33.6.22   qiáng   強
out in public at the crossroads, being good, doing one's
work   33.6.23   xíng   行
—this is boiling sugarcane with fire as follows!—   33.6.24   zhâ   者
  it's flesh-and-meat-handling Being,   33.6.25   yǒu   有
  their will, stepping off from the heart's
  footprint here.   33.6.26   zhì   志

The husk of the initial false guard-petals but not really
the true flower of   33.7.27   bù   不
dropped from a hand,   33.7.28   shī   失
what it holds a basket of...   33.7.29   qí   其
'that place' being intentionally created like any
household gate hewn with an axe   33.7.30   suǒ   所
—this is boiling sugarcane with fire as follows!—   33.7.31   zhâ   者
  it's enduring through time as a person receiving
  moxibustion, that mugwort treatment for
  cramps, turning a breech baby, or other health
  issues.   33.7.32   jiǔ   久

'Dying, a person turning to a pile of bones,'   33.8.33   sǐ   死
yet now, bearded, you're   33.8.34   ér   而
the husk of the initial false guard-petals but *not really*
the true flower of   33.8.35   bù   不
someone *gone*, absent because they've perished or fled
by a knife's edge   33.8.36   wáng   亡
—this is boiling sugarcane with fire as follows!—   33.8.37   zhâ   者

it's longevity, an old man, '*Lǎo*,' sheltering
many mouths."

33.8.38 · shòu · 壽

*I would appear to die but actually become a marquis in
a conquered region removed from the capitol intrigues:
another, entirely new, dual identity.*

Chapter 34: I would be able to perform every role as my own person.

This great big person
walking with the footprint of the loose-haired head

34.1.1 · dà · 大

buck

34.1.2 · dào · 道

and spreading out everywhere like water overflowing
on a commonplace bucket,

34.1.3 · fàn · 氾

hmmm—like wind through tree branches!

34.1.4 · xī · 兮

What it holds a basket of

34.2.5 · qí · 其

is a lip-smackingly genuinely

34.2.6 · kâ · 可

inferior aide position, doing left-handed work
as with a bladed tool,

34.2.7 · zuǒ · 左

in a priority position, right hand over mouth.

34.2.8 · yòu · 右

The best of both worlds.

The medicine-dancing-scorpion insect swarm of

34.3.9 · wàn · 萬

matter (outside one's body, "cut from the cow" by a
bloodied blade),

34.3.10 · wù · 物

a mother—the heart grabbed like by the hand of a
government office or temple worker that was usually a
eunuch in the old days—

34.3.11 · shì · 恃

stepping on from this footprint, it will have this,

34.3.12 · zhī · 之

yet now, bearded, you'll be: 34.3.13 ér 而
sprouting a bud from the ground,   34.3.14 shēng 生
   yet now, bearded, you'll be   34.3.15 ér 而
   the husk of the initial false guard-petals
   but not really the true flower of 34.3.16 bù 不
   using a chisel (the one that marks
   slaves and criminals) to rule as a hand
   from above over a hand with a
   common bucket in a place outside the
   city;   34.3.17 cí 辭

laboring with the force of a blade and the work
of one's arm or a plow   34.4.18 gōng 功
completing, that final 'nail' in a weapon on a
pole,   34.4.19 chéng 成
   the husk of the initial false guard-petals
   but not really the true flower of 34.4.20 bù 不
   that personal name given in childhood
   and still whispered by moonlight, 34.4.21 míng 名
   flesh-and-meat-handling Being; 34.4.22 yǒu 有

clothing, like draping with a robe as the
placental afterbirth hanging from a recently
pregnant woman,   34.5.23 yī 衣
and feeding, mouth over a rice bowl, as
beautiful as a ram's head,   34.5.24 yǎng 養
the medicine-dancing-scorpion insect swarm of 34.5.25 wàn 萬
matter (outside one's body, 'cut from the cow,'
by a bloodied blade),   34.5.26 wù 物
   yet now, bearded, you'll be   34.5.27 ér 而
   the husk of the initial false guard-petals
   but not really the true flower of 34.5.28 bù 不

creating something by hand, carving an
elephant likeness of good fortune and
royal power,   34.5.29   wéi   為
as you, "oh, honored senior official
master," owner, and host of the flame.   34.5.30   zhǔ   主

When this conventional royal administrator wearing a
men's headcloth as his skirt,   34.6.31   cháng 常
as the shamanic dancer with animal tails flowing from
her wrists, Not-Having,   34.6.32   wú   無
is missing, kneeling with a yawning mouth before a
ravine eroded between two mountains, wanting,
lacking   34.6.33   yù   欲
        the lip-smackingly genuinely   34.6.34   kâ   可
        personal name given in childhood and still
        whispered by moonlight,   34.6.35   míng   名
        will be in this place and time, oh, black, icy
        raven sun: 34.6.36   yú   於
                our tiny dear little one, like three grains
                of sand.   34.6.37   xiǎo   小

*Back in Chapter 1, "when the conventional royal
administrator as Not-Having was missing, the
watchtower kept lookout for a young woman with the
mysterious essence of a young prince wafting off her
back." But with this new plan, when my Not-Having
person goes missing, the real me will be with our tiny,
dear little one!*

The medicine-dancing-scorpion insect swarm of   34.7.38   wàn   萬
matter (outside one's body, "cut from the cow" by a
bloodied blade)   34.7.39   wù   物

will be coming back after sweeping troops out of the
soil mound hills to this
here, straightening things out for "nailing" that first
footstep of a journey on the back of this yellow bird
with the "dangling tail" that lives around the Yangtze
and Huai Rivers—right here, huh!—
      yet now, bearded, you'll be
the husk of the initial protective bud casing but
not really the true flower of
creating something by hand, carving an
elephant likeness of good fortune and royal
power,
          as you, "oh, honored senior official
          master," owner, and host of the flame.

The lip-smackingly genuine
personal name given in childhood and still
whispered by moonlight
will be creating something by hand, carving an
elephant likeness of good fortune and royal
power,
          as this great big person.

This is cultivating, like a plow,
what it holds a basket of
is ending like the knot at the end of a thick silk
skein, like winter,
the husk of the initial false guard-petals but not
really the true flower of
as yourself personally, right on the nose,
creating something by hand, carving an
elephant likeness of fortune and royal power,
          as this great big person.

34.7.40	guī	歸
34.7.41	yān	焉
34.7.42	ér	而
34.7.43	bù	不
34.7.44	wéi	為
34.7.45	zhǔ	主
34.8.46	kâ	可
34.8.47	míng	名
34.8.48	wéi	為
34.8.49	dà	大
34.9.50	yǐ	以
34.9.51	qí	其
34.9.52	zhōng	終
34.9.53	bù	不
34.9.54	zì	自
34.9.55	wéi	為
34.9.56	dà	大

I can stop creating as anyone other than myself.

This taps lightly with a tutoring cane and leaves a mark		
on the solid shield of the past:	34.10.57	gù 故
that legendary Hybrid Power of a mythical bear-like		
animal who has the legs of a deer	34.10.58	néng 能
will be completing, that final "nail" in a weapon on a		
pole,	34.10.59	chéng 成
what it holds a basket of,	34.10.60	qí 其
this great big person.	34.10.61	dà 大

Chapter 35: Unlike either of my old lives, it would be safe and moderate.

A kneeling person, arrested and held, arms		
outstretched in handcuffs,	35.1.1	zhí 執
this great big person,	35.1.2	dà 大
like an elephant skeleton to a living elephant, is		
bearing a likeness to something:	35.1.3	xiàng 象
with the heavenly from high above this		
great big person	35.1.4	tiān 天
now here down below,	35.1.5	xià 下
a person is walking slowly toward you		
with the luxuriant footprint of a king,		
the left leg leading the way.	35.1.6	wǎng 往

Uh oh. Not again?!

A person is walking slowly toward you with the		
luxuriant footprint of a king, the left leg leading the		
way,	35.2.7	wǎng 往
yet now, bearded, you'll be	35.2.8	ér 而

the husk of the initial false guard-petals but not
really the true flower of
being harmed as a house in which weeds
sprout from a mouth
      but staying calm as a woman sitting on
      her heels at home,
      pacified, divided, and leveled (as with a
      pestle) until made even,
      the quite greatest biggest person—
      period!

Pleasurably playing, as glad music upon a wooden
instrument's two silk strings,
participating with (a "biting tooth" lifted by a pair of
hands onto strong shoulders, perhaps interfering with
or perhaps supporting)
alluring food made from rice dough (you'd love to put
your mouth over that bowl, 'Âr'),
      what's past and surpassing, maybe "passed
      away," maybe excessive, walking slowly with
      the footprint of a slanting skull mouth
      speaking, the left leg leading the way,
      was entering a house as a guest like you're the
      last one, sticking out like the knot at the end of
      a cord,
      and halting right here in this footprint;

but walking with the footprint of the loose-haired head
buck,
what it has, stepping on from this footprint,
stepping out of their cave
with the words from their mouth

35.2.9	bù	不
35.2.10	hài	害
35.2.11	ān	妄
35.2.12	píng	平
35.2.13	tài	太
35.3.14	lè	樂
35.3.15	yǔ	與
35.3.16	âr	餌
35.3.17	guò	過
35.3.18	kè	客
35.3.19	zhǐ	止
35.4.20	dào	道
35.4.21	zhī	之
35.4.22	chū	出
35.4.23	kǒu	口

as bland as a pair of flames doused by a river of
water | 35.5.24 | dàn | 淡
—PAH, CAN YOU?! | 35.5.25 | hū | 乎
What it holds a basket of | 35.5.26 | qí | 其
is the shamanic dancer with animal tails flowing
from her wrists, Not-Having, | 35.5.27 | wú | 無
tasting, reflecting on a flavor in the mouth
which is still forming like a tree whose top
branches are not yet fully grown. | 35.5.28 | wèi | 味

*No more of either of the old ways—not fearing
authorities and not the fancy life!*

Regarded as by one big eye for a head, kneeling at an
altar, | 35.6.29 | shì | 視
what it will have, stepping on from this footprint, | 35.6.30 | zhī | 之
will be the husk of the initial false *guard-petals
but not really the true flower of* | 35.6.31 | bù | 不
*fully enough, like the whole leg as well as the
footprint* | 35.6.32 | zú | 足
seen by someone with one big eye for a head. | 35.6.33 | jiàn | 見

*This is like the sentiment from Chapter 14, but now I'll
be not really "fully enough" seen. I'll be seen, all right,
but I'll be seen as the Marquis.*

Hearing, an ear listening to voices, perhaps heeding,
allowing, or handling matters of state, | 35.7.34 | tīng | 聽
what it will have, stepping on from this footprint, | 35.7.35 | zhī | 之
will be the husk of the initial false guard-petals
but not really the true flower of | 35.7.36 | bù | 不
fully enough, like the whole leg as well as the
footprint | 35.7.37 | zú | 足

heard at the two-winged gateway and famously
reported on;   35.7.38   wén   聞

doing truly useful work like a water bucket, by means
of carrying-capacity   35.8.39   yòng   用
what it will have, stepping on from this footprint,   35.8.40   zhī   之
    will be the husk of the initial protective bud
    casing but not really the true flower of   35.8.41   bù   不
    fully enough, like the whole leg as well as the
    footprint   35.8.42   zú   足
    "done"—as de facto as a kneeling person
    turning away after eating a bowl of rice, done.   35.8.43   jì   既

**Chapter 36: But first, I had to remain "in the deep
water" for a bit longer. Such is the nature of planning
an escape and of delivering a baby—both involve a
long-term strategy full of seeming opposites.**

*[Chapter 29 began in much the same way as this
chapter, but back then I didn't have this plan.]*

Assured, as if by hand-offering a meat tribute at an
altar, a certain future of   36.1.1   jiāng   將
missing, kneeling with a yawning mouth before a ravine
eroded between two mountains, wanting, lacking,   36.1.2   yù   欲
    while sucking in, coming together, a kneeling
    person with their mouth open, their back
    toward one open mouth atop another mouth
    above a pair of little wings,   36.1.3   xī   歙
    what it has, stepping on from this footprint...   36.1.4   zhī   之

then hands over heart, analytically,	36.2.5	bì	必
solidly, for a long time, keeping as firm to what			
happened in the first place as this land surrounding and			
holding this nation's shield since ancient times,	36.2.6	gù	固
stretch out, like lengthening the bow string,	36.2.7	zhāng	張
what it has, stepping on from this footprint.	36.2.8	zhī	之
Assured a future of	36.3.9	jiāng	將
missing, kneeling with a yawning mouth before a ravine			
eroded between two mountains, wanting, lacking,	36.3.10	yù	欲
while in a delicate state with a pair of fragile			
bows,	36.3.11	ruò	弱
what it has, stepping on from this footprint...	36.3.12	zhī	之
then hands over heart, analytically,	36.4.13	bì	必
solidly keep firm to what happened in the first place,	36.4.14	gù	固
revolving around themself as a powerful bow			
broadening, strengthening, stiff, hard, and			
compelling as a rice weevil, like a tiny			
venomous snake— thwang!—	36.4.15	qiáng	強
what it has, stepping on from this footprint.	36.4.16	zhī	之
Assured a future of	36.5.17	jiāng	將
missing, kneeling with a yawning mouth before a ravine			
eroded between two mountains, wanting, lacking,	36.5.18	yù	欲
while collapsing like a house shot by a bow			
launching—thwang!—and leveling a pair of			
grass sprouts with one's feet as effectively as if			
by hand with a halberd,	36.5.19	fèi	廢
what it has, stepping on from this footprint...	36.5.20	zhī	之
then hands over heart, analytically,	36.6.21	bì	必
solidly keep firm to what happened in the first place,	36.6.22	gù	固

lift together, clasping two pairs of hands
together in front of ones' chests and together
carrying ones' shields,   36.6.23 xìng 興
what it has, stepping on from this footprint. 36.6.24 zhī 之

Assured a future of   36.7.25 jiāng 將
missing, kneeling with a yawning mouth before a ravine
eroded between two mountains, wanting, lacking 36.7.26 yù 欲
  while seizing, snatching 'a spread-winged bird'
  with your forearm where your pulse beats
  strong,   36.7.27 duó 奪
  what it has, stepping on from this footprint... 36.7.28 zhī 之

then hands over heart, analytically,   36.8.29 bì 必
solidly keep firm to what happened in the first place, 36.8.30 gù 固
  participating with (a "biting tooth" lifted by a
  pair of hands onto strong shoulders, perhaps
  interfering with or perhaps supporting) 36.8.31 yǔ 與
  what it has, stepping on from this footprint. 36.8.32 zhī 之

This baby footprint on bamboo-slip pages, 36.9.33 shì 是
by the nitty-gritty, grinding gizzard of a fowl, what
that's called,   36.9.34 wèi 謂
  "trifling," a slight thing, this admired beauty
  wearing a ram's horn headdress and stepping
  slowly with only the left leg leading, a tutoring
  cane lightly tapping their hair, combing out or
  "splitting hairs," not having much, 36.9.35 wēi 微
    is bright as dawn rising on a crescent
    moon, enlightened,   36.9.36 míng 明

  softening to be as supple as a tree that can be
  cut with a spear   36.10.37 róu 柔

in a delicate state with a pair of fragile bows   36.10.38   ruò   弱
    is able to withstand entirely, to be
    victorious as a splendid piece of
    jewelry, an omen or the royal "We"
    mending something on a boat with two
    hands by the strength of an arm,
    bladed tool, or a plow,   36.10.39   shèng   勝
    firm, like a web of mountain within a
    net as strong as a blade,   36.10.40   gāng   剛
    while revolving around itself as a
    powerful bow broadening,
    strengthening, stiff, hard, and
    compelling as a rice weevil, like a tiny
    venomous snake— thwang!   36.10.41   qiáng   強

Fish   36.11.42   yú   魚
    are the husk of the initial false guard-petals but
    not really the true flower of   36.11.43   bù   不
    lip-smackingly genuinely   36.11.44   kâ   可
    freely exchanging the meat of their matter,
    stripping themself like a smiling breathy older
    brother of,   36.11.45   tuō   脫
    in this place and time, oh, black, icy raven sun,   36.11.46   yú   於
        deep water;   36.11.47   yuān   淵

likewise, our domestic enclave, defended by a weapon
on a pole,   36.12.48   guó   國
what it has, stepping on from this footprint,   36.12.49   zhī   之
in reaping benefits in the manner of a sharp-edged
blade slicing grain...   36.12.50   lì   利
a set of highly regarded vessels with lots of capacity,
worthy of a guard dog,   36.12.51   qì   器

is the husk of the initial false guard-petals but
not really the true flower of | 36.13.52 | bù | 不
lip-smackingly genuinely | 36.13.53 | kâ | 可
cultivating, like a plow, | 36.13.54 | yǐ | 以
    being displayed on an altar, | 36.13.55 | shì | 示
    that person. | 36.13.56 | rén | 人

Chapter 37: The plan for living as a marquis king

*"Walking with the footprint of the loose-haired head
buck* | 37.1.1 | dào | 道
*as the conventional royal administrator wearing a
men's headcloth for his skirt,* | 37.1.2 | cháng | 常
    the shamanic dancer with animal tails flowing
    from her wrists, Not-Having, | 37.1.3 | wú | 無
    is creating something by hand, carving an
    elephant likeness of good fortune and royal
    power, | 37.1.4 | wéi | 為

    yet, now you're bearded, | 37.2.5 | ér | 而
    shaman-dancing Not-Having | 37.2.6 | wú | 無
    is the husk of the initial false guard-petals but
    not really the true flower of | 37.2.7 | bù | 不
    creating something by hand, carving an
    elephant likeness of good fortune and royal
    power. | 37.2.8 | wéi | 為

As a marquis, 'arrow in the cave' | 37.3.9 | hóu | 侯
*king, with his ceremonial jade axe or crown, connecting
the three levels of heaven, man, and earth?"* | 37.3.10 | wáng | 王
    A Certain Someone compliantly combing her
    loose hair seems to be saying "this is as if | 37.3.11 | ruò | 若

using that legendary Hybrid Power of a
mythical bear-like animal who has the legs of a
deer for   37.3.12   néng   能
hand-defending this building   37.3.13   shǒu   守
what it has, stepping on from this footprint: 37.3.14   zhī   之

The medicine-dancing-scorpion insect swarm of   37.4.15   wàn   萬
matter (outside one's body, 'cut from the cow,' by a
bloodied blade),   37.4.16   wù   物
    is assured, as if by hand-offering a meat tribute
    at an altar, a certain future of   37.4.17   jiāng   將
    yourself personally, right on the nose,   37.4.18   zì   自
    transforming as a right-side-up person into an
    upside-down person...   37.4.19   huà   化

    transforming as a right-side-up person into an
    upside-down person,   37.5.20   huà   化
    yet, now you're bearded,   37.5.21   ér   而
        missing, kneeling with a yawning
        mouth before a ravine eroded between
        two mountains, wanting, lacking,   37.5.22   yù   欲
        while recently, exactly, having
        immediately folded from one straight
        rod into two.   37.5.23   zuò   作

Counting up on all five fingers, aren't I   37.6.24   wú   吾
    assured, as if by hand-offering a meat tribute at
    an altar, a certain future of   37.6.25   jiāng   將
    calming, sedating, chilling with genuine ancient
    axed-copper-alloy divination spoon and
    cauldron for a long time,   37.6.26   zhèn   鎮
    what it has, stepping on from this footprint,   37.6.27   zhī   之
        and, cultivating, like a plow,   37.6.28   yǐ   以

the shaman-dancing Not-Having
personal name given in childhood and
still whispered by moonlight,
what it has, stepping on from this
footprint...
that 'piece of wood' in the dense,
unpolished, sticking, natural state of a
thicket of oak trees?

37.6.29	wú	無
37.6.30	míng	名
37.6.31	zhī	之
37.6.32	pǔ	樸

"The shaman-dancing Not-Having
personal name,
what it has, stepping on from this footprint,
that 'piece of wood' in the dense, unpolished, sticking,
natural state of a thicket of oak trees...
in fact, that is to say This Grown Man with hairpin and
public courtesy name"
—both armpits sweat this too!—
is assured, as if by hand-offering a meat tribute
at an altar, a certain future of
shaman-dancing Not-Having
missing, kneeling with a yawning mouth before
a ravine eroded between two mountains,
wanting, lacking...

37.7.33	wú	無
37.7.34	míng	名
37.7.35	zhī	之
37.7.36	pǔ	樸
37.7.37	fū	夫
37.7.38	yì	亦
37.7.39	jiāng	將
37.7.40	wú	無
37.7.41	yù	欲

the husk of the initial protective bud casing but
not really the true flower of
missing, kneeling with a yawning mouth before
a ravine eroded between two mountains,
wanting, lacking,
this is cultivating, like a plow,
calm peace, the clear blue-green
growth of the sedative cinnabar plant

37.8.42	bù	不
37.8.43	yù	欲
37.8.44	yǐ	以
37.8.45	jìng	靜

quieting a dispute between two hands
on a plowshare.

The heavenly from high above this great big person   37.9.46   tiān   天
now here down below   37.9.47   xià   下
    is assured, as if by hand-offering a meat tribute
    at an altar, a certain future of   37.9.48   jiāng   將
    yourself personally, right on the nose,   37.9.49   zì   自
    being as stable and determined as when one
    puts a roof over their departure, *'nailing' that*
    first step of the journey."   37.9.50   dìng   定

What could be better than to be assured that the beloved heavenly
spirit and I could stay together with me solid and ready to go—ready to
end that very busy part of my life in which I went from the wild-haired
head buck to the emperor's Handpicked Gem, "Being," a secret mother.
I was set to live the rest of my life as yet another new man, a marquis
living the Dé.

This was the last chapter of my original writings since the book of the
Dé came before the book of the Dào. The next section describes my
plans for that Dé *life.*

<u>*Dé*</u>

Walking In Alignment with Your Eyes Looking Forward, Directly Over Your Heart

Chapter 38: My old high life with the emperor vs. the new, humbler life I set up for myself

On top,	38.1.1	shàng	上
walking with the footprint of someone who's in alignment (eyes looking forward, directly over the heart, left leg slowly leading the way),	38.1.2	dé	德
the husk of the initial protective bud casing but not really the true flower of	38.1.3	bù	不
walking with the footprint of someone who's in alignment:	38.1.4	dé	德
this baby footprint on bamboo-slip pages,	38.2.5	shì	是
this is cultivating, like a plow,	38.2.6	yǐ	以
flesh-and-meat-handling "Being"	38.2.7	yǒu	有
walking with the footprint of someone who's in alignment.	38.2.8	dé	德
Now here down below,	38.3.9	xià	下
walking with the footprint of someone who's in alignment,	38.3.10	dé	德
the husk of the initial protective bud casing but not really the true flower of	38.3.11	bù	不
dropped from a hand,	38.3.12	shī	失
walking with the footprint of someone who's in alignment:	38.3.13	dé	德

this baby footprint on bamboo-slip pages, 38.4.14 shì 是
this is cultivating, like a plow, 38.4.15 yǐ 以
a shamanic dancer with animal tails
flowing from her wrists, "Not-Having," 38.4.16 wú 無
walking with the footprint of someone
who's in alignment. 38.4.17 dé 德

*As I wrote this for Yinxi on my way out of the
country, I reflected on how, in the high life with the
emperor, my Being persona hadn't been heart-
aligned even though I worked to make sure it
looked that way. So, in my new humbler station, I
wouldn't be dropping alignment, really. In fact, I
felt sure that my true Not-Having self would have
the chance to be genuinely aligned at last.*

On top, 38.5.18 shàng 上
walking with the footprint of someone who's in
alignment 38.5.19 dé 德
and shaman-dancing Not-Having 38.5.20 wú 無
creating something by hand, carving an elephant
likeness of good fortune and royal power, 38.5.21 wéi 為
    yet, now you're bearded, 38.5.22 ér 而
    shaman-dancing Not-Having 38.5.23 wú 無
    is the husk of the initial protective bud
    casing but not really the true flower of 38.5.24 bù 不
    creating something by hand, carving an
    elephant likeness of good fortune and
    royal power. 38.5.25 wéi 為

Now here down below, 38.6.26 xià 下
walking with the footprint of someone who's in
alignment 38.6.27 dé 德

and creating something by hand, carving an
elephant likeness of good fortune and royal power,   38.6.28   wéi   為
    what it has, stepping on from this
    footprint,   38.6.29   zhī   之
    yet, now you're bearded,   38.6.30   ér   而
    is flesh-and-meat-handling Being   38.6.31   yǒu   有
    cultivating, like a plow,   38.6.32   yǐ   以
    creating something by hand, carving an
    elephant likeness of good fortune and
    royal power.   38.6.33   wéi   為

On top, I'd hid the true self that was creating
something. In a lower position, my Being person
could cultivate that process. Which would be nice
because that high life had deteriorated...

On top,   38.7.34   shàng   上
a kernel of humanity—a person seated over not
just one but two, a different *èr*—   38.7.35   rén   仁
and creating something by hand, carving an
elephant likeness of good fortune and royal power,   38.7.36   wéi   為
    what it has, stepping on from this
    footprint,   38.7.37   zhī   之
    yet, now you're bearded,   38.7.38   ér   而
    is shaman-dancing Not-Having,   38.7.39   wú   無
    cultivating, like a plow,   38.7.40   yǐ   以
    creating something by hand, carving an
    elephant likeness of good fortune and
    royal power.   38.7.41   wéi   為

Once the emperor knew exactly who I was, things
changed: when I got pregnant again, he knew

exactly what was happening, and so things went
very differently than they had the first time...

On top,
sacrificing a ram with that rake-like weapon we use
to defend ourselves and our opinions, righteous,
and creating something by hand, carving an
elephant likeness of good fortune and royal power,
    what it has, stepping on from this
    footprint,
    yet, now you're bearded,
    is flesh-and-meat-handling Being
    cultivating, like a plow,
    creating something by hand, carving an
    elephant likeness of good fortune and
    royal power;

38.8.42	shàng	上
38.8.43	yì	義
38.8.44	wéi	為
38.8.45	zhī	之
38.8.46	ér	而
38.8.47	yǒu	有
38.8.48	yǐ	以
38.8.49	wéi	為

At first, when the emperor knew my Being self
actually was a pregnant woman, he let me
continue the duties of the life I had created, albeit
with a lot of sacrifice. But...

On top,
making ritual offerings of honor at an altar with
two strings of jade and a feathered drum in the lap
of luxury
and creating something by hand, carving an
elephant likeness of good fortune and royal power,
    what it has, stepping on from this
    footprint,
    yet, now you're bearded,
    like the sun sinking down in four bushes...
    you must not be—cannot be, eh?—

38.9.50	shàng	上
38.9.51	lǐ	禮
38.9.52	wéi	為
38.9.53	zhī	之
38.9.54	ér	而
38.9.55	mò	莫

what it has, stepping on from this
footprint,   38.9.56   zhī   之
agreeably echoing an answer like a heart in
a habitable cliff cave with a bird of prey, a
bird with a dangling tail together with a
small-tailed bird.   38.9.57   yīng 應

*Going through all the motions, it was important I
not actually and lose my self in agreeing with the
emperor. But I did.*

After following this sacrificial blade-and-cauldron-
like ritual regulation,   38.10.58   zé   則
a hand is rolling up a sleeve, helping to undress   38.10.59   rǎng 攘
an arm, the meat of a ruler or dead husband who
administered and punished, marking a kneeling
slave or criminal with a chisel,   38.10.60   bì   臂
   yet, now you're bearded,   38.10.61   ér   而
   the hand rather unexpectedly throws away
   what it holds,   38.10.62   réng 扔
      what it has, stepping on from this
      footprint. 38.10.63   zhī   之

*Here's the history of what happened each time I
rolled up my sleeves and threw away what I had…*

This taps lightly with a tutoring cane and leaves a
mark on the solid shield of the past…   38.11.64   gù   故
dropped from a hand,   38.11.65   shī   失
walking with the footprint of the loose-haired head
buck,   38.11.66   dào   道
   yet, now you're bearded,   38.11.67   ér   而

walking slowly with just the left leg leading
the way, and leaving behind this tiny silk
thread footprint like a knot in a thread, a
descendant, at the end:　　　　　　　　38.11.68　hòu　後
       walking with the footprint of
       someone who's in alignment;　　38.11.69　dé　德

dropped from a hand,　　　　　　　　　38.12.70　shī　失
walking with the footprint of someone who's in
alignment,　　　　　　　　　　　　　　38.12.71　dé　德
    yet, now you're bearded,　　　　　38.12.72　ér　而
    leaving this descendant at the end:　38.12.73　hòu　後
       a kernel of humanity—a person
       seated over not just one but two, a
       different *èr*;　　　　　　　　38.12.74　rén　仁

dropped from a hand,　　　　　　　　　38.13.75　shī　失
a kernel of humanity—a person seated over not
just one but two, a different *èr*—　　　38.13.76　rén　仁
    yet, now you're bearded,　　　　　38.13.77　ér　而
    leaving this descendant at the end:　38.13.78　hòu　後
       sacrificing a ram with that rake-like
       weapon we use to defend
       ourselves and our opinions,
       righteous;　　　　　　　　　　38.13.79　yì　義

and dropped from a hand,　　　　　　　38.14.80　shī　失
sacrificing a ram with that rake-like weapon we use
to defend ourselves and our opinions, righteous,　38.14.81　yì　義
    yet, now you're bearded,　　　　　38.14.82　ér　而
    leaving this descendant at the end:　38.14.83　hòu　後

       making ritual offerings of honor at
       an altar with two strings of jade

and a feathered drum in the lap of
luxury.   38.14.84   lǐ   禮

In fact, that is to say *"This Grown Man"* with
hairpin and public courtesy name: 38.15.85   fū   夫
making ritual offerings of honor at an altar with
two strings of jade and a feathered drum, in the lap
of luxury—   38.15.86   lǐ   禮
—this is boiling sugarcane with fire as follows!— 38.15.87   zhâ   者
    that centered heart, like that drum with a
    flagpole placed in the middle of a field to
    gather the people,   38.15.88   zhōng   忠
    giving one's word to a person...   38.15.89   xìn   信
        what it has, stepping on from this
        footprint, it has this   38.15.90   zhī   之
        thin covering of two sprouts of
        grass, not really covering the
        widespread river of a man's public
        courtesy name, reduced to one
        short inch the size of that spot on
        the forearm where the pulse beats
        strong,   38.15.91   bó   薄

yet, now you're bearded,   38.16.92   ér   而
trying to govern in chaos, two people
disentangling a roll of threads using their
hands with the help of a comb or beater...   38.16.93   luàn   亂
        what it has, stepping on from this
        footprint, it has this   38.16.94   zhī   之
        face of the mythical loose-haired
        head buck;   38.16.95   shǒu   首

at the front (that place in battle where a step could mean your feet get cut off as punishment),	38.17.96	qián 前
intimately known, speaking of what's gathered with a tone from the mouth by a dagger-ax, marked and remembered	38.17.97	shí 識
—this is boiling sugarcane with fire as follows!—	38.17.98	zhâ 者
walking with the footprint of the loose-haired head buck,	38.17.99	dào 道
what it has, stepping on from this footprint,	38.17.100	zhī 之
is a decorative brilliant magnificence, a flower blooming,	38.17.101	huá 華
yet, now you're bearded, a heart like that trampling monkey with the head of a ghost,	38.18.102	ér 而
	38.18.103	yú 愚
what it has, stepping on from this footprint,	38.18.104	zhī 之
is conceiving, a woman kneeling, happy, speaking of gathering herself from three sides.	38.18.105	shĭ 始

I moved from Dào *into* Dé *when I needed safety during my first pregnancy. But then, step by step, I sacrificed more and more and ended up in a life of empty ritual. Once the emperor knew the truth of who I was, my cover was thinned, and I was left trying to straighten out chaos with my true face revealed. Instead of being the soldier and advisor I*

once was, I found myself "intimately known" at the
frontlines, the Dào *now merely a decorative flourish*
and my bearded, foolish heart conceiving a baby.
Again.

This baby footprint on bamboo-slip pages,   38.19.106   shì   是
this is cultivating, like a plow,   38.19.107   yǐ   以
this great big person   38.19.108   dà   大
and a respected man or husband from whom one
maintains a distance of ten feet,   38.19.109   zhàng 丈
in fact, that is to say "This Grown Man" with
hairpin and public courtesy name: 38.19.110   fū   夫

disappearing like a tiger head at home, footprint
pointed back down by a table, staying here, chaste,
rather than accepting a government position or
getting married,   38.20.111   chù   處
    what it holds a basket of   38.20.112   qí   其
    is a jug in a habitable cave in a cliff, *thick*
    and generous...   38.20.113   hòu   厚

the husk of the initial protective bud casing but not
really the true flower of   38.21.114   bù   不
staying put here, sitting over the solid shield of the
past at this birthplace, where   38.21.115   jū   居
    what it holds a basket of   38.21.116   qí   其
    is a *thin covering* of two sprouts of grass,
    not really covering the widespread river of
    a man's public courtesy name, reduced to
    one short inch the size of that spot on the
    forearm where the pulse beats strong;   38.21.117   bó   薄

disappearing like a tiger head at home, footprint
pointed back down by a table, staying here, chaste,
rather than accepting a government position or
getting married,   38.22.118   chù   處
          what it holds a basket of   38.22.119   qí   其
          is filling, like a truly rich building crammed
          with jade and cowry-shells...   38.22.120   shí   實

the husk of the initial protective bud casing but not
really the true flower of   38.23.121   bù   不
staying put here, sitting over the solid shield of the
past at this birthplace, where   38.23.122   jū   居
          what it holds a basket of   38.23.123   qí   其
          is a *decorative* brilliant magnificence, a
          flower blooming.   38.23.124   huá   華

This taps lightly with a tutoring cane and leaves a
mark on the solid shield of the past: 38.24.125   gù   故
a person with a cave mouth between their legs, is
leaving   38.24.126   qù   去
          that fur stripped by hand from its pelt on
          the road where they stepped slowly, the
          left leg leading the way,   38.24.127   bǐ   彼
and is getting hold of, grabbing the ear of   38.24.128   qù   取
          this here—the foot stops a person here on
          this footprint!   38.24.129   cǐ   此

*As a "well-respected man" who also happened to
be pregnant, it was better to disappear rather than
perform empty rituals or run off to the front.*

*But when I became pregnant the second time, I
could no longer disappear within that life I'd*

created, like I had in my first pregnancy. After all, the emperor knew. To disappear, I'd have to leave that life completely. That's why I'd decided to appoint myself, under yet another new identity, to be a marquis king in one of the emperor's holdings outside of the capitol. I had it all planned out.

Chapter 39: I had an idealized pregnancy plan based on my life as the chosen one, but as delivery drew closer and I considered going through that again, much less doing it as my own Not-Having self while implementing my new marquis strategy, panic hit.

Ancient times, when floods covered the sun,	39.1.1	xī	昔
stepping on from this footprint, it had this	39.1.2	zhī	之
Hand-Picked Gem, like cowry-shell-riches			
discovered along the road,	39.1.3	dé	得
"The One"	39.1.4	yī	一
—this is boiling sugarcane with fire as follows!	39.1.5	zhâ	者

Regarding the heavenly from high above this great big person,	39.2.6	tiān	天
The Hand-Picked Gem,	39.2.7	dé	得
The One,	39.2.8	yī	一
was cultivating, like a plow,	39.2.9	yǐ	以
the clarity of still bright blue-green water, the color resembling the growth of that sedative cinnabar plant;	39.2.10	qīng	清

regarding here in this earthly womb,   39.3.11   dì   地

    The Hand-Picked Gem,   39.3.12   dé   得

    The One,   39.3.13   yī   一

        was cultivating, like a plow,   39.3.14   yǐ   以
        being as settled as when a married
        woman visits her parents' home,
        her heart under their roof with
        food and wine, and she exhales;   39.3.15   níng   寧

regarding that magical god spirit lightning, the
divine spark,   39.4.16   shén   神

    The Hand-Picked Gem,   39.4.17   dé   得

    The One,   39.4.18   yī   一

        was cultivating, like a plow,   39.4.19   yǐ   以
        being nimble as a god or spirit, a
        cloudburst raining two pairs of
        misty little drops into three bigger
        drops above two pieces of jade
        crossed over each other like a
        shaman-witch uses or perhaps a
        coffin;   39.4.20   líng   靈

regarding being in a difficult position in a ravine, in
an emptied, eroded valley mouth between two
mountains,   39.5.21   gǔ   谷

    The Hand-Picked Gem,   39.5.22   dé   得

    The One,   39.5.23   yī   一

        was cultivating, like a plow,   39.5.24   yǐ   以
        a vessel full to overflowing;   39.5.25   yíng   盈

regarding the medicine-dancing-scorpion insect
swarm of   39.6.26   wàn   萬

matter (outside one's body, "cut from the cow" by
a bloodied blade),   39.6.27   wù   物
    The Hand-Picked Gem,   39.6.28   dé   得
    The One,   39.6.29   yī   一
        was cultivating, like a plow,   39.6.30   yǐ   以
        sprouting a bud from the ground;   39.6.31   shēng   生

regarding a marquis, "arrow in the cave"   39.7.32   hóu   侯
king, with his ceremonial jade axe or crown,
connecting the three levels of heaven, man, and
earth,   39.7.33   wáng   王
    The Hand-Picked Gem,   39.7.34   dé   得
    The One,   39.7.35   yī   一
        was cultivating, like a plow,   39.7.36   yǐ   以
        creating something by hand,
        carving an elephant likeness of
        good fortune and royal power,   39.7.37   wéi   為
        the heavenly from high above this
        great big person   39.7.38   tiān   天
        now here down below,   39.7.39   xià   下
        like an ancient divination cauldron,
        faithful, pure, and chaste as a
        proper woman.   39.7.40   zhēn   貞

But what it holds a basket of   39.8.41   qí   其
*thoroughly delivering, exhausting, arriving at the
extreme* (like an arrow stuck in the ground and
tapped lightly with a tutoring cane so as to leave a
mark),   39.8.42   zhì   致
stepping on from this footprint, it has this: 39.8.43   zhī   之

regarding the heavenly from high above this great
big person,   39.9.44   tiān   天
    the shamanic dancer with animal tails
    flowing from her wrists, Not-Having,   39.9.45   wú   無
    cultivating, like a plow,   39.9.46   yǐ   以
    the clarity of still bright blue-green water   39.9.47   qīng   清
        is assured, as if by hand-offering a
        meat tribute at an altar, *a certain*
        future of   39.9.48   jiāng   將
        fearing (their heart like a
        commonplace dish scraped with a
        blade)   39.9.49   kǒng   恐
        being rendered, a blade tearing a
        robe or the placental afterbirth
        hanging from a recently pregnant
        woman;   39.9.50   liè   裂

regarding now down here in this earthly womb,   39.10.51   dì   地
    shaman-dancing Not-Having   39.10.52   wú   無
    cultivating, like a plow,   39.10.53   yǐ   以
    being as settled as when a married woman
    visits her parents' home, her heart under
    their roof with food and wine, and she
    exhales,   39.10.54   níng   寧
        is assured a certain future of   39.10.55   jiāng   將
        fearing   39.10.56   kǒng   恐
        being shot by a bow launching—
        "thwang!"—and leveling grass
        underfoot as effectively as if by
        hand with a halberd;   39.10.57   fā   發

regarding that magical god spirit lightning, the
divine ,   39.11.58   shén   神
    shaman-dancing Not-Having   39.11.59   wú   無
    cultivating, like a plow,   39.11.60   yǐ   以
    being nimble as a god or spirit   39.11.61   líng   靈
        is assured a certain future of   39.11.62   jiāng   將
        fearing   39.11.63   kǒng   恐
        fading, a mouth begging for alms
        behind a kneeling person with
        their mouth open too;   39.11.64   xié   歇

regarding being in a difficult position in a ravine, in
an emptied, eroded valley mouth between two
mountains,   39.12.65   gǔ   谷
    shaman-dancing Not-Having   39.12.66   wú   無
    cultivating, like a plow,   39.12.67   yǐ   以
    full to overflowing your vessel   39.12.68   yíng   盈
        is assured a certain future of   39.12.69   jiāng   將
        fearing   39.12.70   kǒng   恐
        being drained, exhausted as a
        person standing on solid ground
        making a yawning sound;   39.12.71   jié   竭

regarding the medicine-dancing-scorpion insect
swarm of   39.13.72   wàn   萬
matter (outside one's body, "cut from the cow" by
a bloodied blade),   39.13.73   wù   物
    shaman-dancing Not-Having   39.13.74   wú   無
    cultivating, like a plow,   39.13.75   yǐ   以
    sprouting a bud from the ground   39.13.76   shēng   生
        is assured a certain future of   39.13.77   jiāng   將
        fearing   39.13.78   kǒng   恐

being obliterated as a fire
sheltered by a cliff with a habitable
cave extinguished by water just as
surely as any weapon on a pole;   39.13.79   miè   滅

regarding a marquis, "arrow in the cave"   39.14.80   hóu   侯
king, with his ceremonial jade axe or crown,
connecting the three levels of heaven, man, and
earth,   39.14.81   wáng   王
    shaman-dancing Not-Having   39.14.82   wú   無
cultivating, like a plow,   39.14.83   yǐ   以
being held in high regard, like when two
hands are wrapped around a person atop
cowry-shell-riches   39.14.84   guì   貴
way up, as in a two-story building outside
the city, high above what's faced with
admiration and echoed in there,   39.14.85   gāo   高
is assured a certain future of   39.14.86   jiāng   將
    fearing   39.14.87   kǒng   恐
toppling down—an upside-down
person falling in a habitable cave in
a cliff next to a kneeling person
with their mouth, a full leg and
foot just outside!   39.14.88   jué   蹶

*I became afraid in general, as is typical for any
pregnant woman, and felt especially traumatized
from my difficult first pregnancy. I specifically
worried that my marquis status wouldn't work.*

This taps lightly with a tutoring cane and leaves a
mark on the solid shield of the past: 39.15.89   gù   故

"being held in high regard, like when two hands are
wrapped around a person atop cowry-shell-riches"   39.15.90   guì   貴
cultivating, like a plow,   39.15.91   yǐ   以
accumulating lowly cowry-shell riches, like a couple
tiny pole weapons stacked together trying to be an
arsenal,   39.15.92   jiàn   賤
    is creating something by hand, carving an
    elephant likeness of good fortune and
    royal power,   39.15.93   wéi   為
    the root system, the foundation of that
    tree,   39.15.94   bân   本

and "way up, as in a two-story building outside the
city, high above what's faced with admiration and
echoed in there,"   39.16.95   gāo   高
cultivating, like a plow,   39.16.96   yǐ   以
now here down below   39.16.97   xià   下
    is creating something by hand, carving an
    elephant likeness of good fortune and
    royal power,   39.16.98   wéi   為
    the undisturbed earth or clay foundation
    under that basket.   39.16.99   jī   基

*That high status seemed foundational to my
pregnancy. Happily, a solution was right there for
the having...*

This baby footprint on bamboo-slip pages   39.17.100   shì   是
is cultivating, like a plow,   39.17.101   yǐ   以
a marquis, "arrow in the cave"   39.17.102   hóu   侯
king, with his ceremonial jade axe or crown,
connecting the three levels of heaven, man, and
earth,   39.17.103   wáng   王

yourself personally, right on the nose,
by the nitty-gritty, grinding gizzard of a fowl, being called
          a big-headed, legs-swaddled baby left as a
          melon on the vine, an *orphan*,
          the loose-haired head buck who
          differentiates right from wrong kneeling in
          a house alone like a *widow*,
          and the husk of the initial false guard-
          petals but not really the true flower of
          the hub of a wheel, that working part of a
          carriage you tend to with a hand tool...

this here—the foot stops a person here on this
footprint!— this
wrings to backward the two wings of,
this is cultivating, like a plow,
          accumulating lowly cowry-shell riches, like
          a couple tiny pole weapons stacked
          together trying to be an arsenal,
          creating something by hand, carving an
          elephant likeness of good fortune and
          royal power,
          the root system, the foundation of that
          tree,
                    as unwholesome in nature as the
                    disease-causing environment
                    around Elephant, Tusk Town,
                    Lángyá.

"Wring to backward the two wings
—PAH, CAN YOU?!"

39.17.104	zì	自
39.17.105	wèi	謂
39.17.106	gū	孤
39.17.107	guǎ	寡
39.17.108	bù	不
39.17.109	gǔ	轂
39.18.110	cǐ	此
39.18.111	fēi	非
39.18.112	yǐ	以
39.18.113	jiàn	賤
39.18.114	wéi	為
39.18.115	bǎn	本
39.18.116	yé	邪
39.19.117	fēi	非
39.19.118	hū	乎

This taps lightly with a tutoring cane and leaves a
mark on the solid shield of the past: 39.20.119   gù   故
in thoroughly delivering, exhausting, arriving at the
extreme (like an arrow stuck in the ground and
tapped lightly with a tutoring cane so as to leave a
mark),   39.20.120   zhì   致
adding up to that (tapping lightly with a tutoring
cane up through the stack from a kneeling woman
to a round center drum with a flagpole and then a
suckling mother)   39.20.121   shǔ   數
while being carried in a carriage's sedan chair
supported on shoulders, upheld by two hands like
the territory and the public,   39.20.122   yú   輿
     then shaman-dancing Not-Having,   39.20.123   wú   無
     being carried in a carriage's sedan chair
     supported on shoulders, upheld by two
     hands like the territory and the public,   39.20.124   yú   輿

     is the husk of the initial false guard-petals
     but not really the true flower of   39.21.125   bù   不
     missing, kneeling with a yawning mouth
     before a ravine eroded between two
     mountains, wanting, lacking,   39.21.126   yù   欲

this precious stone carved like jade
in the manner wood is shaped as a
water filter   39.21.127   lù   瑇
—this precious stone carved like
jade in the manner wood is shaped
as a water filter,   39.21.128   lù   瑇
like a kneeling woman with breasts
doing as told,   39.21.129   rú   如
is a pure jade totem—   39.21.130   yù   玉

or this particular weird precious
stone, pedestrian as the sole of a
foot on a mouth   39.22.131   luò   珞
—this particular weird precious
stone, pedestrian as the sole of a
foot on a mouth,   39.22.132   luò   珞
like a kneeling woman with breasts
doing as told,   39.22.133   rú   如
is a gem in a habitable cave in a
rock cliff.   39.22.134   shí   石

*If I let myself get carried around in a palanquin as
"a cheaply carved, odd, pedestrian stone…" well,
that would perpetuate that lonely and
unremarkable reputation, but the real me, the
"pure jade, a gem safe in the cozy cave," would
remain intact and safe.*

Chapter 41: Looking back at the three phases that got me here, I decided to keep borrowing the useful bits from every part of me and my journey.

Chapter 40 comes after Chapter 42 in the oldest known versions.

<table>
<tr><td>

On top,
an ax-wielding bachelor-soldier-scholar-official
appointed by the emperor
heard at the two-winged gateway and famously
reported on as
*walking with the footprint of the loose-haired head
buck*
      is exerting with force, working hard with
      the strong force of an arm, a bladed tool,
      or a plow on the soil,
      yet, now you're bearded,
            out in public at the crossroads,
            being good, doing one's work,
            what that has, stepping on from
            this footprint.

</td></tr>
</table>

41.1.1	shàng	上
41.1.2	shì	士
41.1.3	wén	聞
41.1.4	dào	道
41.1.5	qín	勤
41.1.6	ér	而
41.1.7	xíng	行
41.1.8	zhī	之

In the center, that drum with a flagpole placed in
the middle of a field to gather the people and
detect wind,
an ax-wielding bachelor-soldier-scholar-official
appointed by the emperor
heard at the two-winged gateway and famously
reported on as
*walking with the footprint of the loose-haired head
buck*

41.2.9	zhōng	中
41.2.10	shì	士
41.2.11	wén	聞
41.2.12	dào	道

is, A Certain Someone compliantly combing
her loose hair seemed to say, "as if   41.2.13   ruò   若
continuing to exist, a baby with health
issues, maybe a large head, but still a seed
sprouting…"   41.2.14   cún   存
    A Certain Someone compliantly
    combing her loose hair seemed to
    say "this is as if   41.2.15   ruò   若
    someone gone, absent because
    they'd perished or fled by a knife's
    edge."   41.2.16   wáng   亡

Now here down below,   41.3.17   xià   下
an ax-wielding bachelor-soldier-scholar-official
appointed by the emperor   41.3.18   shì   士
heard at the two-winged gateway and famously
reported on as   41.3.19   wén   聞
walking with the footprint of the loose-haired head
buck   41.3.20   dào   道
    is this great big person   41.3.21   dà   大
    laughing like a dog in a pair of grass
    sprouts,   41.3.22   xiào   笑
    what that has, stepping on from this
    footprint.   41.3.23   zhī   之

If the husk of the initial protective bud
casing but not really the true flower of   41.4.24   bù   不
laughing like a dog in a pair of grass
sprouts,   41.4.25   xiào   笑
    then the husk of the initial
    protective bud casing but not really
    the true flower of   41.4.26   bù   不

fully enough, like the whole leg as
well as the footprint,	41.4.27	zú	足
this is cultivating, like a plow,	41.4.28	yǐ	以
creating something by hand,
carving an elephant likeness of
good fortune and royal power,	41.4.29	wéi	為
walking with the footprint of the
loose-haired head buck.	41.4.30	dào	道

*On top with the emperor, my head-buck self was
associated with doing good work. In the middle
phase, I followed my invaluable midwife friend's
advice to appear to be gone to survive. Finally, in
my new life, I could be just another odd, laughable,
lower-level imperial appointee. And underneath it
all, I was just a pregnant person getting a kick out
of all of it! Know this: if they're not laughing or
you're not laughing, it means you're "not fully
enough supporting the free-haired head buck
creating that little royal elephant."*

This taps lightly with a tutoring cane and leaves a
mark on the solid shield of the past...	41.5.31	gù	故
*A striding person establishing, hand-planting a
pole,*	41.5.32	jiàn	建
speaking out loud:	41.5.33	yán	言
    flesh-and-meat-handling Being,	41.5.34	yǒu	有
    has that, stepping on from this footprint.	41.5.35	zhī	之

*Confidently marching around saying what I wanted
was what my Being persona did. Of course, living
the Dào is very different in appearance and
reality...*

As bright as dawn rising on a crescent moon, enlightened,
walking with the footprint of the loose-haired head buck:
>A Certain Someone compliantly combing her loose hair seems to say this is as if dark as "the eight earthly branches" phase of the waxing moon before it's really full, like a tree that's upper branches aren't fully grown, not yet mature but venturing out, perhaps violating, coveting.

Walking slowly forward on the footprint of a "short-tailed bird," the left leg leading the way, walking with the footprint of the loose-haired head buck:
>A Certain Someone compliantly combing her loose hair seems to say this is as if withdrawing, walking with the footprint of a person slowly retreating from the table after eating, like the ending of a thread in a knot, their eye looking backward, the left leg leading the way.

"Foreign," part of the great barbarian tribe of the east carrying bows, leveling and razing, walking with the footprint of the loose-haired head buck:
>A Certain Someone compliantly combing her loose hair seems to say this is as if

41.6.36	míng	明
41.6.37	dào	道
41.6.38	ruò	若
41.6.39	mèi	昧
41.7.40	jìn	進
41.7.41	dào	道
41.7.42	ruò	若
41.7.43	tuì	退
41.8.44	yí	夷
41.8.45	dào	道
41.8.46	ruò	若

a flaw knotting the thread, that kneeling
loose-haired head buck person with rice
kernels on a skein of fine silk.   41.8.47   lèi   纇

And what about the Dé, you might ask? Well,
here's its approach...

On top,   41.9.48   shàng   上
walking with the footprint of someone who's in
alignment (eyes looking forward, directly over the
heart, left leg slowly leading the way):   41.9.49   dé   德
    A Certain Someone compliantly combing
    her loose hair seems to say this is as if   41.9.50   ruò   若
    in the common practices of the people
    from that difficult position in the valley
    between two mountains...   41.9.51   sú   俗

    this great big person,   41.10.52   dà   大
    and a little white, blank acorn, pure,
    gratuitous...   41.10.53   bái   白
        A Certain Someone compliantly
        combing her loose hair seems to
        say this is as if   41.10.54   ruò   若
        hanging from a cliff above a hand
        underneath, shaking, humiliated.   41.10.55   rǔ   辱

The Dé life, when I was living the high life with the
emperor, left me vulnerable.

Widespread, a person with a large belly in a
habitable cave in a cliff,   41.11.56   guǎng   廣
walking with the footprint of someone who's in
alignment: 41.11.57   dé   德

A Certain Someone compliantly combing
her loose hair seems to say this is as if   41.11.58   ruò   若
the husk of the initial protective bud casing
but not really the true flower of   41.11.59   bù   不
fully enough, like the whole leg as well as
the footprint.   41.11.60   zú   足

*In my situation, the Dé wasn't enough. But combine
it with the confidence of my Being persona…*

*A striding person establishing, hand-planting a
pole,*   41.12.61   jiàn   建
*AND walking with the footprint of someone who's
in alignment:*   41.12.62   dé   德
A Certain Someone compliantly combing
her loose hair seems to say this is as if   41.12.63   ruò   若
covertly sneaking, a person standing with
their back to someone gathering
themselves together from three sides after
a blade cut off their foot as punishment,
like from adultery…   41.12.64   tōu   偷

what matters, with the keen and weighty
quality of two axes over a cowry held as
hostage,   41.13.65   zhì   質
genuinely getting into it, like using a fork to
get food right from the cauldron…   41.13.66   zhēn   真
A Certain Someone compliantly
combing her loose hair seems to
say this is as if   41.13.67   ruò   若
as changeable as a river flowing
against someone gathering
themselves together from three

sides after a blade cut off their foot
as punishment, like from adultery.   41.13.68   yū   渝

With this combination of styles, important
conditions and outcomes could be changed easily
when needed. And there are more advantages...

With this great big person   41.14.69   dà   大
like the wide, parallel side of a tipped blade,   41.14.70   fāng   方
    the shamanic dancer with animal tails
    flowing from her wrists, Not-Having,   41.14.71   wú   無
    is in a corner, that remote place by the big
    soil mound with that trampling monkey
    with the head of a ghost,   41.14.72   yú   隅

and this great big person,   41.15.73   dà   大
a set of highly regarded vessels with lots of
capacity, worthy of a guard dog...   41.15.74   qì   器
    in late evening, when the sun on a man in a
    hat is being removed,   41.15.75   wǎn   晚
    is completing that final "nail" in a weapon
    on a pole.   41.15.76   chéng   成

With this great big person   41.16.77   dà   大
singing one tone from their mouth,   41.16.78   yīn   音
    "barely there," as sparse as the few
    interconnecting threads in the gendered
    head-cloth we wear after reaching
    adulthood, rarely seen or heard,   41.16.79   xī   希
    are the many sounds you'd hear when
    hitting chimes with a weapon in your right
    hand, going right through a person,   41.16.80   shēng   聲

and this great big person,
like an elephant skeleton to a living elephant,
bearing a likeness to something...
    shaman-dancing Not-Having
    is shaping as finely and level as two shields
    side by side with measuring lines of three
    hairs' breadth.

*Walking with the footprint of the loose-haired head
buck*
secreted, hiding behind a soil mound as careful and
compassionate as a claw-like hand grabbing from
above the real work of a bladed tool over a pig-
head heart,
    shaman-dancing Not-Having
    that personal name given in childhood and
    still whispered by moonlight...

in fact, that is to say This Grown Man with hairpin
and public courtesy name,
"Oh, YES, Ma'am," says the "short-tailed bird,"
*walking with the footprint of the loose-haired head
buck,*
the traditionally virtuous, offering up a ram's head
while speaking back and forth, tongues waggling,
loaned like a retrievable arrow attached to a string
with cowry riches...
    is lasting over time as the erect manhood
    of a male ancestor
    completing that final "nail" in a weapon on
    a pole.

41.17.81	dà	大
41.17.82	xiàng	象
41.17.83	wú	無
41.17.84	xíng	形
41.18.85	dào	道
41.18.86	yǐn	隱
41.18.87	wú	無
41.18.88	míng	名
41.19.89	fū	夫
41.19.90	wéi	唯
41.19.91	dào	道
41.19.92	shàn	善
41.19.93	dài	貸
41.19.94	qiâ	且
41.19.95	chéng	成

*It seemed wise to combine the best of all three of
these lifestyles—Being, Dào and Dé—and secret my
wild buck self when I was really big and wide. This
would allow me to "borrow" the virtuous life to
help me last through completing my pregnancy.*

Chapter 42: Feeling physically depleted gave me a surprising advantage in achieving my goal.

Walking with the footprint of the loose-haired head buck	42.1.1	dào	道
sprouted a bud from the ground...	42.1.2	shēng	生
The One.	42.1.3	yī	一
The One	42.2.4	yī	一
sprouted a bud from the ground...	42.2.5	shēng	生
two.	42.2.6	èr	二
Two	42.3.7	èr	二
sprouted a bud from the ground...	42.3.8	shēng	生
Three.	42.3.9	sān	三
Three	42.4.10	sān	三
sprouted a bud from the ground...	42.4.11	shēng	生
the medicine-dancing-scorpion insect swarm of	42.4.12	wàn	萬
matter (outside one's body, "cut from the cow" by a bloodied blade).	42.4.13	wù	物
The medicine-dancing-scorpion insect swarm of	42.5.14	wàn	萬
matter (outside one's body, "cut from the cow" by a bloodied blade),	42.5.15	wù	物

is carried by (as cowry-riches toted by a much
smaller person or a knife in the kind of load-
bearing that can lead to suffering, neglect,
betrayal, and repudiation)   42.5.16   fù   負
the feminine *yīn* principle (what's hidden and
overcast, as when what's being said in the mouth
now, in modern times, is said when it's dusky, with
clouds covering a big soil mound),   42.5.17   yīn   陰
    yet now, bearded, you're   42.5.18   ér   而
    bundling it all up together in both arms
    into   42.5.19   bào   抱
    the male *yáng* principle of sun shining on a
    big soil mound,   42.5.20   yáng 陽

    pouring from the center, like a stream from
    the hollow drum at the base of a flagpole,   42.6.21   chōng 沖
    that vital qì energy, the breath of life, that
    air flow that's like a gift of rice: 42.6.22   qì   氣
        this is cultivating, like a plow,   42.6.23   yǐ   以
        creating something by hand,
        carving an elephant likeness of
        good fortune and royal power,   42.6.24   wéi   為
        and warming, wetting, and stickily
        kneading together, harmonizing
        like breath blown into a reed-pipe
        mouth organ.   42.6.25   hé   和

    I began to leak prematurely again, as I did
    with my first pregnancy.

That person,   42.7.26   rén   人
what it has, stepping on from this footprint, it has
this: 42.7.27   zhī   之

"that place" being intentionally created like any
household gate hewn with an axe
     is like a tomb built over the heart,

     "oh, YES, Ma'am," says the "short-tailed
     bird,"
     "an *orphan*, a big-headed, legs-swaddled
     baby left as a melon on the vine,
     the loose-haired head buck who
     differentiates right from wrong kneeling in
     a house alone like a *widow*...
     and the husk of the initial false guard-
     petals but *not really* the true flower of
     the hub of a wheel, that working part of a
     carriage you tend to with a hand tool."

Having another fragile pregnancy felt like a death
sentence. I simply didn't have the strength to be
the center of activity. But then, remember back in
Chapter 39, my assignment was exactly this: to be
an unassuming leader.

Yet now, bearded, you're
a king with his ceremonial jade axe or crown
connecting the three levels of heaven, man, and
earth
as publicly fair and impartial as a high-ranking older
man who's "got balls," a duke,
     and this is cultivating, like a plow,
     creating something by hand, carving an
     elephant likeness of good fortune and
     royal power,

42.7.28	suǒ	所
42.7.29	wù	惡
42.8.30	wéi	唯
42.8.31	gū	孤
42.8.32	guǎ	寡
42.8.33	bù	不
42.8.34	gǔ	穀
42.9.35	ér	而
42.9.36	wáng	王
42.9.37	gōng	公
42.9.38	yǐ	以
42.9.39	wéi	為

and being weighed, like a claw-like hand
grabbing from above, holding rice or grain
on a scale, and called out *as exactly that.*   42.9.40   chēng   稱

This taps lightly with a tutoring cane and leaves a
mark on the solid shield of the past: 42.10.41   gù   故
matter outside one's body, "cut from the cow" by a
bloodied blade,   42.10.42   wù   物
in this particular enclave that's defended by a
weapon on a pole,   42.10.43   huò   或
diminishing, like hands and fingers injured by the
top edge of the three-legged cauldron that's like
the great members of the monarchy government   42.10.44   sǔn   損
what it has, stepping on from this footprint, it has
this: 42.10.45   zhī   之
          yet now, bearded, you're   42.10.46   ér   而
          overflowing like water from a vessel;   42.10.47   yì   益

in this particular enclave,   42.11.48   huò   或
overflowing, like water from a vessel,   42.11.49   yì   益
what it has, stepping on from this footprint, it has
this: 42.11.50   zhī   之
          yet now, bearded, you're   42.11.51   ér   而
          diminishing.   42.11.52   sǔn   損

That person,   42.12.53   rén   人
what it has, stepping on from this footprint, it has
this: 42.12.54   zhī   之
          "that place" being intentionally created like
          any household gate hewn with an axe   42.12.55   suǒ   所

          is lessons learned the hard way, like a child
          being taught counting with bamboo slips or

divination with yarrow stalks, tapping them
lightly with a tutoring cane.

*My delicate pregnancy, rather than being a
tomb, turned out to be the way for me to
learn some important things. Remember
me pointedly* not *specifying any of those
hardlearned lessons, back in line 2.10 of
the Dào? Here's perhaps the main learning
to which I was referring...*

Holding a rake-like weapon to defend
myself and my opinion
—both armpits sweat this too!—
*a lesson learned the hard way, like a child
being taught counting with bamboo slips or
divination with yarrow stalks, tapping them
lightly with a tutoring cane,*
what it has, stepping on from this
footprint, it has this:

*"Revolving around oneself as a powerful
bow broadening, strengthening, stiff, hard,
and compelling as a rice weevil, like a tiny
venomous snake—thwang!—*
*where wood bridges water with the help of
a double-edged sword, like a beam
("Liáng," like the state located where the
south-flowing Yellow River enters the
Guanzhong Plain)*
*—this is boiling sugarcane with fire as
follows!—*

42.12.56	jiào	教
42.13.57	wǒ	我
42.13.58	yì	亦
42.13.59	jiào	教
42.13.60	zhī	之
42.14.61	qiáng	強
42.14.62	liáng	梁
42.14.63	zhâ	者

the husk of the initial false guard-petals but
not really the true flower of   42.14.64   bù   不
The Hand-Picked Gem, like cowry-shell-
riches discovered along the road,   42.14.65   dé   得
what it holds a basket of...   42.14.66   qí   其
dying, a person turning to a pile of bones."   42.14.67   sǐ   死

This lesson can mean many things, including:

"Strengthening like a beam or sword, the valued
one won't really die.

Or, "Across the bridge to Liáng *in the final firming-*
up phase of pregnancy, the treasured one doesn't
really die."

Or, "Powerful violence means a not-good death."

Or, "With a strong double-edged sword, what's
not-really-precious dies."

Or, maybe hard lessons themselves are like double
edged swords you can use as a bridge to cross from
one place to another when you're strengthening
yourself rather than dying as The Chosen One.

All these interpretations have been useful and
important to me at some time, and, as with this
whole book, I hope you find that to be the case for
you, too.

Counting up on all five fingers, aren't I
assured, as if by hand-offering a meat tribute at an
altar, a certain future of,
this is cultivating, like a plow,
> creating something by hand, carving an
> elephant likeness of good fortune and
> royal power,
> with this lesson learned the hard way, like
> a child being taught counting with bamboo
> slips or divination with yarrow stalks,
> tapping them lightly with a tutoring cane,
>> and then a "Respected Father," a
>> hand holding a working stone
>> blade axe?

42.15.68	wú 吾
42.15.69	jiāng 將
42.15.70	yǐ 以
42.15.71	wéi 為
42.15.72	jiào 教
42.15.73	fù 父

*That provocative, evocative, layered lesson is like a
respected elder or father.*

*Plus, it assured I was transformed into a respected
father—and that meant safety when I needed it
most and a stable lifestyle that would last.*

Chapter 40: Returning to the best parts of my cave-self and easily doing my most useful work, even in that most delicate state

As a different-sounding *Fǎn*, turning your palm
over in a habitable cave in a cliff, reversing,
returning, reflecting, maybe countering with the
opposite
—this is boiling sugarcane with fire as follows!—

40.1.1	fǎn 反
40.1.2	zhâ 者

walking with the footprint of the loose-haired head buck,
what it has, stepping on from this footprint, it has this:

    easily doing work as hard as moving a
    heavy bag tied at both ends with the
    strong force of an arm or plow.

In a delicate state with a pair of fragile bows
—this is boiling sugarcane with fire as follows!—
walking with the footprint of the loose-haired head buck,
what it has, stepping on from this footprint, it has this:

    doing truly useful work like a water bucket,
    by means of carrying-capacity.

    Meaning…

    With the heavenly from high above this
    great big person
    now here down below,
        the medicine-dancing-scorpion
        insect swarm of
        matter (outside one's body, "cut
        from the cow" by a bloodied
        blade),
        is sprouting a bud from the ground
        in this place and time, oh, black, icy
        raven sun:
            flesh-and-meat-handling
            Being;

40.1.3	dào	道
40.1.4	zhī	之
40.1.5	dòng	動
40.2.6	ruò	弱
40.2.7	zhâ	者
40.2.8	dào	道
40.2.9	zhī	之
40.2.10	yòng	用
40.3.11	tiān	天
40.3.12	xià	下
40.3.13	wàn	萬
40.3.14	wù	物
40.3.15	shēng	生
40.3.16	yú	於
40.3.17	yǒu	有

and flesh-and-meat-handling Being   40.4.18   yǒu   有
is sprouting a bud from the ground   40.4.19   shēng   生
in this place and time, oh, black, icy
raven sun: 40.4.20   yú   於
> the shamanic dancer with
> animal tails flowing from
> her wrists, Not-Having.   40.4.21   wú   無

*My Not-Having self could once again host a Being
persona, and that Being could host the next child.*

Chapter 43: In this transitional time and space, I needed to be both supple and a confident leader.

The heavenly from high above this great big person   43.1.1   tiān   天
now here down below,   43.1.2   xià   下
> what it has, stepping on from this
> footprint,   43.1.3   zhī   之
> arriving at the end (the extreme climax,
> like an arrow straight into the clay soil)   43.1.4   zhì   至
> softening to be as supple as a tree that can
> be cut with a spear   43.1.5   róu   柔

is galloping—"oh yeah, 'feminine funnel!'"—   43.2.6   chí   馳
like a horse given free rein by a chivalrous martial
warrior (that knight with a pair of helmets and a
sharp exhalation), galloping all over   騁
the heavenly   43.2.7   châng
now here down below,   43.2.8   tiān   天
> what it has, stepping on from this   43.2.9   xià   下
> footprint,   43.2.10   zhī   之
> arriving at the end   43.2.11   zhì   至

hardening, drying and forming a crust, hard
as the clay soil underneath a finger in an
eye cast down in surrender.   43.2.12   jiān   堅

The shamanic dancer with animal tails flowing from
her wrists, Not-Having,   43.3.13   wú   無
        with flesh-and-meat-handling *Being*   43.3.14   yǒu   有
                entering like an arrowhead
                inserting or maybe joining the
                imperial government   43.3.15   rù   入
        and shaman-dancing *Not-Having*   43.3.16   wú   無
                in an interstitial, transitional space
                or time where moonlight's peeking
                through a double-winged gateway,   43.3.17   jiān   間

counting up on all five fingers, aren't I   43.4.18   wú   吾
this little acorn plant's footprint,   43.4.18   shì   是
this is cultivating, like a plow,   43.4.20   yǐ   以
speaking as a great big person to a baby,
distinguishing, imparting, and administering
wisdom confidently and intimately,   43.4.21   zhī   知
        and then shaman-dancing Not-Having,   43.4.22   wú   無
                creating something by hand,
                carving an elephant likeness of
                good fortune and royal power,   43.4.23   wéi   為
        what it has, stepping on from this
        footprint,   43.4.24   zhī   之
        is flesh-and-meat-handling Being   43.4.25   yǒu   有
                overflowing like water from a
                vessel?   43.4.26   yì   益

Versus…

The husk of the initial false guard-petals but *not
really* the true flower of
speaking out loud,
what it has, stepping on from this footprint,
lessons learned the hard way, like a child being
taught counting with bamboo slips or divination
with yarrow stalks, tapping them lightly with a
tutoring cane...

>*then shaman-dancing Not-Having,*
>>creating something by hand,
>>carving an elephant likeness of
>>good fortune and royal power,
>>what it has, stepping on from this
>>footprint,
>>*is overflowing like water from a*
>>*vessel,*

and, the heavenly
now here down below,
>>*is "barely there,"* as sparse as the
>>few interconnecting threads in the
>>gendered head-cloth we wear after
>>reaching adulthood, *rarely seen or*
>>*heard*
>>*finally reaching, hand-grabbing*
>>*and holding onto a person,*
>>what it has, stepping on from this
>>footprint.

43.5.27	bù	不
43.5.28	yán	言
43.5.29	zhī	之
43.5.30	jiào	教
43.6.31	wú	無
43.6.32	wéi	為
43.6.33	zhī	之
43.6.34	yì	益
43.7.35	tiān	天
43.7.36	xià	下
43.7.37	xī	希
43.7.38	jí	及
43.7.39	zhī	之

*In my newest post as a marquis, if I was speaking
as that confident leader while creating the little
elephant likeness, then my public persona could fill*

to overflowing. (There always have been plenty of chubby sages, so that wasn't an issue!)

But if I was not speaking up about those lessons that I'd learned the hard way while creating the little elephant likeness, then my private persona would be all I had while I was filling up. And as we've seen, beginning in Chapter 3, Not-Having creating the elephant likeness on her own as that shamanic dance has never been "flowing the River Happy."

You remember from Chapter 2 that keeping silent about the insights gained from my unorthodox situation was part of my "ideal sage" plan during my first pregnancy, and it worked well. But that strategy wasn't going to allow successfully grabbing hold of a little one the second time around.

So, what were the important lessons I learned the hard way? My entire Dé lifestyle and this whole book are those very lessons...

Chapter 44: Trying to do it all felt impossible, especially while pregnant and sick.

That personal name given in childhood and still whispered by moonlight

44.1.1   míng   名

participating with (a "biting tooth" lifted by a pair of hands onto strong shoulders, perhaps interfering with or perhaps supporting)

44.1.2   yǔ   與

your pregnant self,
       which kneeling person is using both arms
       for paying tribute to an ancestral shrine,
       fully processing
       an intimate one, a beloved who's suffering,
       like from that chisel used to mark slaves
       and criminals, you see up close with one
       big eye for a head?

       How could I be known as my real self, be
       pregnant, and also be someone's beloved?

Your pregnant self
participating with (a "biting tooth" lifted by a pair
of hands onto strong shoulders, perhaps
interfering with or perhaps supporting)
a transformation from a right-side-up person to an
upside-down person atop cowry-shell riches,
       which kneeling person is using both arms
       for paying tribute to an ancestral shrine,
       fully processing
       having more, like two pieces of meat?

       How could I be transformed into someone
       else, be pregnant, and also be dealing with
       this "double serving" of kids?

"A Hand-Picked Gem," like cowry-shell-riches
discovered along the road,
participating with (a "biting tooth" lifted by a pair
of hands onto strong shoulders, perhaps
interfering with or perhaps supporting)

44.1.3	shēn	身
44.1.4	shú	孰
44.1.5	qīn	親
44.2.6	shēn	身
44.2.7	yǔ	與
44.2.8	huò	貨
44.2.9	shú	孰
44.2.10	duō	多
44.3.11	dé	得
44.3.12	yǔ	與

someone gone, absent because they've perished or
fled by a knife's edge,   44.3.13   wáng   亡
    which kneeling person is using both arms
    for paying tribute to an ancestral shrine,
    fully processing   44.3.14   shú   孰
    ill as one carried on a stretcher?   44.3.15   bìng   病

    How could I be the missing precious Gem
    and also be so sick?

This baby footprint on bamboo-slip pages,   44.4.16   shì   是
this taps lightly with a tutoring cane and leaves a
mark on the solid shield of the past: 44.4.17   gù   故
in pairing like one-half of a double-yoked harness
as pleasant as something sweet in the mouth and
therefore extra   44.4.18   shèn   甚
loving, kneeling with your head turned this way
and your heart in your throat,   44.4.19   ài   愛
    hands over heart, analytically,   44.4.20   bì   必
    this great big person   44.4.21   dà   大
    is lavishly, rather wastefully, expended, like
    two sticks tied together to start a fire over
    cowry-riches;   44.4.22   fèi   費

in having more, like two pieces of meat,   44.5.23   duō   多
hiding, stored like weapons on a pole that can kill
by piercing the eye under a bamboo bed below a
pair of grass sprouts, stolen goods, or slaves,   44.5.24   cáng   藏
    hands over heart, analytically,   44.5.25   bì   必
    a jug in a habitable cave in a cliff, thick and
    generous,   44.5.26   hòu   厚
    is someone gone, absent because they've
    perished or fled by a knife's edge.   44.5.27   wáng   亡

"Speaking as a great big person to a baby,
distInguishing, imparting, and administering
wisdom confidently and intimately,   44.6.28   zhī   知
fully enough, like the whole leg as well as the
footprint..."   44.6.29   zú   足

*[In Chapter 33 of the Dào, I used this same phrase.
There, I said it was "wealthy," and now I say...]*

> ...it's the husk of the initial protective bud
> casing but not really the true flower of   44.6.30   bù   不
> hanging from a cliff above a hand
> underneath, shaking, humiliated.   44.6.31   rǔ   辱

"Speaking as a great big person to a baby,
distinguishing, imparting, and administering
wisdom confidently and intimately,   44.7.32   zhī   知
halting right here in this footprint...   44.7.33   zhǐ   止
> it's the husk of the initial protective bud
> casing but not really the true flower of   44.7.34   bù   不
> endangered as human remains, spoken of
> privately, revolving around yourself."   44.7.35   dài   殆

In Chapter 32 of the Dào, I said the same thing.

> Lip-smackingly genuinely,   44.8.36   kâ   可
> this is cultivating, like a plow,   44.8.37   yǐ   以
>> lengthening as long as hair that has
>> to be tied with a brooch, like a
>> loose-haired old man,   44.8.38   cháng 長
>
> enduring through time as a person
> receiving moxibustion, that

mugwort treatment for cramps,
turning a breech baby, or other
health issues.   44.8.39   jiǔ   久

*In the critical transition time, my safety lay not in
diving hard into love nor in hiding out but rather in
that role of the wise speaker, a role at which I had
become skilled.*

Chapter 45: A Certain Someone said I was capable of doing everything necessary. In fact, the time was at hand.

This great big person   45.1.1   dà   大
completing that final "nail" in a weapon on a pole?   45.1.2   chéng   成
A Certain Someone compliantly combing her loose
hair seems to be saying "this is as if   45.1.3   ruò   若
a lidded earthen pot with a gap broken by a
resolute hand with a fork, incomplete and lacking…   45.1.4   quē   缺

    what it holds a basket of   45.2.5   qí   其
    doing truly useful work like a water bucket,
    by means of carrying-capacity   45.2.6   yòng   用
        is the husk of the initial false
        guard-petals but not really the true
        flower of   45.2.7   bù   不
        fraud, a drawback like both hands
        supporting a tattered traditional
        gendered head-cloth that's been
        hit lightly."   45.2.8   bì   弊

This great big person,   45.3.9   dà   大
full to overflowing their vessel?   45.3.10   yíng   盈
A Certain Someone compliantly combing her loose
hair seems to be saying "this is as if   45.3.11   ruò   若
pouring water from the center like a stream from
the hollow drum at the base of a flagpole...   45.3.12   chōng 沖

    what it holds a basket of   45.4.13   qí   其
    doing truly useful work like a water bucket,
    by means of carrying-capacity   45.4.14   yòng   用
        is the husk of the initial false
        guard-petals but not really the true
        flower of   45.4.15   bù   不
        thoroughly used up and destitute,
        like your pregnant self buried with
        a bow."   45.4.16   qióng 窮

You don't have to be perfect. Especially because
outcomes aren't always as you'd expect.
Sometimes reality is paradoxical. And as we've
seen, the accommodations that were made
necessary by my pregnancy were what caused me
to develop my unique style and ability to thrive.

This great big person   45.5.17   dà   大
looking straight on, forward?   45.5.18   zhí   直
A Certain Someone compliantly combing her loose
hair seems to be saying "this is as if   45.5.19   ruò   若
    bending like one who represents the dead
    in a rite, flexing to step out of a cave."   45.5.20   qū   屈

This great big person
having the craftiness of a bladed tool on exhaled
air?   45.6.21   dà   大

A Certain Someone compliantly combing her loose   45.6.22   qiǎo   巧
hair seems to be saying "this is as if   45.6.23   ruò   若
        clumsy, stepping out of their cave all hands
        and fingers."   45.6.24   zhuō   拙

This great big person   45.7.25   dà   大
discussing and debating, speaking in the middle of
two chisels used to brand slaves or criminals?   45.7.26   biàn   辯
A Certain Someone compliantly combing her loose
hair seems to be saying "this is as if   45.7.27   ruò   若
        words entering a city through its outskirts,
        mumbling or stammering."   45.7.28   nè   訥

"The fidgety, impetuous as the footprint of three
birds chirping in a tree,   45.8.29   zào   躁
        is able to withstand entirely (to be
        victorious as a splendid piece of jewelry, an
        omen or the royal 'We' mending
        something on a boat with two hands by the
        strength of an arm, bladed tool, or a plow)   45.8.30   shèng   勝
        sleeping under a desolate roof amidst a
        pair of grass sprouts to protect themselves
        from winter chill, a cold humble person;   45.8.31   hán   寒

and calm peace, the clear blue-green growth of the
sedative cinnabar plant quieting a dispute between
two hands on a plowshare,   45.9.32   jìng   靜
        is able to withstand entirely (to be
        victorious as a splendid piece of jewelry, an
        omen or the royal 'We' mending   45.9.33   shèng   勝

something on a boat with two hands by the
strength of an arm, bladed tool, or a plow)
a hot fire under a tree tipped and planted
by a person in the clay soil.   45.9.34   rè   熱

The clarity of still bright blue-green water, the
color resembling the growth of that sedative
cinnabar plant,   45.10.35   qīng   清
and calm peace, the clear blue-green growth of the
sedative cinnabar plant quieting a dispute between
two hands on a plowshare,   45.10.36   jìng   靜
    creating something by hand, carving an
    elephant likeness of good fortune and
    royal power,   45.10.37   wéi   為
    the heavenly from high above this great big
    person   45.10.38   tiān   天
    now here down below,   45.10.39   xià   下
        is straightening up, straightening
        things out for 'nailing' that first
        footstep of a journey."   45.10.40   zhèng   正

*She reassured me that I was ready to set out on this
journey! (See the last line of the Dào in Chapter 37.)*

Chapter 46: My friend reminded me she wasn't referring to me "taking a journey" in my previous head buck style.

"The heavenly from high above this great big
person   46.1.1   tiān   天
now here down below,   46.1.2   xià   下
    if flesh-and-meat-handling Being   46.1.3   yǒu   有

is walking with the footprint of the loose-
haired head buck
      and withdrawing like a kneeling
      person from within that valley
      mouth between two mountains,
      taking off, rising up, passing on like
      a young man running over a
      snake...
that's a horse
cultivating, like a plow,
manure like the rice kernels of a differently-
masked person!

The heavenly from high above this great big person
now here down below,
      if the shamanic dancer with animal tails
      flowing from her wrists, Not-Having,
      is walking with the footprint of the loose-
      haired head buck
          and armed with a shield and a
          weapon on a pole...
that's a horse
sprouting a bud from the ground
in this place and time, oh, black, icy raven
sun,
outside of town where a person sits with
crossed legs at a big soil mound.

With my toddler in tow, if I went the route of Being
running away, I'd inevitably die young... that's
horse shit!

46.1.4	dào	道
46.1.5	què	卻
46.1.6	zǒu	走
46.1.7	mǎ	馬
46.1.8	yǐ	以
46.1.9	fèn	糞
46.2.10	tiān	天
46.2.11	xià	下
46.2.12	wú	無
46.2.13	dào	道
46.2.14	róng	戎
46.2.15	mǎ	馬
46.2.16	shēng	生
46.2.17	yú	於
46.2.18	jiāo	郊

*But also, if I once again went to war with the
emperor… well, we've seen from the past that
might mean end up with me pregnant again!*

My friend definitely knew my default modes.

It's guilty, suffering, sinful, or even criminal, with a
webbed net over two wings wrung backwards!   46.3.19   zuì   罪
Like the sun sinking down in four bushes, one must
not be—cannot be, eh?—   46.3.20   mò   莫
this great big person   46.3.21   dà   大
in this place and time, oh, black, icy raven sun,   46.3.22   yú   於
     lip-smackingly genuinely   46.3.23   kâ   可
     missing, kneeling with a yawning mouth
     before a ravine eroded between two
     mountains, wanting, lacking.   46.3.24   yù   欲

It's disaster like the slanting mouth of a skull on a
sacrifice altar!   46.4.25   huò   禍
Like the sun sinking down in four bushes, one must
not be—cannot be, eh?—   46.4.26   mò   莫
this great big person   46.4.27   dà   大
in this place and time, oh, black, icy raven sun,   46.4.28   yú   於
     the husk of the initial protective bud casing
     but *not really* the true flower of   46.4.29   bù   不
     'speaking as a great big person to a baby,
     distinguishing, imparting, and
     administering wisdom confidently and
     intimately,   46.4.30   zhī   知
     fully enough, like the whole leg as well as
     the footprint.'   46.4.31   zú   足

*I couldn't leave. And, reiterating the advice in 44.6,
I couldn't not be fully speaking as a leader. It'd be a
disaster.*

A person following this upside-down footprint sees
its calamity!   46.5.32 jiù 咎
Like the sun sinking down in four bushes, one must
not be—cannot be, eh?—   46.5.33 mò 莫
this great big person   46.5.34 dà 大
in this place and time, oh, black, icy raven sun,   46.5.35 yú 於
      a missing, kneeling with a yawning mouth
      before a ravine eroded between two
      mountains, wanting, lacking,   46.5.36 yù 欲
      'Hand-Picked Gem,' like cowry-shell-riches
      discovered along the road.   46.5.37 dé 得

This taps lightly with a tutoring cane and leaves a
mark on the solid shield of the past...   46.6.38 gù 故
speaking as a great big person to a baby,
distinguishing, imparting, and administering
wisdom confidently and intimately,   46.6.39 zhī 知
fully enough, like the whole leg as well as the
footprint,   46.6.40 zú 足
      what it has, stepping on from this
      footprint, it has this,   46.6.41 zhī 之
      fully enough, like the whole leg as well as
      the footprint: 46.6.42 zú 足

      the conventional royal administrator
      wearing a men's headcloth as his skirt,   46.7.43 cháng 常
      fully enough, like the whole leg as well as
      the footprint   46.7.44 zú 足

—I swear, an arrow revolving around
oneself, that's it!"   46.7.45   yǐ   矣

*I needed to be a royal administrator. I needed to
stick with the marquis plan.*

Chapter 47: But I did not need to be public with my child or my true identity while doing my wise-administrator work.

If the husk of the initial protective bud casing but
not really the true flower of   47.1.1   bù   不
stepping out of that cave,   47.1.2   chū   出
the single-gate doorway to a household,   47.1.3   hù   戶
    speaking as a great big person to a baby,
    distinguishing, imparting, and
    administering wisdom confidently and
    intimately,   47.1.4   zhī   知
      with the heavenly from high above
      this great big person   47.1.5   tiān   天
      now here down below,   47.1.6   xià   下

and the husk of the initial protective bud casing but
not really the true flower of   47.2.7   bù   不
that is to say, in fact, this particular grown man
with a hairpin and public courtesy name being in
the two-winged gateway with a person who has
one big eye for a head, flashing a look at   47.2.8   kuī   闚
a window, like a boudoir window's sliver of wood
that's half of a two-winged gateway and lets the
moon shine in on the family's primordial father,
ten spindles hanging,   47.2.9   yǒu   牖

seen by someone with one big eye for a
head,   47.2.10   jiàn   見
       with the heavenly from high above
       this great big person,   47.2.11   tiān   天
       walking with the footprint of the
       loose-haired head buck…   47.2.12   dào   道

then what it holds a basket of   47.3.13   qí   其
stepping out of that cave   47.3.14   chū   出
       is *relaxing one's bow* as for repair with a
       loom, threads crossing this way, right here,
       for more, for *filling or covering*   47.3.15   mí   彌
       the much distant, *not intimate or near but*
       profound way of slowly walking with the
       footprint of a big round spindle with a long
       robe hanging like the afterbirth from a
       postpartum woman, the left leg leading the
       way;   47.3.16   yuǎn   遠

what it holds a basket of   47.4.17   qí   其
speaking as a great big person to a baby,
distinguishing, imparting, and administering
wisdom confidently and intimately,   47.4.18   zhī   知
       is *relaxing one's bow as for repair* with a
       loom, threads crossing this way, right here,
       for more, for *filling or covering*   47.4.19   mí   彌
       being belittled, considered to be
       insignificant as four tiny dots like a young
       master's youthful period.   47.4.20   shǎo   少

I could step out and be non-defensive. I could be
private so no one could see whether I was pregnant
or post-partum or in any other reproductive

category, and I could be a wise leader without anyone seeing and demeaning my Dào self or the young heir.

This baby footprint on bamboo-slip pages,	47.5.21	shì	是
this is cultivating, like a plow,	47.5.22	yǐ	以
an ideal grounded sage known for his civilian			
petition to authority, standing straight, speaking,			
and being listened to,	47.5.23	shèng	聖
that person	47.5.24	rén	人
would be the husk of the initial protective bud			
casing but not really the true flower of	47.5.25	bù	不
out in public at the crossroads, being good, doing			
one's work,	47.5.26	xíng	行
yet now, bearded, you're	47.5.27	ér	而
speaking as a great big person to a baby,			
distinguishing, imparting, and			
administering wisdom confidently and			
intimately;	47.5.28	zhī	知
would be the husk of the initial protective bud			
casing but not really the true flower of	47.6.29	bù	不
seen by someone with one big eye for a head,	47.6.30	jiàn	見
yet now, bearded, you're	47.6.31	ér	而
that personal name given in childhood and			
still whispered by moonlight;	47.6.32	míng	名
would be the husk of the initial protective bud			
casing but not really the true flower of	47.7.33	bù	不
creating something by hand, carving an elephant			
likeness of good fortune and royal power,	47.7.34	wéi	為
yet now, bearded, you're	47.7.35	ér	而

completing, that final "nail" in a weapon
on a pole.   47.7.36   chéng   成

Chapter 48: The wild-haired buck lifestyle alone didn't provide what I needed at this point. A royal administrator role did.

Creating something by hand, carving an elephant
likeness of good fortune and royal power,   48.1.1   wéi   為
while learning and understanding with divination
or tally marks held between one's hands and a
child safe beneath a roof...   48.1.2   xué   學
    then the entire day, the full sun,   48.1.3   rì   日
    is overflowing like water from a vessel;   48.1.4   yì   益

creating something by hand, carving an elephant
likeness of good fortune and royal power,   48.2.5   wéi   為
while walking with the footprint of the loose-
haired head buck...   48.2.6   dào   道
    then the entire day, the full sun,   48.2.7   rì   日
    is diminishing, like hands and fingers
    injured by the top edge of the three-legged
    cauldron that's like the great members of
    the monarchy government...   48.2.8   sǔn   損

diminishing, like hands and fingers injured
by the top edge of the three-legged
cauldron that's like the great members of
the monarchy government,   48.3.9   sǔn   損
what it has, stepping on from this
footprint, it has this   48.3.10   zhǐ   之
    again, on the right hand,   48.3.11   yòu   又

diminishing like hands and fingers
injured by the top edge of the
cauldron that is the monarchy
government   48.3.12   sǔn   損

cultivating, like a plow,   48.4.13   yǐ   以
arriving at the end, the extreme
climax, like an arrow straight into
the clay soil,   48.4.14   zhì   至
in this place and time, oh, black, icy
raven sun: 48.4.15   yú   於
with the shamanic dancer with
animal tails flowing from her
wrists, Not-Having,   48.4.16   wú   無
creating something by hand,
carving an elephant likeness of
good fortune and royal power.   48.4.17   wéi   為

*As we have seen, beginning in Chapter 3,
creating as my shaman-dancing nobody
Not-Having self wasn't safe. But...*

Shaman-dancing Not-Having   48.5.18   wú   無
creating something by hand, carving an elephant
likeness of good fortune and royal power,   48.5.19   wéi   為
    yet, now you're bearded,   48.5.20   ér   而
    shaman-dancing Not-Having   48.5.21   wú   無
    the husk of the initial protective bud casing
    but *not really* the true flower of   48.5.22   bù   不
    creating something by hand, carving an
    elephant likeness of good fortune and
    royal power,   48.5.23   wéi   為

getting hold of, grabbing the ear of 48.6.24 qǔ 取
the heavenly from high above this great big person 48.6.25 tiān 天
now here down below, 48.6.26 xià 下
as the conventional royal administrator wearing a
men's headcloth as his skirt, 48.6.27 cháng 常
  is cultivating, like a plow, 48.6.28 yǐ 以
  shaman-dancing Not-Having, 48.6.29 wú 無
  their task, what they do with a weapon,
  flag, or pen in hand. 48.6.30 shì 事

Finally reaching, hand-grabbing and holding onto a
person, 48.7.31 jí 及
what it holds a basket of, 48.7.32 qí 其
  flesh-and-meat-handling Being, 48.7.33 yǒu 有
  their task, what they do with a weapon,
  flag, or pen in hand, 48.7.34 shì 事
    is the husk of the initial protective
    bud casing but not really the true
    flower of 48.8.35 bù 不
    fully enough, like the whole leg as
    well as the footprint, 48.8.36 zú 足
    this is cultivating, like a plow, 48.8.37 yǐ 以
    getting hold of, grabbing the ear of 48.8.38 qǔ 取
    the heavenly, from high above this
    great big person 48.8.39 tiān 天
    now here down below. 48.8.40 xià 下

*My true Not-Having self needed support to really
grab onto that new person. And my old Being
persona wasn't enough either. I needed my own
official position.*

Chapter 49: Specific ideas on my Not-Having-self operating as the marquis administrator while bringing a heavenly one down to this level: virtue and honesty cannot be the only traits involved.

An ideal grounded sage known for his civilian
petition to authority, standing straight, speaking,
and being listened to,

that person,

   would be the shamanic dancer with animal
   tails flowing from her wrists, Not-Having,
   the conventional royal administrator
   wearing a men's headcloth as his skirt,
     in their heart,

   cultivating, like a plow,
   a hundred
   family names that a kneeling woman
   sprouts from the ground,
     in their heart,
   creating something by hand, carving an
   elephant likeness of good fortune and
   royal power,
     in their heart:

Traditionally virtuous, offering up a ram's
head while speaking back and forth,
tongues waggling?
This is boiling sugarcane with fire as
follows!
Counting up on all five fingers, aren't I

49.1.1	shèng	聖
49.1.2	rén	人
49.1.3	wú	無
49.1.4	cháng	常
49.1.5	xīn	心
49.2.6	yǐ	以
49.2.7	bǎi	百
49.2.8	xìng	姓
49.2.9	xīn	心
49.2.10	wéi	為
49.2.11	xīn	心
49.3.12	shàn	善
49.3.13	zhâ	者
49.3.14	wú	吾

traditionally virtuous, offering up a
ram's head while speaking back
and forth, tongues waggling,
stepping on from this footprint
with this*?!*

49.3.15   shàn   善

49.3.16   zhī   之

The husk of the initial protective bud
casing but *not really* the true flower of
traditionally virtuous, offering up a ram's
head while speaking back and forth,
tongues waggling?
This is boiling sugarcane with fire as
follows!
Counting up on all five fingers, aren't I
—both armpits sweat this too!—
traditionally virtuous, offering up a
ram's head while speaking back
and forth, tongues waggling,
stepping on from this footprint
with this*?!*

49.4.17   bù   不

49.4.18   shàn   善

49.4.19   zhâ   者
49.4.20   wú   吾
49.4.21   yì   亦

49.4.22   shàn   善

49.4.23   zhī   之

Walking with the footprint of someone who's in
alignment, eyes directly above the heart and
looking forward, the left leg slowly leading the way,
and traditionally virtuous, offering up a ram's head
while speaking back and forth, tongues waggling:

49.5.24   dé   德

49.5.25   shàn   善

Giving one's word to a person?
This is boiling sugarcane with fire as
follows!
Counting up on all five fingers, aren't I
giving my word to a person,

49.6.26   xìn   信
49.6.27   zhâ   者
49.6.28   wú   吾
49.6.29   xìn   信

stepping on from this footprint
with this*?!*

| | 49.6.30 | zhī | 之 |

The husk of the initial protective bud
casing but not really the true flower of
giving one's word to a person?
This is boiling sugarcane with fire as
follows!
Counting up on all five fingers, aren't I
—both armpits sweat this too!—
giving my word to a person,
stepping on from this footprint
with this*?!*

	49.7.31	bù	不
	49.7.32	xìn	信
	49.7.33	zhâ	者
	49.7.34	wú	吾
	49.7.35	yì	亦
	49.7.36	xìn	信
	49.7.37	zhī	之

Walking with the footprint of someone who's in
alignment, eyes directly above the heart and
looking forward, the left leg slowly leading the way,
and giving one's word to a person:

| | 49.8.38 | dé | 德 |
| | 49.8.39 | xìn | 信 |

an ideal grounded sage known for his
civilian petition to authority, standing
straight, speaking, and being listened to,
that person,
with that existing sprouting of seedlings
and talents, here on earth, of
the heavenly from high above this great big
person
now here down below

	49.9.40	shèng	聖
	49.9.41	rén	人
	49.9.42	zài	在
	49.9.43	tiān	天
	49.9.44	xià	下

sucking in, coming together a kneeling
person with their mouth open, their back
toward one open mouth atop another
mouth above a pair of little wings,

| | 49.10.45 | xī | 歙 |

sucking in

here, straightening things out for "nailing"
that first footstep of a journey on the back
of this yellow bird with the "dangling tail"
that lives around the Yangtze and Huai

Rivers—right here, huh!—
creating something by hand, carving an
elephant likeness of good fortune and

royal power,
the heavenly, from high above this great

big person
now here down below

would be muddying like river water
spouting from an army of surrounding carts
what it holds a basket of
            in their heart.

Given these circumstances a wise person would
muddy the water.

Regarding a hundred
family names that a kneeling woman sprouts from
the ground,
what gossip, comparing two people like there was
something oh so sweet in their mouth, says...
            it fills up, like a river and you, honored
            senior official master, owner and host of
            the lamp's flame, or your spouse or
            princess daughter, with
            what it holds a basket of,
            their ear ("âr"),
            and what the eye sees;

regarding an ideal grounded sage known for his
civilian petition to authority, standing straight,
speaking, and being listened to,   49.13.61   shèng   聖
that person,   49.13.62   rén   人
what gossip, comparing two people like there was
something oh so sweet in their mouth, says...   49.13.63   jiē   皆
    would be a baby animal, giggling,   49.13.64   hái   孩
    stepping on from this footprint with this.   49.13.65   zhī   之

*Gossip started this whole odyssey, as you
remember from Chapter 2, and it turns out to be
easy enough to control with a little muddying of the
waters. Forgive me if I chuckle a little bit.*

Chapter 50: The odds for surviving childbirth and soldiering are slim. To live, I'd need to avoid wild beasts and war.

Stepping out of one's cave   50.1.1   chū   出
    and sprouting a bud from the ground,   50.1.2   shēng   生
vs. entering like an arrowhead inserting (or maybe
joining the imperial government!)   50.1.3   rù   入
    and dying, a person turning to a pile of
    bones?   50.1.4   sǐ   死

Sprouting a bud from the ground...   50.2.5   shēng   生
stepping on from this footprint   50.2.6   zhī   之
walking with the footprint of merely a foot soldier,
afoot on the clay soil: 50.2.7   tú   徒
    of ten   50.2.8   shí   十
    flesh-and-meat-handling Beings,   50.2.9   yǒu   有

three are that.	50.2.10	sān	三
Dying, a person turning to a pile of bones...	50.3.11	sǐ	死
stepping on from this footprint	50.3.12	zhī	之
walking with the footprint of merely a foot soldier,			
afoot on the clay soil:	50.3.13	tú	徒
of ten	50.3.14	shí	十
flesh-and-meat-handling Beings,	50.3.15	yǒu	有
three are that.	50.3.16	sān	三
That person	50.4.17	rén	人
stepping on from this footprint	50.4.18	zhī	之
sprouting a bud from the ground	50.4.19	shēng	生
easily doing that work as hard as moving a			
heavy bag tied at both ends with the			
strong force of an arm or plow,	50.4.20	dòng	動
and stepping on from this footprint	50.4.21	zhī	之
dying, a person turning to a pile of bones	50.4.22	sǐ	死
now down here in this earthly womb	50.4.23	dì	地
—both armpits sweat this too!—	50.5.24	yì	亦
of ten	50.5.25	shí	十
flesh-and-meat-handling Beings,	50.5.26	yǒu	有
three are that.	50.5.27	sān	三
In fact, that is to say *This Grown Man* with hairpin			
and public courtesy name,	50.6.28	fū	夫
that one, that very one shouldering a weapon,	50.6.29	hé	何
this taps lightly with a tutoring cane and leaves a			
mark on the solid shield of the past,	50.6.30	gù	故
is cultivating, like a plow,	50.7.31	yǐ	以
stepping on from this footprint	50.7.32	qí	其

sprouting a bud from the ground:	50.7.33	shēng	生
sprouting a bud from the ground,	50.7.34	shēng	生
stepping on from this footprint,	50.7.35	zhī	之
a jug in a habitable cave in a cliff, thick and generous,	50.7.36	hòu	厚
and covering, as a pair of grass sprouts and clay soil thatch atop a chalice and its lid,	50.8.37	gài	蓋
what's heard at the two-winged gateway and famously reported on as	50.8.38	wén	聞
the traditionally virtuous, offering up a ram's head while speaking back and forth, tongues waggling,	50.8.39	shàn	善
taking well in hand, hearing three times over,	50.8.40	shè	攝
sprouting a bud from the ground.	50.8.41	shēng	生
This is boiling sugarcane with fire as follows!	50.8.42	zhâ	者
On the land where two divided pieces of soil are next to a big soil mound,	50.9.43	lù	陸
out in public at the crossroads, being good, doing one's work,	50.9.44	xíng	行
he's the husk of the initial protective bud casing but not really the true flower of	50.9.45	bù	不
walking slowly with the footprint of that trampling monkey with the head of a ghost, the left leg leading the way,	50.9.46	yù	遇
with fearsome buffalo	50.9.47	sì	兕
and fierce tigers.	50.9.48	hǔ	虎

Entering, like an arrowhead inserting or maybe
joining the imperial government,   50.10.49   rù   入
an army of surrounding carts,   50.10.50   jūn   軍
    he's the husk of the initial protective bud
    casing but not really the true flower of   50.10.51   bù   不
    wearing, like a robe or the placental
    afterbirth hanging from a recently
    pregnant woman made of fur stripped by
    hand from its pelt,   50.10.52   bèi   被
        a turtle shell shield   50.10.53   jiǎ   甲
        and carrying a short ax with two
        hands like a soldier or pawn.   50.10.54   bīng   兵

As opposed to…

If, around fearsome buffalo,   50.11.55   sì   兇
the shamanic dancer with animal tails flowing from
her wrists, Not-Having,   50.11.56   wú   無
with "this place" being intentionally created like
any household gate hewn with an axe   50.11.57   suǒ   所
    is throwing (expertly by hand like handling
    a *shū* weapon)   50.11.58   tóu   投
    what it holds a basket of,   50.11.59   qí   其
    an angled horn;   50.11.60   jiǎo   角

if, around fierce tigers,   50.12.61   hǔ   虎
the shaman-dancing Not-Having   50.12.62   wú   無
with "this place" being intentionally created like
any household gate hewn with an axe   50.12.63   suǒ   所
    is arranging (like hand-placing two strips of
    meat to dry in the sun)   50.12.64   cuò   措
    what it holds a basket of,   50.12.65   qí   其
    a claw like a hand grabbing from above;   50.12.66   zhào   爪

if, carrying a short ax with two hands like a soldier
or pawn,   50.13.67   bīng   兵
the shaman-dancing Not-Having   50.13.68   wú   無
with "this place" being intentionally created like
any household gate hewn with an axe   50.13.69   suǒ   所
      is having an outward public container of
      private parts, like a building housing an
      important, older man who's "got balls," a
      duke,   50.13.70   róng   容
      and what holds a basket of   50.13.71   qí   其
      is a blade?   50.13.72   rèn   刃

In fact, that is to say This Grown Man with hairpin
and public courtesy name,   50.14.73   fū   夫
that one, that very one shouldering a weapon,   50.14.74   hé   何
this taps lightly with a tutoring cane and leaves a
mark on the solid shield of the past,   50.14.75   gù   故

is cultivating, like a plow,   50.15.76   yǐ   以
what it holds a basket of,   50.15.77   qí   其
shaman-dancing Not-Having: 50.15.78   wú   無
      dying, a person turning to a pile of bones, 50.15.79   sǐ   死
      now down here in this earthly womb. 50.15.80   dì   地

***Chapter 51: Don't get me wrong, I honor Dào,
even when choosing a highly regarded Dé life
because everything began there.***

Walking with the footprint of the loose-haired
head buck…   51.1.1   dào   道
      sprouting a bud from the ground,   51.1.2   shēng   生

what it had, stepping on from this
footprint, it had this...   51.1.3   zhī   之

walking with the footprint of someone who's in
alignment (eyes looking forward, directly over the
heart, left leg slowly leading the way)...   51.2.4   dé   德
     tying animals and raising them in a pen,   51.2.5   xù   畜
     what it had, stepping on from this
     footprint, it had this...   51.2.6   zhī   之

matter (outside one's body, "cut from the cow" by
a bloodied blade),   51.3.7   wù   物
     shaping as finely and level as two shields
     side by side with measuring lines of three
     hairs' breadth,   51.3.8   xíng   形
     what it had, stepping on from this
     footprint, it had this...   51.3.9   zhī   之

planting power, like holding a forceful arm, a
bladed tool, or a plow on the soil to seed like
testicles,   51.4.10   shì   勢
     completing that final "nail" in a weapon on
     a pole   51.4.11   chéng   成
     what it had, stepping on from this
     footprint, it had this.   51.4.12   zhī   之

This baby footprint on bamboo-slip pages   51.5.13   shì   是
cultivating, like a plow,   51.5.14   yǐ   以
the medicine-dancing-scorpion insect swarm of   51.5.15   wàn   萬
matter (outside one's body, "cut from the cow" by
a bloodied blade),   51.5.16   wù   物
like the sun sinking down in four bushes, must not
be—cannot be, eh?—   51.5.17   mò   莫

the husk of the initial protective bud casing but not
really the true flower of
honoring, like offering by hand the ritual alcohol
vessel with the chief in charge of its preparation,
walking with the footprint of the loose-haired head
buck,
       yet now, bearded, you're
       held in high regard, like when two hands
       are wrapped around a person atop cowry-
       shell-riches,
       walking with the footprint of someone
       who's in alignment (eyes looking forward,
       directly over the heart, left leg slowly
       leading the way).

Walking with the footprint of the loose-haired
head buck...
what it has, stepping on from this footprint, it has
this...
       honoring, like offering by hand the ritual
       alcohol vessel with the chief in charge of its
       preparation;

walking with the footprint of someone who's in
alignment (eyes looking forward, directly over the
heart, left leg slowly leading the way)...
what it has, stepping on from this footprint, it has
this...
       being held in high regard, like when two
       hands are wrapped around a person atop
       cowry-shell-riches.

51.6.18	bù	不
51.6.19	zūn	尊
51.6.20	dào	道
51.6.21	ér	而
51.6.22	guì	貴
51.6.23	dé	德
51.7.24	dào	道
51.7.25	zhī	之
51.7.26	zūn	尊
51.8.27	dé	德
51.8.28	zhī	之
51.8.29	guì	貴

In fact, that is to say This Grown Man with hairpin
and public courtesy name,   51.9.30   fū   夫
like the sun sinking down in four bushes, it must
not be—cannot be, eh?—that   51.9.31   mò   莫
what it has, stepping on from this footprint, it has
this   51.9.32   zhī   之
destiny, what has to be, like a command from a
magistrate speaking, joining from three sides over
a kneeling person,   51.9.33   mìng 命
    yet now, bearded, you're   51.9.34   ér   而
    the conventional royal administrator
    wearing a men's headcloth as his skirt,   51.9.35   cháng 常
      oneself personally, right on the
      nose   51.9.36   zì   自
      accomplishing this thus, as
      naturally as dog meat over a fire.   51.9.37   rán   然

*This wasn't a "destiny" I could have
accomplished on my own. It took both Dào
and Dé...*

This taps lightly with a tutoring cane and leaves a
mark on the solid shield of the past: 51.10.38   gù   故
"walking with the footprint of the loose-haired
head buck,   51.10.39   dào   道
    sprouting a bud from the ground,   51.10.40   shēng 生
    what it had, stepping on from this
    footprint, it had this...   51.10.41   zhī   之

walking with the footprint of someone who's in
alignment (eyes looking forward, directly over the
heart, left leg slowly leading the way),   51.11.42   dé   德
    tying animals and raising them in a pen   51.11.43   xù   畜

what it had, stepping on from this
footprint, it had this…"   51.11.44   zhī   之

lengthening as long as hair that has to be tied with
a brooch, a loose-haired old man,   51.12.45   zháng   長
what it had, stepping on from this footprint, it had
this…   51.12.46   zhī   之

birthing an upside-down baby below the
moon   51.12.47   yù   育
what it had, stepping on from this
footprint, it had this…   51.12.48   zhī   之

sheltering like a person in a pavilion or in a
checkpoint,   51.13.49   tíng   亭
what it had, stepping on from this footprint, it had
this…   51.13.50   zhī   之

army banner made with feathers and hair,
like a feathered headdress on a kneeling
woman, like the one used on the
emperor's or a king's carriage   51.13.51   dú   毒
what it had, stepping on from this
footprint, it had this…   51.13.52   zhī   之

feeding a meal, mouth over a rice bowl, as
beautiful as a ram's head,   51.14.53   yǎng   養
what it had, stepping on from this footprint, it had
this…   51.14.54   zhī   之

covering the walking forth and then
returning, doubling back like the gut,
stepping slowly with only one's left leg
leading the way,   51.14.55   fù   覆
what it had, stepping on from this
footprint, it had this…   51.14.56   zhī   之

sprouting a bud from the ground,   51.15.57   shēng   生
yet now, bearded, you're   51.15.58   ér   而
          the husk of the initial protective bud casing
          but not really the true flower of   51.15.59   bù   不
          flesh-and-meat-handling Being…   51.15.60   yǒu   有

creating something by hand, carving an elephant
likeness of good fortune and royal power,   51.16.61   wéi   為
yet now, bearded, you're   51.16.62   ér   而
          the husk of the initial protective bud casing
          but not really the true flower of   51.16.63   bù   不
          a mother—the heart grabbed like by the
          hand of a government office or temple
          worker that was usually a eunuch in the
          old days…   51.16.64   shì   恃

lengthening as long as hair that has to be tied with
a brooch, a loose-haired old man,   51.17.65   zháng   長
yet now, bearded, you're   51.17.66   ér   而
          the husk of the initial protective bud casing
          but not really the true flower of   51.17.67   bù   不
          dominating as the house of that chisel used
          to mark slaves and criminals.   51.17.68   zǎi   宰

Like in Chapter 2 and in Chapter 10.

"This baby footprint on bamboo-slip pages,   51.18.69   shì   是
by the nitty-gritty, grinding gizzard of a fowl, what
that's called,   51.18.70   wèi   謂
this hard-to-see structure of a double-looped,
figure-eight skein of string-dyed-black,   51.18.71   xuán   玄

walking with the footprint of someone
who's in alignment (eyes looking forward,
directly over the heart, left leg slowly
leading the way)."   51.18.72   dé   德

Verbatim from the end of Chapter 10.

Chapter 52: How to avoid danger and difficulty
(spoiler: don't be a follower)

The heavenly from high above this great big person   52.1.1   tiān   天
now here down below,   52.1.2   xià   下
    and flesh-and-meat-handling Being   52.1.3   yǒu   有
    conceiving, a woman kneeling, happy,
    speaking of gathering herself from three
    sides,   52.1.4   shǐ   始

    this is cultivating, like a plow,   52.2.5   yǐ   以
    creating something by hand, carving an
    elephant likeness of good fortune and
    royal power,   52.2.6   wéi   為
        the heavenly, from high above this
        great big person   52.2.7   tiān   天
        now here down below, 52.2.8   xià   下
        suckling, a woman kneeling with
        breasts full of milk. 52.2.9   mǔ   母

"Done"—as de facto as a kneeling person turning
away after eating a bowl of rice—done with   52.3.10   jì   既
The Hand-Picked Gem, like cowry-shell-riches
discovered along the road,   52.3.11   dé   得
what it holds a basket of,   52.3.12   qí   其

suckling, a woman kneeling with breasts full of
milk,   52.3.13   mǔ   母
    this is cultivating, like a plow,   52.3.14   yǐ   以
    speaking as a great big person to a baby,
    distinguishing, imparting, and
    administering wisdom confidently and
    intimately,   52.3.15   zhī   知
        what it holds a basket of,   52.3.16   qí   其
        a baby with arms wide open and
        legs swaddled, *Zǐ.*   52.3.17   zǐ   子

"Done" with   52.4.18   jì   既
speaking as a great big person to a baby,
distinguishing, imparting, and administering
wisdom confidently and intimately,   52.4.19   zhī   知
what it holds a basket of,   52.4.20   qí   其
a baby with arms wide open and legs swaddled,
"*Zǐ,*"   52.4.21   zǐ   子
    someone walking with a footprint of slowly
    returning with the left leg leading the way,
    doubling back (like the gut) on one's
    footprint *to*   52.4.22   fù   復
    hand-defending this building,   52.4.23   shǒu   守
        what it holds a basket of,   52.4.24   qí   其
        suckling, a woman kneeling with
        breasts full of milk: 52.4.25   mǔ   母
        "no longer, as if diving into the
        water, knife in hand, it's gone,   52.4.26   mò   沒
        your pregnant self...   52.4.27   shēn   身
        the husk of the initial protective
        bud casing but not really the true
        flower of   52.4.28   bù   不

endangered as human remains,
spoken of privately, revolving
around yourself."   52.4.29   dài   殆

Direct quote from Chapter 16.

Blocking like a fortress along the northern border
made by two hands stuffing items into a house,
cramming full,   52.5.30   sāi   塞
what it holds a basket of,   52.5.31   qí   其
       a person with a clear open mouth,
       breathing, freely exchanging like air,
       smiling   52.5.32   duì   兑

and obstructing the two-winged gateway with
sprouting seeds, blocking entry to   52.6.33   bì   閉
what it holds a basket of,   52.6.34   qí   其
       this two-winged gateway: 52.6.35   mén   門

       then ending like the knot at the end of a
       thick silk skein, like winter,   52.7.36   zhōng   終
       your pregnant self...   52.7.37   shēn   身
          the husk of the initial protective
          bud casing but not really the true
          flower of   52.7.38   bù   不
          exerting with force, working hard
          with the strong force of an arm, a
          bladed tool, or a plow on the soil.   52.7.39   qín   勤

But two hands unlatching that two-winged
gateway,   52.8.40   kāi   開
what it holds a basket of,   52.8.41   qí   其

a person with a clear open mouth,
breathing, freely exchanging like air,
smiling,   52.8.42   duì   兌

and helping (like ferrying across the River *Qi* in the
kingdom of that same name, which means a field
as even and deferential as two identical stalks of
grain under the chisel, like a pair showing piety
before offering sacrifices and other ceremonies)   52.9.43   jì   濟
what it holds a basket of,   52.9.44   qí   其
          their task, what they do with a weapon,
flag, or pen in hand: 52.9.45   shì   事

          then ending like the knot at the end of a
          thick silk skein, like winter,   52.10.46   zhōng 終
          your pregnant self...   52.10.47   shēn   身
                    the husk of the initial protective
                    bud casing but not really the true
                    flower of   52.10.48   bù   不
          tapping lightly with a tutoring cane
          a fur coat, saving by forbidding.   52.10.49   jiù   救

Seen by someone with one big eye for a head,   52.11.50   jiàn   見
our tiny dear little one, like three grains of sand,   52.11.51   xiǎo   小
          that's called, when issued on a breath from
          the mouth   52.11.52   yuē   曰
               "as bright as dawn rising on a crescent
          moon, enlightened,"   52.11.53   míng   明

and hand-defending this building,   52.12.54   shǒu   守
softening to be as supple as a tree that can be cut
with a spear   52.12.55   róu   柔

that's called, when issued on a breath from
the mouth.
"revolving around itself as a powerful bow

      52.12.56   yuē   曰

broadening, strengthening, stiff, hard, and
compelling as a rice weevil, like a tiny
venomous snake—thwang;"

      52.12.57   qiáng   強

doing truly useful work like a water bucket, by
means of carrying-capacity,

      52.13.58   yòng   用

what it holds a basket of,

      52.13.59   qí   其

      that shining fire over the head of a
      kneeling person

      52.13.60   guāng   光

and someone walking with a footprint of slowly
returning with the left leg leading the way,
doubling back (like the gut) on one's footprint,

      52.13.61   fù   復

coming back after sweeping troops out of the soil
mound hills to this,

      52.13.62   guī   歸

what it holds a basket of,

      52.13.63   qí   其

      "as bright as dawn rising on a crescent
      moon, enlightened:"

      52.13.64   míng   明

this shamanic dancer with animal tails flowing from
her wrists, Not-Having,

      52.14.65   wú   無

is walking with the footprint of someone slowly
leaving behind cowry-like riches after *dying*, the
left leg leading the way with two hands are
wrapped around them, dragging them off,

      52.14.66   yí   遺

      your pregnant self

      52.14.67   shēn   身

      harmed by evil misfortune, the bone
      remnants of a pleading person with their
      head in the middle of a pole over their
      shoulders with two things on either end.

      52.14.68   yáng   殃

This baby footprint on bamboo-slip pages
is creating something by hand, carving an
elephant likeness of good fortune and
royal power,

        fluttering both wings high above
        the sun, learning to fly, a loyal
        follower practicing
        the conventional royal
        administrator wearing a men's
        headcloth as his skirt.

52.15.69	shì	是
52.15.70	wéi	為
52.15.71	xí	習
52.15.72	cháng	常

*Why did I write so many chapters explaining why I
needed to strike out as my own version of a royal
administrator rather than continuing to be a loyal
follower? Was I justifying it to Yinxi and posterity,
or was I talking myself into something that was
hard for me to do? Both?*

Chapter 53: My role as a follower hurt the Dào. It made me nothing more than an extravagant thief.

That low-ranking government official, his hand
holding a pen, sent as a messenger or an envoy,
putting to work, using in every way you can think
of, directing,
I, holding a rake-like weapon to defend myself and
my opinion:
firmly as a person seated between two things,
perhaps shells, connecting them, armored by
them,

53.1.1	shǐ	使
53.1.2	wǒ	我
53.1.3	jiè	介

am accomplishing this thus, as naturally as dog
meat over a fire…   53.1.4   rán   然
    flesh-and-meat-handling Being   53.1.5   yǒu   有
    speaking as a great big person to a baby,
    distinguishing, imparting, and
    administering wisdom confidently and
    intimately,   53.1.6   zhī   知

    out in public at the crossroads, being good,
    doing my work,   53.2.7   xíng   行
    in this place and time, oh, black, icy raven
    sun…   53.2.8   yú   於
        this great big person   53.2.9   dà   大
        walking with the footprint of the
        loose-haired head buck.   53.2.10   dào   道

"Oh, YES, Ma'am," says the "short-tailed bird,"   53.3.11   wéi   唯
flying flags over—yes, that too, "female funnel"—
spreading, reproducing   53.3.12   shī   施
this baby footprint on bamboo-slip pages,   53.3.13   shì   是
    is scared—like of a ghost with a stick.   53.3.14   wèi   畏

"This great big person   53.4.15   dà   大
walking with the footprint of the loose-haired head
buck"   53.4.16   dào   道
    pairing like one-half of a double-yoked
    harness as pleasant as something sweet in
    the mouth and therefore extra   53.4.17   shèn   甚
    foreign," part of the great barbarian tribe
    of the east carrying bows, leveling and
    razing,   53.4.18   yí   夷

yet now, bearded, you're
one of our folk, the people enslaved by blinding
with a dagger: 53.5.20   mín   民
        as good as a woman with a child   53.5.21   hǎo   好
        taking a short-cut pathway straight across,
        stepping slowly with the left leg over an
        underground stream.   53.5.22   jìng   徑

Beginning the morning when the sun's just rising
out of the grass alongside a river, perhaps paying a
visit to the emperor,   53.6.23   cháo   朝
        pairing like one-half of a double-yoked
        harness as pleasant as something sweet in
        the mouth and therefore extra   53.6.24   shèn   甚
        in a new posting in a thatched cottage by a
        soil mountain,   53.6.25   chú   除

a field   53.7.26   tián   田
        pairing like one-half of a double-yoked
        harness as pleasant as something sweet in
        the mouth and therefore extra   53.7.27   shèn   甚
        thick as a pair of grass sprouts growing
        from Not-Having, dancing with long tails
        flowing from her wrists like turnips from an
        unused field,   53.7.28   wú   蕪

granaries, food stored in one's house,   53.8.29   cāng   倉
        pairing like one-half of a double-yoked
        harness as pleasant as something sweet in
        the mouth and therefore extra   53.8.30   shèn   甚
        empty, like a tiger head upon a mound...   53.8.31   xū   虛

yet now, bearded, you're   53.5.19   ér   而

wearing clothes like a mourning dress, a person
hand-subdued to kneeling before a commonplace
plate,   53.9.32   fú   服
          covering with this pattern, like a tattoo on
          the chest of a great big man,   53.9.33   wén   文
          a skein of silk dyed many colors with fruit
          hand-picked from a tree,   53.9.34   cǎi   綵

a belt made of the traditional gendered head-cloth
we wrap around our hair once we receive our
public courtesy names   53.10.35   dài   帶
          reaping benefits in the manner of a sharp-
          edged blade slicing grain,   53.10.36   lì   利
          a double-edged sword like a blade with
          two people and their mouths all together,
          gathering themselves from three sides,   53.10.37   jiàn   劍

sated like a dog with meat in its mouth, fed up,   53.11.38   yàn   厭
          drinking, leaning over a vase for making
          alcohol with one's mouth,   53.11.39   yǐn   飲
          eating, mouth over a bowl of rice on a
          stand;   53.11.40   shí   食

and sprouting riches, cowry currency, like seeds,   53.12.41   cái   財
the transformation from a right-side-up person to
an upside-down person atop cowry-shell riches,   53.12.42   huò   貨
          flesh-and-meat-handling Being   53.12.43   yǒu   有
          having leftover excess food remains in
          their house...   53.12.44   yú   餘

this baby footprint on bamboo-slip pages,   53.13.45   shì   是
by the nitty-gritty, grinding gizzard of a fowl, what
that's called,   53.13.46   wèi   謂

spitting into a bowl like in an oath among robbers,
"thick as thieves,"

    53.13.47   dào   盗

> as extravagant as this great big person
> blowing air.

    53.13.48   kuā   夸

> It wrings to backward the two wings of
> walking with the footprint of the loose-
> haired head buck

    53.14.49   fēi   非
    53.14.50   dào   道

> —yes, that too, oh "female funnel!"

    53.14.51   yâ   也

> I say, "Oh, indeed, that hurts, a weapon on
> a pole wounding sprouting seeds and
> talents."

    53.14.52   zāi   哉

Chapter 54: But I was loathe to give up being highly regarded.

The traditionally virtuous, offering up a ram's head
while speaking back and forth, tongues waggling,

    54.1.1   shàn   善

a striding person establishing, hand-planting a pole

    54.1.2   jiàn   建

—this is boiling sugarcane with fire as follows!—

    54.1.3   zhâ   者

> is the husk of the initial protective bud
> casing but not really the true flower of

    54.1.4   bù   不

> pulled up so expertly by hand that it's like a
> running dog arriving;

    54.1.5   bá   拔

the traditionally virtuous

    54.2.6   shàn   善

bundling it all up together in both arms

    54.2.7   bào   抱

—this is boiling sugarcane with fire as follows!—

    54.2.8   zhâ   者

> is the husk of the initial protective bud
> casing but not really the true flower of

    54.2.9   bù   不

freely exchanging the meat of their matter,
stripping themself like a smiling breathy
older brother.   54.2.10   tuō   脫

A baby with arms wide open and legs swaddled,
"Zǐ,"   54.3.11   zǐ   子
an infant boy, maybe a grandson like a thin silk
skein as tiny as three grains of sand: 54.3.12   sūn   孫
this is cultivating, like a plow,   54.3.13   yǐ   以
a ceremony making a meat offering by hand at an
altar,   54.3.14   jì   祭
sacrificing with something like a fetus upon an
altar,   54.3.15   sì   祀
        is the husk of the initial protective bud
        casing but not really the true flower of   54.3.16   bù   不
        halting like a person with hands for feet
        handling a chariot.   54.3.17   chuò   輟

*Even my son didn't stop me from that ritual life. But
what I needed to develop every aspect of myself
was to live the Dé...*

If a person develops (warned, built, mended,
embellished by being lightly hitting on the back
with a tutor cane and three strands of hair)   54.4.18   xiū   修
what it has, stepping on from this footprint   54.4.19   zhī   之
in this place and time, oh, black, icy raven sun...   54.4.20   yú   於
your pregnant self,   54.4.21   shēn   身
        what it holds a basket of   54.4.22   qí   其
        walking with the footprint of someone
        who's in alignment (eyes looking forward,
        directly over the heart, left leg slowly
        leading the way)...   54.4.23   dé   德

only then do you get
genuinely getting into it, like using a fork to
get food right from the cauldron.

	54.4.24	nǎi　乃
	54.4.25	zhēn　真

If a person develops
what it has, stepping on from this footprint
in this place and time, oh, black, icy raven sun...
a home, complete with a pig under the roof,
　　what it holds a basket of
　　walking with the footprint of someone
　　who's in alignment...
　　only then do you get
leftover excess food remaining in their
house.

	54.5.26	xiū　修
	54.5.27	zhī　之
	54.5.28	yú　於
	54.5.29	jiā　家
	54.5.30	qí　其
	54.5.31	dé　德
	54.5.32	nǎi　乃
	54.5.33	yú　餘

If a person develops
what it has, stepping on from this footprint
in this place and time, oh, black, icy raven sun...
a village, a rural community where people face one
another over a food vessel, feasting,
　　what it holds a basket of
　　walking with the footprint of someone
　　who's in alignment...
　　only then do you get
lengthening as long as hair that has to be
tied with a brooch, like a loose-haired old
man.

	54.6.34	xiū　修
	54.6.35	zhī　之
	54.6.36	yú　於
	54.6.37	xiāng　鄉
	54.6.38	qí　其
	54.6.39	dé　德
	54.6.40	nǎi　乃
	54.6.41	cháng　長

If a person develops
what it has, stepping on from this footprint
in this place and time, oh, black, icy raven sun...
our domestic enclave, defended by a weapon on a
pole,

	54.7.42	xiū　修
	54.7.43	zhī　之
	54.7.44	yú　於
	54.7.45	guó　國

what it holds a basket of			
walking with the footprint of someone			
who's in alignment…	54.7.47	dé	德
only then do you get	54.7.48	nǎi	乃
luxury as lush as a pot holding a pair of			
blooming flowers.	54.7.49	fēng	豐

---

what it holds a basket of — 54.7.46 — qí — 其
walking with the footprint of someone
who's in alignment… — 54.7.47 — dé — 德
only then do you get — 54.7.48 — nǎi — 乃
luxury as lush as a pot holding a pair of
blooming flowers. — 54.7.49 — fēng — 豐

If a person develops — 54.8.50 — xiū — 修
what it has, stepping on from this footprint — 54.8.51 — zhī — 之
in this place and time, oh, black, icy raven sun… — 54.8.52 — yú — 於
the heavenly from high above this great big person — 54.8.53 — tiān — 天
now here down below, — 54.8.54 — xià — 下
what it holds a basket of — 54.8.55 — qí — 其
walking with the footprint of someone
who's in alignment… — 54.8.56 — dé — 德
only then do you get — 54.8.57 — nǎi — 乃
the general, the universal, the vast
lusterlessness of two arrows blocking the
sun, (a different pǔ). — 54.8.58 — pǔ — 普

This taps lightly with a tutoring cane and leaves a
mark on the solid shield of the past: — 54.9.59 — gù — 故
cultivating, like a plow, — 54.9.60 — yǐ — 以
your pregnant self, — 54.9.61 — shēn — 身
someone with one big eye for a head
kneeling on a stork-like temple or
watchtower, is keeping lookout for — 54.9.62 — guān — 觀
your pregnant self; — 54.9.63 — shēn — 身

cultivating, like a plow, — 54.10.64 — yǐ — 以
a home, complete with a pig under the roof, — 54.10.65 — jiā — 家

someone with one big eye for a head
kneeling on a stork-like temple or
watchtower, is keeping lookout for   54.10.66   guān   觀
a home, complete with a pig under the
roof;   54.10.67   jiā   家

cultivating, like a plow,   54.11.68   yǐ   以
a village, a rural community where people face one
another over a food vessel, feasting,   54.11.69   xiāng   鄉
    someone with one big eye for a head
    kneeling on a stork-like temple or
    watchtower, is keeping lookout for   54.11.70   guān   觀
    a village, a rural community where people
    face one another over a food vessel,
    feasting;   54.11.71   xiāng   鄉

cultivating, like a plow,   54.12.72   yǐ   以
our domestic enclave, defended by a weapon on a
pole,   54.12.73   guó   國
    someone with one big eye for a head
    kneeling on a stork-like temple or
    watchtower, is keeping lookout for   54.12.74   guān   觀
    our domestic enclave, defended by a
    weapon on a pole;   54.12.75   guó   國

cultivating, like a plow,   54.13.76   yǐ   以
the heavenly from high above this great big person   54.13.77   tiān   天
now here down below,   54.13.78   xià   下
    someone with one big eye for a head
    kneeling on a stork-like temple or
    watchtower, is keeping lookout for   54.13.79   guān   觀
    the heavenly from high above this great big
    person   54.13.80   tiān   天

now here down below... 54.13.81 xià 下

counting up on all five fingers, aren't I 54.14.82 wú 吾
that one—that very one shouldering a weapon— 54.14.83 hé 何
cultivating, like a plow, 54.14.84 yǐ 以
speaking as a great big person to a baby,
distinguishing, imparting, and administering
wisdom confidently and intimately, 54.14.85 zhī 知
> *with the heavenly, from high above this*
> *great big person* 54.14.86 tiān 天
> *now here down below,* 54.14.87 xià 下
> accomplishing this thus, as naturally as dog
> meat over a fire? 54.14.88 rán 然
> I say, "Oh, indeed, that hurts, a weapon on
> a pole wounding sprouting seeds and
> talents." 54.14.89 zāi 哉

What I was developing was my boss talk.

This is cultivating, like a plow, 54.15.90 yǐ 以
this here—the foot stops a person here on this
footprint! 54.15.91 cǐ 此

**Chapter 55: Living the Dé works beautifully, and
that usually does mean being an official… but not
a high-ranking official.**

Keeping what's being said in the mouth *now*, in
modern times, stuffed in like jade, pearls, and
gems in a corpse's mouth, 55.1.1 hán 含
> *walking with the footprint of someone*
> *who's in alignment (eyes looking forward,* 55.1.2 dé 德

directly over the heart, left leg slowly
leading the way),
what it has, stepping on from this
footprint,   55.1.3   zhī   之
a jug in a habitable cave in a cliff, thick and
generous,   55.1.4   hòu   厚

compares, like two people right next to each other,
to   55.2.5   bǐ   比
this place and time, oh, black, icy raven sun...   55.2.6   yú   於
a bare naked and red (as this great big person on
fire)   55.2.7   chì   赤
baby with arms wide open and legs swaddled, "*Zǐ:*" 55.2.8   zǐ   子

A bee (like a snaky animal with "a knot in a thread"
in lush bushes)   55.3.9   féng   蜂
scorpion   55.3.10   chài   蠆
venomous snake (that will cut off one's foot)-   55.3.11   huǐ   虺
serpent (a snake as crooked as certain gentlemen
or emperors),   55.3.12   shé   蛇
    is the husk of the initial protective bud
    casing but not really the true flower of   55.3.13   bù   不
    stinging—both armpits sweat this too!—as
    when hit lightly by a snake;   55.3.14   shì   螫

a vigorous and ferocious (as a dog of an eldest
brother, that baby son in the chalice),   55.4.15   mǎng   猛
predator (like a dog attacking an animal)   55.4.16   shòu   獸
    is the husk of the initial protective bud
    casing but not really the true flower of   55.4.17   bù   不
    taking possession of as an expert hand with
    tigers or boars fighting one another;   55.4.18   jù   據

grabbing with claws like a big round expert hand
with two nervous eyes over "a short-tailed bird"
hand,   55.4.19   juē   攫
a bird with a dangling tail, paying attention already,   55.4.20   niǎo   鳥
     is the husk of the initial protective bud
     casing but not really the true flower of   55.4.21   bù   不
     rolling around by hand, modeling or
     monopolizing (like a hand turning a big
     round spindle over an inch-sized spot
     that's as small as that spot on your forearm
     where your pulse beats strong).   55.4.22   bó   搏

A strong framework, like bones,   55.5.23   gǔ   骨
     in a delicate state with a pair of fragile
     bows,   55.5.24   ruò   弱
and sinew, tendons, muscles, or even veins that
stand out like two bamboo stalks on a rib or the
meat of an arm that sticks out from the body like a
plow   55.5.25   jīn   筋
     softening to be as supple as a tree that can
     be cut with a spear,   55.5.26   róu   柔
yet now you're bearded,   55.5.27   ér   而
     gripping—grasping as onto a room, a roof
     covering an arrow straight in the clay soil,
     having arrived at the end, in the extreme
     climax—   55.5.28   wò   握
     solidly, for a long time, keeping as firm to
     what happened in the first place as this
     land surrounding and holding this nation's
     shield since ancient times.   55.5.29   gù   固

Like a tree whose top branches aren't yet fully			
grown, *not yet*	55.6.30	wèi	未
speaking as a great big person to a baby,			
distinguishing, imparting, and			
administering wisdom confidently and			
intimately,	55.6.31	zhī	知
and the spoon of a cow or "a woman's valley,"	55.6.32	pìn	牝
and a bull soil, "male parts,"	55.6.33	mǔ	牡
what they have, stepping on from this			
footprint,	55.6.34	zhī	之
joining together from three sides over a			
mouth, like having sex,	55.6.35	hé	合
yet now you're bearded,	55.6.36	ér	而
whole like a piece of pure jade, entire as it			
arrived,	55.6.37	quán	全
recently, exactly, having immediately			
folded from one straight rod into two,	55.6.38	zuò	作
a strong essence or soul, like polished raw rice,			
seminal fluid, or spring's blue-green lush ripening			
of the sedative cinnabar plant,	55.7.39	jīng	精
is what it has, stepping on from this			
footprint,	55.7.40	zhī	之
in arriving at the end, the extreme climax,			
like an arrow straight into the clay soil	55.7.41	zhì	至
—yes, that too, oh "female funnel!	55.7.42	yâ	也
Ending like the knot at the end of a thick silk skein,			
like winter,	55.8.43	zhōng	終
the entire day—the full sun—	55.8.44	rì	日
roaring like a puffing tiger head,	55.8.45	háo	號
yet now you're bearded,	55.8.46	ér	而

the husk of the initial protective bud casing
but *not really* the true flower of   55.8.47   bù   不
hoarse as the mouth of a man under a
scorching sun,   55.8.48   shà   嘎

warming, wetting, and stickily kneading together,
harmonizing like breath blown into a reed-pipe
mouth organ,   55.9.49   hé   和
     is what it has, stepping on from this
     footprint,   55.9.50   zhī   之
     in arriving at the end, the extreme climax,
     like an arrow straight into the clay soil   55.9.51   zhì   至
—yes, that too, oh "female funnel!"   55.9.52   yâ   也

*Living the Dé can mean being an imperial
administrator…*

Speaking as a great big person to a baby,
distinguishing, imparting, and administering
wisdom confidently and intimately,   55.10.53 zhī   知
     warming, wetting, and stickily kneading
     together, harmonizing like breath blown
     into a reed-pipe mouth organ,   55.10.54 hé   和
what that's called when issued on a breath from
the mouth   55.10.55 yuē   曰
     is "the conventional royal administrator
     wearing a men's headcloth as his skirt;" 55.10.56 cháng 常

speaking as a great big person to a baby,
distinguishing, imparting, and administering
wisdom confidently and intimately,   55.11.57 zhī   知
     the conventional royal administrator
     wearing a men's headcloth as his skirt,   55.11.58 cháng 常

what that's called when issued on a breath from
the mouth   55.11.59   yuē   曰
       is "as bright as dawn rising on a crescent
       moon, enlightened;"   55.11.60   míng   明

overflowing like water from a vessel,   55.12.61   yì   益
       sprouting a bud from the ground,   55.12.62   shēng   生
what that's called when issued on a breath from
the mouth   55.12.63   yuē   曰
       is "a good omen like a ram's head at an
       altar."   55.12.64   xiáng   祥

But it works only with a humble position...

In their heart,   55.13.65   xīn   心
that *low-ranking* government official, his hand
holding a pen, sent as a messenger or an envoy,
putting to work, using in every way you can think
of, directing,   55.13.66   shǐ   使
that vital *qì* energy, the breath of life, that air flow
that's like a gift of rice,   55.13.67   qì   氣
what that's called when issued on a breath from
the mouth   55.13.68   yuē   曰
       is "revolving around itself as a powerful
       bow broadening, strengthening, stiff, hard,
       and compelling as a rice weevil, like a tiny
       venomous snake—thwang!"   55.13.69   qiáng   強

But matter outside one's body, "cut from the cow"
by a bloodied blade,   55.14.70   wù   物
when you're strong as a *high-rank*ing bachelor
soldier-scholar-official, appointed by the emperor,   55.14.71   zhuàng   壯

like battle-axe-hewn-wood, like one burn of a
moxa in moxibustion?
After following this sacrificial blade-and-cauldron-
like ritual regulation,   55.14.72   zé   則
the honorable loose-haired elder bent over an
arrow as a cane,   55.14.73   lǎo   老

by the nitty-gritty, grinding gizzard of a fowl, what
that's called,   55.15.74   wèi   謂
    what it has, stepping on from this
    footprint,   55.15.75   zhǐ   之
    is the husk of the initial false guard-petals
    but *not really* the true flower of   55.15.76   bù   不
    walking with the footprint of the loose-
    haired head buck;   55.15.77   dào   道

and the husk of the initial protective bud casing but
not really the true flower of   55.16.78   bù   不
walking with the footprint of the loose-haired head
buck,   55.16.79   dào   道
    it's early, premature as sunrise above an
    acorn on the jujube, that thorny plant
    that's used for insomnia and contraception
    and causes midterm miscarriages,   55.16.80   zǎo   早
    already finishing it in the womb. 55.16.81   yǐ   已

***Chapter 56: Rather than speaking out loud,
"putting a sock in it" would let me be truly a wise
speaker with the new little life surviving alongside
the heavenly one already here.***

Speaking as a great big person to a baby,
distinguishing, imparting, and administering
wisdom confidently and intimately,   56.1.1   zhī   知
—this is boiling sugarcane with fire as follows!—   56.1.2   zhâ   者
    the husk of the initial protective bud casing
    but not really the true flower of   56.1.3   bù   不
    speaking out loud;   56.1.4   yán   言
speaking out loud   56.1.5   yán   言
—this is boiling sugarcane with fire as follows!—   56.1.6   zhâ   者
    the husk of the initial protective bud casing
    but not really the true flower of   56.1.7   bù   不
    speaking as a great big person to a baby,
    distinguishing, imparting, and
    administering wisdom confidently and
    intimately.   56.1.8   zhī   知

"Both hands stuffing items into the house,
cramming full,   56.2.9   sāi   塞
what it holds a basket of...   56.2.10   qí   其
    a person with a clear open mouth,
    breathing, freely exchanging like air,
    smiling;   56.2.11   duì   兌

obstructing the two-winged gateway with
sprouting seeds, blocking entry to,   56.3.12   bì   閉
what it holds a basket of...   56.3.13   qí   其
    this two-winged gateway:"   56.3.14   mén   門

[...as suggested in Chapter 52]

"pushing down to seated, on the ground,   56.4.15   cuò   挫
what it holds a basket of...   56.4.16   qí   其
a person speaking like an axe being
sharpened on metal, pointed;   56.4.17   ruì   銳

cutting, like a blade removing an ox's horn,   56.5.18   jiǎ   解
what it holds a basket of...   56.5.19   qí   其
unravelling, a blade dividing a skein of silk
into disorderliness;   56.5.20   fēn   紛

harmonizing, like breath blown into a reed-
pipe mouth organ,   56.6.21   hé   和
what it holds a basket of...   56.6.22   qí   其
that shining fire over the head of a
kneeling person;   56.6.23   guāng   光

and what's known as '*Fán*, one and the
same,' when spoken of as ordinarily and
generally as any commonplace bucket,   56.7.24   tóng   同
what it holds a basket of...   56.7.25   qí   其
is leaving one billionth of a trace like the
dust raised by deer running across the dirt,
streaked with soil."   56.7.26   chén   塵

*These are the same words as when I
learned my first baby would survive in
Chapter 4.*

This baby footprint on bamboo-slip pages,   56.8.27   shì   是
by the nitty-gritty, grinding gizzard of a fowl, what
that's called,   56.8.28   wèi   謂

this hard-to-see structure of a double-
looped, figure-eight skein of string-dyed-
black,   56.8.29   xuán   玄
     what's known as '*Fán*, one and the same,'
when spoken of as ordinarily and generally
as any commonplace bucket,   56.8.30   tóng   同

[Just like in the beginning, in 1.13.]

this taps lightly with a tutoring cane and leaves a
mark on the solid shield of the past: 56.9.31   gù   故
the husk of the initial protective bud casing but not
really the true flower of   56.9.32   bù   不
lip-smackingly genuinely   56.9.33   kâ   可
The Hand-Picked Gem, like cowry-shell-riches
discovered along the road,   56.9.34   dé   得
          yet now, you're bearded,   56.9.35   ér   而
          an intimate one, a beloved whose
          suffering, like from that chisel used to mark
          slaves and criminals, you see up close with
          one big eye for a head...   56.9.36   qīn   親

          the husk of the initial protective bud casing
          but not really the true flower of   56.10.37   bù   不
lip-smackingly genuinely   56.10.38   kâ   可
The Hand-Picked Gem, like cowry-shell-
riches discovered along the road,   56.10.39   dé   得
          yet now, you're bearded,   56.10.40   ér   而
          thinned, obstructions cleared—
          fully enough, like a complete leg
          and foot, an upside-down baby is
          upside down with amniotic fluid
          streaming below;   56.10.41   shū   疏

the husk of the initial protective bud casing but not
really the true flower of   56.11.42   bù   不
lip-smackingly genuinely   56.11.43   kâ   可
The Hand-Picked Gem, like cowry-shell-riches
discovered along the road,   56.11.44   dé   得
    yet now, you're bearded,   56.11.45   ér   而
    reaping benefits (in the manner of a sharp-
    edged blade slicing grain)...   56.11.46   lì   利

    the husk of the initial protective bud casing
    but not really the true flower of   56.12.47   bù   不
    lip-smackingly genuinely   56.12.48   kâ   可
    The Hand-Picked Gem, like cowry-shell-
    riches discovered along the road,   56.12.49   dé   得
        yet now, you're bearded,   56.12.50   ér   而
        being harmed as a house in which
        weeds sprout from a mouth;   56.12.51   hài   害

the husk of the initial protective bud casing but not
really the true flower of   56.13.52   bù   不
lip-smackingly genuinely   56.13.53   kâ   可
The Hand-Picked Gem, like cowry-shell-riches
discovered along the road,   56.13.54   dé   得
    yet now, you're bearded,   56.13.55   ér   而
    held in high regard, like when two hands
    are wrapped around a person atop cowry-
    shell-riches;   56.13.56   guì   貴

    the husk of the initial protective bud casing
    but not really the true flower of   56.14.57   bù   不
    lip-smackingly genuinely   56.14.58   kâ   可

The Hand-Picked Gem, like cowry-shell-
riches discovered along the road,   56.14.59 dé 得
   yet now, you're bearded,   56.14.60 ér 而
   accumulating, like a couple tiny
   pole weapons stacked together
   trying to be an arsenal, lowly
   cowry-shell riches...   56.14.61 jiàn 賤

this taps lightly with a tutoring cane and leaves a
mark on the solid shield of the past: 56.15.62 gù 故
creating something by hand, carving an elephant
likeness of good fortune and royal power, 56.15.63 wéi 為
with the heavenly, from high above this great big
person   56.15.64 tiān 天
now here down below,   56.15.65 xià 下
   held in high regard, like when two hands
   are wrapped around a person atop cowry-
   shell-riches.   56.15.66 guì 貴

*I could be who I really was—"Fán," that person
who stepped out of a cave in Chapter 1. Without
the niceties of being "The Handpicked One," I could
avoid the drawbacks.*

Chapter 57: I led two very different lives at once as I got ready to leave.

Cultivating, like a plow,   57.1.1 yǐ 以
straightening up, straightening things out for
"nailing" that first footstep of a journey... 57.1.2 zhèng 正

and flowing the River Happy, speaking of
gathering oneself from three sides,
managing
in our domestic enclave, defended by a
weapon on a pole;

cultivating, like a plow,
remarkable cunning like this great big person atop
that very one shouldering a weapon that tastes lip-
smackingly genuinely like the one…
    and doing truly useful work like a water
    bucket, by means of carrying-capacity,
    carrying a short ax with two hands like a
    soldier or pawn;

cultivating, like a plow,
the shamanic dancer with animal tails flowing from
her wrists, Not-Having,
their task, what they do with a weapon, flag, or
pen in hand…
    and getting hold of, grabbing the ear of
    the heavenly, from high above this great
    big person
    now here down below:

"counting up on all five fingers, aren't I
that one—that very one shouldering a weapon,
cultivating, like a plow,
speaking as a great big person to a baby,
distinguishing, imparting, and administering
wisdom confidently and intimately,"
    what it holds a basket of,

57.1.3	zhì	治
57.1.4	guó	國
57.2.5	yǐ	以
57.2.6	qí	奇
57.2.7	yòng	用
57.2.8	bīng	兵
57.3.9	yǐ	以
57.3.10	wú	無
57.3.11	shì	事
57.3.12	qù	取
57.3.13	tiān	天
57.3.14	xià	下
57.4.15	wú	吾
57.4.16	hé	何
57.4.17	yǐ	以
57.4.18	zhī	知
57.4.19	qí	其

accomplishing this thus, as naturally as dog
meat over a fire?   57.4.20   rán   然
I say, "Oh, indeed, that hurts, a weapon on
a pole wounding sprouting seeds and
talents."   57.4.21   zāi   哉

*Doing all of that at the same time and also acting
the part of the wise advisor was... problematic.*

This is cultivating, like a plow,   57.5.22   yǐ   以
this here—the foot stops a person here on this
footprint!   57.5.23   cǐ   此

The heavenly from high above this great big person   57.6.24   tiān   天
now here down below,   57.6.25   xià   下
    having more, like two pieces of meat,   57.6.26   duō   多
    binding one's heart with a silk rope—
    mourning, prohibiting, afraid, avoiding—   57.6.27   jì   忌
    with words we avoid, like taking footsteps
    around an enclosure, taboo words like the
    name of a deceased emperor or elder: 57.6.28   huì   諱
        yet, now you're bearded,   57.6.29   ér   而
        one of our folk, the people
        enslaved by blinding with a dagger, 57.6.30   mín   民
        relaxing their bow as for repair
        with a loom, threads crossing this
        way, right here, for more, for filling
        or covering   57.6.31   mí   彌
        being separated by a knife from
        cowry-riches, poor;   57.6.32   pín   貧

one of our folk, the people enslaved by blinding
with a dagger,   57.7.33 mín 民
   having more, like two pieces of meat, 57.7.34 duō 多
   reaping benefits (in the manner of a sharp-
   edged blade slicing grain),   57.7.35 lì 利
   a set of highly regarded vessels with lots of
   capacity, worthy of a guard dog: 57.7.36 qì 器
      our domestic enclave, defended by
      a weapon on a pole,   57.7.37 guó 國
      home, complete with a pig under
      the roof,   57.7.38 jiā 家
      is increasingly as a river of <u>double</u>
      the hard-to-see dark structure—
      two figure-eight skeins of string-
      dyed-black—   57.7.39 zī 滋
      darkening as the sun bowing down
      to the ground;   57.7.40 hūn 昏

that person,   57.8.41 rén 人
   having more, like two pieces of meat, 57.8.42 duō 多
   underhandedly tricky like that person with
   their right hand supporting ten, 57.8.43 jì 伎
   crafty as a bladed tool on exhaled air 57.8.44 qiǎo 巧
   with remarkable cunning like this great big
   person atop that very one shouldering a
   weapon that tastes lip-smackingly
   genuinely like the one: 57.8.45 qí 奇
      matter (outside one's body, "cut
      from the cow" by a bloodied
      blade),   57.8.46 wù 物
      is flowing a river of hard-to-see
      dark structure, a figure-eight skein 57.8.47 zī 滋

of string-dyed-black, *crying tears,*
glistening like dew,
taking off, rising up, possibly
passing on early like a young man
running over a snake.   57.8.48   qǐ   起

Like the mythical head buck who distinguishes right
and wrong kneeling at the river flowing by a person
with a mouth or cave between their legs, leaving,
this comes from and emulates the standards or
even magic of   57.9.49   fǎ   法
controlling (joining together from three sides over
a kneeling person and ordering an action or
perhaps sending off to somewhere),   57.9.50   lìng   令
    increasingly as a river of double the hard-
    to-see dark structure (two figure-eight
    skeins of string-dyed-black)   57.9.51   zī   滋
    shining forth as obviously clear and
    "enlightened" as the hair on a person
    standing on the ground in the early
    morning sun over the thorny jujube plant
    that's used for insomnia and contraception
    and causes midterm miscarriages: 57.9.52   zhāng 彰
        spitting into a bowl like in an oath
        among robbers, "thick as thieves,"   57.9.53   dào   盜
        is using a weapon on a pole to
        harm that sacrificial blade-and-
        cauldron-like ritual regulation, like
        an insect that eats at the joints and
        roots of a plant, destroying,   57.9.54   zéi   賊
        having more, like two pieces of
        meat,   57.9.55   duō   多
        flesh-and-meat-handling Being.   57.9.56   yǒu   有

Back in 19.6, both my Being and Not-Having personas were getting harmed this way. That was bad enough, but now it's even worse: both babies are involved. Honestly, an ideal sage would develop a plan for using a beard to change, leave, become financially stable, and get to the end of pregnancy safely...

This taps lightly with a tutoring cane and leaves a
mark on the solid shield of the past:

57.10.57	gù	故

an ideal grounded sage known for his civilian
petition to authority, standing straight, speaking,
and being listened to,

57.10.58	shèng	聖

that person

57.10.59	rén	人

would be saying like a cloud:

57.10.60	yún	云

"I, holding a rake-like weapon to defend myself and
my opinion,

57.11.61	wǒ	我

am shaman-dancing Not-Having

57.11.62	wú	無

creating something by hand, carving an elephant
likeness of good fortune and royal power,"

57.11.63	wéi	為

    yet, now you're bearded,

57.11.64	ér	而

    one of our folk, the people enslaved by
    blinding with a dagger,

57.11.65	mín	民

    yourself personally, right on the nose

57.11.66	zì	自

    transforming as a right-side-up person into
    an upside-down person;

57.11.67	huà	化

"I, holding a rake-like weapon to defend myself and
my opinion,

57.12.68	wǒ	我

am as good as a woman with a child,

57.12.69	hǎo	好

calm peace, the clear blue-green growth of the
sedative cinnabar plant quieting a dispute between
two hands on a plowshare,"   57.12.70   jìng   靜
    yet, now you're bearded,   57.12.71   ér   而
    one of our folk, the people enslaved by
    blinding with a dagger,   57.12.72   mín   民
    yourself personally, right on the nose 57.12.73   zì   自
    straightening up, straightening things out
    for "nailing" that first footstep of a journey;   57.12.74   zhèng   正

"I, holding a rake-like weapon to defend myself and
my opinion,   57.13.75   wǒ   我
am shaman-dancing Not-Having,   57.13.76   wú   無
their task, what they do with a weapon, flag, or
pen in hand,"   57.13.77   shì   事
    yet, now you're bearded,   57.13.78   ér   而
    one of our folk, the people enslaved by
    blinding with a dagger,   57.13.79   mín   民
    yourself personally, right on the nose, 57.13.80   zì   自
    wealthy, a home full of valuable vessels
    with lots of capacity;   57.13.81   fù   富

"I, holding a rake-like weapon to defend myself and
my opinion,   57.14.82   wǒ   我
am shaman-dancing Not-Having   57.14.83   wú   無
missing, kneeling with a yawning mouth before a
ravine eroded between two mountains, wanting,
lacking,"   57.14.84   yù   欲
    yet, now you're bearded,   57.14.85   ér   而
    one of our folk, the people enslaved by
    blinding with a dagger,   57.14.86   mín   民
    yourself personally, right on the nose, 57.14.87   zì   自

that "piece of wood" in the dense,
unpolished, sticking, natural state of a
thicket of oak trees. 57.14.88 pǔ 樸

Chapter 58: Getting ready for this new journey in this condition meant there were a lot of paradoxes. What looked like disaster was a blessing, and vice versa.

What it holds a basket of, 58.1.1 qí 其
governing or editing, tapping lightly with a tutoring
cane to straighten up and "nail" setting out by foot
on a long journey or campaign, preparing the
ground for it, 58.1.2 zhèng 政
one's heart right in the middle of the two-winged
gateway, dark and melancholy... 58.1.3 mèn 悶
one's heart right in the middle of the two-winged
gateway, dark and melancholy: 58.1.4 mèn 悶

what it holds a basket of 58.2.5 qí 其
is one of our folk, the people enslaved by blinding
with a dagger, 58.2.6 mín 民
    honest as the river of thick-tasting
    enjoyment of an ancestral shrine, offering,
    or tribute... 58.2.7 chún 淳
    honest as the river of thick-tasting
    enjoyment of an ancestral shrine, offering,
    or tribute. 58.2.8 chún 淳

What it holds a basket of, 58.3.9 qí 其
governing or editing, tapping lightly with a tutoring
cane to straighten up and "nail" setting out by foot 58.3.10 zhèng 政

on a long journey or campaign, preparing the
ground for it,
carefully discerning, studying at home, making a
meat offering by hand at an altar...   58.3.11   chá   察
carefully discerning, studying at home, making a
meat offering by hand at an altar: 58.3.12   chá   察

what it holds a basket of   58.4.13   qí   其
is one of our folk, the people enslaved by blinding
with a dagger,   58.4.14   mín   民
        a lidded earthen pot with a gap broken by
        a resolute hand with a fork, incomplete
        and lacking...   58.4.15   quē   缺
        a lidded earthen pot with a gap broken by
        a resolute hand with a fork, incomplete
        and lacking.   58.4.16   quē   缺

Disaster like the slanting mouth of a skull on a
sacrifice altar?   58.5.17   huò   禍
        Hmmm—like wind through tree branches! 58.5.18   xī   兮
        Blessings and good fortune, a full vessel on
        display on an altar,   58.5.19   fú   福
        stepping on from this footprint has this, 58.5.20   zhī   之
                "this place" being intentionally
                created like any household gate
                hewn with an axe   58.5.21   suǒ   所
                that's something leaned on, relied
                on by a person who's remarkable
                as the great big person that's lip-
                smackingly genuinely the one. 58.5.22   yǐ   倚

Blessings and good fortune, a full vessel on display
on an altar?   58.6.23   fú   福
    Hmmm—like wind through tree branches!   58.6.24   xī   兮
    Disaster like the slanting mouth of a skull
    on a sacrifice altar,   58.6.25   huò   禍
    stepping on from this footprint has this,   58.6.26   zhī   之
        "this place" being intentionally
        created like any household gate
        hewn with an axe   58.6.27   suǒ   所
        that's something lying in wait like a
        dog waiting to ambush a person.   58.6.28   fú   伏

Which kneeling person using both arms for paying
tribute to an ancestral shrine is fully processing   58.7.29   shú   孰
speaking as a great big person to a baby,
distinguishing, imparting, and administering
wisdom confidently and intimately,   58.7.30   zhī   知
    what it holds a basket of   58.7.31   qí   其
    in the utmost position, a person pressing
    urgently against a double-beamed wooden
    ridgepole that's high as a tree?   58.7.32   jí   極

What it holds a basket of   58.8.33   qí   其
is the shamanic dancer with animal tails flowing
from her wrists, Not-Having,   58.8.34   wú   無
straightening up, straightening things out for
"nailing" that first footstep of a journey…   58.8.35   zhèng 正

Straightening up, straightening things out for
"nailing" that first footstep of a journey: 58.9.36   zhèng 正
someone walking with a footprint of slowly
returning with the left leg leading the way,
doubling back (like the gut) on one's footprint,   58.9.37   fù   復

is creating something by hand, carving an elephant
likeness of good fortune and royal power,
      and remarkable cunning like this great big
      person atop that very one shouldering a
      weapon that tastes lip-smackingly
      genuinely like the one.

Traditionally virtuous, offering up a ram's head
while speaking back and forth, tongues waggling:
someone walking with a footprint of slowly
returning with the left leg leading the way,
doubling back (like the gut) on one's footprint,
is creating something by hand, carving an elephant
likeness of good fortune and royal power,
      and spooky and evil as gorgeous demons, a
      kneeling woman chased by a running
      young man who may die young.

That person
stepping on from this footprint has this
getting lost, slowly walking with the footprint of
raw rice scattered on the footprint, the left leg
leading the way, bewitched, infatuated...

      what it holds a basket of
      is the entire day—the full sun—
      solidly (for a long time, keeping as firm to
      what happened in the first place as this
      land surrounding and holding this nation's
      shield since ancient times)
      enduring through time as a person
      receiving moxibustion, that mugwort

58.9.38	wéi	為
58.9.39	qí	奇
58.10.40	shàn	善
58.10.41	fù	復
58.10.42	wéi	為
58.10.43	yāo	妖
58.11.44	rén	人
58.11.45	zhī	之
58.11.46	mí	迷
58.12.47	qí	其
58.12.48	rì	日
58.12.49	gù	固
58.12.50	jiǔ	久

treatment for cramps, turning a breech
baby, or other health issues.

This baby footprint on bamboo-slip pages,   58.13.51   shì   是
this is cultivating, like a plow,   58.13.52   yǐ   以
an ideal grounded sage known for his civilian
petition to authority, standing straight, speaking,
and being listened to,   58.13.53   shèng   聖
that person...   58.13.54   rén   人

would be like the wide, parallel side of a tipped
blade,   58.14.55   fāng   方
    yet, now you're bearded,   58.14.56   ér   而
    the husk of the initial protective bud casing
    but not really the true flower of   58.14.57   bù   不
    cutting apart a harmful house in which
    lush, abundant plant growth is spoken of;   58.14.58   gē   割

would be holding two stalks of grain, doing two
things at once in a habitable cliff cave, clean and
incorruptible,   58.15.59   lián   廉
    yet, now you're bearded,   58.15.60   ér   而
    the husk of the initial protective bud casing
    but not really the true flower of   58.15.61   bù   不
    knifing two feet and a battle ax, pacing,
    marking the passage of a year, another
    harvest;   58.15.62   guì   劌

would be looking straight on, forward,   58.16.63   zhí   直
    yet, now you're bearded,   58.16.64   ér   而
    the husk of the initial protective bud casing
    but not really the true flower of   58.16.65   bù   不

undisciplined as long hair so lengthy it be
brushed by hand;   58.16.66   sì   肆

would be that shining fire over the head of a
kneeling person,   58.17.67   guāng   光
      yet, now you're bearded,   58.17.68   ér   而
      the husk of the initial protective bud casing
      but not really the true flower of   58.17.69   bù   不
      brilliant as that shining fire over the head
      of a kneeling person when it's like the
      plumes of a long-tailed cock pheasant.   58.17.70   yào   燿

Chapter 59: But complication struck, and my
strategy fell apart.

In flowing the River Happy, speaking of gathering
oneself from three sides, managing,   59.1.1   zhì   治
that person,   59.1.2   rén   人
their task, what they do with a weapon, flag, or
pen in hand,   59.1.3   shì   事
the heavenly from high above this great big person   59.1.4   tiān   天
      like the sun sinking down in four bushes,
      they must not be—cannot be, eh?—   59.1.5   mò   莫
      A Certain Someone compliantly combing
      her loose hair seems to be saying, "as if   59.1.6   ruò   若
      like someone stockpiling wheat in a
      granary rather than letting it flow, as if
      there's not enough of what they cherish."   59.1.7   sè   嗇

In fact, that is to say if This Grown Man with
hairpin and public courtesy name,   59.2.8   fū   夫
"Oh, YES, Ma'am," says the "short-tailed bird,"   59.2.9   wéi   唯

is like someone stockpiling wheat in a granary
rather than letting it flow, as if there's not enough
of what they cherish,   59.2.10   sè   嗇
this baby footprint on bamboo-slip pages,   59.2.11   shì   是
by the nitty-gritty, grinding gizzard of a fowl, what
that's called…   59.2.12   wèi   謂
    early, *premature* as sunrise above an acorn
    on the jujube, that thorny plant that's used
    for insomnia and contraception and causes
    midterm miscarriages,   59.2.13   zǎo   早
    wearing clothes like a *mourning* dress, a
    person hand-subdued to kneeling before a
    commonplace plate;   59.2.14   fú   服

and early, premature as sunrise above an acorn on
the jujube, that thorny plant that's used for
insomnia and contraception and causes midterm
miscarriages   59.3.15   zǎo   早
wearing clothes like a mourning dress, a person
hand-subdued to kneeling before a commonplace
plate,   59.3.16   fú   服
by the nitty-gritty, grinding gizzard of a fowl, what
that's called…   59.3.17   wèi   謂
    what it has, stepping on from this
    footprint,   59.3.18   zhī   之
    is the seriously heavy (like a bag tied at
    both ends, so weighty that a man has to
    kneel to put it on his back)   59.3.19   zhòng 重
    accumulating, amassing grain plants like
    cowry-riches under a thorn tree, like
    indigestion,   59.3.20   jī   積
    while walking with the footprint of
    someone who's in alignment (eyes looking   59.3.21   dé   德

forward, directly over the heart, left leg
slowly leading the way).

The seriously heavy   59.4.22   zhòng   重
accumulating, amassing grain plants like cowry-
riches under a thorn tree, like indigestion,   59.4.23   jī   積
when walking with the footprint of someone who's
in alignment (eyes looking forward, directly over
the heart, left leg slowly leading the way)...   59.4.24   dé   德
    after following this sacrificial blade-and-
    cauldron-like ritual regulation,   59.4.25   zé   則
    the shamanic dancer with animal tails
    flowing from her wrists, Not-Having,   59.4.26   wú   無
    is the husk of the initial protective bud
    casing but not really the true flower of   59.4.27   bù   不
    conquering, a kneeling person wearing a
    battle helmet;   59.4.28   kè   克

and if this shaman-dancing Not-Having   59.5.29   wú   無
is the husk of the initial protective bud casing but
not really the true flower of   59.5.30   bù   不
conquering, a kneeling person wearing a battle
helmet,   59.5.31   kè   克
    after following this sacrificial blade-and-
    cauldron-like ritual regulation,   59.5.32   zé   則
    like the sun sinking down in four bushes,
    one must not be—cannot be, eh?—   59.5.33   mò   莫
    "speaking as a great big person to a baby,
    distinguishing, imparting, and
    administering wisdom confidently and
    intimately,   59.5.34   zhī   知
    what it holds a basket of   59.5.35   qí   其

59.5.36   jí   極

*When the heavenly is your responsibility,
accumulating excess weight is not a good idea, and
not just for health reasons. In this shape, I couldn't
stay in the confident wisdom-speaker role as I got
toward delivery, as I hoped in the last chapter.*

"Like the sun sinking down in four bushes, one
must not be—cannot be, eh?—   59.6.37   mò   莫
speaking as a great big person to a baby,
distinguishing, imparting, and administering
wisdom confidently and intimately,   59.6.38   zhī   知
what it holds a basket of   59.6.39   qí   其
in the utmost position, a person pressing urgently
against a double-beamed wooden ridgepole that's
high as a tree..."   59.6.40   jí   極
    lip-smackingly genuinely   59.6.41   kâ   可
    this cultivates, like a plow: 59.6.42   yǐ   以
    flesh-and-meat-handling Being   59.6.43   yǒu   有
    in our domestic enclave, defended by a
    weapon on a pole;   59.6.44   guó   國

*Not in the "speaking wisdom confidently" role
when in the ultimate end position, then my Being
persona was confined to home. (In Chapter 1 we
saw that this domestic space was for my Not-
Having persona, not for my Being persona.)*

"Flesh-and-meat-handling Being   59.7.45   yǒu   有
in our domestic enclave, defended by a weapon on
a pole,"   59.7.46   guó   國
what it has, stepping on from this footprint,   59.7.47   zhī   之
suckling, a woman kneeling with breasts full of
milk...   59.7.48   mǔ   母
    lip-smackingly genuinely   59.7.49   kâ   可
    this cultivates, like a plow,   59.7.50   yǐ   以
    lengthening as long as hair that has to be
    tied with a brooch, like a loose-haired old
    man,   59.7.51   cháng 長
    enduring through time as a person
    receiving moxibustion, that mugwort
    treatment for cramps, turning a breech
    baby, or other health issues.   59.7.52   jiǔ   久

This baby footprint on bamboo-slip pages,   59.8.53   shì   是
by the nitty-gritty, grinding gizzard of a
fowl, what that's called: 59.8.54   wèi   謂
deep as far water,   59.8.55   shēn 深
    the root of the family tree, like an
    ancestor's manhood,   59.8.56   gēn   根
    is solidly (for a long time, keeping
    as firm to what happened in the
    first place as this land surrounding
    and holding this nation's shield
    since ancient times)   59.8.57   gù   固
    rooted like a tree—a person
    standing on the ground bowing to
    their lineage.   59.8.58   dǐ   柢

Lengthening as long as hair that has to be tied with
a brooch, like a loose-haired old man,

59.9.59   cháng   長

sprouting a bud from the ground,

59.9.60   shēng   生

enduring through time as a person receiving
moxibustion, that mugwort treatment for cramps,
turning a breech baby, or other health issues,

59.9.61   jiǔ   久

> *regarded as by one big eye for a head,*
> *kneeling at an altar,*

59.9.62   shì   視

> what it has, stepping on from this
> footprint:

59.9.63   zhī   之

> walking with the footprint of the loose-
> haired head buck.

59.9.64   dào   道

I stayed at home for that extended time, known by
"the eye" as that wild-haired head buck.

Chapter 60: Being at home under these circumstances was not good for the baby. Or me.

Flowing the River Happy, speaking of gathering
oneself from three sides, managing,

60.1.1   zhì   治

this great big person

60.1.2   dà   大

in our domestic enclave, defended by a weapon on
a pole,

60.1.3   guó   國

> A Certain Someone compliantly combing
> her loose hair seems to be saying this is as
> if

60.1.4   ruò   若

> boiling alive, a baby crying over the fire,

60.1.5   pēng   烹

> our tiny dear little one, like three grains of
> sand,

60.1.6   xiǎo   小

> a delicacy such as fresh fish or ram's head.

60.1.7   xiān   鮮

This is cultivating, like a plow,   60.2.8   yǐ   以
walking with the footprint of the loose-haired head
buck   60.2.9   dào   道
in a good position like someone standing on solid
ground drying up water under cover of a pair of
grass sprouts or arriving at an official ceremony,
managing, supervising,   60.2.10   lì   蒞
    the heavenly, from high above this great
    big person   60.2.11   tiān   天
    now here down below...   60.2.12   xià   下

what it holds a basket of   60.3.13   qí   其
is a ghost,   60.3.14   guǐ   鬼
    the husk of the initial protective bud casing
    but not really the true flower of   60.3.15   bù   不
    that magical god spirit "lightning," the
    divine spark.   60.3.16   shén   神

Wring to backward the two wings of   60.4.17   fēi   非
    "what it holds a basket of,   60.4.18   qí   其
    a ghost   60.4.19   guǐ   鬼
    that's the husk of the initial protective bud
    casing but not really the true flower of   60.4.20   bù   不
    that magical god spirit 'lightning,' the
    divine spark,"   60.4.21   shén   神

    and what it holds a basket of,   60.5.22   qí   其
    that magical god spirit "lightning," the
    divine spark,   60.5.23   shén   神
    that's the husk of the initial protective bud
    casing but not really the true flower of   60.5.24   bù   不

hurting, like someone in front of that male
principle of the sun shining on a sacrificial
altar,   60.5.25   shāng   傷
that person.   60.5.26   rén   人

Wring to backward the two wings of   60.6.27   fēi   非
    "what it holds a basket of,   60.6.28   qí   其
    that magical god spirit 'lightning,' the
    divine spark,   60.6.29   shén   神
    that's the husk of the initial protective bud
    casing but not really the true flower of   60.6.30   bù   不
    hurting, like someone in front of that male
    principle of the sun shining on a sacrificial
    altar,   60.6.31   shāng   傷
    that person,"   60.6.32   rén   人

and an ideal grounded sage known for his civilian
petition to authority, standing straight, speaking,
and being listened to,   60.7.33   shèng   聖
that person   60.7.34   rén   人
—both armpits sweat this too!—   60.7.35   yì   亦
    would be the husk of the initial protective
    bud casing but not really the true flower of   60.7.36   bù   不
    hurting, like someone in front of that male
    principle of the sun shining on a sacrificial
    altar,   60.7.37   shāng   傷
    that person.   60.7.38   rén   人

This life in which I was at home on bed rest and
also the head buck managing official business (with
a little child!) was unhealthy. I was holding a ghost
with no divine spark. I wanted to undo it such that

the little divine spark wasn't hurt. But also, I
wanted to undo it such that I was unhurt.

In fact, that is to say This Grown Man with hairpin
and public courtesy name,   60.8.39   fū   夫
these two, this pair of traditional, adult, gendered
head-cloths *covered by "The One,"*   60.8.40   liǎng   兩
    are the husk of the initial protective bud
    casing but *not really* the true flower of,   60.8.41   bù   不
    like a seen tree and the eye seeing it (or
    like a well-tended lord and his attentive
    attendant), when taken *together, creating*
    this singular phenomenon...   60.8.42   xiāng   相
    hurting (like someone in front of that male
    principle of the sun shining on a sacrificial
    altar).   60.8.43   shāng   傷

They were the same! This life didn't need to hurt
anything.

This taps lightly with a tutoring cane and leaves a
mark on the solid shield of the past: 60.9.44   gù   故
walking with the footprint of someone who's in
alignment, eyes looking forward, directly over the
heart, left leg slowly leading the way,   60.9.45   dé   德
intersecting with this—picture a big-bellied person
sitting crossed-legged making a relationship with
this,   60.9.46   jiāo   交
    is coming back after sweeping troops out
    of the soil mound hills to this   60.9.47   guī   歸
    here, straightening things out for "nailing"
    that first footstep of a journey on the back
    of this yellow bird with the "dangling tail"

that lives around the Yangtze and Huai Rivers—right here, huh!

60.9.48 yān 焉

The Dé life was the solution.

Chapter 61: As a royal administrator, I could be pregnant at home, deliver, and successfully have the little one. And the little one could have me too. We'd both be okay <u>if</u> we gave up that Hand-Picked Gem role and went for a more humble version of the same type of thing.

This great big person
in our domestic enclave, defended by a weapon on
a pole

61.1.1 dà 大

61.1.2 guó 國

—this is boiling sugarcane with fire as follows!—

61.1.3 zhâ 者

now here down below

61.1.4 xià 下

flowing—a baby coming out headfirst in a river of watery waste:

61.1.5 liú 流

the heavenly from high above this great big person

61.2.6 tiān 天

now here down below,

61.2.7 xià 下

stepping on from this footprint, it has this intersecting with this—picture a big-bellied person sitting crossed-legged making a relationship with this;

61.2.8 zhī 之

61.2.9 jiāo 交

the heavenly from high above this great big person

61.3.10 tiān 天

now here down below

61.3.11 xià 下

stepping on from this footprint, it has this

61.3.12 zhī 之

spoon of a cow, or "a woman's valley."

61.3.13 pìn 牝

The spoon of a cow, or "a woman's valley,"   61.4.14   pìn   牝
as the conventional royal administrator wearing a
men's headcloth as his skirt, nobly assisting the
emperor, dividing up and differentiating what's
faced with admiration and echoed under that roof: 61.4.15   cháng   常
this is cultivating, like a plow,   61.4.16   yǐ   以
    calm peace, the clear blue-green growth of
    the sedative cinnabar plant quieting a
    dispute between two hands on a
    plowshare,   61.4.17   jìng   靜
    able to withstand entirely (to be victorious
    as a splendid piece of jewelry, an omen or
    the royal 'We' mending something on a
    boat with two hands by the strength of an
    arm, bladed tool, or a plow)   61.4.18   shèng   勝
    a bull soil, "male parts,"   61.4.19   mǔ   牡

this is cultivating, like a plow,   61.5.20   yǐ   以
    calm peace   61.5.21   jìng   靜
    creating something by hand, carving an
    elephant likeness of good fortune and
    royal power,   61.5.22   wéi   為
    now here down below.   61.5.23   xià   下

This taps lightly with a tutoring cane and leaves a
mark on the solid shield of the past...   61.6.24   gù   故
This great big person   61.6.25   dà   大
in our domestic enclave, defended by a weapon on
a pole,   61.6.26   guó   國
cultivating, like a plow,   61.6.27   yǐ   以
    now here down below,   61.6.28   xià   下
    our tiny dear little one, like three grains of
    sand,   61.6.29   xiǎo   小

in our domestic enclave, defended by a weapon on a pole:	61.6.30	guó	國
after following this sacrificial blade-and-cauldron- like ritual regulation,	61.7.31	zé	則
it's getting hold of, grabbing the ear of	61.7.32	qù	取
our tiny dear little one, like three grains of sand,	61.7.33	xiǎo	小
in our domestic enclave, defended by a weapon on a pole.	61.7.34	guó	國
Our tiny dear little one, like three grains of sand,	61.8.35	xiǎo	小
in our domestic enclave, defended by a weapon on a pole,	61.8.36	guó	國
cultivating, like a plow,	61.8.37	yǐ	以
now here down below,	61.8.38	xià	下
this great big person	61.8.39	dà	大
in our domestic enclave, defended by a weapon on a pole:	61.8.40	guó	國
after following this sacrificial blade-and-cauldron- like ritual regulation,	61.9.41	zé	則
it's getting hold of, grabbing the ear of	61.9.42	qù	取
this great big person	61.9.43	dà	大
in our domestic enclave, defended by a weapon on a pole.	61.9.44	guó	國
This taps lightly with a tutoring cane and leaves a mark on the solid shield of the past:	61.10.45	gù	故
in this particular enclave that's defended by a weapon on a pole,	61.10.46	huò	或
now here down below	61.10.47	xià	下
cultivating, like a plow,	61.10.48	yǐ	以

getting hold of, grabbing an ear,   61.10.49   qù 取

in this particular enclave that's defended by a
weapon on a pole,   61.11.50   huò 或
now here down below   61.11.51   xià 下
    yet now, bearded, you're   61.11.52   ér 而
    getting hold of, grabbing an ear.   61.11.53   qù 取

This *great big person*   61.12.54   dà 大
in our domestic enclave, defended by a weapon on
a pole,   61.12.55   guó 國
the husk of the initial protective bud casing but *not
really* the true flower of   61.12.56   bù 不
*what's past and surpassing, maybe "passed away,"
maybe excessive,* walking slowly with the footprint
of a slanting skull mouth speaking, the left leg
leading the way,   61.12.57   guò 過
missing, kneeling with a yawning mouth before a
ravine eroded between two mountains, wanting,
lacking: 61.12.58   yù 欲
    that hand holding two stalks of grain, doing
    two things at once,   61.12.59   jiān 兼
    is rearing animals, feeding them from a bag
    tied with a rope,   61.12.60   chù 畜
    that person.   61.12.61   rén 人

Our *tiny dear little one,* like three grains of sand,   61.13.62   xiǎo 小
in our domestic enclave, defended by a weapon on
a pole,   61.13.63   guó 國
the husk of the initial protective bud casing but *not
really* the true flower of   61.13.64   bù 不
*what's past and surpassing, maybe "passed away,"
maybe excessive,* walking slowly with the footprint   61.13.65   guò 過

of a slanting skull mouth speaking, the left leg
leading the way,
missing, kneeling with a yawning mouth before a
ravine eroded between two mountains, wanting,
lacking: 61.13.66   yù   欲
    entering like an arrowhead or maybe
    joining the imperial government   61.13.67   rù   入
    is their task, what they do with a weapon,
    flag, or pen in hand,   61.13.68   shì   事
    that person.   61.13.69   rén   人

In fact, that is to say if This Grown Man with
hairpin and public courtesy name,   61.14.70   fū   夫
these two, this pair of traditional, adult, gendered
head-cloths covered by "The One"   61.14.71   liǎng   兩
—this is boiling sugarcane with fire as follows!—   61.14.72   zhâ   者
that particular one, unusual as the knot coming at
the end of a cord sticking out from a mouth,   61.14.73   gè   各
The Hand-Picked Gem, like cowry-shell-riches
discovered along the road,   61.14.74   dé   得
    what it holds a basket of   61.14.75   qí   其
      is "that place" being intentionally created
    like any household gate hewn with an axe,   61.14.76   suǒ   所
    missing, kneeling with a yawning mouth
    before a ravine eroded between two
    mountains, wanting, lacking,   61.14.77   yù   欲

then this great big person   61.15.78   dà   大
—this is boiling sugarcane with fire as follows!—   61.15.79   zhâ   者
    is two pieces of meat on a sacrificial altar,
    seemingly, properly   61.15.80   yí   宜

creating something by hand, carving an
eformat

elephant likeness of good fortune and
royal power,   61.15.81   wéi   為
now here down below.   61.15.82   xià   下

With my "Handpicked Gem" persona and her
womb missing, I would be free to create new life in
my new humbler life.

Chapter 62: How I ended up in that high life

Walking with the footprint of the loose-haired head
buck—   62.1.1   dào   道
this is boiling sugarcane with fire as follows: 62.1.2   zhâ   者
the medicine-dancing-scorpion insect swarm of   62.1.3   wàn   萬
matter (outside one's body, "cut from the cow" by
a bloodied blade),   62.1.4   wù   物
what it has, stepping on from this footprint   62.1.5   zhī   之
    is this secret corner, a sanctuary like that
    backwater place on the city outskirts
    where grain's arriving and divided by this
    great big person;   62.1.6   ào   奧

the traditionally virtuous, offering up a ram's head
while speaking back and forth, tongues waggling,   62.2.7   shàn   善
that person,   62.2.8   rén   人
what it has, stepping on from this footprint   62.2.9   zhī   之
    are treasures like a house containing
    cowry-riches, jade, and a lidded pot;   62.2.10   bǎo   寶

husk of the initial protective bud casing but not
really the true flower of
the traditionally virtuous, offering up a ram's head
while speaking back and forth, tongues waggling,
that person,
what it has, stepping on from this footprint
    is this "place" being intentionally created
    like any household gate hewn with an axe
    safeguarding, like carrying a child on their
    back.

62.3.11	bù	不
62.3.12	shàn	善
62.3.13	rén	人
62.3.14	zhī	之
62.3.15	suǒ	所
62.3.16	bǎo	保

But...

An admired beauty, a person wearing a ram's horn
headdress
speaking out loud,
    lip-smackingly genuinely
    cultivating, like a plow,
    a marketplace (like a bustling city at the
    forked tree)

62.4.17	mâi	美
62.4.18	yán	言
62.4.19	kâ	可
62.4.20	yǐ	以
62.4.21	shì	市

and honoring, like offering by hand the ritual
alcohol vessel with the chief in charge of its
preparation,
out in public at the crossroads, being good, doing
one's work,
    lip-smackingly genuinely
    cultivating, like a plow,
    piling on more with strenuous effort,
    puffing with a plow or arm,
    that person...

62.5.22	zūn	尊
62.5.23	xíng	行
62.5.24	kâ	可
62.5.25	yǐ	以
62.5.26	jiā	加
62.5.27	rén	人

that person,   62.6.28   rén   人
    what it has, stepping on from this footprint   62.6.29   zhī   之
        is the husk of the initial protective
        bud casing but not really the true
        flower of   62.6.30   bù   不
        traditionally virtuous, offering up a
        ram's head while speaking back
        and forth, tongues waggling;   62.6.31   shàn   善

    that one, that very one shouldering a
    weapon,   62.7.32   hé   何
    tossing out, two hands throwing a baby
    from a basket,   62.7.33   qì   棄
    what it has, stepping on from this footprint   62.7.34   zhī   之
        is flesh-and-meat-handling Being.   62.7.35   yǒu   有

This taps lightly with a tutoring cane and leaves a
mark on the solid shield of the past: 62.8.36   gù   故
a person standing straight up on the ground,   62.8.37   lì   立
        the heavenly from high above this great big
        person,   62.8.38   tiān   天
        a baby with arms wide open and legs
        swaddled, "Zǐ,"   62.8.39   zǐ   子

was put in place, like a webbed net over an eye
directed straight forward, by   62.9.40   zhì   置
        three   62.9.41   sān   三
        publicly fair and impartial men like high-
        ranking older men who've "got balls,"
        dukes,   62.9.42   gōng   公

and immediately adjacent (like a venomous snake			
with "a short-tailed bird," right next to it) to	62.10.43	suī	雖
flesh-and-meat-handling Being	62.10.44	yǒu	有
arching around and holding aloft (like the			
area enclosed by two hands folded in front			
of the chest)	62.10.45	gǒng	拱
the ruling system, the penal code, or the			
monarch himself marking the back of			
kneeling slaves or criminals with a chisel.	62.10.46	bì	璧

I got to this place of standing tall and holding the baby via the dukes and via my Being persona upholding the system.

Cultivating, like a plow,	62.11.47	yǐ	以
leading, long before, stepping off from this			
footprint, *an ancestor*	62.11.48	xiān	先
driving (like handling four horses that pull a			
chariot)	62.11.49	sì	駟
that horse,	62.11.50	mǎ	馬

was the husk of the initial protective bud casing			
but *not really* the true flower of	62.12.51	bù	不
a kneeling woman with breasts doing as told,	62.12.52	rú	如
sitting here, two people staying here,	62.12.53	zuò	坐
walking slowly forward on the footprint of			
a "short-tailed bird," the left leg leading			
the way to	62.12.54	jìn	進
this here—the foot stops a person here on			
this footprint!—	62.12.55	cǐ	此
walking with the footprint of the loose-haired head buck.	62.12.56	dào	道

I did not get to that place of safety via the Dào life.

Speaking of the solid shield of the *past,*	62.13.57	gǔ 古
what it had, stepping on from this footprint:	62.13.58	zhī 之
"This place" being intentionally created like any		
household gate hewn with an axe,	62.13.59	suǒ 所
cultivating, like a plow,	62.13.60	yǐ 以
being held in high regard, like two hands are		
wrapped around a person atop cowry-shell-riches,	62.13.61	guì 貴
"this here—the foot stops a person here		
on this footprint!—	62.13.62	cǐ 此
walking with the footprint of the loose-		
haired head buck"	62.13.63	dào 道
—this is boiling sugarcane with fire as		
follows!—	62.13.64	zhâ 者
that one—that very one shouldering a		
weapon	62.13.65	hé 何
was the husk of the initial protective bud		
casing but not really the true flower of	62.14.66	bù 不
what's called when issued on a breath		
from the mouth,	62.14.67	yuē 曰
"looking for, coveting like a centipede,	62.15.68	qiú 求
cultivating, like a plow,	62.15.69	yǐ 以
The Hand-Picked Gem, like cowry-shell-		
riches discovered along the road."	62.15.70	dé 得

Pregnant, the head buck, I not really
looking for The Handpicked Gem life.

Flesh-and-meat-handling Being,	62.16.71	yǒu 有
guilty, suffering, sinful, or even criminal, with a		
webbed net over two wings wrung backwards,	62.16.72	zuì 罪

cultivating, like a plow,

being wounded, like a man taking off a hat,

as unwholesome in nature as the disease-causing
environment around Elephant, Tusk Town, *Lángyá*,

    this tapped lightly with a tutoring cane and
    left a mark on the solid shield of the past...
    creating something by hand, carving an
    elephant likeness of good fortune and
    royal power,

        the heavenly from high above this
        great big person
        now here down below,

was held in high regard, like when two
hands are wrapped around a person atop
cowry-shell-riches.

62.16.73	yǐ	以
62.16.74	miǎn	免
62.16.75	yé	邪
62.17.76	gù	故
62.17.77	wéi	為
62.17.78	tiān	天
62.17.79	xià	下
62.17.80	guì	貴

*But my guilty, wounded Being persona took me
there, to that high-status life when I was pregnant
and had a child.*

**Chapter 63: Because I was judged harshly in
creating this little elephant as my real self, the Dé
life was a better way to go. With that approach, I
could change things easily.**

When creating something by hand, carving an
elephant likeness of good fortune and royal power,

    *as the shamanic dancer with animal tails
    flowing from her wrists, Not-Having,*

63.1.1	wéi	為
63.1.2	wú	無

creating something by hand, carving an
elephant likeness of good fortune and
royal power: 63.1.3   wéi   為

their task, what it is they do with a weapon, flag, or
pen in hand,   63.2.4   shì   事
          is the shaman-dancing Not-Having   63.2.5   wú   無
          task, what it is they do with a weapon, flag,
          or pen in hand;   63.2.6   shì   事

tasting, reflecting on a flavor in the mouth which is
still forming like a tree whose top branches are not
yet fully grown,   63.3.7   wèi   味
          is shaman-dancing Not-Having   63.3.8   wú   無
          tasting, reflecting on a flavor in the mouth
          which is still forming like a tree whose top
          branches are not yet fully grown;   63.3.9   wèi   味

and this great big person   63.4.10   dà   大
and our tiny dear little one, like three grains of
sand,   63.4.11   xiǎo   小
          are having more, like two pieces of meat,   63.4.12   duō   多
          belittled, considered to be insignificant as
          four tiny dots like a young master's
          youthful period.   63.4.13   shǎo   少

Judgment handcuffing and subduing a kneeling
person with a hand to the back, making them
answer for what's happened,   63.5.14   bào   報
and resentment, the heart under an animal lying
down to die,   63.5.15   yuàn   怨
are cultivating, like a plow,   63.5.16   yǐ   以

walking with the footprint of someone who's in
alignment (eyes looking forward, directly over the
heart, left leg slowly leading the way):   63.5.17   dé   德

charting, like drawing a city wall around a lowly
rural granary,   63.6.18   tú   圖
the solid (like that hard yellow earth with two little
grass tufts next to River Han, where "short-tailed
birds" find no food)   63.6.19   nán   難
    in this place and time, oh, black, icy raven
    sun,   63.6.20   yú   於
    what it holds a basket of,   63.6.21   qí   其
    is easily changeable as switching from
    saying "don't," serious as three drops of
    blood on a blade, to shining like the sun;   63.6.22   yì   易

and creating something by hand, carving an
elephant likeness of good fortune and royal power,   63.7.23   wéi   為
this great big person   63.7.24   dà   大
    in this place and time, oh, black, icy raven
    sun,   63.7.25   yú   於
    what it holds a basket of,   63.7.26   qí   其
    is a small skein-of-silk fontanelle. 63.7.27   xì   細

A person living the Dé life can manage the solid to
be easily flexible, and their pregnancy can create a
little youngster. That seemed ideal in my situation...

With the heavenly from high above this great big
person   63.8.28   tiān   天
now here down below,   63.8.29   xià   下
    solid   63.8.30   nán   難

is their task, what it is they do with a
weapon, flag, or pen in hand;   63.8.31   shì   事

    hands over heart, analytically,   63.9.32   bì   必
    recently, exactly, having immediately
    folded from one straight rod into two,   63.9.33   zuò   作
    in this place and time, oh, black, icy raven
    sun,   63.9.34   yú   於
        it's easily changeable as switching
        from saying "don't," serious as
        three drops of blood on a blade, to
        shining like the sun;   63.9.35   yì   易

with the heavenly, from high above this great big
person   63.10.36   tiān   天
now here down below,   63.10.37   xià   下
    this great big person   63.10.38   dà   大
    is their task, what it is they do with a
    weapon, flag, or pen in hand;   63.10.39   shì   事

    hands over heart, analytically,   63.11.40   bì   必
    recently, exactly, having immediately
    folded from one straight rod into two,   63.11.41   zuò   作
    in this place and time, oh, black, icy raven
    sun,   63.11.42   yú   於
        it's a small skein-of-silk fontanelle. 63.11.43   xì   細

This baby footprint on bamboo-slip pages,   63.12.44   shì   是
this is cultivating, like a plow,   63.12.45   yǐ   以
an *ideal grounded sage* known for his civilian
petition to authority, standing straight, speaking,
and being listened to,   63.12.46   shèng   聖
that person   63.12.47   rén   人

*would be ending, like the knot at the end of a thick
silk skein, like winter,*   63.12.48   zhōng   終

    *the husk of the initial protective bud casing
but not really the true flower of*   63.12.49   bù   不
    *creating something by hand, carving an
elephant likeness of good fortune and royal
power,*   63.12.50   wéi   為

    as this great big person.   63.12.51   dà   大

This taps lightly with a tutoring cane and leaves a
mark on the solid shield of the past: 63.13.52   gù   故
they would be using that *legendary Hybrid Power*
of a mythical bear-like animal who has the legs of a
deer *for*   63.13.53   néng   能
completing that final "nail" in a weapon on a pole,   63.13.54   chéng   成
    what it holds a basket of,   63.13.55   qí   其
    this great big person.   63.13.56   dà   大

*It was best not to finish up as a great big pregnant
person but instead to complete the pregnancy
using that hybrid power I'd perfected.*

In fact, that is to say This Grown Man with hairpin
and public courtesy name: 63.14.57   fū   夫
if a lightweight, like a light carriage, portable,
running through the whole like a lengthwise warp
thread of something woven, like menses, like a
classic text,   63.14.58   qīng   輕
assenting by speaking out loud like A Certain
Someone compliantly combing her loose hair
saying, "this seems is as if, yeah, definitely,"   63.14.59   nuò   諾
    hands over heart, analytically,   63.14.60   bì   必

he's the loose-haired head buck who
differentiates right from wrong kneeling in
a house *alone,* like a widow,

63.14.61	guǎ	寡

giving their word to a person;

63.14.62	xìn	信

if having more, like two pieces of meat,

63.15.63	duō	多

easily changeable as switching from saying "don't,"
serious as three drops of blood on a blade to
shining like the sun,

63.15.64	yì	易

     hands over heart, analytically,

63.15.65	bì	必

     he's having more, like two pieces of meat,

63.15.66	duō	多

     solid (like that hard yellow earth with two
     little grass tufts next to River Han, where
     "short-tailed birds" find no food).

63.15.67	nán	難

When I was a fragile person giving promises, I
ended up being the wild-haired head buck who was
alone and too trusting. (And as we saw in the
adage from Chapters 23 and 17, that wasn't
enough.)

But if my "double duty" self was able to easily
change things, then that same self was free to be
solid. That is to say...

This baby footprint on bamboo-slip pages,

63.16.68	shì	是

this is cultivating, like a plow,

63.16.69	yǐ	以

an ideal grounded sage known for his civilian
petition to authority, standing straight, speaking,
and being listened to,

63.16.70	shèng	聖

that person,

63.16.71	rén	人

would be, in the same manner as the unlikely rise
of a dog monkey to the top of the alcohol vat to
become chief of brewing,
solid,
what it has, stepping on from this footprint,

and, this taps lightly with a tutoring cane and
leaves a mark on the solid shield of the past,
ending, like the knot at the end of a thick silk skein,
like winter,
> *as shaman-dancing Not-Having*
> *solid (like that hard yellow earth with two*
> *little grass tufts next to River Han, where*
> *"short-tailed birds" find no food)*
> *—I swear, an arrow revolving around*
> *oneself… that's it!*

This is how Not-Having could end up being the solid
one.

Chapter 64: Of course, easy change can go too far and end up on the wrong direction.

What it holds a basket of,
staying calm as a woman sitting on her heels at
home,
> is easily changeable as switching from
> saying "don't," serious as three drops of
> blood on a blade, to shining like the sun, to
> grasping, like a government office or
> temple holding onto what comes from this
> footprint with the very skillful human hand

63.16.72	yóu	猶
63.16.73	nán	難
63.16.74	zhī	之
63.17.75	gù	故
63.17.76	zhōng	終
63.17.77	wú	無
63.17.78	nán	難
63.17.79	yǐ	矣
64.1.1	qí	其
64.1.2	ān	妄
64.1.3	yì	易

of that official (usually a eunuch in the old
days);

    64.1.4   chí   持

what it holds a basket of,
like a tree whose top branches aren't yet fully
grown, not yet
an omen, the cracks on a divination shell,
        is easily changeable as switching from
        saying "don't," serious as three drops of
        blood on a blade, to shining like the sun, to
        plotting a scheme, like speaking with a
        certain humble so-and-so sweet-in-the-
        mouth plum tree;

what it holds a basket of,
fragile as crisp meat on a roof, precariously high
above a kneeling person,
        is easily changeable as switching from
        saying "don't," serious as three drops of
        blood on a blade, to shining like the sun, to
        dissolving as half a beef in the river (as our
        "Zhou" dynasty's school is named);

what it holds a basket of,
"trifling," a slight thing, this admired beauty
wearing a ram's horn headdress and stepping
slowly with only the left leg leading, a tutoring cane
lightly tapping their hair, combing out or "splitting
hairs," not having much
        is easily changeable as switching from
        saying "don't," serious as three drops of
        blood on a blade, to shining like the sun, to

64.2.5	qí	其
64.2.6	wèi	未
64.2.7	zhǎo	兆
64.2.8	yì	易
64.2.9	móu	謀
64.3.10	qí	其
64.3.11	cuì	脆
64.3.12	yì	易
64.3.13	pàn	泮
64.4.14	qí	其
64.4.15	wēi	微
64.4.16	yì	易

scattered like a pair of bamboo stalks atop
the crescent moon, tapped lightly with a
tutoring cane by hand.   64.4.17   sàn   散

Creating something by hand, carving an elephant
likeness of good fortune and royal power,   64.5.18   wéi   為
what it has, stepping on from this footprint,   64.5.19   zhī   之
in this place and time, oh, black, icy raven sun: 64.5.20   yú   於
        it's like a tree whose top branches aren't
        yet fully grown, not yet   64.5.21   wèi   未
        flesh-and-meat-handling Being;   64.5.22   yǒu   有

flowing the River Happy, speaking of gathering
oneself from three sides, managing,   64.6.23   zhì   治
what it has, stepping on from this footprint,   64.6.24   zhī   之
in this place and time, oh, black, icy raven sun: 64.6.25   yú   於
        it's like a tree whose top branches aren't
        yet fully grown, not yet   64.6.26   wèi   未
        trying to govern in chaos, two people
        disentangling a roll of threads using their
        hands with the help of a comb or beater;   64.6.27   luàn   亂

joining together from three sides over a mouth,
like having sex,   64.7.28   hé   合
and bundling it all up together in both arms,   64.7.29   bào   抱
what it has, stepping on from this footprint,   64.7.30   zhī   之
tree branches and roots   64.7.31   mù   木

sprouting a bud from the ground   64.8.32   shēng   生
in this place and time, oh, black, icy raven sun: 64.8.33   yú   於
        it's tiny as the fine hair covering below the
        mouth   64.8.34   háo   毫
        tip-top, tree-top;   64.8.35   mò   末

nine (the elbow, in that old way of counting)   64.9.36   jiǔ   九
layers piling up (like how a person representing the
dead in a rite, flexing to step out of a cave, has
bent over the steam cooker many times),   64.9.37   céng   層
what it has, stepping on from this footprint,   64.9.38   zhī   之
that it says, revolving around itself, as its place
name,   64.9.39   tái   台

taking off, rising up, possibly passing on early like a
young man running over a snake   64.10.40   qǐ   起
in this place and time, oh, black, icy raven sun: 64.10.41   yú   於
        it's repeatedly building up, like a skein of
        silk or fatigue after work in the field,   64.10.42   lâi   累
        clay soil;   64.10.43   tǔ   土

and where a person reaches when extending their
counting, that is, one thousand   64.11.44   qiān   千
traditional miles that villagers use to measure
fields on the clay soil,   64.11.45   lǐ   里
what it has, stepping on from this footprint,   64.11.46   zhī   之
out in public at the crossroads, being good, doing
one's work,   64.11.47   xíng   行

conceiving, a woman kneeling, happy, speaking of
gathering herself from three sides,   64.12.48   shǐ   始
in this place and time, oh, black, icy raven sun: 64.12.49   yú   於
        it's fully enough, like the whole leg as well
        as the footprint   64.12.50   zú   足
        now here down below.   64.12.51   xià   下

*Enough. A thousand miles in this condition is too
much.*

Creating something by hand, carving an elephant
likeness of good fortune and royal power?   64.13.52   wéi   為
This is boiling sugarcane with fire as follows!   64.13.53   zhâ   者
Being defeated, riches hit lightly by hand, failing,
decaying,   64.13.54   bài   敗
is what it has, stepping on from this footprint.   64.13.55   zhī   之

A kneeling person, arrested and held, arms
outstretched in handcuffs?   64.14.56   zhí   執
This is boiling sugarcane with fire as follows!   64.14.57   zhâ   者
Dropped from a hand,   64.14.58   shī   失
is what it has, stepping on from this footprint.   64.14.59   zhī   之

This baby footprint on bamboo-slip pages,   64.15.60   shì   是
this is cultivating, like a plow,   64.15.61   yǐ   以
an ideal grounded sage known for his civilian
petition to authority, standing straight, speaking,
and being listened to,   64.15.62   shèng   聖
that person: 64.15.63   rén   人
    as the shamanic dancer with animal tails
    flowing from her wrists, Not-Having,   64.15.64   wú   無
    creating something by hand, carving an
    elephant likeness of good fortune and
    royal power,   64.15.65   wéi   為
        this taps lightly with a tutoring
        cane and leaves a mark on the
        solid shield of the past...   64.15.66   gù   故
        shaman-dancing Not-Having   64.15.67   wú   無
        would be defeated, riches hit
        lightly by hand, failing, decaying;   64.15.68   bài   敗

    as shaman-dancing Not-Having   64.16.69   wú   無

a kneeling person, arrested and held, arms
outstretched in handcuffs,   64.16.70   zhí   執
     this taps lightly with a tutoring
     cane and leaves a mark on the
     solid shield of the past...   64.16.71   gù   故
     shaman-dancing Not-Having   64.16.72   wú   無
     would be dropped from a hand.   64.16.73   shī   失

Stepping on from this footprint, it has this,   64.17.75   zhī   之
following in this footprint, *slowly* walking directly
after another person, the left leg leading the way,   64.17.76   cóng   從
their task, what they do with a weapon, flag, or
pen in hand,   64.17.77   shì   事
as the conventional royal administrator wearing a
men's headcloth as his skirt   64.17.78   cháng   常
in this place and time, oh, black, icy raven sun: 64.17.79   yú   於
     it's like two little silk threads separated by
     the sword of a garrison guard—so, so near   64.17.80   jǐ   幾
     completing, that final "nail" in a weapon
     on a pole,   64.17.81   chéng   成
          yet now bearded, you're   64.17.82   ér   而
          defeated, riches hit lightly by hand,
          failing, decaying,   64.17.83   bài   敗
          stepping on from this footprint, it
          has this.   64.17.84   zhī   之

Full of care, your heart acting sincerely with care
like using your fork to get food right from the
cauldron,   64.18.85   shèn   慎
ending, like the knot at the end of a thick silk skein,
like winter,   64.18.86   zhōng   終
     a kneeling woman with breasts doing as
     told   64.18.87   rú   如

conceiving, a woman kneeling, happy,
speaking of gathering herself from three
sides?   64.18.88   shǐ   始

After following this sacrificial blade-and-
cauldron-like ritual regulation,   64.19.89   zé   則
shaman-dancing Not-Having   64.19.90   wú   無
        is defeated, riches hit lightly by
        hand, failing, decaying   64.19.91   bài   敗
        in their task, what they do with a
        weapon, flag, or pen in hand.   64.19.92   shì   事

This baby footprint on bamboo-slip pages,   64.20.93   shì   是
this is cultivating, like a plow,   64.20.94   yǐ   以
an ideal grounded sage known for his civilian
petition to authority, standing straight, speaking,
and being listened to,   64.20.95   shèng   聖
that person   64.20.96   rén   人
would be missing, kneeling with a yawning mouth
before a ravine eroded between two mountains,
wanting, lacking,   64.20.97   yù   欲
        the husk of the initial protective bud casing
        but not really the true flower of   64.20.98   bù   不
        missing, kneeling with a yawning mouth
        before a ravine eroded between two
        mountains, wanting, lacking: 64.20.99   yù   欲
would be the husk of the initial protective bud
casing but not really the true flower of   64.20.100   bù   不
held in high regard, like when two hands are
wrapped around a person atop cowry-shell-riches,   64.20.101   guì   貴
        the solid (like that hard yellow earth with
        two little grass tufts next to River Han,
        where "short-tailed birds" find no food)   64.20.102   nán   難

"Hand-Picked Gem," like cowry-shell-riches
discovered along the road,   64.20.103   dé   得
and what it has, stepping on from this
footprint, its   64.20.104   zhī   之
transformation from a right-side-up person
to an upside-down person atop cowry-shell
riches;   64.20.105   huò   貨

would be learning and understanding with
divination or tally marks held between one's hands
and a child safe beneath a roof,   64.21.106   xué   學
        the husk of the initial protective bud casing
        but not really the true flower of   64.21.107   bù   不
        learning and understanding with divination
        or tally marks held between one's hands
        and a child safe beneath a roof.   64.21.108   xué   學
Someone walking with a footprint of slowly
returning with the left leg leading the way,
doubling back (like the gut) on one's footprint,   64.21.109   fù   復
the sun, shining down like an eye on the people,
sees all this, sees,   64.21.110   zhòng   眾
        that person,   64.21.111   rén   人
        what it has, stepping on from this
        footprint...   64.21.112   zhī   之
        "that place" being intentionally created like
        any household gate hewn with an axe   64.21.113   suǒ   所
        past and surpassing, maybe "passed
        away," maybe excessive, walking slowly
        with the footprint of a slanting skull mouth
        speaking, the left leg leading the way.   64.21.114   guò   過

There was no returning to that Hand-Picked Gem
life. It was time to go.

This is cultivating, like a plow,   64.22.115   yǐ   以
assisting, like the wooden bars that help prevent a
carriage from over-turning or a carriage with a
man's courtesy name that he gets when he
becomes a man,   64.22.116   fǔ   輔
the medicine-dancing-scorpion insect swarm of   64.22.117   wàn   萬
matter (outside one's body, "cut from the cow" by
a bloodied blade),   64.22.118   wù   物
what it has, stepping on from this footprint,   64.22.119   zhī   之
oneself personally, right on the nose,   64.22.120   zì   自
accomplishing this thus... as naturally as dog meat
over a fire,   64.22.121   rán   然
      yet now, bearded, you're   64.22.122   ér   而
      the husk of the initial protective bud casing
      but not really the true flower of   64.22.123   bù   不
      venturing to be bold, even a little bit and
      ultra-politely hunting a boar as pleasantly
      as if you had something sweet in your
      mouth,   64.22.124   gǎn   敢
      creating something by hand, carving an
      elephant likeness of good fortune and
      royal power.   64.22.125   wéi   為

*It was time to go—it was essential for the kids—yet
I wasn't being bold enough. But could I live as the
wild-haired buck and still be "good?" No...*

Chapter 65: Trying to live the virtuous life at the same time as the Dào had already proven to cause issues. But here's the plan for solving that problem. (Spoiler: the Dé)

Speaking of the solid shield of the *past,*	65.1.1	gǔ	古
what it had stepping on from this footprint,	65.1.2	zhī	之
the traditionally virtuous, offering up a ram's head			
while speaking back and forth, tongues waggling,	65.1.3	shàn	善
creating something by hand, carving an elephant			
likeness of good fortune and royal power,	65.1.4	wéi	為
AND walking with the footprint of the loose-haired			
head buck	65.1.5	dào	道
—this is boiling sugarcane with fire as follows:	65.1.6	zhâ	者
wringing to backward the two wings of	65.2.7	fēi	非
cultivating, like a plow,	65.2.8	yǐ	以
as bright as dawn rising on a crescent			
moon, enlightened,	65.2.9	míng	明
one of our folk, the people enslaved by			
blinding with a dagger,	65.2.10	mín	民
it's assured, as if by hand-offering a meat			
tribute at an altar, a certain future of	65.3.11	jiāng	將
cultivating, like a plow,	65.3.12	yǐ	以
a heart like that trampling monkey			
with the head of a ghost,	65.3.13	yú	愚
what it has stepping on from this			
footprint.	65.3.14	zhī	之
One of our folk, the people enslaved by			
blinding with a dagger,	65.4.15	mín	民
what it has stepping on from this footprint,	65.4.16	zhī	之

solid, like that hard yellow earth
with two little grass tufts next to
River Han, where "short-tailed
birds" find no food,
flowing the River Happy, speaking
of gathering oneself from three
sides, managing,

is cultivating, like a plow,
what it holds a basket of
      oh, so very pleasantly speaking
      with that wise knowledge passed
      on from a great big person to a
      baby, as if something sweet in the
      mouth,
      having more, like two pieces of
      meat.

This taps lightly with a tutoring cane and leaves a
mark on the solid shield of the past:
cultivating, like a plow,
"oh, so very pleasantly speaking with that wise
knowledge passed on from a great big person to a
baby, as if something sweet in the mouth,"
while flowing the River Happy, speaking of
gathering oneself from three sides, managing,
in our domestic enclave, defended by a weapon on
a pole,

      our domestic enclave, defended by a
      weapon on a pole,
      what it has, stepping on from this
      footprint,

65.4.17	nán	難
65.4.18	zhì	治
65.5.19	yǐ	以
65.5.20	qí	其
65.5.21	zhì	智
65.5.22	duō	多
65.6.23	gù	故
65.6.24	yǐ	以
65.6.25	zhì	智
65.6.26	zhì	治
65.6.27	guó	國
65.7.28	guó	國
65.7.29	zhī	之

is using a weapon on a pole to
harm that sacrificial blade-and-
cauldron-like ritual regulation, like
an insect that eats at the joints and
roots of a plant, destroying.　　65.7.30　　zéi　賊

But the husk of the initial protective bud casing but
not really the true flower of,　　65.8.31　　bù　不
"cultivating, like a plow,　　65.8.32　　yǐ　以
oh, so very pleasantly speaking with that wise
knowledge passed on from a great big person to a
baby, as if something sweet in the mouth,　　65.8.33　　zhì　智
while flowing the River Happy, speaking of
gathering oneself from three sides, managing　　65.8.34　　zhì　治
in our domestic enclave, defended by a weapon on
a pole,"　　65.8.35　　guó　國

then our domestic enclave, defended by a
weapon on a pole,　　65.9.36　　guó　國
what it has, stepping on from this
footprint,　　65.9.37　　zhī　之
is blessings and good fortune, a full
vessel on display on an altar.　　65.9.38　　fú　福

*Trying to live as the <u>wild-haired buck</u> while also
being a <u>traditionally virtuous person hand-making
my little elephant</u>, I was being oh so very sweet at
work, even though I was having a hard time
"flowing the River Happy" at home... and that ate
away at everything. I needed a different approach.*

Speaking as a great big person to a baby,
distinguishing, imparting, and administering
wisdom confidently and intimately,   65.10.39   zhī   知
—this here, the foot stops a person here on this
footprint!—   65.10.40   cǐ   此
these two, this pair of traditional, adult, gendered
head-cloths covered by "The One?"   65.10.41   liǎng 兩
This is boiling sugarcane with fire as follows!   65.10.42   zhâ   者

> Both armpits sweat this too!   65.11.43   yì   亦
> A loose-haired head buck is examining, like
> it's some delicious food or maybe an
> intention or imperial decree, investigating   65.11.44   jī   稽
> a model example, like a bladed tool and a
> retrievable arrow attached to a string for
> effective shooting and catching!   65.11.45   shì   式

But as a conventional royal administrator wearing a
men's headcloth as his skirt   65.12.46   cháng 常
speaking as a great big person to a baby,
distinguishing, imparting, and administering
wisdom confidently and intimately,   65.12.47   zhī   知
> the loose-haired head buck examining like
> it's some delicious food or maybe an
> intention or imperial decree, investigating   65.12.48   jī   稽
> a model example, like a bladed tool and a
> retrievable arrow attached to a string for
> effective shooting and catching...   65.12.49   shì   式

> this baby footprint on bamboo-slip pages,   65.13.50   shì   是
> by the nitty-gritty, grinding gizzard of a
> fowl, what that's called,   65.13.51   wèi   謂

*this hard-to-see structure of a double-
looped, figure-eight skein of string-dyed-
black,*   65.13.52   xuán   玄
*walking with the footprint of someone
who's in alignment (eyes looking forward,
directly over the heart, left leg slowly
leading the way).*   65.13.53   dé   德

*If the wild-haired buck takes a good look at the
cultural models from inside, <u>as a royal
administrator,</u> that works. That "participant-
observer" strategy always had been the foundation
of my unseen double life living the Dé. And that
needed to continue somehow.*

*"This hard-to-see structure of a double-looped,
figure-eight skein of string-dyed-black,*   65.14.54   xuán   玄
*walking with the footprint of someone who's in
alignment (eyes looking forward, directly over the
heart, left leg slowly leading the way):"*   65.14.55   dé   德
    It's deep as far water   65.14.56   shēn   深
        —I swear, an arrow revolving
        around oneself, that's it!   65.14.57   yǐ   矣
    It's the much distant, not intimate or near
    but profound way of slowly walking with
    the footprint of a big round spindle with a
    long robe hanging like the afterbirth from a
    postpartum woman, the left leg leading the
    way   65.14.58   yuǎn   遠
        —I swear, an arrow revolving
        around oneself, that's it!   65.14.59   yǐ   矣

It's participating with (a "biting tooth"
lifted by a pair of hands onto strong
shoulders, perhaps interfering with or
perhaps supporting)   65.15.60   yǔ   與
matter (outside one's body, "cut from the
cow" by a bloodied blade)   65.15.61   wù   物
as a different-sounding *Fǎn*, turning your
palm over in a habitable cave in a cliff,
reversing, returning, reflecting, maybe
countering with the opposite   65.15.62   fǎn   反
    —I swear, an arrow revolving
    around oneself, that's it!   65.15.63   yǐ   矣

Accomplishing this thus, as naturally as dog meat
over a fire,   65.16.64   rán   然
walking slowly with just the left leg leading the
way, leaving behind this tiny silk thread footprint
like a knot in a thread, a descendant, at the end, 65.16.65   hòu   後
only then do you get,   65.16.66   nǎi   乃
in arriving at the end, the extreme climax, like an
arrow straight into the clay soil,   65.16.67   zhì   至
    this great big person   65.16.68   dà   大
    smoothly going along like the loose-haired
    head buck kneeling at a river.   65.16.69   shùn   順

That's the only way I could flow easily through to
delivery.

Chapter 66: But in the hundred-fold more extreme situation in which I would be suckling AND pregnant AND operating my own marquessate, could my hybrid solution work again?

The Yangtze River (the river that works like a stone
axe) flowing into   66.1.1   jiāng   江
a lushness like that of a river of new life sprouting
from a nursing mother, like the ocean: 66.1.2   hǎi   海
*"that place" being intentionally created like any
household gate hewn with an axe...*   66.1.3   suǒ   所
    this is cultivating, like a plow,   66.1.4   yǐ   以
    using that legendary Hybrid Power of a
    mythical bear-like animal who has the legs
    of a deer for   66.1.5   néng   能
    creating something by hand, carving an
    elephant likeness of good fortune and
    royal power,   66.1.6   wéi   為
    a hundred times   66.1.7   bǎi   百
    in a difficult position in a ravine, in an
    emptied, eroded valley mouth between
    two mountains,   66.1.8   gǔ   谷
        as a king, with his ceremonial jade
        axe or crown, connecting the three
        levels of heaven, man, and earth?   66.1.9   wáng   王
        This is boiling sugarcane with fire
        as follows!   66.1.10   zhâ   者

This is cultivating, like a plow,   66.2.11   yǐ   以
what it holds a basket of,   66.2.12   qí   其
the *traditionally virtuous*, offering up a ram's head
while speaking back and forth, tongues waggling,   66.2.13   shàn   善
now here down below,   66.2.14   xià   下

what it has, stepping on from this footprint...	66.2.15	zhī	之
this taps lightly with a tutoring cane and			
leaves a mark on the solid shield of the			
past:	66.3.16	gù	故
"using that legendary Hybrid Power of a			
mythical bear-like animal who has the legs			
of a deer for	66.3.17	néng	能
creating something by hand, carving an			
elephant likeness of good fortune and			
royal power,	66.3.18	wéi	為
a hundred times	66.3.19	bǎi	百
in a difficult position in a ravine, in an			
emptied, eroded valley mouth between			
two mountains	66.3.20	gǔ	谷
as a king with his ceremonial jade			
axe or crown connecting the three			
levels of heaven, man, and earth."	66.3.21	wáng	王
This baby footprint on bamboo-slip pages,	66.4.22	shì	是
this is cultivating, like a plow,	66.4.23	yǐ	以
an ideal grounded sage known for his civilian			
petition to authority, standing straight, speaking,			
and being listened to,	66.4.24	shèng	聖
that person:	66.4.25	rén	人
would be missing, kneeling with a yawning mouth			
before a ravine eroded between two mountains,			
wanting, lacking,	66.4.26	yù	欲
on top,	66.4.27	shàng	上
one of our folk, the people enslaved by blinding			
with a dagger,	66.4.28	mín	民
and hands over heart, analytically,	66.4.29	bì	必
this is cultivating, like a plow,	66.4.30	yǐ	以

speaking out loud	66.4.31	yán	言
now here down below,	66.4.32	xià	下
what it has, stepping on from this			
footprint;	66.4.33	zhī	之

would be missing, kneeling with a yawning mouth			
before a ravine eroded between two mountains,			
wanting, lacking,	66.5.34	yù	欲
leading, long before, stepping off from this			
footprint an *ancestor,*	66.5.35	xiān	先
one of our folk, the people enslaved by blinding			
with a dagger,	66.5.36	mín	民
and hands over heart, analytically,	66.5.37	bì	必
cultivating, like a plow,	66.5.38	yǐ	以
your pregnant self	66.5.39	shēn	身
walking slowly with just the left leg leading			
the way, leaving behind this tiny silk thread			
footprint like a knot in a thread, a			
descendant, at the end,	66.5.40	hòu	後
what it has, stepping on from this			
footprint.	66.5.41	zhī	之

This baby footprint on bamboo-slip pages,	66.6.42	shì	是
this is cultivating, like a plow,	66.6.43	yǐ	以
an ideal grounded sage known for his civilian			
petition to authority, standing straight, speaking,			
and being listened to,	66.6.44	shèng	聖
that person:	66.6.45	rén	人
would be disappearing like a tiger head at home,			
footprint pointed back down by a table, staying			
here, chaste, rather than accepting a government			
position or getting married	66.6.46	chù	處
on top,	66.6.47	shàng	上

yet now, bearded, you,
one of our folk, the people enslaved by
blinding with a dagger,
are the husk of the initial protective bud
casing but not really the true flower of
the seriously heavy (like a bag tied at both
ends, so weighty that a man has to kneel to
put it on his back);

would be disappearing like a tiger head at home,
footprint pointed back down by a table, staying
here, chaste, rather than accepting a government
position or getting married,
at the front (that place in battle where a step could
mean your feet get cut off as punishment),
yet now, bearded, you,
one of our folk, the people enslaved by
blinding with a dagger,
are the husk of the initial protective bud
casing but not really the true flower of
harmed as a house in which weeds sprout
from a mouth.

This baby footprint on bamboo-slip pages,
this is cultivating, like a plow,
with the heavenly from high above this great big
person
now here down below,
pleasurably playing (as glad music upon a wooden
instrument's two silk strings)
promoting along (like hand-pushing that "short-
tailed bird"),
yet now, bearded, you're

66.6.48	ér	而
66.6.49	mín	民
66.6.50	bù	不
66.6.51	zhòng	重
66.7.52	chù	處
66.7.53	qián	前
66.7.54	ér	而
66.7.55	mín	民
66.7.56	bù	不
66.7.57	hài	害
66.8.58	shì	是
66.8.59	yǐ	以
66.8.60	tiān	天
66.8.61	xià	下
66.8.62	lè	樂
66.8.63	tuī	推
66.8.64	ér	而

the husk of the initial protective bud casing
but not really the true flower of
sated like a dog with meat in its mouth, fed
up...

66.8.65	bù	不
66.8.66	yàn	厭

this is cultivating, like a plow,
what it holds a basket of,
    the husk of the initial protective bud casing
    but not really the true flower of
    competing, two hands clawing over a
    plowshare.

66.9.67	yǐ	以
66.9.68	qí	其
66.9.69	bù	不
66.9.70	zhēng	爭

This taps lightly with a tutoring cane and leaves a
mark on the solid shield of the past:
with the heavenly from high above this great big
person
now here down below,
like the sun sinking down in four bushes, one must
not be—*cannot be, eh?*—
using that legendary Hybrid Power of a mythical
bear-like animal who has the legs of a deer for
participating with (a "biting tooth" lifted by a pair
of hands onto strong shoulders, perhaps
interfering with or perhaps supporting)
what it has, stepping on from this footprint, this
competing, two hands clawing over a plowshare.

66.10.71	gù	故
66.10.72	tiān	天
66.10.73	xià	下
66.10.74	mò	莫
66.10.75	néng	能
66.10.76	yǔ	與
66.10.77	zhī	之
66.10.78	zhēng	爭

*Yes. The hybrid power could be used in a humbler
marquis king position to accomplish my goals
without that grinding competition. In fact, it was
vital that it be done pleasantly, without overdoing
it, and without competing.*

Chapter 80: Meanwhile, the head buck all alone at home with the baby had this deceptive appearance...

This chapter and the next were located here, after Chapter 66, in the oldest known versions of my book.

Our tiny dear little one, like three grains of sand,
in our domestic enclave defended by a weapon on
a pole,
and the loose-haired head buck who differentiates
right from wrong, kneeling in a house like a widow,
alone,
one of our folk, the people enslaved by blinding
with a dagger:

That low-ranking government official, his hand
holding a pen, sent as a messenger or an envoy,
putting to work, using in every way you can think
of, directing,
flesh-and-meat-handling Being...
    ten people,
    counts (acorns like eldest brothers or
    paternal uncles),
    this is what they have, stepping on from
    this footprint, as their
    "set of highly regarded vessels with lots of
    capacity, worthy of a guard dog,"

    yet now bearded, you're
    the husk of the initial protective bud casing
    but not really the true flower of

80.1.1	xiǎo	小
80.1.2	guó	國
80.1.3	guǎ	寡
80.1.4	mín	民
80.2.5	shǐ	使
80.2.6	yǒu	有
80.2.7	shí	什
80.2.8	bó	伯
80.2.9	zhī	之
80.2.10	qì	器
80.3.11	ér	而
80.3.12	bù	不

doing truly useful work like a water bucket,
by means of carrying-capacity.

80.3.13   yòng   用

That low-ranking government official, his hand
holding a pen, sent as a messenger or an envoy,
putting to work, using in every way you can think
of, directing,

80.4.14   shǐ   使

one of our folk, the people enslaved by blinding
with a dagger,

80.4.15   mín   民

is seriously heavy (like a bag tied at both
ends, so weighty that a man has to kneel to
put it on his back)

80.4.16   zhòng   重

dying, a person turning to a pile of bones,

80.4.17   sǐ   死

yet now, bearded, you're

80.5.18   ér   而

the husk of the initial protective bud casing
but *not really* the true flower of

80.5.19   bù   不

the much *distant*, not intimate or near but
profound way of slowly walking with the
footprint of a big round spindle with a long
robe hanging like the afterbirth from a
postpartum woman, the left leg leading the
way,

80.5.20   yuǎn   遠

moving, shifting, *migrating* like feces
leaving a living person representing the
dead in a rite.

80.5.21   xǐ   徙

I looked ill, like I couldn't do useful work, and I
appeared to be dying. But I wouldn't really passing
on. When my funeral was going on in one place, I
would be somewhere else...

Immediately adjacent (like a venomous snake with
"a short-tailed bird," right next to it) to   80.6.22   suī   雖
flesh-and-meat-handling Being   80.6.23   yǒu   有
riding in a boat, a dugout canoe,   80.6.24   zhōu   舟
and carried in a carriage's sedan chair supported
on shoulders, upheld by two hands like the
territory and the public,   80.6.25   yú   輿

    the shamanic dancer with animal tails
    flowing from her wrists, Not-Having,   80.7.26   wú   無
    "that place" being intentionally created like
    any household gate hewn with an axe: 80.7.27   suǒ   所
        a four-horse military carriage,   80.7.28   shèng   乘
        is what they have, stepping on
        from this footprint, as theirs.   80.7.29   zhī   之

Immediately adjacent (like a venomous snake with
"a short-tailed bird," right next to it) to   80.8.30   suī   雖
flesh-and-meat-handling Being   80.8.31   yǒu   有
with a turtle shell shield   80.8.32   jiǎ   甲
and carrying a short ax with two hands like a
soldier or pawn,   80.8.33   bīng   兵

    the shaman-dancing Not-Having,   80.9.34   wú   無
    "that place" being intentionally created like
    any household gate hewn with an axe: 80.9.35   suǒ   所
        the exhibition of an old eastern
        landowner, a bag tied at both
        ends, on display near a big mound
        of soil, as in the ancient vassal
        state of Chén,   80.9.36   chén   陳
        is what they have, stepping on
        from this footprint, as theirs..   80.9.37   zhī   之

That low-ranking government official, his hand
holding a pen, sent as a messenger or an envoy,
putting to work, using in every way you can think
of, directing,   80.10.38   shǐ   使
one of our folk, the people enslaved by blinding
with a dagger,   80.10.39   mín   民
      is someone walking with a footprint of
      slowly *returning* with the left leg leading
      the way, doubling back (like the gut) on
      one's footprint *to*   80.10.40   fù   復
      tying, joining with an emotional knot, a
      skein of silk with the auspicious empty
      mouth of a bachelor soldier-scholar-official
      appointed by the emperor,   80.10.41   jié   結
      a skein of silk around a striving toad,   80.10.42   shéng   繩

yet now, bearded, you're   80.11.43   ér   而
doing truly useful work like a water bucket, by
means of carrying-capacity,   80.11.44   yòng   用
is what you have, stepping on from this footprint,
as yours.   80.11.45   zhǐ   之

With my new life as a marquis I once more was
binding myself with a skein of silk, as described
before in Chapters 14 and 27, but it allowed me to
do that useful carrying work of pregnancy. And it
involved some changes from the luxury and
admiration I'd been used to having...

Sweet-tasting in the mouth,   80.12.46   gān   甘
what it holds a basket of   80.12.47   qí   其

is eating, mouth over a bowl of rice on a
stand;   80.12.48   shí   食

an admired beauty, a person wearing a ram's horn
headdress,   80.13.49   mâi   美
what it holds a basket of   80.13.50   qí   其
        is wearing clothes like a mourning dress, a
        person hand-subdued to kneeling before a
        commonplace plate;   80.13.51   fú   服

staying calm as a woman sitting on her heels at
home,   80.14.52   ān   妄
what it holds a basket of   80.14.53   qí   其
        is staying put here, sitting over the solid
        shield of the past at this birthplace;   80.14.54   jū   居

pleasurably playing as glad music upon a wooden
instrument's two silk strings,   80.15.55   lè   樂
what it holds a basket of   80.15.56   qí   其
        is the common practices of the people
        from that difficult position in the valley
        between two mountains.   80.15.57   sú   俗

The neighboring countries, appealing as the will o'
wisp light emanating from a corpse attracting a
kneeling person to a grave,   80.16.58   lín   鄰
and our domestic enclave, defended by a weapon
on a pole,   80.16.59   guó   國
like a seen tree and the eye seeing it (or like a well-
tended lord and his attentive attendant), when
taken together, are creating this singular
phenomenon of   80.16.60   xiāng   相

gazing from a distance (like a good human
standing on soil below the cutting edge of
a knife and the crescent moon);   80.16.61   wàng   望

and a rooster (a "short-tailed bird," this great big
person, their tiniest silk thread child is grabbed by
a hand from above like a female sex worker)   80.17.62   jī   雞
and a dog,   80.17.63   quǎn   犬
what they have, stepping on from this footprint, as
theirs   80.17.64   zhī   之
many sounds you hear when hitting chimes with a
weapon in your right hand, going right through a
person,   80.17.65   shēng   聲
like a seen tree and the eye seeing it (or like a well-
tended lord and his attentive attendant), when
taken together, are creating this singular
phenomenon of   80.17.66   xiāng   相
          being heard at the two-winged gateway
          and famously reported on...   80.17.67   wén   聞

but one of our folk, the people enslaved by
blinding with a dagger,   80.18.68   mín   民
arriving at the end, the extreme climax, like an
arrow straight into the clay soil,   80.18.69   zhì   至
          and an honorable loose-haired elder bent
          over an arrow as a cane,   80.18.70   lǎo   老
          dying, a person turning to a pile of bones,   80.18.71   sǐ   死

are the husk of the initial protective bud casing but
not really the true flower of   80.19.72   bù   不
like a seen tree and the eye seeing it (or like a well-
tended lord and his attentive attendant), when   80.19.73   xiāng   相

taken together, creating this singular phenomenon
of

> a person walking slowly toward you with
> the luxurious footprint of a king, the left
> leg leading the way
> coming like a stalk of wheat.

80.19.74	wǎng	往
80.19.75	lái	來

*My new place was within sight and sound. But I
could reach full term there because my honorable-
old-man persona could seem to die, meaning the
king would never cross this short distance to where
I really was.*

Chapter 81: I could be done with Being and the system I'd been part of.

Giving one's word to a person,
speaking out loud

> is the husk of the initial protective bud
> casing but not really the true flower of
> an admired beauty, a person wearing a
> ram's horn headdress;

81.1.1	xìn	信
81.1.2	yán	言
81.1.3	bù	不
81.1.4	mâi	美

an admired beauty, a person wearing a ram's horn
headdress,
speaking out loud

> is the husk of the initial protective bud
> casing but not really the true flower of
> giving one's word to a person.

81.2.5	mâi	美
81.2.6	yǎn	言
81.2.7	bù	不
81.2.8	xìn	信

The traditionally virtuous, offering up a ram's head
while speaking back and forth, tongues waggling
—this is boiling sugarcane with fire as follows!—
    it's the husk of the initial protective bud
    casing but not really the true flower of
    discussing and debating, speaking in the
    middle of two chisels used to brand slaves
    or criminals;

discussing and debating, speaking in the middle of
two chisels used to brand slaves or criminals
—this is boiling sugarcane with fire as follows!—
    it's the husk of the initial protective bud
    casing but not really the true flower of
    the traditionally virtuous, offering up a
    ram's head while speaking back and forth,
    tongues waggling.

Speaking as a great big person to a baby,
distinguishing, imparting, and administering
wisdom confidently and intimately,
—this is boiling sugarcane with fire as follows!—
    it's the husk of the initial protective bud
    casing but not really the true flower of
    widely winning (like ten times a courtesy
    name a man takes upon becoming a man,
    as small as that inch-sized spot where you
    measure the pulse in your wrist);

widely winning (like ten times a courtesy name a
man takes upon becoming a man, as small as that
inch-sized spot where you measure the pulse in
your wrist)

81.3.9	shàn	善
81.3.10	zhâ	者
81.3.11	bù	不
81.3.12	biàn	辯
81.4.13	biàn	辯
81.4.14	zhâ	者
81.4.15	bù	不
81.4.16	shàn	善
81.5.17	zhī	知
81.5.18	zhâ	者
81.5.19	bù	不
81.5.20	bó	博
81.6.21	bó	博

—this is boiling sugarcane with fire as follows!—
　　it's the husk of the initial protective bud
　　casing but not really the true flower of
　　speaking as a great big person to a baby,
　　distinguishing, imparting, and
　　administering wisdom confidently and
　　intimately.

An ideal grounded sage known for his civilian
petition to authority, standing straight, speaking,
and being listened to,
that person
　　would be the husk of the initial protective
　　bud casing but not really the true flower of
　　accumulating, amassing grain plants like
　　cowry-riches under a thorn tree, like
　　indigestion:

"done"—as de facto as a kneeling person turning
away after eating a bowl of rice, done with,
cultivating, like a plow,
creating something by hand, carving an elephant
likeness of good fortune and royal power,
that person
　　themselves, privately, personally bound
　　with a silk rope,
　　a person after an illness who is gathering
　　themself together from three sides by
　　moonlight over their heart after a blade cut
　　off their foot as punishment and now,
　　they've recovered,
　　　　　　"flesh-and-meat-handling Being;"

81.6.22	zhâ	者
81.6.23	bù	不
81.6.24	zhī	知
81.7.25	shèng	聖
81.7.26	rén	人
81.7.27	bù	不
81.7.28	jī	積
81.8.29	jì	既
81.8.30	yǐ	以
81.8.31	wéi	為
81.8.32	rén	人
81.8.33	jǐ	己
81.8.34	yù	愈
81.8.35	yǒu	有

and "done"—as de facto as a kneeling person
turning away after eating a bowl of rice, done with,   81.9.36   jì   既
cultivating, like a plow,   81.9.37   yǐ   以
participating with (a "biting tooth" lifted by a pair
of hands onto strong shoulders, perhaps
interfering with or perhaps supporting),   81.9.38   yǔ   與
that person,   81.9.39   rén   人
        themselves, privately, personally bound
        with a silk rope,   81.9.40   jǐ   己
        a person after an illness who is gathering
        themself together from three sides by
        moonlight over their heart after a blade cut
        off their foot as punishment and now,
        they've recovered,   81.9.41   yù   愈
                having more, like two pieces of
                meat...   81.9.42   duō   多

the heavenly from high above this great big person   81.10.43   tiān   天
what it has, stepping on from this footprint, it has
this,   81.10.44   zhī   之
walking with the footprint of the loose-haired head
buck,   81.10.45   dào   道
reaping benefits (in the manner of a sharp-edged
blade slicing grain),   81.10.46   lì   利
        yet now, bearded, you're   81.10.47   ér   而
        the husk of the initial protective bud casing
        but not really the true flower of   81.10.48   bù   不
        being harmed as a house in which weeds
        sprout from a mouth.   81.10.49   hài   害

An ideal grounded sage known for his civilian
petition to authority, standing straight, speaking,
and being listened to,   81.11.50   shèng   聖

that person,
what it would have, stepping on from this
footprint, it would have this:
*walking with the footprint of the loose-haired head
buck*
*creating something by hand, carving an elephant
likeness of good fortune and royal power,*
>yet now, bearded, you're
>the husk of the initial protective bud casing
>but not really the true flower of
>competing, two hands clawing over a
>plowshare.

	81.11.51	rén	人
	81.11.52	zhī	之
	81.11.53	dào	道
	81.11.54	wéi	為
	81.11.55	ér	而
	81.11.56	bù	不
	81.11.57	zhēng	爭

*I could be done creating as the Being persona and
done participating with the system as that "double
serving." The heavenly spirit itself could have the
wild-haired head buck, reaping benefits and safe.
And I could be not only that wild-haired head buck
again but also hand-making my next little elephant
without danger and without competing.*

**Chapter 67: My cover was deep and effective
during that first pregnancy. And though I was
going to "die" out of that persona, it had
transformed me at a deeper level.**

*The heavenly from high above this great big person
now here down below,*
gossip, comparing two people like there was
something oh so sweet in their mouth, said,
>by the nitty-gritty, grinding gizzard of a
>fowl, what that's called:

	67.1.1	tiān	天
	67.1.2	xià	下
	67.1.3	jiē	皆
	67.1.4	wèi	謂

I, holding a rake-like weapon to defend
myself and my opinion,   67.1.5   wǒ   我
walking with the footprint of the loose-
haired head buck,   67.1.6   dào   道
this great big person,   67.1.7   dà   大

was resembling, like how a person and a
turned fetus, side-by-side look alike,   67.2.8   sì   似
the husk of the initial protective bud casing
but *not really* the true flower of   67.2.9   bù   不
our tiny dear little one, three grains of sand
being the likeness of meat.   67.2.10   xiào   肖

In fact, that is to say This Grown Man with hairpin
and public courtesy name,   67.3.11   fū   夫
"Oh, YES, Ma'am," says the "short-tailed bird,"   67.3.12   wéi   唯
this great big person...   67.3.13   dà   大

this taps lightly with a tutoring cane and
leaves a mark on the solid shield of the
past,   67.4.14   gù   故
"resembling, like how a person and a
turned fetus, side-by-side look alike,   67.4.15   sì   似
the husk of the initial protective bud casing
but not really the true flower of   67.4.16   bù   不
like our tiny dear little one, three grains of
sand being the likeness of meat..."   67.4.17   xiào   肖

A Certain Someone compliantly combing
her loose hair seems to be saying "this is as
if   67.5.18   ruò   若
our tiny dear little one, three grains of sand
being the likeness of meat,   67.5.19   xiào   肖

enduring through time as a person
receiving moxibustion, that mugwort
treatment for cramps, turning a breech
baby, or other health issues
—I swear, an arrow revolving around
oneself, that's it!

What it holds a basket of,
a small, skein-of-silk fontanelle
—yes, that too, oh 'female funnel!'—
in fact, that is to say This Grown Man with
hairpin and public courtesy name."

I, holding a rake-like weapon to defend myself and
my opinion,
as flesh-and-meat-handling Being,
    three,
    treasures (like a house containing cowry-
    riches, jade, and a lidded pot)

grasped, like a government office or
temple holding what comes from this
footprint with the very skillful human hand
of that official (usually a eunuch in the old
days),
        yet, now you're bearded,
        safeguarding, like carrying a child
        on one's back,
        what it has, stepping on from this
        footprint.

67.6.20	jiǔ	久
67.6.21	yǐ	矣
67.7.22	qí	其
67.7.23	xì	細
67.7.24	yâ	也
67.7.25	fū	夫
67.8.26	wǒ	我
67.8.27	yǒu	有
67.8.28	sān	三
67.8.29	bǎo	寶
67.9.30	chí	持
67.9.31	ér	而
67.9.32	bǎo	保
67.9.33	zhī	之

The One,
what it's called when issued on a breath from the
mouth,   67.10.34   yī   一

       is "benevolent as a mother, two loops of   67.10.35   yuē   曰
       string-dyed-black over the heart;"   67.10.36   cí   慈

two   67.11.37   èr   二
what it's called when issued on a breath from the
mouth,   67.11.38   yuē   曰

       is "moderate (like one humble person next
       to two people and two mouths, altogether,
       gathering from three sides perhaps during
       a poor harvest);"   67.11.39   jiǎn 儉

three   67.12.40   sān   三
what it's called when issued on a breath from the
mouth,   67.12.41   yuē   曰

       is "the husk of the initial protective bud
       casing but not really the true flower of   67.12.42   bù   不
       venturing to be bold, even a little bit and
       ultra-politely hunting a boar as pleasantly
       as if you had something sweet in your
       mouth,   67.12.43   gǎn   敢
       creating something by hand, carving an
       elephant likeness of good fortune and
       royal power,   67.12.44   wéi   為
       the heavenly from high above this great big
       person   67.12.45   tiān 天
       now here down below,   67.12.46   xià   下
       leading, long before, stepping off from this
       footprint... an *ancestor*."   67.12.47   xiān 先

"Benevolent as a mother, two loops of string-dyed-
black over the heart…"   67.13.48   cí   慈
this taps lightly with a tutoring cane and leaves a
mark on the solid shield of the past: 67.13.49   gù   故
        using that legendary Hybrid Power of a
        mythical bear-like animal who has the legs
        of a deer for,   67.13.50   néng   能
        like the handle of a bell, being courageous
        and sturdy as a soldier, strong as an arm,
        bladed tool, or a plow.   67.13.51   yǒng   勇

"Moderate (like one humble person next to two
people and two mouths altogether, gathering from
three sides perhaps during a poor harvest)…"   67.14.52   jiǎn   儉
this taps lightly with a tutoring cane and leaves a
mark on the solid shield of the past: 67.14.53   gù   故
        using that legendary Hybrid Power of a
        mythical bear-like animal who has the legs
        of a deer for   67.14.54   néng   能
        being widespread, like a person with a
        large belly in a habitable cave in a cliff.   67.14.55   guǎng   廣

"The husk of the initial protective bud casing but
not really the true flower of   67.15.56   bù   不
venturing to be bold, even a little bit and ultra-
politely hunting a boar as pleasantly as if you had
something sweet in your mouth   67.15.57   gǎn   敢
creating something by hand, carving an elephant
likeness of good fortune and royal power,   67.15.58   wéi   為
the heavenly, from high above this great big person   67.15.59   tiān   天
now here down below,   67.15.60   xià   下
leading, long before, stepping off from this
footprint… an ancestor…"   67.15.61   xiān   先

this taps lightly with a tutoring cane and leaves a
mark on the solid shield of the past: 67.15.62   gù   故
    using that legendary Hybrid Power of a
    mythical bear-like animal who has the legs
    of a deer for   67.15.63   néng   能
    completing, that final "nail" in a weapon
    on a pole,   67.15.64   chéng   成
        a set of highly regarded vessels
        with lots of capacity, worthy of a
        guard dog,   67.15.65   qì   器
        lengthening as long as hair that has
        to be tied with a brooch, like a
        loose-haired old man.   67.15.66   cháng   長

Gathering from three sides over this now, *in
current times*:   67.16.67   jīn   今
stopping, like at a thatched inn (usually located
every thirty of the ancient miles), humble,   67.16.68   shâ   舍
being benevolent as a mother, two loops of string-
dyed-black over the heart...   67.16.69   cí   慈
    lasting over time as the erect manhood of
    a male ancestor   67.16.70   qiâ   且
    like the handle of a bell, being courageous
    and sturdy as a soldier, strong as an arm,
    bladed tool, or a plow;   67.16.71   yǒng   勇

stopping, like at a thatched inn (usually located
every thirty of the ancient miles), humble,   67.17.72   shâ   舍
being moderate (like one humble person next to
two people and two mouths altogether, gathering
from three sides perhaps during a poor harvest)...   67.17.73   jiǎn   儉
    lasting over time as the erect manhood of
    a male ancestor   67.17.74   qiâ   且

widespread, like a person with a large belly
in a habitable cave in a cliff;   67.17.75   guǎng   廣

stopping, like at a thatched inn (usually located
every thirty of the ancient miles), humble   67.18.76   shâ   舍
walking slowly with just the left leg leading the
way, leaving behind this tiny silk thread footprint
like a knot in a thread, *a descendant*, at the end…   67.18.77   hòu   後
        lasting over time as the erect manhood of
        a male ancestor   67.18.78   qiâ   且
        leading, long before, stepping off from this
        footprint an *ancestor*…   67.18.79   xiān   先

        dying, a person turning to a pile of bones   67.19.80   sǐ   死
        —I swear, an arrow revolving around
        oneself, that's it!   67.19.81   yǐ   矣

In fact, that is to say This Grown Man with hairpin
and public courtesy name,   67.20.82   fū   夫
benevolent as a mother, two loops of string-dyed-
black over the heart: 67.20.83   cí   慈
this is cultivating, like a plow,   67.20.84   yǐ   以
battling, using a net for catching animals against a
weapon on a pole…   67.20.85   zhàn   戰
        after following this sacrificial blade-and-
        cauldron-like ritual regulation, becomes   67.20.86   zé   則
        able to withstand entirely, to be victorious
        as a splendid piece of jewelry, an omen or
        the royal 'We' mending something on a
        boat with two hands by the strength of an
        arm, bladed tool, or a plow;   67.20.87   shèng   勝

this is cultivating, like a plow,   67.21.88 yǐ 以
hand-defending this building…   67.21.89 shǒu 守
  after following this sacrificial blade-and-
  cauldron-like ritual regulation, becomes 67.21.90 zé 則
  solidly, for a long time, keeping as firm to
  what happened in the first place as this
  land surrounding and holding this nation's
  shield since ancient times,   67.21.91 gù 固

  the heavenly, from high above this great
  big person   67.22.92 tiān 天
  assured, as if by hand-offering a meat
  tribute at an altar, a certain future of 67.22.93 jiāng 將
  tapping lightly with a tutoring cane a fur
  coat, saving by forbidding 67.22.94 jiù 救
  what it has, stepping on from this
  footprint…   67.22.95 zhī 之

this is cultivating, like a plow, 67.23.96 yǐ 以
benevolent as a mother, two loops of string-dyed-
black over the heart…   67.23.97 cí 慈
  guarding like with footsteps around an
  enclosure at a public at the crossroads 67.23.98 wèi 衛
  what it has, stepping on from this
  footprint.   67.23.99 zhī 之

Those practices I had adopted the first time around,
especially being benevolent as a mother, left me as
someone who could withstand anything, be
victorious, and do whatever it took for
safeguarding my little ones.

Chapter 68: How to get to that ultimate end (it's not angry warfare but rather the Dé)

The traditionally virtuous, offering up a ram's head
while speaking back and forth, tongues waggling,   68.1.1   shàn   善
creating something by hand, carving an elephant
likeness of good fortune and royal power,   68.1.2   wéi   為
as an ax-wielding bachelor-soldier-scholar-official
appointed by the emperor   68.1.3   shì   士
—this is boiling sugarcane with fire as follows!—   68.1.4   zhâ   者
    is the husk of the initial protective bud
    casing but not really the true flower of   68.1.5   bù   不
    setting out by foot with spear as one for a
    long journey like the military.   68.1.6   wǔ   武

The traditionally virtuous, offering up a ram's head
while speaking back and forth, tongues waggling,   68.2.7   shàn   善
battling, using a net for catching animals against a
weapon on a pole   68.2.8   zhàn   戰
—this is boiling sugarcane with fire as follows!—   68.2.9   zhâ   者
    is the husk of the initial protective bud
    casing but not really the true flower of   68.2.10   bù   不
    angry like the heart beneath a hand
    capturing a woman to be a slave.   68.2.11   nù   怒

The traditionally virtuous, offering up a ram's head
while speaking back and forth, tongues waggling,   68.3.12   shàn   善
able to withstand entirely, to be victorious as a
splendid piece of jewelry, an omen or the royal
'We' mending something on a boat with two hands
by the strength of an arm, bladed tool, or a plow,   68.3.13   shèng   勝
hostilely resisting the enemy (tapping lightly with a
tutoring cane the mere speaking of "God of   68.3.14   dí   敵

Heaven" as we call our emperors, for they're like
flower sepals connecting to above with that
traditional gendered head-cloth, the one we wrap
around our hair once we receive our public
courtesy names)
—this is boiling sugarcane with fire as follows!—   68.3.15   zhâ   者
        is the husk of the initial protective bud
        casing but not really the true flower of   68.3.16   bù   不
        participating (a "biting tooth" lifted by a
        pair of hands onto strong shoulders,
        perhaps interfering with or perhaps
        supporting).   68.3.17   yǔ   與

The traditionally virtuous, offering up a ram's head
while speaking back and forth, tongues waggling,   68.4.18   shàn   善
doing truly useful work like a water bucket, by
means of carrying-capacity,   68.4.19   yòng   用
that person   68.4.20   rén   人
—this is boiling sugarcane with fire as follows!—   68.4.21   zhâ   者
        is creating something by hand, carving an
        elephant likeness of good fortune and
        royal power,   68.4.22   wéi   為
        what it has, stepping on from this
        footprint,   68.4.23   zhī   之
        now here down below.   68.4.24   xià   下

This baby footprint on bamboo-slip pages,   68.5.25   shì   是
by the nitty-gritty, grinding gizzard of a fowl, what
that's called,   68.5.26   wèi   謂
the husk of the initial protective bud casing but not
really the true flower of   68.5.27   bù   不
competing, two hands clawing over a plowshare,   68.5.28   zhēng   爭
what it has, stepping on from this footprint: 68.5.29   zhī   之

walking with the footprint of someone
who's in alignment (eyes looking forward,
directly over the heart, left leg slowly
leading the way).   68.5.30   dé   德

This baby footprint on bamboo-slip pages,   68.6.31   shì   是
by the nitty-gritty, grinding gizzard of a fowl, what
that's called,   68.6.32   wèi   謂
doing truly useful work like a water bucket, by
means of carrying-capacity,   68.6.33   yòng 用
that person,   68.6.34   rén   人
what it has, stepping on from this footprint: 68.6.35   zhī   之
    forceful as with the strength of an arm, a
    bladed tool, or a plow.   68.6.36   lì   力

This baby footprint on bamboo-slip pages,   68.7.37   shì   是
by the nitty-gritty, grinding gizzard of a fowl, what
that's called,   68.7.38   wèi   謂
matching with the right mix (kneeling by an alcohol
vat to allocate, arrange, and prepare, like you
would a compounded prescription or the perfect
dish to go with rice)   68.7.39   pèi   配
the heavenly, from high above this great big
person,   68.7.40   tiān 天

speaking of the solid shield of the *past,*   68.8.41   gǔ   古
what it has, stepping on from this footprint: 68.8.42   zhī   之
    being in the utmost position, a person
    pressing urgently against a double-beamed
    wooden ridgepole that's high as a tree.   68.8.43   jí   極

***Chapter 69: But still, even pregnant, it was hard
for me to avoid war, speaking out, or any of the
other things I was used to doing.***

Doing truly useful work like a water bucket, by
means of carrying-capacity,   69.1.1   yòng   用
    carrying a short ax with two hands like a
    soldier or pawn,   69.1.2   bīng   兵
    flesh-and-meat-handling Being   69.1.3   yǒu   有
    speaking out loud: 69.1.4   yán   言

counting up on all five fingers, aren't I: 69.2.5   wú   吾
the husk of the initial protective bud casing but not
really the true flower of   69.2.6   bù   不
venturing to be bold, even a little bit and ultra-
politely hunting a boar as pleasantly as if you had
something sweet in your mouth   69.2.7   gǎn   敢
creating something by hand, carving an elephant
likeness of good fortune and royal power,   69.2.8   wéi   為
as you, "oh, honored senior official master,"
owner, and host of the flame,   69.2.9   zhǔ   主

    yet now, bearded, you're   69.3.10   ér   而
    creating something by hand, carving an
    elephant likeness of good fortune and
    royal power,   69.3.11   wéi   為
    entering a house as a *guest* like you're the
    last one, sticking out like the knot at the
    end of a cord;   69.3.12   kè   客

the husk of the initial protective bud casing but not really the true flower of	69.4.13	bù	不
venturing to be bold, even a little bit and ultra-politely hunting a boar as pleasantly as if you had something sweet in your mouth	69.4.14	gǎn	敢
walking slowly *forward* on the footprint of a "short-tailed bird," the left leg leading the way	69.4.15	jìn	進
one short inch (that spot on the forearm where the pulse beats strong).	69.4.16	cùn	寸
yet now, bearded, you're	69.5.17	ér	而
withdrawing, walking with the footprint of a person slowly retreating from the table after eating, like the ending of a thread in a knot, their eye looking backward, the left leg leading the way,	69.5.18	tuì	退
one foot (measured with a bent person)?	69.5.19	chǐ	尺
This baby footprint on bamboo-slip pages, by the nitty-gritty, grinding gizzard of a fowl, what that's called:	69.6.20 / 69.6.21	shì / wèi	是 / 謂
out in public at the crossroads, being good, doing one's work...	69.6.22	xíng	行
the shamanic dancer with animal tails flowing from her wrists, Not-Having,	69.6.23	wú	無
out in public at the crossroads, being good, doing one's work:	69.6.24	xíng	行
one's hand is rolling up a sleeve, helping to undress...	69.7.25	rǎng	攘
the shaman-dancing Not-Having	69.7.26	wú	無
arm, like the meat of a ruler or dead husband who administered and punished,	69.7.27	bì	臂

marking a kneeling slave or criminal with a
chisel;

a hand unexpectedly throwing away what it holds...	69.8.28	réng	扔
shaman-dancing Not-Having	69.8.29	wú	無
hostilely resisting the enemy (tapping			
lightly with a tutoring cane the mere			
speaking of "God of Heaven" as we call our			
emperors, for they're like flower sepals			
connecting to above with that traditional			
gendered head-cloth, the one we wrap			
around our hair once we receive our public			
courtesy names);	69.8.30	dí	敵

a kneeling person, arrested and held, arms			
outstretched in handcuffs...	69.9.31	zhí	執
shaman-dancing Not-Having,	69.9.32	wú	無
carrying a short ax with two hands like a			
soldier or pawn.	69.9.33	bīng	兵

Disaster like the slanting mouth of a skull on a			
sacrifice altar!	69.10.34	huò	禍
Like the sun sinking down in four bushes, one must			
not be—cannot be, eh?—	69.10.35	mò	莫
this great big person	69.10.36	dà	大
in this place and time, oh, black, icy raven sun:	69.10.37	yú	於
a lightweight, like a light carriage, portable,			
running through the whole like a			
lengthwise warp thread of something			
woven (like menses, like a classic text)	69.10.38	qīng	輕
hostilely resisting the enemy (tapping			
lightly with a tutoring cane the mere			
speaking of "God of Heaven" as we call our			

emperors, for they're like flower sepals
connecting to above with that traditional
gendered head-cloth (the one we wrap
around our hair once we receive our public
courtesy names).   69.10.39   dí   敵

A lightweight, like a light carriage, portable,
running through the whole like a lengthwise warp
thread of something woven (like menses, like a
classic text)   69.11.40   qīng   輕
hostilely resisting the enemy (tapping lightly with a
tutoring cane the mere speaking of "God of
Heaven" as we call our emperors, for they're like
flower sepals connecting to above with that
traditional gendered head-cloth, the one we wrap
around our hair once we receive our public
courtesy names)   69.11.41   dí   敵
is like two little silk threads separated by the sword
of a garrison guard, so, so near   69.11.42   jǐ   幾
many mouths clamoring on a mulberry tree,
grieving the dead: 69.11.43   sāng   喪
    counting up on all five fingers, aren't I,   69.11.44   wú   吾
    those treasures like a house containing
    cowry-riches, jade, and a lidded pot?   69.11.45   bǎo   寶

Remember the three treasures from Chapter 67?

This taps lightly with a tutoring cane and leaves a
mark on the solid shield of the past: 69.12.46   gù   故
opposing, raising resistance, lifting a hand to some
high, arrogant extreme like a neck or the ridge of a
roof   69.12.47   kàng   抗

and carrying a short ax with two hands like a
soldier or pawn,   69.12.48   bīng   兵
     like a seen tree and the eye seeing it (or
     like a well-tended lord and his attentive
     attendant), when taken together, create
     this singular phenomenon...   69.12.49   xiāng   相
     piling on more with strenuous effort,
     puffing with a plow or arm.   69.12.50   jiā   加

Lamenting from the chest, under one's roof?   69.13.51   āi   哀
This is boiling sugarcane with fire as follows!   69.13.52   zhâ   者
     Able to withstand entirely, to be victorious
     as a splendid piece of jewelry, an omen or
     the royal 'We' mending something on a
     boat with two hands by the strength of an
     arm, bladed tool, or a plow   69.13.53   shèng   勝
     —I swear, an arrow revolving around
     oneself, that's it!   69.13.54   yǐ   矣

*Opposing this system and fighting its war were
exhausting. Winning was sorrow. Sorrow was
winning.*

Chapter 70: This wasn't the time for speaking out
in public.

Counting up on all five fingers, aren't I,   70.1.1   wú   吾
speaking out loud...   70.1.2   yán   言
pairing (like one-half of a double-yoked harness as
pleasant as something sweet in the mouth) and
therefore extra   70.1.3   shèn   甚

easily changeable (like switching from saying
"don't," serious as three drops of blood on a blade,
to shining like the sun) to   70.1.4   yì   易
        speaking as a great big person to a baby,
        distinguishing, imparting, and
        administering wisdom confidently and
        intimately;   70.1.5   zhī   知

pairing (like one-half of a double-yoked harness as
pleasant as something sweet in the mouth) and
therefore extra   70.2.6   shèn   甚
easily changeable (like switching from saying
"don't," serious as three drops of blood on a blade,
to shining like the sun) to   70.2.7   yì   易
        being out in public at the crossroads, being
        good, doing one's work?   70.2.8   xíng   行

With the heavenly from high above this great big
person   70.3.9   tiān   天
now here down below: 70.3.10   xià   下
like the sun sinking down in four bushes, one must
not be—cannot be, eh?—   70.3.11   mò   莫
using that legendary Hybrid Power of a mythical
bear-like animal who has the legs of a deer for   70.3.12   néng   能
        speaking as a great big person to a baby,
        distinguishing, imparting, and
        administering wisdom confidently and
        intimately;   70.3.13   zhī   知

like the sun sinking down in four bushes, one must
not be—cannot be, eh?—   70.4.14   mò   莫
using that legendary Hybrid Power of a mythical
bear-like animal who has the legs of a deer for   70.4.15   néng   能

being out in public at the crossroads, being
good, doing one's work.   70.4.16   xíng   行

Speaking up, in my situation, easily ended up with
me speaking as a sage, out in public doing good.
And that was NOT what I should have been doing
at this stage.

Talking out loud,   70.5.17   yán   言
      is the flesh-and-meat-handling Being   70.5.18   yǒu   有
      ancestral temple;   70.5.19   zōng   宗

their task, what they do with a weapon, flag, or
pen in hand,   70.6.20   shì   事
      is the flesh-and-meat-handling Being   70.6.21   yǒu   有
      lord prince, his hand holding a rod over a
      mouth.   70.6.22   jūn   君

In fact, that is to say This Grown Man with hairpin
and public courtesy name,   70.7.23   fū   夫
"Oh, YES, Ma'am," says the "short-tailed bird,"   70.7.24   wéi   唯
the shamanic dancer with animal tails flowing from
her wrists, Not-Having,   70.7.25   wú   無
speaking as a great big person to a baby,
distinguishing, imparting, and administering
wisdom confidently and intimately...   70.7.26   zhī   知

      this baby footprint on bamboo-slip pages,   70.8.27   shì   是
      this is cultivating, like a plow,   70.8.28   yǐ   以
      I, holding a rake-like weapon to defend
      myself and my opinion,   70.8.29   wǒ   我
      am the husk of the initial protective bud
      casing but not really the true flower of   70.8.30   bù   不

speaking as a great big person to a baby,
distinguishing, imparting, and
administering wisdom confidently and
intimately.   70.8.31   zhī   知

Speaking as a great big person to a baby,
distinguishing, imparting, and administering
wisdom confidently and intimately,   70.9.32   zhī   知
I, holding a rake-like weapon to defend myself and
my opinion   70.9.33   wǒ   我
—this is boiling sugarcane with fire as follows!—   70.9.34   zhâ   者
am "barely there," as sparse as the few
interconnecting threads in the gendered head-
cloth we wear after reaching adulthood, rarely
seen or heard...   70.9.35   xī   希

    after following this sacrificial blade-and-
    cauldron-like ritual regulation,   70.10.36   zé   則
    I, holding a rake-like weapon to defend
    myself and my opinion   70.10.37   wǒ   我
    —this is boiling sugarcane with fire as
    follows!—   70.10.38   zhâ   者
    am held in high regard, like when two
    hands are wrapped around a person atop
    cowry-shell-riches.   70.10.39   guì   貴

This baby footprint on bamboo-slip pages,   70.11.40   shì   是
this is cultivating, like a plow,   70.11.41   yǐ   以
an ideal grounded sage known for his civilian
petition to authority, standing straight, speaking,
and being listened to,   70.11.42   shèng 聖
that person   70.11.43   rén   人

would be wearing (like a robe or the placental
afterbirth hanging from a recently pregnant
woman made of fur stripped by hand from its pelt)
dull brown like coarse clothing, placental afterbirth
hanging from a recently pregnant woman, or a
robe on the torso used to bundle up and hide

and carrying deep in one's bosom, affectionately
concealed in one's heart by clothing like a webbed
net over a river,
a pure jade totem.

The less I spoke or looked like a boss or important,
the higher my reputation.

Chapter 71: If I didn't publicly speak when sick, I could pass as a wise sage who doesn't get sick.

Speaking as a great big person to a baby,
distinguishing, imparting, and administering
wisdom confidently and intimately
    but the husk of the initial protective bud
    casing *and not really* the true flower of
    speaking as a great big person to a baby,
    distinguishing, imparting, and
    administering wisdom confidently and
    intimately
    on top:

70.11.44	bèi	被
70.11.45	hè	褐
70.12.46	huái	懷
70.12.47	yù	玉
71.1.1	zhī	知
71.1.2	bù	不
71.1.3	zhī	知
71.1.4	shàng	上

the husk of the initial protective bud casing
but *not really* the true flower of   71.2.5   bù   不
speaking as a great big person to a baby,
distinguishing, imparting, and
administering wisdom confidently and
intimately   71.2.6   zhī   知

    is speaking as a great big person to
    a baby, distinguishing, imparting,
    and administering wisdom
    confidently and intimately,   71.2.7   zhī   知
    while ill as one carried on a
    stretcher.   71.2.8   bìng   病

In fact, that is to say if This Grown Man with
hairpin and public courtesy name,   71.3.9   fū   夫
"Oh, YES, Ma'am," says the "short-tailed bird,"   71.3.10   wéi   唯
    is "*ill*   71.3.11   bìng   病
    ill…"   71.3.12   bìng   病

    this baby footprint on bamboo-slip pages,   71.4.13   shì   是
    this is cultivating, like a plow,   71.4.14   yǐ   以
    "the husk of the initial protective bud
    casing but not really the true flower of   71.4.15   bù   不
    ill."   71.4.16   bìng   病

I had to try to look not-sick because…

An ideal grounded sage known for his civilian
petition to authority, standing straight, speaking,
and being listened to,   71.5.17   shèng   聖
that person,   71.5.18   rén   人

would be the husk of the initial protective
bud casing but not really the true flower of   71.5.19   bù   不
ill.   71.5.20   bìng   病

And so I made sure that when I was really sick-sick,
I didn't look sick:

    This is cultivating, like a plow,   71.6.21   yǐ   以
    what it holds a basket of...   71.6.22   qí   其
        "ill   71.6.23   bìng   病
        ill..."   71.6.24   bìng   病

    this baby footprint on bamboo-slip pages,   71.7.25   shì   是
    this is cultivating, like a plow,   71.7.26   yǐ   以
    "the husk of the initial protective bud
    casing but not really the true flower of   71.7.27   bù   不
    ill."   71.7.28   bìng   病

Chapter 72: If I could be unafraid of domination
and be satisfied, then I could arrive at the end
sprouting a little bud—wise and loving but not
famously well regarded.

If one of our folk, the people enslaved by blinding
with a dagger,   72.1.1   mín   民
is the husk of the initial protective bud casing but
not really the true flower of   72.1.2   bù   不
scared—like of a ghost with a stick—of   72.1.3   wèi   畏
an axe held with power and pomp over a kneeling
woman,   72.1.4   wēi   威

after following this sacrificial blade-and-cauldron-
like ritual regulation,   72.2.5   zé   則
this great big person,   72.2.6   dà   大
an axe held with power and pomp over a kneeling
woman,   72.2.7   wēi   威
    is arriving at the end, the extreme climax,
    like an arrow straight into the clay soil.   72.2.8   zhì   至

The shamanic dancer with animal tails flowing from
her wrists, Not-Having,   72.3.9   wú   無
behaving intimately (maybe disrespectfully,
teasingly, or improperly so, like a dog with a turtle
shell)...   72.3.10   xiá   狎
    what it holds a basket of   72.3.11   qí   其
    is "that place" being intentionally created
    like any household gate hewn with an axe   72.3.12   suǒ   所
        staying put here, sitting over the
        solid shield of the past at this
        birthplace;   72.3.13   jū   居

shaman-dancing Not-Having   72.4.14   wú   無
sated like a dog with meat in its mouth, fed up...   72.4.15   yàn   厭
    what it holds a basket of   72.4.16   qí   其
    is "that place" being intentionally created
    like any household gate hewn with an axe   72.4.17   suǒ   所
        sprouting a bud from the ground.   72.4.18   shēng   生

In fact, that is to say if This Grown Man with
hairpin and public courtesy name,   72.5.19   fū   夫
"Oh, YES, Ma'am," says the "short-tailed bird,"   72.5.20   wéi   唯
    is the husk of the initial protective bud
    casing but not really the true flower of   72.5.21   bù   不

sated like a dog with meat in its mouth, fed
up...   72.5.22   yàn   厭

then this baby footprint on bamboo-slip pages,   72.6.23   shì   是
this is cultivating, like a plow,   72.6.24   yǐ   以
        the husk of the initial protective bud casing
        but not really the true flower of   72.6.25   bù   不
        sated like a dog with meat in its mouth, fed
        up.   72.6.26   yàn   厭

This baby footprint on bamboo-slip pages,   72.7.27   shì   是
this is cultivating, like a plow,   72.7.28   yǐ   以
an ideal grounded sage known for his civilian
petition to authority, standing straight, speaking,
and being listened to,   72.7.29   shèng   聖
that person: 72.7.30   rén   人
would be as themself personally, right on the nose,   72.7.31   zì   自
speaking as a great big person to a baby,
distinguishing, imparting, and administering
wisdom confidently and intimately,   72.7.32   zhī   知

        and the husk of the initial protective bud
        casing but not really the true flower of   72.8.33   bù   不
        as themself personally, right on the nose,   72.8.34   zì   自
        being seen by someone with one big eye
        for a head;   72.8.35   jiàn   見

would be as themself personally, right on the nose,   72.9.36   zì   自
loving, kneeling with your head turned this way
and your heart in your throat,   72.9.37   ài   愛

and the husk of the initial protective bud
casing but not really the true flower of
as themself personally, right on the nose,
being held in high regard, like when two
hands are wrapped around a person atop
cowry-shell-riches.

	72.10.38	bù	不
	72.10.39	zì	自
	72.10.40	guì	貴

This taps lightly with a tutoring cane and leaves a
mark on the solid shield of the past:
leave (like a person with a cave mouth between
their legs)
that—that fur stripped by hand from its pelt on the
road where they stepped slowly, the left leg
leading the way—
and get hold of, grab the ear of, "marry"
this here—the foot stops a person here on this
footprint!

	72.11.41	gù	故
	72.11.42	qù	去
	72.11.43	bǐ	彼
	72.11.44	qù	取
	72.11.45	cǐ	此

Chapter 73: Be brave, but don't be a bold hunter— not even a sweet one.

Like the handle of a bell, being courageous and
sturdy as a soldier, strong as an arm, bladed tool,
or plow
in this place and time, oh, black, icy raven sun,
venturing to be bold, even a little bit and ultra-
politely hunting a boar as pleasantly as if you had
something sweet in your mouth...
    after following this sacrificial blade-and-
    cauldron-like ritual regulation,
    it's killing, like impaling a boar by hand;

	73.1.1	yǒng	勇
	73.1.2	yú	於
	73.1.3	gǎn	敢
	73.1.4	zé	則
	73.1.5	shā	殺

like the handle of a bell, being courageous and
sturdy as a soldier, strong as an arm, bladed tool,
or a plow   73.2.6   yǒng   勇
in this place and time, oh, black, icy raven sun,   73.2.7   yú   於
the husk of the initial protective bud casing but not
really the true flower of   73.2.8   bù   不
venturing to be bold, even a little bit and ultra-
politely hunting a boar as pleasantly as if you had
something sweet in your mouth...   73.2.9   gǎn   敢
       after following this sacrificial blade-and-
       cauldron-like ritual regulation,   73.2.10   zé   則
       it's really living, like a tongue or bell-
       clapper licking the river water.   73.2.11   huó   活

This here—the foot stops a person here on this
footprint!—   73.3.12   cǐ   此
these two, this pair of traditional, adult, gendered
head-cloths covered by "The One"   73.3.13   liǎng   兩
—this is boiling sugarcane with fire as follows!   73.3.14   zhâ   者
in *this* particular enclave that's defended by a
weapon on a pole   73.3.15   huò   或
       reap benefits (in the manner of a sharp-
       edged blade slicing grain),   73.3.16   lì   利
and in *this* particular enclave that's defended by a
weapon on a pole   73.3.17   huò   或
       are harmed as a house in which weeds
       sprout from a mouth.   73.3.18   hài   害

       The heavenly from high above this great
       big person,   73.4.19   tiān   天
       what it has, stepping on from this
       footprint, it has this   73.4.20   zhī   之

"place" being intentionally created like any
household gate hewn with an axe — 73.4.21 · suǒ · 所
like a tomb built over the heart. — 73.4.22 · wù · 惡

Whichever kneeling person using both arms for
paying tribute to an ancestral shrine is fully
processing — 73.5.23 · shú · 孰
speaking as a great big person to a baby,
distinguishing, imparting, and administering
wisdom confidently and intimately, — 73.5.24 · zhī · 知
    what it holds a basket of... — 73.5.25 · qí · 其
    this taps lightly with a tutoring cane and
    leaves a mark on the solid shield of the
    past... — 73.5.26 · gù · 故

this baby footprint on bamboo-slip pages, — 73.6.27 · shì · 是
this is cultivating, like a plow, — 73.6.28 · yǐ · 以
an ideal grounded sage known for his civilian
petition to authority, standing straight, speaking,
and being listened to, — 73.6.29 · shèng · 聖
that person — 73.6.30 · rén · 人
would be, in the same manner as the unlikely rise
of a dog monkey to the top of the alcohol vat to
become chief of brewing, like — 73.6.31 · yóu · 猶
    solid (like that hard yellow earth with two
    little grass tufts next to River Han, where
    "short-tailed birds" find no food), — 73.6.32 · nán · 難
    what it has, stepping on from this
    footprint, it has this. — 73.6.33 · zhī · 之

What I should have been doing as the head buck
with a little one vs. what I was doing as I acted the

*part of the bearded virtuous person were two very
different things:*

The heavenly,
*what it has, stepping on from this footprint, it has
this*
*walking with the footprint of the loose-haired head
buck:*
the husk of the initial protective bud casing but not
really the true flower of
competing, two hands clawing over a plowshare,
> yet now bearded, you're
> the traditionally virtuous, offering up a
> ram's head while speaking back and forth,
> tongues waggling,
> able to withstand entirely, to be victorious
> as a splendid piece of jewelry, an omen or
> the royal 'We' mending something on a
> boat with two hands by the strength of an
> arm, bladed tool, or a plow;

the husk of the initial protective bud casing but not
really the true flower of
speaking out loud,
> yet now bearded, you're
> the traditionally virtuous, offering up a
> ram's head while speaking back and forth,
> tongues waggling,
> agreeably echoing an answer like a heart in
> a habitable cliff cave with a bird of prey, a
> bird with a dangling tail together with a
> small-tailed bird;

73.7.34	tiān	天
73.7.35	zhī	之
73.7.36	dào	道
73.7.37	bù	不
73.7.38	zhēng	爭
73.7.39	ér	而
73.7.40	shàn	善
73.7.41	shèng	勝
73.8.42	bù	不
73.8.43	yán	言
73.8.44	ér	而
73.8.45	shàn	善
73.8.46	yīng	應

the husk of the initial protective bud casing but not
really the true flower of
convening when an imperial summons calls
everyone together like a blade out of a mouth,
       yet now bearded, you're
       yourself personally, right on the nose,
       coming like a stalk of wheat;

easy-going as a solitary individual who uses a net of
loose silk with weights to catch animals
accomplishing this thus, as naturally as dog meat
over a fire,
       yet now bearded, you're
       the traditionally virtuous, offering up a
       ram's head while speaking back and forth,
       tongues waggling,
       plotting a scheme, like speaking with a
       certain humble so-and-so sweet-in-the-
       mouth plum tree.

       So there I was, being a tough guy, agreeing
       with the predators, coming when called,
       and scheming.

The heavenly
thin silk webbing
is vast as an expanded heart restored from ashes,
from fire that can be touched by hand...
vast as an expanded heart restored from ashes,
from fire that can be touched by hand
and thinned, obstructions cleared—fully enough,
like a complete leg and foot, an upside-down baby,

73.9.47	bù	不
73.9.48	zhāo	召
73.9.49	ér	而
73.9.50	zì	自
73.9.51	lái	來
73.10.52	chǎn	繟
73.10.53	rán	然
73.10.54	ér	而
73.10.55	shàn	善
73.10.56	móu	謀
73.11.57	tiān	天
73.11.58	wǎng	網
73.11.59	huī	恢
73.11.60	huī	恢
73.12.61	shū	疏

upside down with amniotic fluid streaming
below—

        yet now bearded, you're   73.12.62   ér   而
        the husk of the initial protective bud casing
        but not really the true flower of   73.12.63   bù   不
        dropped from a hand.   73.12.64   shī   失

        I kept hanging on even though delivery was
        very close.

**Chapter 74: As I learned, if you cultivate fear of
death, no matter how cunning you are, you
yourself creep up on killing people.**

If one of our folk, the people enslaved by blinding
with a dagger,   74.1.1   mín   民
        is the husk of the initial protective bud
        casing but not really the true flower of 74.1.2   bù   不
        scared—like of a ghost with a stick—of 74.1.3   wèi   畏
        dying, a person turning to a pile of bones: 74.1.4   sǐ   死

how, how, indeed is he bearing it, this great big
person on an altar,   74.2.5   nài   奈
that one, that very one shouldering a weapon, 74.2.6   hé   何
cultivating, like a plow,   74.2.7   yǐ   以
dying, a person turning to a pile of bones,   74.2.8   sǐ   死
        frightened (like the heart of two panicked
        eyes over "a short-tailed bird") of   74.2.9   jù   懼
        what it has, stepping on from this
        footprint?!   74.2.10   zhī   之

A Certain Someone compliantly combing her loose			
hair seems to be saying this is as if	74.3.11	ruò	若
that low-ranking government official, his hand			
holding a pen, sent as a messenger or an envoy, is			
putting to work, using in every way you can think			
of, directing,	74.3.12	shǐ	使
one of our folk, the people enslaved by blinding			
with a dagger,	74.3.13	mín	民
a conventional royal administrator wearing a men's			
headcloth as his skirt,	74.3.14	cháng	常
is scared—like of a ghost with a stick—of	74.3.15	wèi	畏
dying, a person turning to a pile of bones,	74.3.16	sǐ	死
yet now, bearded, you're	74.4.17	ér	而
"creating something by hand, carving an			
elephant likeness of good fortune and			
royal power,	74.4.18	wéi	為
and remarkably cunning like this great big			
person atop that very one shouldering a			
weapon that tastes lip-smackingly			
genuinely like the one."	74.4.19	qí	奇
This is boiling sugarcane with fire as			
follows!	74.4.20	zhâ	者

*You remember me referring to this same
cunning back in Chapters 57 and 59.*

Counting up on all five fingers, aren't I	74.5.21	wú	吾
The Hand-Picked Gem, like cowry-shell-riches			
discovered along the road,	74.5.22	dé	得
a kneeling person, arrested and held, arms			
outstretched in handcuffs,	74.5.23	zhí	執
yet now, bearded, you're	74.5.24	ér	而

killing, like impaling a boar by hand,
what it has, stepping on from this
footprint?

74.5.25   shā   殺

74.5.26   zhī   之

Which kneeling person using both arms for
paying tribute to an ancestral shrine is fully
processing

74.6.27   shú   孰

venturing to be bold, even a little bit and
ultra-politely hunting a boar as pleasantly
as if you had something sweet in your
mouth?

74.6.28   gǎn   敢

*I once was the arrested one, and then I
became the killer?! Who could do that?*

The conventional royal administrator wearing a
men's headcloth as his skirt,

74.7.29   cháng   常

flesh-and-meat-handling Being,

74.7.30   yǒu   有

    a reversed royal speaker like a queen or
    king

74.7.31   sī   司

    killing, like impaling a boar by hand?

74.7.32   shā   殺

    This is boiling sugarcane with fire as
    follows!

74.7.33   zhâ   者

        Killing, like impaling a boar by
        hand!

74.7.34   shā   殺

In fact, that is to say This Grown Man with hairpin
and public courtesy name

74.8.35   fū   夫

    taking the place of (like a person with a
    retrievable arrow attached to a string or an
    era or a dynasty lineage)

74.8.36   dài   代

    a reversed royal speaker like a queen or
    king

74.8.37   sī   司

killing, like impaling a boar by hand?
This is boiling sugarcane with fire as
follows!— 74.8.38 shā 殺
 74.8.39 zhâ 者
    Killing, like impaling a boar by
    hand! 74.8.40 shā 殺

This baby footprint on bamboo-slip pages, 74.9.41 shì 是
by the nitty-gritty, grinding gizzard of a fowl, what
that's called, 74.9.42 wèi 謂
    taking the place of, like a person with a
    retrievable arrow attached to a string or an
    era or a dynasty lineage, 74.9.43 dài 代
    this great big person, 74.9.44 dà 大
    a master craftsmen who builds a box with
    an ax, 74.9.45 jiàng 匠
    chopping like a keen axe cutting a stone
    flagon. 74.9.46 zhuō 斲

In fact, that is to say This Grown Man with hairpin
and public courtesy name 74.10.47 fū 夫
    taking the place of, like a person with a
    retrievable arrow attached to a string or an
    era or a dynasty lineage, 74.10.48 dài 代
    this great big person, 74.10.49 dà 大
    a master craftsmen who builds a box with
    axe, 74.10.50 jiàng 匠
    chopping like a keen axe cutting a stone
    flagon? 74.10.51 zhuō 斲
    This is boiling sugarcane with fire as
    follows! 74.10.52 zhâ 者

    Barely there, as sparse as the few
    interconnecting threads in the gendered 74.11.53 xī 希

head-cloth we wear after reaching
adulthood, rarely seen or heard
is flesh-and-meat-handling Being 74.11.54 yǒu 有
the husk of the initial protective bud casing
but not really the true flower of 74.11.55 bù 不
hurting (like someone in front of that male
principle of the sun shining on a sacrificial
altar) 74.11.56 shāng 傷
    what it holds a basket of, 74.11.57 qí 其
    their expert, convenient hand 74.11.58 shǒu 手
    —I swear, an arrow revolving
    around oneself, that's it! 74.11.59 yǐ 矣

Chances are, Being will end up hurting themselves.

Chapter 75: Why I had a hard time stepping away
from what felt like security

If one of our folk, the people enslaved by blinding
with a dagger, 75.1.1 mín 民
what it has, stepping on from this footprint, 75.1.2 zhī 之
is a time of famine, having a meal with one's
mouth over a bowl of rice on a stand carefully
watched over with the smallest things, two tiny silk
threads, under separate guard by a man with a
spear, by a garrison, 75.1.3 jī 饑

they're cultivating, like a plow, 75.2.4 yǐ 以
what it holds a basket of... 75.2.5 qí 其
on top 75.2.6 shàng 上
    eating, mouth over a bowl of rice on a
    stand, 75.2.7 shí 食

open mouthed like a smiling, breathy older
brother next to a rice plant, that is, taxing
what it has, stepping on from this
footprint,
having more, like two pieces of meat.

This baby footprint on bamboo-slip pages
is cultivating, like a plow,
a time of famine, having a meal with one's
mouth over a bowl of rice on a stand
carefully watched over with the smallest
things, two tiny silk threads, under
separate guard by a man with a spear, by a
garrison.

*If you're starving, you try to have more
food than you know what to do with! And
then you end up hungry.*

If one of our folk, the people enslaved by blinding
with a dagger,
what it has, stepping on from this footprint,
is solid (like that hard yellow earth with two little
grass tufts next to River Han, where "short-tailed
birds" find no food)
flowing the River Happy, speaking of gathering
oneself from three sides, managing,

they're cultivating, like a plow,
what it holds a basket of...
on top,
what it has, stepping on from this
footprint,

flesh-and-meat-handling Being   75.5.22   yǒu   有
creating something by hand, carving an
elephant likeness of good fortune and royal
power.   75.5.23   wéi   為

This baby footprint on bamboo-slip pages   75.6.24   shì   是
is cultivating, like a plow,   75.6.25   yǐ   以
solid   75.6.26   nán   難
flowing the River Happy, speaking of
gathering oneself from three sides,
managing.   75.6.27   zhì   治

If one of our folk, the people enslaved by blinding
with a dagger,   75.7.28   mín   民
what it has, stepping on from this footprint,   75.7.29   zhī   之
is a lightweight, like a light carriage, portable,
running through the whole like a lengthwise warp
thread of something woven (like menses, like a
classic text)   75.7.30   qīng   輕
dying, a person turning to a pile of bones,   75.7.31   sǐ   死

they're cultivating, like a plow,   75.8.32   yǐ   以
what it holds a basket of...   75.8.33   qí   其
looking for, *coveting* like a centipede,   75.8.34   qiú   求
sprouting a bud from the ground,   75.8.35   shēng   生
what it has, stepping on from this
footprint,   75.8.36   zhī   之
a jug in a habitable cave in a cliff, thick and
generous.   75.8.37   hòu   厚

This baby footprint on bamboo-slip pages   75.9.38   shì   是
is cultivating, like a plow,   75.9.39   yǐ   以
a lightweight   75.9.40   qīng   輕

dying, a person turning to a pile of bones.   75.9.41   sǐ   死

*If your pregnancy might end in death, you
try to have a beginning that's safe and
sound like a fat jug in a cozy cave! And
then you end up in a pregnancy that might
mean death.*

In fact, that is to say This Grown Man with hairpin
and public courtesy name,   75.10.42   fū   夫
"Oh, YES, Ma'am," says the "short-tailed bird,"   75.10.43   wéi   唯
the shamanic dancer with animal tails flowing from
her wrists, Not-Having,   75.10.44   wú   無
    cultivating, like a plow,   75.10.45   yǐ   以
    sprouting a bud from the ground,   75.10.46   shēng   生
    *creating something by hand, carving an
    elephant likeness of good fortune and royal
    power?*   75.10.47   wéi   為
This is boiling sugarcane with fire as
follows!   75.10.48   zhâ   者

    This baby footprint on bamboo-slip pages,   75.11.49   shì   是
    their eye cleverly, solidly, looking down
    from atop cowry-like riches,   75.11.50   xián   賢
    in this place and time, oh, black, icy raven
    sun,   75.11.51   yú   於
    *is held in high regard, like when two hands
    are wrapped around a person atop cowry-
    shell-riches*   75.11.52   guì   貴
    sprouting a bud from the ground.   75.11.53   shēng   生

*Despite the other plans we had hatched, it was
hard to step away from the status that felt like*

security even though it clearly hadn't worked to make me secure.

Chapter 76: Continuing on top as a soldier can work up to a point. But for that final stiffening phase, it's disaster. Then it's time not only to disappear but to do so down at the lower level I had planned for myself.

That person,

what it has stepping on from this footprint, it has this...

sprouting a bud from the ground

—yes, that too, oh "female funnel!"—
    softening to be as supple as a tree that can
    be cut with a spear
        in a delicate state with a pair of
        fragile bows,

what it holds a basket of...

dying, a person turning to a pile of bones

—yes, that too, oh "female funnel!"—
    hardening, drying and forming a crust, hard
    as the clay soil underneath a finger in an
    eye cast down in surrender,
        revolving around itself as a
        powerful bow broadening,
        strengthening, stiff, hard, and
        compelling as a rice weevil, like a
        tiny venomous snake—thwang!

Glosses:

76.1.1 rén 人
76.1.2 zhī 之
76.1.3 shēng 生
76.1.4 yâ 也
76.1.5 róu 柔
76.1.6 ruò 弱

76.2.7 qí 其
76.2.8 sǐ 死
76.2.9 yâ 也
76.2.10 jiān 堅
76.2.11 qiáng 強

The medicine-dancing-scorpion insect swarm of
matter outside one's body, "cut from the cow" by a
bloodied blade,

early (like a pair of grass sprouts that are
premature as sunrise above an acorn on the jujube,
that thorny plant that's used for insomnia and
contraception and causes midterm miscarriages)
tree branches and roots,
what it has stepping on from this footprint, it has
this…
sprouting a bud from the ground
—yes, that too, oh "female funnel!"—
    softening to be as supple as a tree that can
    be cut with a spear,
        fragile as crisp meat on a roof,
        precariously high above a kneeling
        person,

what it holds a basket of…
dying, a person turning to a pile of bones
—yes, that too, oh "female funnel!"—
    dried and withered, like an ancient tree of
    ten generations,
        meagre and withered like a tree
        high above (a two-story building in
        the city outskirts).

This taps lightly with a tutoring cane and leaves a
mark on the solid shield of the past:
"hardening, drying and forming a crust, hard as the
clay soil underneath a finger in an eye cast down in
surrender,

76.3.12	wàn	萬
76.3.13	wù	物
76.3.14	cǎo	草
76.3.15	mù	木
76.3.16	zhī	之
76.3.17	shēng	生
76.3.18	yâ	也
76.3.19	róu	柔
76.3.20	cuì	脆
76.4.21	qí	其
76.4.22	sǐ	死
76.4.23	yâ	也
76.4.24	kū	枯
76.4.25	gǎo	槁
76.5.26	gù	故
76.5.27	jiān	堅

revolving around itself as a powerful bow
broadening, strengthening, stiff, hard, and
compelling as a rice weevil, like a tiny venomous
snake—thwang?!"
This is boiling sugarcane with fire as follows!
    Dying, a person turning to a pile of bones,
    what it has stepping on from this footprint,
    it has this...
    walking with the footprint of merely *a foot
    soldier*, afoot on the clay soil.

"Softening to be as supple as a tree that can be cut
with a spear
in a delicate state with a pair of fragile bows?"
This is boiling sugarcane with fire as follows!
    Sprouting a bud from the ground,
    what it has stepping on from this footprint,
    it has this...
    walking with the footprint of merely a foot
    soldier, afoot on the clay soil.

This baby footprint on bamboo-slip pages,
this is cultivating, like a plow:
*carrying a short ax with two hands, like a soldier or
pawn,*
revolving around itself as a powerful bow
broadening, strengthening, stiff, hard, and
compelling as a rice weevil, like a tiny venomous
snake—thwang!—
    after following this sacrificial blade-and-
    cauldron-like ritual regulation
    is the husk of the initial protective bud
    casing but not really the true flower of

76.5.28	qiáng	強
76.5.29	zhâ	者
76.5.30	sǐ	死
76.5.31	zhī	之
76.5.32	tú	徒
76.6.33	róu	柔
76.6.34	ruò	弱
76.6.35	zhâ	者
76.6.36	shēng	生
76.6.37	zhī	之
76.6.38	tú	徒
76.7.39	shì	是
76.7.40	yǐ	以
76.7.41	bīng	兵
76.7.42	qiáng	強
76.7.43	zé	則
76.7.44	bù	不

able to withstand entirely, to be victorious
as a splendid piece of jewelry, an omen or
the royal 'We' mending something on a
boat with two hands by the strength of an
arm, bladed tool, or a plow;   76.7.45   shèng   勝

tree branches and roots   76.8.46   mù   木
revolving around themself as a powerful bow
broadening, strengthening, stiff, hard, and
compelling as a rice weevil, like a tiny venomous
snake—thwang!—   76.8.47   qiáng   強
    after following this sacrificial blade-and-
    cauldron-like ritual regulation   76.8.48   zé   則
    are breaking off, a tree cut in half with an
    axe.   76.8.49   zhé   折

Revolving around itself as a powerful bow
broadening, strengthening, stiff, hard, and
compelling as a rice weevil, like a tiny venomous
snake—thwang!—   76.9.50   qiáng   強
this great big person,   76.9.51   dà   大
    they're disappearing like a tiger head at
    home, footprint pointed back down by a
    table, staying here, chaste, rather than
    accepting a government position or getting
    married,   76.9.52   chù   處
    now here down below;   76.9.53   xià   下

softening to be as supple as a tree that can be cut
with a spear   76.10.54   róu   柔
in a delicate state with a pair of fragile bows,   76.10.55   ruò   弱
    they're disappearing like a tiger head at
    home, footprint pointed back down by a   76.10.56   chù   處

table, staying here, chaste, rather than
accepting a government position or getting
married,
on top.   76.10.57   shàng   上

Chapter 77: But I wondered if I could go back to being a wandering loose-haired head buck with my little one at my side...

The heavenly high above this great person,   77.1.1   tiān   天
what it has stepping on from this footprint   77.1.2   zhī   之
walking with the footprint of the loose-haired head
buck...   77.1.3   dào   道

what it holds a basket of,   77.2.4   qí   其
in the same manner as the unlikely rise of a dog
monkey to the top of the alcohol vat to become
chief of brewing, it's   77.2.5   yóu   猶
stretching out, lengthening like a bowstring,   77.2.6   zhāng   張
like a bow,   77.2.7   gōng   弓
when participating with someone, a "biting tooth"
lifted by two hands onto strong shoulders, perhaps
interfering with or perhaps supporting: 77.2.8   yǔ   與

    way up, as in a two-story building outside
    the city, high above what's faced with
    admiration and echoed in there   77.3.9   gāo   高
    —this is boiling sugarcane with fire as
    follows!—   77.3.10   zhâ   者
        it's suppressing like a hand pushing
        down on a kneeling person   77.3.11   yì   抑

what it has, stepping on from this
footprint, it has this;   77.3.12   zhī   之

now here down below   77.4.13   xià   下
—this is boiling sugarcane with fire as
follows!—   77.4.14   zhâ   者
    it's lifting up, supporting, offering
    to shoulder (above a fang)   77.4.15   jǔ   舉
    what it has stepping on from this
    footprint.   77.4.16   zhī   之

Flesh-and-meat-handling Being   77.5.17   yǒu   有
having leftover excess food remaining in
their house   77.5.18   yú   餘
—this is boiling sugarcane with fire as
follows!—   77.5.19   zhâ   者
    it's diminishing, like hands and
    fingers injured by the top edge of
    the three-legged cauldron that's
    like the great members of the
    monarchy government,   77.5.20   sǔn   損
    what it has stepping on from this
    footprint;   77.5.21   zhī   之

the husk of the initial protective bud casing
but not really the true flower of   77.6.22   bù   不
fully enough, like the whole leg as well as
the footprint   77.6.23   zú   足
—this is boiling sugarcane with fire as
follows!—   77.6.24   zhâ   者
    it's mending (like clothing such as a
    robe, especially that worn on the
    torso like the placental afterbirth   77.6.25   bǔ   補

            hanging from a recently pregnant
            woman, being fixed by the
            courtesy name of a man)
            what it has stepping on from this
            footprint.   77.6.26   zhī   之

The heavenly from high above this great big person   77.7.27   tiān   天
what it has stepping on from this footprint   77.7.28   zhī   之
walking with the footprint of the loose-haired head
buck: 77.7.29   dào   道
            It's diminishing, like hands and fingers
            injured by the top edge of the three-legged
            cauldron that's like the great members of
            the monarchy government,   77.7.30   sǔn   損
            flesh-and-meat-handling Being   77.7.31   yǒu   有
            having leftover excess food remains in
            their house;   77.7.32   yú   餘

yet, now you're bearded: 77.8.33   ér   而
            mending (like clothing such as a robe,
            especially that worn on the torso like the
            placental afterbirth hanging from a
            recently pregnant woman, being fixed by
            the courtesy name of a man)   77.8.34   bǔ   補
            that which is the husk of the initial
            protective bud casing but *not really* the
            true flower of   77.8.35   bù   不
            fully enough, like the whole leg as well as
            the footprint.   77.8.36   zú   足

And I also considered the idea of going out again
alone as the head buck. Alas, it would have the
opposite effect...

That person,
what it has stepping on from this footprint
walking with the footprint of the loose-haired head
buck,

    after following this sacrificial blade-and-
    cauldron-like ritual regulation, becomes
    the husk of the initial protective bud casing
    but not really the true flower of
    accomplishing this thus, as naturally as dog
    meat over a fire:

it's diminishing, like hands and fingers
injured by the top edge of the three-legged
cauldron that's like the great members of
the monarchy government,
that which is the husk of the initial
protective bud casing but not really the
true flower of
fully enough, like the whole leg as well as
the footprint,
    and cultivating, like a plow,
    offering a lush growth of plants
    with two hands to
    flesh-and-meat-handling Being
    when leftover excess food remains
    in their house.

And increasing Being's excess lifestyle doesn't seem
like a great choice. Unless…

77.9.37	rén	人
77.9.38	zhī	之
77.9.39	dào	道
77.9.40	zé	則
77.9.41	bù	不
77.9.42	rán	然
77.10.43	sǔn	損
77.10.44	bù	不
77.10.45	zú	足
77.10.46	yǐ	以
77.10.47	fèng	奉
77.10.48	yǒu	有
77.10.49	yú	餘

Which kneeling person using both arms for paying
tribute to an ancestral shrine is fully processing   77.11.50   shú   孰
using that legendary Hybrid Power of a mythical
bear-like animal who has the legs of a deer for   77.11.51   néng   能
flesh-and-meat-handling Being   77.11.52   yǒu   有
having leftover excess food remaining in their
house,   77.11.53   yú   餘
> cultivating, like a plow,   77.11.54   yǐ   以
> offering a lush growth of plants with two
> hands to   77.11.55   fèng   奉
> *the heavenly, from high above this great*
> *big person*   77.11.56   tiān   天
> *now here down below?*   77.11.57   xià   下

> *So, is there anyone who could use those*
> *Hybrid Powers in a way that Being's*
> *leftovers help the heavenly one?*

"Oh, YES, Ma'am," says the "short-tailed bird,"   77.12.58   wéi   唯
flesh-and-meat-handling Being,   77.12.59   yǒu   有
walking with the footprint of the loose-haired
head buck   77.12.60   dào   道
—this is boiling sugarcane with fire as follows!   77.12.61   zhâ   者

Back in Chapters 24, 31, and 46, the combination of
Being AND living like a free, wild-haired head buck,
absolutely was not a good idea. But now...

This baby footprint on bamboo-slip pages,   77.13.62   shì   是
this is cultivating, like a plow,   77.13.63   yǐ   以
an ideal grounded sage known for his civilian
petition to authority, standing straight, speaking,
and being listened to,   77.13.64   shèng   聖

that person   77.13.65   rén   人
would be creating something by hand, carving an
elephant likeness of good fortune and royal power,   77.13.66   wéi   為
         yet, now you're bearded,   77.13.67   ér   而
         the husk of the initial protective bud casing
         but not really the true flower of   77.13.68   bù   不
         a mother—the heart grabbed like by the
         hand of a government office or temple
         worker that was usually a eunuch in the
         old days;   77.13.69   shì   恃

would be laboring with the force of a blade and the
work of one's arm or a plow   77.14.70   gōng   功
completing, that final "nail" in a weapon on a pole, 77.14.71   chéng   成
         yet, now you're bearded,   77.14.72   ér   而
         "the husk of the initial protective bud
         casing but not really the true flower of   77.14.73   bù   不
         disappearing like a tiger head at home,
         footprint pointed back down by a table,
         staying here, chaste, rather than accepting
         a government position or getting married."   77.14.74   chù   處

*"Not really disappearing into the home" is exactly
how "Being walking with the footprint of the wild-
haired head buck" was described in 24.10 and 31.3.
Back then, that wasn't a good thing. But my
situation had changed, and this strategy became
more appealing.*

What it holds a basket of   77.15.75   qí   其
is the husk of the initial protective bud casing but
not really the true flower of   77.15.76   bù   不

missing, kneeling with a yawning mouth before a
ravine eroded between two mountains, wanting,
lacking,

and seen by someone with one big eye for a head,
their eye cleverly, solidly, looking down from atop
cowry-like riches.

*It would mean not being seen by the big boss man
as missing. And that's a god thing.*

Chapter 78: I couldn't stay there doing what I'd been doing. I needed a new, humbler kind of hybrid life.

The heavenly from high above this great big person
now here down below:
Like the sun sinking down in four bushes, one must
not be—*cannot be*, eh?—
"softening to be as supple as a tree that can be cut
with a spear
in a delicate state with a pair of fragile bows"
in this place and time, oh, black, icy raven sun:
    water flowing right in the center a river,
    spraying up on both sides...

    yet, now you're bearded,
        attacking, hitting lightly
          with a bladed tool,
"hardening, drying and forming a crust,
hard as the clay soil underneath a finger in
an eye cast down in surrender.

77.15.77	yù	欲
77.15.78	jiàn	見
77.15.79	xián	賢
78.1.1	tiān	天
78.1.2	xià	下
78.1.3	mò	莫
78.1.4	róu	柔
78.1.5	ruò	弱
78.1.6	yú	於
78.1.7	shuǐ	水
78.2.8	ér	而
78.2.9	gōng	攻
78.2.10	jiān	堅

while revolving around itself as a powerful
bow broadening, strengthening, stiff, hard,
and compelling as a rice weevil, like a tiny
venomous snake—thwang!"   78.2.11   qiáng   強
This is boiling sugarcane with fire as
follows!   78.2.12   zhâ   者

Like the sun sinking down in four bushes, one must
not be—*cannot be*, eh?—   78.3.13   mò   莫
what it has stepping on from this footprint,   78.3.14   zhī   之
using that legendary Hybrid Power of a mythical
bear-like animal who has the legs of a deer for 78.3.15   néng   能
    being able to withstand entirely, to be
    victorious as a splendid piece of jewelry, an
    omen or the royal 'We' mending
    something on a boat with two hands by the
    strength of an arm, bladed tool, or a plow.   78.3.16   shèng   勝

What it holds a basket of…   78.4.17   qí   其
the shamanic dancer with animal tails flowing from
her wrists, Not-Having,   78.4.18   wú   無
cultivating, like a plow,   78.4.19   yǐ   以
    being easily changeable as switching from
    saying "don't," serious as three drops of
    blood on a blade, to shining like the sun,   78.4.20   yì   易
    what it has, stepping on from this
    footprint…   78.4.21   zhī   之

    "in a delicate state with a pair of fragile
    bows,"   78.5.22   ruò   弱
    what it has, stepping on from this
    footprint,   78.5.23   zhī   之

is able to withstand entirely, to be victorious as a splendid piece of jewelry, an omen or the royal 'We' mending something on a boat with two hands by the strength of an arm, bladed tool, or a plow,

78.5.24   shèng   勝

"revolving around itself as a powerful bow broadening, strengthening, stiff, hard, and compelling as a rice weevil, like a tiny venomous snake—thwang;"

78.5.25   qiáng   強

"softening to be as supple as a tree that can be cut with a spear,

78.6.26   róu   柔

what it has, stepping on from this footprint,

78.6.27   zhī   之

is able to withstand entirely, to be victorious as a splendid piece of jewelry, an omen or the royal 'We' mending something on a boat with two hands by the strength of an arm, bladed tool, or a plow,

78.6.28   shèng   勝

the firm like a web of mountain within a net as strong as a blade."

78.6.29   gāng   剛

This sentiment was also in 36.10 when I described the advantages of the plan to become a marquis king.

The heavenly from high above this great big person   78.7.30   tiān   天
now here down below...   78.7.31   xià   下
like the sun sinking down in four bushes, one must not be—cannot be, eh?—   78.7.32   mò   莫

the husk of the initial protective bud casing
but not really the true flower of
speaking as a great big person to a baby,
distinguishing, imparting, and
administering wisdom confidently and
intimately;

like the sun sinking down in four bushes, one must
not be—cannot be, eh?—
using that legendary Hybrid Power of a
mythical bear-like animal who has the legs
of a deer for
out in public at the crossroads, being good,
doing one's work.

*Those two imperatives seem to be at odds. You
might ask: how can one both be a wise speaker and
not be out in public? Here's how...*

This baby footprint on bamboo-slip pages,
this is cultivating, like a plow,
an ideal grounded sage known for his civilian
petition to authority, standing straight, speaking,
and being listened to,
that person
would be saying like a cloud:

receiving and bearing (a hand over a commonplace
bucket with a hand below, on bottom),
in our domestic enclave, defended by a weapon on
a pole,
what it has, stepping on from this
footprint,

78.7.33	bù	不
78.7.34	zhī	知
78.8.35	mò	莫
78.8.36	néng	能
78.8.37	xíng	行
78.9.38	shì	是
78.9.39	yǐ	以
78.9.40	shèng	聖
78.9.41	rén	人
78.9.42	yún	云
78.10.43	shòu	受
78.10.44	guó	國
78.10.45	zhī	之

dirt, like the soil, the clay earth, the shame
of a ruler, especially an empress *hòu*, a
person giving birth to a successor,   78.10.46   gòu   垢

this baby footprint on bamboo-slip pages,   78.11.47   shì   是
by the nitty-gritty, grinding gizzard of a fowl, what
that's called,   78.11.48   wèi   謂
the god of the soil to whom we build altars,   78.11.49   shè   社
the god of plants,   78.11.50   jì   稷
        you, "oh, honored senior official master,"
        owner, and host of the flame;   78.11.51   zhǔ   主

receiving and bearing (a hand over a commonplace
bucket with a hand below, on bottom),   78.12.52   shòu   受
in our domestic enclave, defended by a weapon on
a pole,   78.12.53   guó   國
        the husk of the initial protective bud casing
        but not really the true flower of   78.12.54   bù   不
        a good omen like a ram's head at an altar...   78.12.55   xiáng   祥

this baby footprint on bamboo-slip pages,   78.13.56   shì   是
by the nitty-gritty, grinding gizzard of a fowl, what
that's called,   78.13.57   wèi   謂
the heavenly from high above this great big person   78.13.58   tiān   天
now here down below,   78.13.59   xià   下
        the king with his ceremonial jade axe or
        crown connecting the three levels of
        heaven, man, and earth.   78.13.60   wáng   王

*By accepting humbler circumstances, I could be
master and king.*

Straightening up, straightening things out for
"nailing" that first footstep of a journey,
speaking out loud:

> A Certain Someone compliantly combing
> her loose hair seems to be saying this is as
> if
> a different-sounding *"Fǎn,"* turning your
> palm over in a habitable cave in a cliff,
> reversing, returning, reflecting, maybe
> countering with the opposite.

Getting ready to leave, to return to my origins,
"Fǎn," in a way, but in a different.

Chapter 79: And so we set off to live fully and less famously ever after.

Harmonizing, like breath blown into a reed-pipe
mouth organ,

> with this great big person
> full of resentment (the heart under an
> animal lying down to die),

hands over heart, analytically,

> flesh-and-meat-handling Being,
> even having leftover excess food remains
> in their house,
> is full of resentment (the heart under an
> animal lying down to die).

And that's no way to live, as we've seen.

	78.14.61	zhèng	正
	78.14.62	yán	言
	78.14.63	ruò	若
	78.14.64	fǎn	反
	79.1.1	hé	和
	79.1.2	dà	大
	79.1.3	yuàn	怨
	79.2.4	bì	必
	79.2.5	yǒu	有
	79.2.6	yú	餘
	79.2.7	yuàn	怨

Staying calm as a woman sitting on her heels at
home,   79.3.8   ān   妄
lip-smackingly genuinely   79.3.9   kâ   可
cultivating, like a plow,   79.3.10   yǐ   以
    creating something by hand, carving an
    elephant likeness of good fortune and
    royal power,   79.3.11   wéi   為
    traditionally virtuous, offering up a ram's
    head while speaking back and forth,
    tongues waggling...   79.3.12   shàn   善

this baby footprint on bamboo-slip pages,   79.4.13   shì   是
this is cultivating, like a plow,   79.4.14   yǐ   以
an ideal grounded sage known for his civilian
petition to authority, standing straight, speaking,
and being listened to,   79.4.15   shèng   聖
that person,   79.4.16   rén   人
    would be a kneeling person arrested and
    held, arms outstretched in handcuffs,   79.4.17   zhí   執
    in an inferior aide position, doing left-
    handed work as with a bladed tool,   79.4.18   zuǒ   左
    engraving, writing, this great big person
    carving agreements or contracts like a
    blade cutting weeds,   79.4.19   qì   契

yet, now you're bearded,   79.5.20   ér   而
    the husk of the initial protective bud casing
    but not really the true flower of   79.5.21   bù   不
    poked as if by a tree with thorns over
    cowry-riches, interrogated, or ordered to
    do things   79.5.22   zé   責
    in this place and time, oh, black, icy raven
    sun,   79.5.23   yú   於

that person.   79.5.24   rén   人

The sage accomplishes this neat hat trick of being
*safely "inferior" enough to write as he likes _and_*
also not be jabbed or questioned too closely.
(Remember the discussion in Chapter 31 of how
much luckier it is to be in a lower position!) It looks
like this:

Flesh-and-meat-handling Being   79.6.25   yǒu   有
walking with the footprint of someone who's in
alignment (eyes looking forward, directly over the
heart, left leg slowly leading the way)   79.6.26   dé   德
    is a reversed royal speaker like a queen or
    king,   79.6.27   sī   司
        this great big person engraving, writing,
        carving agreements or contracts like a
        blade cutting weeds;   79.6.28   qì   契

the shamanic dancer with animal tails flowing from
her wrists, Not-Having,   79.7.29   wú   無
walking with the footprint of someone who's in
alignment (eyes looking forward, directly over the
heart, left leg slowly leading the way)   79.7.30   dé   德
    is a reversed royal speaker like a queen or
    king   79.7.31   sī   司
        walking slowly, the left leg leading the way,
        with the footprint of a woman giving birth
        to an inverted baby, lightly hit by a hand; 79.7.32   chè   徹

the heavenly from high above this great big person   79.8.33   tiān   天
walking with the footprint of the loose-haired head
buck   79.8.34   dào   道

is a shaman-dancing Not-Having
intimate one, a beloved whose suffering,
like from that chisel used to mark slaves
and criminals, you see up close with one
big eye for a head;

and the conventional royal administrator wearing a
men's headcloth as his skirt
participating, a "biting tooth" lifted by two hands
onto strong shoulders, perhaps interfering with or
perhaps supporting,
       is traditionally virtuous, offering up a ram's
       head while speaking back and forth,
       tongues waggling,
       that person.

*So that's how this royal administrator came to the
truly virtuous. It's been a great way to live.*

*Thank you for reading—for being open to seeing
this life and me. May you, too, live a life prosperous
in all the ways that matter.*

79.8.35	wú	無
79.8.36	qīn	親
79.9.37	cháng	常
79.9.38	yǔ	與
79.9.39	shàn	善
79.9.40	rén	人

THANK YOU

I offer deep thanks to those who've been most vital to this project:

Heavenly spirits, happily here down below, Caitlin, Annie, and Trace Addlesperger were my first cheerleaders. I'm so grateful for and lucky to have not only their interest in the *Dào Dé Jīng* but also their interest in my interest in it. This is equally true of Erik Hoversten. I'm so glad that he—and then Hazel!—came into our family. My husband, John, supported all of us during this project just as steadfastly as he has done for our entire relationship. I love these people so much.

Renée Ballard and Kimberly Gee have been with me through this entire eight-year journey with love, enthusiasm, confidence, and the considerable fruits of their wildly creative minds.

Wendy Mead Hammond, the inspired writer, therapist, and coach inspires me daily and believed whole-heartedly in the project's power during the tender, earliest phase as did my beautiful sister-in-love Gail.

I'm so thankful for Lynda Sexson who appeared out of nowhere as proof that one's most ideal reader does exist.

I've had Stephen Mitchell's *Tao Te Ching* within arm's reach since 1996, and I owe him a great deal of thanks.

Hilmar Alquiros, PhD—poet, psychologist, philosopher, and self-described "happy master-survivor in the beautiful Phillipines"—built a Tao Te Ching resource website (tao-te-king.org) that I've used for hours and hours. It was there that I first encountered an etymological reference that changed everything for me. (The character was *shēn*, 身, which is commonly translated as "self." The bronze inscription glyph depicts a pregnant woman in profile.) Ralf Schlüter, PhD—a physicist and Dr. Alquiros' friend, proofreader, and collaborator—helps maintain the site. I have not run my approach nor my imaginings past these gentlemen-scholars, so they should not be held responsible for any of it, but I'm thankful for their work.

Dr. Yi Wu, professor emeritus at the California Institute of Integral Studies wrote a translation of the *Dào Dé Jīng* that feels to me so clear, humble, strong, and based in a sincere effort to represent Lao Tzu. I use it daily and recommend it if you're interested in the master's metaphysical lessons.

With his cover designs, Dave Huebner and Back of Beyond Media made this series of books into art objects that are a delight to look at and hold. I quite simply treasure them. He makes collaboration radically easy, on point, and fun. Thank you so much, Dave.

I offer the deepest thanks and love to my friend and
coach, the artist, writer, podcaster, and founder of The
Art School, Leah Campbell Badertscher. Truly, this
project has been possible because of her and wouldn't
have happened without her. She is a rare blend of
genius, love, beauty, generosity, know-how, fun, power,
and what seems to be magic. I'm so lucky to know her.

Most of all, thank you, Annie, for researching
characters, hand-assembling sub-components when
needed, and reverse-engineering other translators'
versions of the *Dào Dé Jīng*. Collaborating with you is a
dream come true.

Glossary

Pinyin	Modern Chinese	Translation	Bronze Inscription Glyphs	Spots in the text
ài	愛	loving, kneeling with your head turned this way and your heart in your throat		10.7.26 72.9.37 44.4.19 27.16.81 13.14.71
āi	哀	lamenting from the chest, under one's roof		69.13.51 31.17.107
ān	妄	staying calm as a woman sitting on her heels at home		79.3.8 80.14.52 64.1.2 35.2.11 15.14.74
ào	奧	this secret corner, a sanctuary like that backwater place on the city outskirts where grain's arriving and divided by a great big person		62.1.6
bá	拔	pulled up so		54.1.5

		expertly by hand that it's like a running dog arriving		
bái	白	a little white, blank acorn, pure, gratuitous		41.10.53 28.7.26
bài	敗	being defeated, riches hit lightly by hand, failing, decaying		64.19.91 64.17.83 64.15.68 64.13.54 29.5.25
bâi	百	a hundred		66.3.19 66.1.7 49.12.54 49.2.7 5.4.16 10.11.43 19.2.7 17.8.38
bào	抱	bundling it all up together in both arms into		64.7.29 54.2.7 42.5.19 22.7.23 19.9.40 10.1.4
bào	報	judgment,		63.5.14

		handcuffing and subduing a kneeling person with a hand to the back, making them answer for what's happened		
bâo	保	safeguarding, like carrying a child on one's back		67.9.32 62.3.16 15.15.81 9.4.16
bâo	寶	this treasure like a house containing cowry-riches, jade, and a lidded pot		69.11.45 67.8.29 62.2.10
bèi	被	wearing like a robe or the placental afterbirth hanging from a recently pregnant woman made of fur stripped by hand from its pelt		50.10.52 70.11.44
bèi	倍	fold, again and again, turning one's back on another as in betrayal, spitting		19.2.8

		out the words, "just the husk, not really the inner flower!"		
bēi	悲	breaking the two baby wings off one's heart		31.17.108
bên	本	root system, the foundation of that tree		39.18.115 39.15.94
bì	必	hands over heart, analytically		79.2.4 66.5.37 66.4.29 63.15.65 63.14.60 63.11.40 63.9.32 44.5.25 44.4.20 36.8.29 36.6.21 36.4.13 36.2.5 30.5.29
bì	蔽	grassing over, like fatigued raggedy		15.17.94

		clothing cut into rags by tapping lightly with a tutoring cane hiding under a pair of horizontal grass sprouts		
bì	閉	obstructing the two-winged gateway with sprouting seeds, blocking entry to		56.3.12 52.6.33 27.4.18
bì	敝	tattered as one of our traditional gendered head-cloths that's been cut into rags, tapped lightly by a tutoring cane		22.4.10
bì	臂	an arm, the meat of a ruler or dead husband who administered and punished, marking a kneeling slave or criminal with a chisel		69.7.27 38.10.60
bì	弊	fraud, a drawback		45.2.8

		like both hands supporting a tattered traditional gendered head-cloth that's been hit lightly		
bì	璧	the ruling system, the penal code, or the monarch himself marking the back of kneeling slaves or criminals with a chisel		62.10.46
bî	彼	that—that fur stripped by hand from its pelt on the road where they stepped slowly, the left leg leading the way		72.11.43 38.24.127 12.10.47
bî	鄙	a lowly country person, kneeling, receiving from the granary, corralled on all sides		20.26.123
bî	比	it compares, like two people right next to each other,		55.2.5

		to		
biàn	辯	discussing and debating, speaking in the middle of two chisels used to brand slaves or criminals		81.4.13 81.3.12 45.7.26
bīn	賓	receiving as a guest, like a lady of the court		32.4.24
bìng	並	side by side as two arrows pointing up on the ground		16.3.9
bìng	病	ill as one carried on a stretcher		71.7.28 71.6.24 71.6.23 71.5.20 71.4.16 71.3.12 71.3.11 71.2.8 44.3.15
bīng	兵	carrying a short ax		80.8.33

		with two hands like a soldier or pawn		76.7.41 69.12.48 69.9.33 69.1.2 57.2.8 50.13.67 50.10.54 31.6.30 31.5.26 31.1.3 30.2.9
bīng	冰	freezing stream water		15.9.45
bó	泊	mooring in tranquil water, clear and blank as a little white acorn		20.12.49
Pinyin	**MC**	**Translation**	**Bronze Inscription Glyphs**	**Spots in the text**
bó	薄	a thin covering of two sprouts of grass, not really covering the widespread river of		38.21.117 38.15.91

		a man's public courtesy name, reduced to one short inch the size of that spot on the forearm where the pulse beats strong		
bó	搏	Rolled around by hand, modeled or monopolized (like a hand turning a big round spindle over an inch-sized spot as small as that spot on your forearm where your pulse beats strong)		14.5.15 55.4.22
bó	伯	counts—acorns like eldest brothers or paternal uncles		80.2.8
bó	博	widely winning (like ten times a courtesy name a man takes upon becoming a man, as small as that inch-sized spot where you measure		81.6.21 81.5.20

		the pulse in your wrist)		
bō	魄	the physical soul that stays with a body after death, that skull-white ghost with a tail		10.1.3
bù	不	the husk of the initial false guard-petals but not really the true flower of		38.5.24 23.2.8 81.11.56 81.10.48 81.7.27 81.6.23 81.5.19 81.4.15 81.3.11 81.2.7 81.1.3 80.19.72 80.5.19 80.3.12 79.5.21 78.12.54 78.7.33 77.15.76 77.14.73 77.13.68 77.10.44

				77.9.41
				77.8.35
				77.6.22
				76.7.44
				74.11.55
				74.1.2
				73.12.63
				73.9.47
				73.8.42
				73.7.37
				73.2.8
				72.10.38
				72.8.33
				72.6.25
				72.5.21
				72.1.2
				71.7.27
				71.5.19
				71.4.15
				71.2.5 71.1.2
				70.8.30
				69.4.13
				69.2.6
				68.5.27
				68.3.16
				68.2.10
				68.1.5
				67.15.56

				67.12.42
				67.4.16
				67.2.9
				66.9.69
				66.8.65
				66.7.56
				66.6.50
				65.8.31
				64.22.123
				64.21.107
				64.20.100
				64.20.98
				63.12.49
				62.14.66
				62.12.51
				62.6.30
				62.3.11
				61.13.64
				61.12.56
				60.8.41
				60.7.36
				60.6.30
				60.5.24
				60.4.20
				60.3.15
				59.5.30
				59.4.27
				58.17.69

				58.16.65
				58.15.61
				58.14.57
				56.14.57
				56.13.52
				56.12.47
				56.11.42
				56.10.37
				56.9.32
				56.1.7
				56.1.3
				55.16.78
				55.15.76
				55.8.47
				55.4.21
				55.4.17
				55.3.13
				54.3.16
				54.2.9
				54.1.4
				52.10.48
				52.7.38
				52.4.28
				51.17.67
				51.16.63
				51.15.59
				51.6.18
				50.10.51

				50.9.45
				49.7.31
				49.4.17
				48.8.35
				48.5.22
				47.7.33
				47.6.29
				47.5.25
				47.2.7
				47.1.1
				46.4.29
				45.4.15
				45.2.7
				44.7.34
				44.6.30
				43.5.27
				42.14.64
				42.8.33
				41.11.59
				41.4.26
				41.4.24
				39.21.125
				39.17.108
				38.23.121
				38.21.114
				38.3.11
				38.1.3
				36.13.52

				15.15.85
				15.16.90
				15.17.95
				37.8.42
				37.2.7
				36.11.43
				35.8.41
				35.7.36
				35.6.31
				35.2.9
				34.9.53
				34.7.43
				34.5.28
				34.4.20
				34 3 16
				33.8.35
				33.7.27
				32.10.57
				31.11.69
				31.9.53
				31.8.41
				31.6.32
				31.3.17
				31.1.5
				30.15.72
				30.14.70
				30.11.57
				30.7.38

				30.2.7
				29.4.19
				29.2.12
				28.22.85
				28.11.40
				28.5.17
				27.16.80
				27.16.76
				27.15.68
				27.14.63
				27 7 32
				27.5.23
				27.3.13
				26.4.16
				25.6.29
				25.4.20
				25.3.15
				24.10.46
				24.6.27
				24.4.17
				24.3.12
				24.2.7
				24.1.3
				23.18.86
				23.18.82
				23.6.25
				23.3.13
				22.17.52

				22.15.45
				22.13.39
				22.11.34
				22.9.29
				21.14.55
				20.7.27
				19.7.31
				18.3.15
				17.5.26
				17.5.22
				16.19.66
				16.11.40
				15.4.17
				15.3.12
				14.17.74
				14.16.68
				14.11.44
				14.10.40
				14.9.36
				14.7.25
				14.5.17
				14.3.10
				14.1.3
				12.9.42
				10.16.64
				10.15.60
				10.14.56
				9.4.13 9.2.5

				8.13.46
				6.6.24 6.1.3
				5.10.42
				5.7.32
				5.3.13
				5.1.3 4.11.34
				4.2.7
				3.15.66
				3.13.57
				3.6.26
				3.5.19
				3.4.16
				3.3.8 3.2.6
				3.1.1 2.16.87
				2.13.74
				2.12.70
				2.11.66
				2.10.57
				2.2.19
bû	補	mending (clothing such as a robe, especially that worn on the torso like the placental afterbirth hanging from a recently pregnant woman, being fixed		77.8.34 77.6.25

		by the courtesy name of a man)		
cái	財	sprouting riches, cowry currency, like seeds		53.12.41
cǎi	綵	a skein of silk dyed many colors with fruit hand-picked from a tree		53.9.34
cáng	藏	hiding, like storing some weapons on a pole that can kill by piercing the eye under a bamboo bed below a pair of grass sprouts, some stolen goods or slaves,		44.5.24
chá	察	carefully discerning, studying at home, making a meat offering by hand at an altar		58.3.12 58.3.11 20.21.98 20.21.97
chài	蠆	a scorpion		55.3.10

chân	繟	easy-going as a solitary individual who uses a net of loose silk with weights to catch animals		73.10.52
cháng	常	the conventional royal administrator wearing a men's headcloth as his skirt (nobly assisting the emperor dividing up and differentiating what's faced with admiration and echoed under that roof)		79.9.37 74.7.29 74.3.14 65.12.46 64.17.78 61.4.15 55.11.58 55.10.56 52.15.72 51.9.35 49.1.4 48.6.27 46.7.43 3.12.46 37.1.2 34.6.31 32.1.2 28.17.61 28.11.38

				28.5.15
				27.11.47
				27.9.39
				16.13.47
				16.11.42
				16.10.37
				16.9.35
				1.9.33
				1.7.26
				1.4.11 1.2.5
cháng	長	lengthing as long as hair that has to be tied with a brooch, as a loose-haired old man		67.15.66
				59.9.59
				59.7.51
				54.6.41
				44.8.38
				9.4.15
				7.4.21
				7.2.10 7.1.2
				2.5.31
cháo	朝	beginning the morning when the sun's just rising out of the grass alongside a river, perhaps paying a visit to the emperor		53.6.23
				23.2.10
chāo	超	crossing over the far distant via a		26.6.26

		young man running on foot with a blade from the mouth, carrying an imperious decree		
chè	徹	walking slowly with a footprint of someone thoroughly penetrating, like a hand breaking a pot or hitting lightly an inverted baby being birthed, the left leg leading the way (the "taxing" way)		79.7.32
chē	車	a carriage		11.2.11
chén	臣	casting their eye down, humble, subjecting like a slave, vassal, or servile government official		32.2.12 18.4.26
chén	塵	leaving one billionth		56.7.26

		of a trace, like the dust raised by deer running across the dirt, streaked with soil		4.8.27
chén	陳	the exhibition of an old eastern landowner, a bag tied at both ends, on display near a big mound of soil, as in the ancient vassal state of Chén		80.9.36
chéng	成	completing, that final 'nail' in a weapon on a pole		77.14.71 67.15.64 64.17.81 63.13.54 51.4.11 47.7.36 45.1.2 41.19.95 41.15.76 2.4.30 34.10.59 34.4.19 25.1.4 17.7.35

				15.17.97
				7.10.47
				2.14.77
chéng	誠	speaking completely and truly of putting that final nail in a weapon on the pole		22.21.74
chêng	騁	like a horse given free rein by a chivalrous martial warrior, that knight with a pair of helmets and a sharp exhalation, galloping all over		43.2.7 12.4.20
chēng	稱	being weighed, like a claw-like hand grabbing from above, holding rice or grain on a scale and called out as exactly that		42.9.40
chí	持	holding on, like a government office or temple grasping what comes from this footprint with		67.9.30 64.1.4 9.1.1

		the very skillful human hand of that official (usually a eunuch in the old days)		
chí	馳	galloping—'oh yeah, female funnel!'		43.2.6 12.4.19
chì	赤	bare naked and red as a great big person on fire		55.2.7
chǐ	尺	one foot (measured with a bent person)		69.5.19
chǒng	寵	pampered as a favorite concubine in the home of an emperor dragon crowned with the chisel used to mark slaves or criminals		13.7.29 13.4.16 13.3.12 13.1.1
chōng	沖	pouring water from the center like a stream from the		45.3.12 42.6.21 4.1.2

		hollow drum at the base of a flagpole		
chóu	籌	tallying as an old man, measuring the inches aloud with multiple mouths inside		27.3.15
chú	除	in a new posting in a thatched cottage by a soil mountain		53.6.25 10.5.19
chú	芻	merely a pair of grass stalks wrapped up into		5.4.19 5.2.9
chù	畜	rearing animals, feeding them from a bag tied with a rope		61.12.60 10.13.52
chù	處	disappearing, staying in this place at home, chaste like a tiger head, footprint pointed back down by a table rather than		77.14.74 76.10.56 76.9.52 66.7.52 66.6.46 38.22.118 38.20.111

		accepting a government position or getting married		31.3.18 30.4.20 26.6.25 24.10.47 8.4.13 31.18.116 31.16.100 2.9.51
chū	出	stepping out of a cave		50.1.1 47.3.14 47.1.2 35.4.22 18.2.9 5.8.37 1.11.44
chuâi	揣	polishing a vessel by hand		9.3.9
chuān	川	stream		32.12.66 15.6.30
chuī	吹	blowing as hard as wind like a person with their mouth open kneeling at		29.8.40

		another mouth		
chún	淳	honest as the river of thick-tasting enjoyment of an ancestral shrine, offering, or tribute		58.2.8 58.2.7
chūn	春	vital and alive as a pair of grass sprouts sprouting at camp in the spring sunshine		20.11.44
chuò	輟	halting like a person with hands for feet handling a chariot		54.3.17
cí	雌	the female, the foot stopping a person here in the footprint of the 'short-tailed bird'		28.2.6 10.10.40
cí	慈	benevolent as a mother, two loops of string-dyed-black over the heart		67.23.97 67.20.83 67.16.69 67.13.48 67.10.36 19.4.16 18.3.19
cí	辭	using a chisel (the		34.3.17

		one that marks slaves and criminals) to rule as a hand from above over a hand with a common bucket in a place outside the city		2.11.67
cì	次	next (a little more deficient and lacking, like the second yawn)		17.2.8 17.4.18 17.3.14
cǐ	此	this here—the foot stops a person here on this footprint!—this		15.15.82 21.17.71 73.3.12 72.11.45 65.10.40 62.13.62 62.12.55 57.5.23 54.15.91 39.18.110 38.24.129 23.4.18 19.7.25 14.7.22 12.10.49 1.11.40

cī	疵	so ill that she needs to lie on a stretcher		10.6.24
cóng	從	following, slowly walking directly after another person in that footprint, the left leg leading the way, straightening up, straightening things out for 'nailing' that first footstep of a journey or campaign		64.17.76 23.8.34 21.2.8
cuì	脆	fragile as crisp meat on a roof, precariously high above a kneeling person		76.3.20 64.3.11
cún	存	it continues existing, a baby with health issues, maybe a large head, but still a seed sprouting		41.2.14 7.8.38 6.5.21 4.10.32

cùn	寸	one short inch (that spot on the forearm where the pulse beats strong)		69.4.16
cuò	挫	pushing down to seated on the ground		56.4.15 29.10.46 4.5.16
cuò	措	arranging like hand- placing two strips of meat to dry in the sun		50.12.64
dá	達	arriving with the footprint of small lambs walking slowly on their track, the left leg leading the way		10.11.45
dà	大	a great big person		79.1.2 76.9.51 74.10.49 74.9.44 72.2.6 69.10.36 67.3.13 67.1.7

				65.16.68
				63.13.56
				63.12.51
				63.10.38
				63.7.24
				63.4.10
				61.15.78
				61.12.54
				61.9.43
				61.8.39
				61.6.25
				61.1.1 60.1.2
				53.4.15
				53.2.9
				46.5.34
				46.4.27
				46.3.21
				45.7.25
				45.6.21
				45.5.17
				45.3.9
				45.1.1
				44.4.21
				41.17.81
				41.16.77
				41.15.73
				41.14.69
				41.10.52

				41.3.21
				38.19.108
				35.1.2
				34.10.61
				34.9.56
				34.8.49
				34.1.1
				30.5.25
				28.22.83
				27.17.86
				25.13.66
				25.12.61
				25.12.58
				25.12.56
				25.12.54
				25.9.43
				25.8.42
				18.2.11
				18.1.1
				13.9.44
				13.8.36
				13.2.6
dài	殆	endangered as human remains, spoken of privately, revolving around yourself		52.4.29
				44.7.35
				32.10.58
				25.4.21
				16.19.67

dài	貸	lending like a retrievable arrow attached to a string with cowry riches		41.19.93
dài	帶	a belt made of the traditional gendered head-cloth we wrap around our hair once we receive our public courtesy names		53.10.35
dài	代	taking the place of (like a person with a retrievable arrow attached to a string or an era or a dynasty lineage)		74.10.48 74.9.43 74.8.36
dàn	淡	bland as a pair of flames doused by a river of water		35.5.24 31.8.48
dàn	澹	a person talking and talking, looking upward at a person atop		20.23.103

		a cliff with a habitable cave by the rippling water, calmly indifferent to fame and fortune		
dāng	當	equally as suburbs and fields facing one another		11.2.7 11.6.32 11.4.19
dào	盜	spitting into a bowl like in an oath among robbers, 'thick as thieves,'		57.9.53 53.13.47 19.6.21 3.4.18
dào	道	walking with the footprint of the loose-haired "head" buck		81.11.53 81.10.45 79.8.34 77.12.60 77.9.39 77.7.29 77.1.3 73.7.36 67.1.6 65.1.5 62.13.63 62.12.56 62.1.1 60.2.9

				59.9.64
				55.16.79
				55.15.77
				53.14.50
				53.4.16
				53.2.10
				51.10.39
				51.7.24
				51.6.20
				51.1.1 48.2.6
				47.2.12
				46.2.13
				46.1.4
				42.1.1
				41.19.91
				41.18.85
				41.8.45
				41.7.41
				41.6.37
				41.4.30
				41.3.20
				41.2.12
				41.1.4
				40.2.8
				40.1.3
				38.17.99
				38.11.66
				37.1.1

				35.4.20
				34.1.2
				32.11.60
				32.1.1
				31.3.15
				30.15.73
				30.14.71
				30.1.2
				25.17.82
				25.16.81
				25.12.53
				25.7.36
				24.10.44
				24.7.31
				23.13.58
				23.12.56
				23.9.43
				23.9.39
				23.8.37
				21.3.9
				21.2.6
				18.1.2
				16.18.61
				16.17.60
				15.15.83
				14.21.93
				14.18.81
				9.10.39

dé	得			8.5.22 4.1.1
				1.1.1 1.2.6
				1.1.3
dé	得	'Hand-Picked Gem,' like cowry-shell-riches discovered along the road (a different 'Dé')	得	74.5.22
				64.20.103
				62.15.70
				61.14.74
				56.14.59
				56.13.54
				56.12.49
				56.11.44
				56.10.39
				56.9.34
				52.3.11
				46.5.37
				44.3.11
				42.14.65
				39.7.34
				39.6.28
				39.5.22
				39.4.17
				39.3.12
				39.2.7
				39.1.3
				31.11.72
				31.8.42
				30.11.58

				29.2.13
				23.17.79
				23.15.70
				23.13.61
				22.5.15
				14.5.18
				13.5.19
				12.6.29
				3.3.11
dé	德	walking with the footprint of someone who's in alignment (eyes looking forward, directly over the heart, left leg slowly leading the way)		79.7.30
				79.6.26
				68.5.30
				65.14.55
				65.13.53
				63.5.17
				60.9.45
				59.4.24
				59.3.21
				55.1.2
				54.8.56
				54.7.47
				54.6.39
				54.5.31
				54.4.23
				51.18.72
				51.11.42
				51.8.27
				51.6.23

				51.2.4
				49.8.38
				49.5.24
				41.12.62
				41.11.57
				41.9.49
				38.12.71
				38.11.69
				38.6.27
				38.5.19
				38.4.17
				38.3.13
				38.3.10
				38.2.8
				38.1.4
				38.1.2
				28.17.62
				28.11.39
				28.5.16
				23.15.67
				23.14.65
				23.10.48
				23.10.44
				21.1.2
				10.17.69

dēng	登	ascending as one succeeding in imperial exams —'left and right feet reversed, stepping up on a bean- shaped food container!'—		20.11.45
dí	敵	hostilely resisting the enemy (tapping lightly with a tutoring cane the mere speaking of "God of Heaven" as we call our emperors, for they're like flower sepals connecting to above with that traditional gendered head-cloth (the one we wrap around our hair once we receive our		69.11.41 69.10.39 69.8.30 68.3.14

dì	帝	God of Heaven, as we call our emperors, the husk of a flower's initial bud casing connecting them to above, covering the patriarchy's traditional gendered head-cloth (the one we wrap around our hair once we receive our public courtesy names)		4.12.40
		public courtesy names)		
dì	地	down here in this earthly womb		50.15.80 50.4.23 39.10.51 39.3.11 32.5.26 25.15.76 25.14.75

				25.12.57 25.2.7 23.6.23 23.5.21 8.6.25 7.1.3 7.2.6 6.4.16 5.5.22 5.1.2 1.5.16
dǐ	柢	rooted like a tree—a person standing on the ground bowing to their lineage		59.8.58
dí	滌	washing and arranging things, hitting lightly, stripping, and knotting twigs into slips to write on or a broom		10.5.18
dìng	定	as stable and determined as when one puts a roof over their departure, 'nailing' that first step of the journey		37.9.50

dòng	動	easily doing work as hard as moving a heavy bag tied at both ends with the strong force of an arm or plow		50.4.20 40.1.5 15.14.77 8.12.41 5.8.34
dōng	冬	at the end of the year when things ice up, coming at the end like the knot at the end of a cord		15.6.28
dú	獨	alone as a dog, the last one, a 'silkworm caterpillar on a hollyhock leaf,' as we call the Shû province		25.3.13 20.27.125 20.26.120 20.22.100 20.20.92 20.16.74 20.12.48
dú	毒	an army banner made with feathers and hair, like a feathered headdress on a kneeling		51.13.51

		woman, like the one used on the emperor's or a king's carriage		
dū	篤	honestly and sincerely as a horse under two bamboo stalks		16.2.6
duǎn	短	short as an arrow that fits in a bean-shaped food container		2.5.32
duì	兌	a person with a clear open mouth, breathing, freely exchanging like air, smiling		56.2.11 52.8.42 52.5.32
dùn	沌	muddled and murky as water made turbid in the camp or village		20.18.85 20.18.84
dūn	敦	plentiful and esteemed as a ram's head at the ancestral		15.10.49

		shrine or that thick globe-shaped alloy grain vessel studded with three sculptural legs and two handles protruding on each hemisphere so they could be removed and used as bowls		
duó	奪	seizing, snatching 'a spread-winged bird' with your forearm where your pulse beats strong		36.7.27
duō	多	having more, like two pieces of meat		81.9.42 75.2.10 65.5.22 63.15.66 63.15.63 63.4.12 57.9.55

				57.8.42
				57.7.34
				57.6.26
				44.5.23
				44.2.10
				22.6.16
				5.9.38
è	惡	a tomb constructed over the heart		20.4.16 8.4.18 2.1.10
ē	阿	'oh NO, that familiar one, that big soil mountain that— mwah!— tastes truly of the big soil mound I know'		20.2.8
ér	兒	a baby son that still has an open fontanelle		28.6.23 20.13.56 10.4.16

Pinyin	MC	Translation	Bronze Inscription Glyphs	Spots in the text
ér	而	yet now you're bearded	而	29.1.6 81.11.55 81.10.47 80.11.43 80.5.18 80.3.11 79.5.20 78.2.8 77.14.72 77.13.67 77.8.33 74.5.24 74.4.17 73.12.62 73.10.54 73.9.49 73.8.44 73.7.39 69.5.17 69.3.10 67.9.31 66.8.64 66.7.54 66.6.48

Pinyin	MC	Translation	Bronze Inscription Glyphs	Spots in the text
				64.22.122
				64.17.82
				61.11.52
				58.17.68
				58.16.64
				58.15.60
				58.14.56
				57.14.85
				57.13.78
				57.12.71
				57.11.64
				57.6.29
				56.14.60
				56.13.55
				56.12.50
				56.11.45
				56.10.40
				56.9.35
				55.8.46
				55.6.36
				55.5.27
				53.5.19
				51.17.66
				51.16.62

Pinyin	MC	Translation	Bronze Inscription Glyphs	Spots in the text
				51.15.58
				51.9.34
				51.6.21
				48.5.20
				47.7.35
				47.6.31
				47.5.27
				42.11.51
				42.10.46
				42.9.35
				42.5.18
				41.1.6
				38.18.102
				38.16.92
				38.14.82
				38.13.77
				38.12.72
				38.11.67
				38.10.61
				38.9.54
				38.8.46
				38.7.38
				38.6.30
				38.5.22

Pinyin	MC	Translation	Bronze Inscription Glyphs	Spots in the text
				9.1.2 37.5.21
				37.2.5
				35.2.8
				34.7.42
				34.5.27
				34.3.15
				34.3.13
				33.8.34
				32.6.37
				31.10.55
				31.9.52
				31.8.44
				30.12.61
				30.11.56
				30.10.52
				30.9.48
				30.8.44
				30.6.36
				29.2.6
				27.7.31
				27.5.22
				26.8.34
				25.13.67
				25.4.19

Pinyin	MC	Translation	Bronze Inscription Glyphs	Spots in the text
				23.7.28
				22.21.76
				20.28.129
				20.26.118
				20.16.72
				17.2.10
				14.8.31
				10.16.63
				10.15.59
				10.14.55
				9.7.27
				9.3.10
				8.3.10
				7.8.36
				7.6.30
				5.8.35
				5.7.31
				4.1.3
				2.14.78
				2.13.73
				2.12.69
				2.11.65
				1.12.45

èr	二	Two		67.11.37 42.3.7 42.2.6
êr	餌	alluring food made from rice dough (you'd love to put your mouth over that bowl, 'Êr')		35.3.16
êr	耳	their ear ('Êr')		49.12.59 12.2.11
fá	伐	beheading with a weapon on a pole		30.9.50 24.5.20 22.13.41
fâ	法	like the mythical head buck who distinguishes right and wrong kneeling at the river flowing by a person with a mouth or cave between their legs, leaving, comes from and emulates		57.9.49 25.17.83 25.16.80 25.15.77 25.14.74

		the standards or even magic of		
fā	發	shot by a bow launching—'thwang!—and leveling grass underfoot as effectively as if by hand with a halberd		39.10.57 12.5.26
fàn	氾	spreading out everywhere like water overflowing on a commonplace bucket		34.1.3
fân	反	a different-sounding "Fân," turning your palm over in a habitable cave in a cliff, reversing, returning, reflecting, maybe countering with the opposite		78.14.64 65.15.62 40.1.1 25.11.51
fāng	妨	they're oppositional, holding the tip of a sword over a kneeling woman		12.7.35

fāng	方	like the wide, parallel side of a tipped blade		58.14.55 41.14.70
fèi	廢	collapsing like a house shot by a bow launching—thwang!—and leveling a pair of grass sprouts with one's feet as effectively as if by hand with a halberd		36.5.19 18.1.3
fèi	費	lavishly, rather wastefully, expended, like two sticks tied together to start a fire over cowry-riches		44.4.22
fēi	非	wringing to backward the two wings [of]		65.2.7 60.6.27 60.4.17 53.14.49 39.19.117 39.18.111 31.7.36 7.9.39

				1.4.10 1.2.4
fèn	糞	manure like the rice kernels of a differently-masked person		46.1.9
fēn	紛	unravelling, a blade dividing a skein of silk into disorderliness		56.5.20 4.6.21
féng	蜂	a bee (which is like a snaky animal with 'a knot at the end of a thread' in lush bushes)		55.3.9
fèng	奉	offering a lush growth of plants with two hands		77.11.55 77.10.47
fēng	風	blowing as a male majestic legendary bird with three strands of hair or feathers hanging down below and a common, earthly		23.2.7

		bucket above, fluttering insects and animals in the wind		
fēng	豐	luxury as lush as a pot holding a pair of blooming flowers		54.7.49
fú	弗	like sticks that were tied together in a bundle to start a fire —pfft!—and no longer		2.15.83 2.14.79
fú	幅	hem-width strips		11.1.3
fú	服	wearing clothes like a mourning dress, a person hand-subdued to kneeling before a commonplace plate		80.13.51 59.3.16 59.2.14 53.9.32
fú	福	blessings and good fortune, a full vessel on display on an		65.9.38 58.6.23 58.5.19

		altar		
fú	伏	lying in wait like a dog waiting to ambush a person		58.6.28
fù	富	wealthy, a home full of valuable vessels with lots of capacity		57.13.81 33.5.21 9.7.25
fù	父	Respected Father, a hand holding a working stone blade axe		42.15.73 21.16.66 21.15.60
fù	復	someone walking with a footprint of slowly returning, with the left leg leading the way, doubling back (like the gut) on one's footprint to		80.10.40 64.21.109 58.10.41 58.9.37 52.13.61 52.4.22 28.18.65 28.12.42 28.6.19 19.4.14 16.9.32 16.8.30

				16.6.20
				16.4.14
				14.12.47
fù	負	is carried by (as cowry-riches by a much smaller person or knife in the kind of load-bearing that can lead to suffering, neglect, betrayal, and repudiation)		42.5.16
fù	覆	covering the walking forth and then returning, doubling back like the gut, stepping slowly with only one's left leg leading the way		51.14.55
fù	腹	in their gut, doubled back with a piece of meat inside		12.9.41
				3.9.39
fù	輔	assisting like the wooden bars that help prevent a		64.22.116

		carriage from over-turning or a carriage with a man's courtesy name he gets when he becomes a man		
fū	夫	In fact, that is to say, "This Grown Man" with hairpin and public courtesy name,		50.14.73 50.6.28 60.8.39 59.2.8 41.19.89 38.19.110 38.15.85 75.10.42 74.10.47 74.8.35 72.5.19 71.3.9 70.7.23 67.20.82 67.7.25 67.3.11 63.14.57 61.14.70 51.9.30 37.7.37 15.4.15 2.15.81

				32.9.48
				31.11.63
				31.1.1
				22.17.50
				15.16.88
				8.13.44
				3.13.54
gài	蓋	covering, as a pair of grass sprouts and clay soil thatch atop a chalice and its lid		50.8.37
gâi	改	transforming something like a fetus by cracking lightly by hand or binding with a silk rope		25.3.16
gân	敢	venturing to be bold, even a little bit and ultra-politely hunting a boar as pleasantly as if you had something sweet in your mouth		74.6.28
				73.2.9
				73.1.3
				69.4.14
				69.2.7
				67.15.57
				67.12.43
				64.22.124
				30.7.39
				3.13.58

gān	甘	sweet-tasting in the mouth		80.12.46 32.5.31
gāng	剛	the firm, a web of mountain within a net as strong as a blade		78.6.29 36.10.40
gâo	槁	meagre and withered like a tree high above (a two-story building in the city outskirts)		76.4.25
gāo	高	way up, as in a two- story building outside the city, high above what's faced with admiration and echoed in that place		77.3.9 39.16.95 39.14.85 2.6.35
gè	各	a particular one, unusual as the knot coming at the end of a cord sticking out from a mouth		61.14.73 16.6.19

Pinyin	MC	Translation	Bronze Inscription Glyphs	Spots in the text
gē	割	cutting apart a harmful house in which lush, abundant plant growth is spoken of		58.14.58 28.22.86
gēn	根	the root of the family tree, like an ancestor's manhood		59.8.56 26.9.43 26.1.4 16.7.25 16.6.23 6.4.17
gòng	共	share, like two hands holding something aloft		11.1.4
gōng	拱	arching around and holding aloft like the area enclosed by two hands folded in front of the chest		62.10.45

gōng	公	something as publicly fair and impartial as a high ranking older man who's 'got balls,' a duke		62.9.42 42.9.37 16.15.52 16.14.51
gōng	功	laboring with the force of a blade and the work of one's arm or a plow		77.14.70 34.4.18 24.5.23 22.14.44 17.7.34 9.9.33 2.14.76
gōng	弓	like a bow		77.2.7
gōng	攻	attacking (hitting lightly with a bladed tool)		78.2.9
gòu	垢	dirt, like the soil, the clay earth, the shame of a ruler, especially an empress hòu, a person giving		78.10.46

		birth to a successor,		
gôu	狗	a straw dog, a symbolic sacrificial object		5.4.20 5.2.10
gù	故	this taps lightly with a tutoring cane and leaves a mark on the solid shield of the past:		76.5.26 73.5.26 72.11.41 69.12.46 67.15.62 67.14.53 67.13.49 67.4.14 66.10.71 66.3.16 65.6.23 64.16.71 64.15.66 63.17.75 63.13.52 62.17.76 62.8.36 61.10.45 61.6.24

				60.9.44
				57.10.57
				56.15.62
				56.9.31
				54.9.59
				51.10.38
				50.14.75
				50.6.30
				46.6.38
				44.4.17
				42.10.41
				41.5.31
				39.20.119
				39.15.89
				38.24.125
				38.11.64
				34.10.57
				31.3.13
				29.7.31
				28.22.82
				27.14.59
				27.12.51
				27.10.43
				25.12.52
				24.10.42
				23.8.33
				23.2.5
				22.18.54

				22.16.48
				22.14.42
				22.12.37
				22.10.32
				19.8.33
				15.17.92
				15.5.20
				14.8.29
				12.10.45
				11.7.38
				8.14.48
				8.5.19
				7.10.45
				7.4.19
				2.3.22
				1.7.25
gù	固	solidly, for a long time, keeping as firm to what happened in the first place as this land surrounding and holding this nation's shield since ancient times		55.5.29
				67.21.91
				59.8.57
				58.12.49
				36.8.30
				36.6.22
				36.4.14
				36.2.6

gû	轂	hub of a wheel, that working part of a carriage you tend to with a hand tool		42.8.34 39.17.109 11.1.6
gû	谷	in a difficult position in a ravine, in an emptied, eroded valley mouth between two mountains		66.3.20 66.1.8 39.12.65 39.5.21 32.12.67 28.16.60 28.15.56 15.11.58 6.1.1
gû	骨	in the bones, a strong framework		55.5.23 3.11.45
gû	古	speaking of the solid shield of the past		68.8.41 65.1.1 62.13.57 22.19.62 21.13.50 15.1.1 14.20.89 14.18.79

gū	孤	an orphan, a big-headed, legs-swaddled baby left as a melon on the vine		42.8.31 39.17.106
guâ	寡	the mythical loose- haired head buck who differentiates right from wrong, kneeling in a house like a widow, alone		80.1.3 63.14.61 42.8.32 39.17.107 19.10.44
guān	官	working in a government building with many rooms under one roof as an official		28.21.80
guān	觀	that person with big eye for a head kneeling on a stork- like temple or watchtower, keeping lookout for		54.13.79 54.12.74 54.11.70 54.10.66 54.9.62 26.5.23 16.4.13 1.10.37 1.8.30

guān	關	locking, weaving a pair of the tiniest silk thread youngsters, hair still in two tufts, through the two-winged gateway		27.4.20
guâng	廣	widespread, a person with a large belly in a habitable cave in a cliff,		67.17.75 67.14.55 41.11.56
guāng	光	that shining fire over the head of a kneeling person		58.17.67 56.6.23 52.13.60 4.7.24
guì	貴	held in high regard, like when two hands are wrapped around a person atop cowry-shell-riches		75.11.52 72.10.40 70.10.39 64.20.101 62.17.80 62.13.61 56.15.66 56.13.56 51.8.29 51.6.22 39.15.90 39.14.84

				31.5.28
				31.4.23
				27.16.77
				20.28.130
				17.6.32
				13.12.60
				13.8.35
				13.2.5
				9.7.26
				3.3.9
guì	劌	knifing two feet and a battle ax, pacing, marking the passage of a year, another harvest		58.15.62
guî	鬼	a ghost		60.4.19 60.3.14
guī	歸	coming back after sweeping troops out of the soil mound hills to this		60.9.47 52.13.62 34.7.40 28.18.66 28.12.43 28.6.20 22.21.77 20.14.66

				16.7.24
				16.6.21
				14.12.48
guó	國	in our domestic enclave, defended by a weapon on a pole		80.16.59
				80.1.2
				78.12.53
				78.10.44
				65.9.36
				65.8.35
				65.7.28
				65.6.27
				61.13.63
				61.12.55
				61.9.44
				61.8.40
				61.8.36
				61.7.34
				61.6.30
				61.6.26
				61.1.2 60.1.3
				59.7.46
				59.6.44
				57.7.37
				57.1.4
				54.12.75
				54.12.73
				54.7.45
				36.12.48

				10.7.29 18.4.20
guò	過	what's past and surpassing, maybe "passed away," maybe excessive, walking slowly with the footprint of a slanting skull mouth speaking, the left leg leading the way		64.21.114 61.13.65 61.12.57 35.3.17
guô	果	ripened like fruit on the tree by the sun		30.12.60 30.11.55 30.10.51 30.9.47 30.8.43 30.6.35
hái	孩	baby animal, giggling		49.13.64 20.13.59
hài	害	being harmed as a house in which weeds sprout from a mouth		81.10.49 73.3.18 66.7.57 56.12.51 35.2.10

hâi	海	a lushness like that of a river of new life sprouting from a nursing mother, like the ocean		66.1.2 32.12.71 20.23.107
hán	寒	sleeping under a desolate roof amidst a pair of grass sprouts to protect themselves from winter chill, a cold humble person		45.8.31
hán	含	keeping what's being said in the mouth now, in modern times, stuffed in like jade, pearls, and gems in a corpse's mouth		55.1.1
háo	號	roaring like a puffing tiger head		55.8.45
háo	毫	as tiny as the fine hair covering		64.8.34

		below the mouth		
hâo	好	as good as a woman with a child		57.12.69 53.5.21 30.3.15
hé	合	joining together from three sides over a mouth, like having sex		64.7.28 55.6.35 32.5.28
hé	何	that one—that very one shouldering a weapon		74.2.6 62.13.65 62.7.32 57.4.16 54.14.83 50.14.74 50.6.29 26.7.29 21.16.62 20.5.20 20.3.12 13.11.57 13.8.33 13.3.10
hé	闔	shutting it, a great big person with a		10.9.37

	黑	cave mouth between their legs withdrawing from within the two-winged gateway, covering an empty chalice		
hé	和	warming, wetting, and stickily kneading together, harmonizing like breath blown into a reed-pipe mouth organ		79.1.1 56.6.21 55.10.54 55.9.49 42.6.25 18.3.16 4.7.22 2.7.42
hè	褐	dull brown like coarse clothing, placental afterbirth hanging from a recently pregnant woman, or a robe on the torso used to bundle up and hide		70.11.45
hèi	黑	a dark criminal face-tattoo, shady		28.8.29

hóu	侯	a marquis, 'arrow in the cave'		39.17.102 39.14.80 39.7.32 37.3.9 32.3.14
hòu	後	walking slowly with just the left leg leading the way, leaving behind this tiny silk thread footprint like a knot in a thread, a descendant, at the end		67.18.77 66.5.40 65.16.65 38.14.83 38.13.78 38.12.73 38.11.68 30.5.28 14.17.77 7.5.27 2.8.44
hòu	厚	a jug in a habitable cave in a cliff, thick and generous		75.8.37 55.1.4 50.7.36 44.5.26 38.20.113
hù	戶	the single-gate doorway to a household		47.1.3 11.5.27

hû	虎	fierce tiger		50.12.61 50.9.48
hū	乎	—PAH?!—		39.19.118 35.5.25 23.7.32 10.12.49 10.10.41 10.8.33 10.6.25 10.4.17 10.2.9 5.6.29
hū	惚	a heart cut by a heart, elusive and difficult to understand		21.7.27 21.5.17 21.4.16 14.15.64
huá	華	decorative brilliant magnificence, a flower blooming,		38.23.124 38.17.101
huà	化	transforming as a right-side-up		57.11.67 37.5.20

		person into an upside down person		37.4.19
huái	懷	carrying deep in one's bosom, affectionately concealed in one's heart by clothing like a webbed net over a river		70.12.46
huán	還	giving something the eye, frightened, while slowly walking with the footprint of a robe hanging like placental afterbirth from a recently pregnant woman, long like a spindle, the left leg leading the way, and then doing or giving something or going somewhere 'in return'		30.3.16

huàn	患	sick with worry (or worrisomely sick... or both!), two objects strung together over the heart		13.11.58 13.9.45 13.8.37 13.2.7
huàn	渙	dissolving, dispersing like water in the city outskirts where there are so many people		15.9.42
huāng	恍	the heart of a person kneeling with shining fire over their head, brilliant yet incomprehensible		21.7.25 21.5.19 21.4.14 14.15.65
huāng	荒	a desolate wasteland under a pair of grass sprouts atop the watery uncultivated land of the lost dead		20.8.29
huì	慧	bright, intelligent wisdom, having		18.2.7

		hand-swept one's heart with a broom of two bamboo sprouts		
huì	諱	words we avoid like taking footsteps around an enclosure, taboo words like the name of a deceased emperor or elder		57.6.28
huî	虺	a venomous snake (that will cut off one's foot)		55.3.11
huī	隳	getting destroyed around the soil mountain, a left hand by moonlight over one's heart		29.10.48
huī	恢	vast as an expanded heart restored from ashes, from fire that can be touched by hand		73.11.60 73.11.59

hún	渾	muddying like river water spouting from an army of surrounding carts		49.11.51
hùn	混	turbulently blending torrential waters, like a river of insects, muddling along and maybe even stirring up trouble, joking		15.12.59 25.1.3 14.8.30
hūn	昏	darkening as the sun bowing down to the ground		57.7.40 20.20.94 20.20.93 18.4.22
huó	活	really living, like a tongue or bell clapper licking the river water		73.2.11
huò	貨	transformation from a right-side-up person to an upside down person atop cowry-shell riches		64.20.105 53.12.42 44.2.8 12.6.31 3.3.13
huò	或	in this particular		73.3.17

			enclave that's defended by a weapon on a pole	73.3.15 61.11.50 61.10.46 42.11.48 42.10.43 31.2.10 29.10.47 29.10.45 29.9.43 29.9.41 29.8.39 29.8.37 29.7.35 29.7.33 24.9.39 4.10.31 4.2.6
huò	惑	confused as a heart under this particular enclave defended by a weapon on a pole, infatuated		22.6.18
huò	禍	disaster like the slanting mouth of a skull on a sacrifice altar		69.10.34 58.6.25 58.5.17 46.4.25

jí	棘	the 'double thorny jujube, the red date plant, the fruit of which can be used as contraception and causes midterm miscarriages		30.4.22
jí	吉	lucky as an empty and quiet mouth with a soldier's axe above it		31.12.78
jí	及	finally reaching, hand-grabbing and holding onto a person		43.7.38 48.7.31 21.13.51 13.11.51
jí	極	in the utmost position, a person pressing urgently against a double-beamed wooden ridgepole that's high as a tree		68.8.43 59.6.40 59.5.36 58.7.32 28.12.46 16.1.3
jì	紀	binding itself with fine silk thread, a particular written		14.21.94

		story or rule		
jì	寄	a strange great big person exiled to a house in the east as punishment but still counted on to translate there, trusted with		13.13.68
jì	既	'done'—as de facto as a kneeling person turning away after eating a bowl of rice, done with		81.9.36 81.8.29 52.4.18 52.3.10 32.8.46 35.8.43
jì	寂	quiet as hand-husking peas at home		25.3.9
jì	跡	it's leaving tracks with the full leg of the animal, both armpits sweating this too		27.1.5
jì	濟	helping as		52.9.43

		ferrying across the River Qi in the kingdom of that same name (which means a field as even and deferential as two identical stalks of grain under the chisel like a pair showing piety before offering sacrifices and other ceremonies)		
jì	祭	a ceremony making a meat offering by hand at an altar		54.3.14
jì	忌	binding one's heart like with a silk rope, abstaining from		57.6.27
jì	伎	underhandedly tricky like that person with their right hand		57.8.43

		supporting ten		
jì	稷	the god of plants		78.11.50
jî	幾	like two little silk threads separated by the sword of a garrison guard, so, so near		69.11.42 64.17.80 8.5.20 20.3.11
jî	己	themselves, privately, personally bound with a silk rope		81.8.33 81.9.40
jī	基	undisturbed earth or clay foundation under that basket		39.16.99
jī	積	accumulating, amassing grain plants like cowry-riches under a thorn tree, like indigestion		81.7.28 59.4.23 59.3.20

jī	稽	a loose-haired head buck examining like it's some delicious food or maybe an intention or imperial decree, investigating		65.12.48 65.11.44
jī	饑	in a time of famine, having a meal with one's mouth over a bowl of rice on a stand carefully watched over with the smallest things, two tiny silk threads, under separate guard by a man with a spear, by a garrison		75.3.13 75.1.3
jī	雞	a rooster (a "short-tailed bird," this great big person, their tiniest silk thread child is grabbed by a		80.17.62

		hand from above like a female sex worker)		
jiâ	甲	a turtle shell shield		80.8.32 50.10.53
jiā	家	a home, complete with a pig under the roof		57.7.38 54.10.67 54.10.65 54.5.29 18.4.21
jiā	佳	addressing the emperor using a beautiful stacked pair of pointed jade tablets, so very excellent		31.1.2
jiā	加	piling on more with strenuous effort, puffing with a plow or arm		69.12.50 62.5.26
jiàn	楗	a bar, a door bolt, hand-built from a tree by a striding person skillful with a		27.4.21

		bamboo brush		
jiàn	見	seen by someone with one big eye for a head		77.15.78 72.8.35 52.11.50 47.6.30 47.2.10 35.6.33 29.2.10 24.3.10 22.9.31 19.9.38 14.17.75 14.16.69 14.1.4 3.5.20
jiàn	賤	lowly cowry-shell riches (accumulating like a couple tiny pole weapons stacked together trying to be an arsenal)		56.14.61 39.18.113 39.15.92
jiàn	建	a striding person establishing, hand- planting a pole,		54.1.2 41.12.61 41.5.32

jiàn	劍	a double-edged sword like a blade with two people and their mouths all together, gathering themselves from three sides		53.10.37
jiǎn	儉	moderate (like one humble person next to two people and two mouths altogether, gathering from three sides perhaps during a poor harvest)		67.17.73 67.14.52 67.11.39
jiān	間	this interstitial, transitional space where moonlight's peeking through the two-winged gateway		43.3.17 5.5.24
jiān	堅	hardening, drying and forming a crust,		78.2.10 76.5.27 76.2.10

		hard as the clay soil underneath a finger in an eye cast down in surrender		43.2.12
iān	兼	that hand holding two stalks of grain, doing two things at once		61.12.59
jiàng	降	dropping down, honoring with their presence— two feet, upside down, 'falling down a soil mountain' being birthed		32.5.30
jiàng	匠	master craftsmen who builds a box with axe		74.10.50 74.9.45
jiāng	將	assured, as if by hand-offering a meat tribute at an altar, a certain future of		67.22.93 65.3.11 42.15.69 39.14.86 39.13.77 39.12.69

				39.11.62
				39.10.55
				39.9.48
				31.15.92
				31.14.87
				37.9.48
				37.7.39
				37.6.25
				37.4.17
				36.7.25
				36.5.17
				36.3.9
				36.1.1
				32.9.50
				32.4.22
				29.1.1
				15.9.47
jiāng	江	the Yangtze River (the river that works like a stone axe) flowing into		66.1.1 32.12.70
jiào	教	the lessons they learned the hard way, like a child being taught counting with bamboo slips or divination with		43.5.30 42.15.72 42.13.59 42.12.56 2.10.60

		yarrow stalks, tapping them lightly with a tutoring cane		
jiào	徼	a person carefully tracing a frontier border line, walking with the footprint of a musical instrument, an acorn atop the wide side of a blade, lightly plucked or hit by hand, moving slowly, with just the left foot leading the way		1.10.39
jiâo	皭	bright as a blank white acorn stirred like that musical instrument resembling an acorn atop the wide, parallel side of a tipped blade,		14.9.37

jiāo	驕	arrogant, a young person dangerously racing through the city outskirts on a tall horse with its mane flying		30.10.54 9.7.28
jiāo	角	an angled horn		50.11.60
jiāo	郊	outside of town where a person sits with crossed legs at a big soil mound		46.2.18
jiāo	交	intersecting with this—picture a big-bellied person sitting crossed-legged making a relationship with this;		61.2.9 60.9.46
jié	結	tying, joining with an emotional knot,		80.10.41 27.6.27

			a skein of silk with the auspicious empty mouth of a bachelor soldier- scholar- official appointed by the emperor		
jié	詰		someone questioning or interrogating the empty and quiet, lucky mouth with a soldier's axe above it		14.7.28
jiè	介		firmly as a person seated between two things, perhaps shells, connecting them, armored by them		53.1.3
jiĕ	解		cutting like a blade removing an ox's horn		56.5.18 27.7.34 4.6.19
jiē	皆		gossip, comparing two people like there		67.1.3 49.13.63 49.12.56

		was something oh so sweet in their mouth, said		20.25.115 20.15.69 17.8.40 2.2.12 2.1.3
jiē	竭	drained, exhausted as a person standing on solid ground making a yawning sound		39.12.71
jìn	進	walking slowly forward on the footprint of a 'short- tailed bird,' the left leg leading the way		69.4.15 62.12.54 41.7.40
jīn	金	gold joined together from three sides by grinding it like an axe between two blocks of metal		9.5.17
jīn	矜	gathering together from three sides over a kneeling person with a spear as a		30.8.46 24.6.25 22.15.47

		magistrate, commanding		
jīn	今	gathering from three sides over this now, current times		67.16.67 21.13.52 14.19.84
jīn	筋	sinew, tendons, muscles, or even veins that stand out like two bamboo stalks on a rib or the meat of an arm that sticks out from the body like a plow		55.5.25
jìng	靜	calm peace, the clear blue-green growth of the sedative cinnabar plant quieting a dispute between two hands on a plowshare		61.5.21 61.4.17 57.12.70 45.10.36 45.9.32 37.8.45 26.2.5 16.7.27 16.2.5 15.13.68
jìng	徑	taking a short-cut pathway straight across, stepping		53.5.22

		slowly with the left leg over an underground stream		
jīng	驚	startling, making you jump like a horse spooked by the sound of someone tapping a dog lightly with a tutoring cane		13.7.32 13.6.26 13.5.22 13.3.15 13.1.4
jīng	精	a strong essence or soul, like polished raw rice, seminal fluid, or spring's blue-green lush ripening of the sedative cinnabar plant		55.7.39 21.11.42 21.10.40
jīng	荊	the thorny 'chaste tree' whose fruit makes you not want sex and whose canes are used to flog wives, like the punishment of a		30.4.21

		knife by a square well under two sprouts of grass		
jiù	救	tapping lightly with a tutoring cane a fur coat, saving by forbidding		67.22.94 52.10.49 27.11.49 27.9.41
jiù	咎	a person following this upside-down footprint sees its calamity		46.5.32 9.8.32
jiŭ	久	enduring through time as a person receiving moxibustion, that mugwort treatment for cramps, turning a breech baby, or other health issues		67.6.20 59.9.61 59.7.52 58.12.50 44.8.39 33.7.32 23.6.27 16.18.63 15.14.76 7.2.12 7.1.4
jiŭ	九	nine (the elbow in that old way of counting)		64.9.36
jù	據	taking possession		55.4.18

		of as an expert hand with tigers or boars fighting one another		
jù	懼	frightened (like the heart of two panicked eyes over "a short-tailed bird")		74.2.9
jû	舉	lifting up, supporting, offering to shoulder (above a fang)		77.4.15
jū	居	staying put here, sitting over the solid shield of the past at this birthplace, where		80.14.54 72.3.13 38.23.122 38.21.115 31.15.94 31.14.89 31.4.21 25.13.69 8.6.23 2.15.84 2.14.80
jué	絕	slicing apart, like a blade halving each strand of a		20.1.1 19.5.17 19.3.9

		pair of silk threads		19.1.1
jué	蹶	toppling down—a full leg and foot next to a habitable cave in a cliff where an upside down person falls next to a kneeling person with their mouth—		39.14.88
juē	攫	grabbing with claws as a big expert hand with two nervous eyes over 'a short- tailed bird' hand		55.4.19
jūn	均	evened out like soil that's been wrapped up in two parallel lines		32.6.39
jūn	君	a lord prince, his hand holding a rod over a mouth		70.6.22 31.7.37 31.4.19

				26.10.47 26.2.8
jūn	軍	in an army of surrounding carts		50.10.50 31.15.93 31.14.88 30.5.26
kāi	開	coming unlatched, that two-winged gateway with a pair of hands		52.8.40 27.5.25 10.9.36
kàng	抗	opposing, raising resistance, lifting a hand to some high, arrogant extreme like a neck or the ridge of a roof		69.12.47
kè	客	entering a house as a guest like you're the last one, sticking out like the knot at the end of a cord		69.3.12 35.3.18 15.8.41
kè	克	a person wearing a battle helmet,		59.5.31 59.4.28

		conquering		
kê	可	the lip-smackingly genuine		79.3.9
				62.5.24
				62.4.19
				59.7.49
				59.6.41
				56.14.58
				56.13.53
				56.12.48
				56.11.43
				56.10.38
				56.9.33
				46.3.23
				44.8.36
				36.13.53
				36.11.44
				34.8.46
				34.6.34
				34.2.6
				32.10.55
				31.11.70
				29.4.20
				27.7.33
				27.5.24
				25.5.22
				20.7.26

				15.4.18
				15.3.13
				14.11.45
				14.7.26
				13.15.78
				13.13.67
				9.4.14
				3.5.21
				1.3.8 1.1.2
kông	孔	a profound unimpeded fontanelle-type opening, 'Cave'		21.1.1
kông	恐	they're afraid, their heart like a commonplace dish scraped with a blade		39.14.87 39.13.78 39.12.70 39.11.63 39.10.56 39.9.49
kôu	口	the words from their mouth		35.4.23 12.3.17
kū	枯	dried and withered like an ancient tree of ten generations		76.4.24

kuà	跨	overstepping, straddling, like the full leg-cut of an animal, fully enough, this great big person on exhaled air, extravagantly good- looking		24.2.5
kuā	夸	as extravagant as a great big person blowing air		53.13.48
kuáng	狂	a mad dog roaring as insanely, unrestrainedly as a king		12.5.27
kuàng	況	in this river you find yourself in, brother		23.7.29
kuàng	曠	bright, clear, carefree, and spacious as a yellow sun shining on a		15.11.54

		habitable cave in a cliff holding a great big person with a large belly		
kuī	闚	that is to say, in fact, this particular grown man with a hairpin and public courtesy name being in the two-winged gateway with a person who has one big eye for a head, flashing a look at		47.2.8
lái	來	coming like a stalk of wheat		80.19.75 73.9.51
lân	覽	overseeing everything as royalty acting on behalf of the emperor and commanding as 'blood' family bonded by a drop of blood in a		10.5.21

		ceremonial vessel, bent over and looking down, perhaps in seclusion, all eyes		
láo	牢	a sacrificial animal in a pen		20.10.42
lâo	老	the honorable loose-haired elder bent over an arrow as a cane		80.18.70 55.14.73 30.13.67
lè	樂	pleasurably playing as glad music upon a wooden instrument's two silk strings		80.15.55 66.8.62 35.3.14 31.11.64 31.10.60 23.17.78 23.15.69 23.13.60
léi	贏	fleeing by moonlight with one's cowry-shell-riches and dishes		29.9.44

lèi	儽	a worn out person, backed by a figure- eight skein of silk- dyed-black and the soil margin between three croplands, lazy or perhaps fatigued, maybe bound despite being innocent		20.14.61 20.14.60
lèi	纇	a flaw knotting the thread, that kneeling loose- haired head buck person with rice kernels on a skein of fine silk		41.8.47
lêi	累	repeatedly building up like a skein of silk (or fatigue after work) in the field		64.10.42
lí	離	remaining set apart from (as 'a short- tailed bird' from that		28.5.18 26.4.17 10.2.8

			infamous wild animal hunted in the forest with webbed nets)	
lì	立	a person standing straight up on the ground		62.8.37 25.3.14 24.1.4
lì	力	forceful as with the strength of an arm, a bladed tool, or a plow		33.3.13 68.6.36
lì	利	reaps benefits in the manner of a sharp- edged blade slicing grain		81.10.46 73.3.16 57.7.35 56.11.46 53.10.36 11.7.43 36.12.50 19.5.20 19.2.6 8.2.7
lì	莅	with a good position, standing on the ground drying up water under cover a pair of grass		60.2.10

		sprouts, like someone arriving at an official ceremony, managing, supervising		
lǐ	禮	making ritual offerings of honor at an altar with two strings of jade and a feathered drum in the lap of luxury		38.15.86 38.14.84 38.9.51 31.18.115 31.16.99
lǐ	里	traditional miles that villagers use to measure fields on the clay soil		64.11.45
lián	廉	holding two stalks of grain, doing two things at once in a habitable cliff cave, clean and incorruptible		58.15.59
liáng	梁	where wood bridges water with the help of a double-edged		42.14.62

		sword, like a beam ("Liáng," as in the state located where the south-flowing Yellow River enters the Guanzhong Plain)		
liâng	兩	these two, this pair of traditional, adult, gendered head- cloths covered by "The One,"		73.3.13 65.10.41 61.14.71 60.8.40 1.11.41
liáo	寥	deserted as a house through which blows the wind like two wings with two strands of hair hanging down in front		25.3.11
liáo	飂	wafting with the wind in a high place, drifting like three insects blowing below a		20.24.108

		commonplace bucket between two aligned wings and a couple people with two strands of hair hanging down in front		
liè	獵	a bristly dog beating the game toward you for the hunt, a witch hunt		12.4.22
liè	裂	being rendered, a blade tearing a robe or the placental afterbirth hanging from a recently pregnant woman		39.9.50
lín	鄰	the neighboring countries, appealing as the will o' wisp light emanating from a corpse attracting a kneeling person		80.16.58 15.7.36

		to a grave		
líng	靈	being nimble as a god or spirit, a cloudburst raining two pairs of misty little drops into three bigger drops above two pieces of jade crossed over each other like a shaman-witch uses, or perhaps a coffin		39.11.61 39.4.20
lìng	令	when someone is controlling, joining together from three sides over a kneeling person and ordering an action or perhaps sending off to somewhere		57.9.50 12.5.23 32.6.36 19.8.34 12.7.32 12.3.15 12.2.9 12.1.3
liú	流	it's flowing—a baby coming out headfirst in a river of watery waste		61.1.5

liù	六	six		18.3.13
lóng	聾	deaf as a dragon with an ice-cold wing ear		12.2.12
lù	露	dew like rain falling in two pairs of misty little drops onto the full leg of an animal, enough, each foot and mouth		32.5.32
lù	琭	this precious stone like jade carved in the manner wood is shaped into a water filter		39.21.128 39.21.127
lù	陸	on the land where two divided pieces of soil are next to a big soil mound		50.9.43
luàn	亂	trying to govern in		64.6.27

		chaos, two people disentangling a roll of threads using their hands with the help of a comb or beater		38.16.93 18.4.23 3.6.27
luò	珞	this particular weird precious stone, pedestrian like the sole of a foot on a mouth		39.22.132 39.22.131
mâ	馬	that horse		62.11.50 46.2.15 46.1.7
mân	滿	like arrowheads tightly wrapped in the traditional gendered head-cloth to protect them from water, packed in		9.5.19
máng	盲	what their eye sees is lost, blind		12.1.6

mèi	昧	dark as "the eight earthly branches" phase of the waxing moon before it's really full, like a tree that's upper branches aren't fully grown, not yet mature but venturing out, perhaps violating, coveting		41.6.39 14.10.41
mêi	美	an admired beauty, a person wearing a ram's horn headdress		81.2.5 81.1.4 80.13.49 62.4.17 31.10.56 31.9.54 2.1.8 2.1.5
mén	門	this two-winged gateway		1.15.59 56.3.14 52.6.35 10.9.35 6.3.12
mèn	悶	having one's heart right in the		58.1.4 58.1.3

		middle of the two-winged gateway, dark and melancholy		20.22.102 20.22.101
mêng	猛	vigorous and ferocious as a dog of an eldest brother (that baby son in the chalice)		55.4.15
mí	迷	getting lost, slowly walking with the footprint of raw rice scattered on the footprint, the left leg leading the way, bewitched, infatuated		58.11.46 27.17.87
mí	彌	relaxing one's bow as for repair with a loom, threads crossing this way, right here, for more, for filling or covering		57.6.31 47.4.19 47.3.15
mián	綿	barely perceptible, like the fine, white silk		6.5.19 6.5.18

		threads making up the traditional gendered head-cloth		
miǎn	免	like a man taking off a hat, wounded		62.16.74
miào	妙	a young woman kneeling in a mist, four tiny drops belittled as a rich young master, that subtle, ingenious, exquisite aura		27.18.91 15.2.8 1.15.57 1.8.32
miè	滅	obliterated as a fire sheltered by a cliff with a habitable cave, extinguished by water as surely as any weapon on a pole		39.13.79
mín	民	one of our folk, the people enslaved by blinding with a dagger		80.10.39 53.5.20 80.18.68 80.4.15 80.1.4

				75.7.28
				75.4.14
				75.1.1
				74.3.13
				74.1.1 72.1.1
				66.7.55
				66.6.49
				66.5.36
				66.4.28
				65.4.15
				65.2.10
				64.17.74
				58.4.14
				58.2.6
				57.14.86
				57.13.79
				57.12.72
				57.11.65
				57.7.33
				57.6.30
				32.6.33
				19.4.13
				19.2.5
				10.7.27
				3.12.48
				3.6.24
				3.4.15 3.2.5
míng	冥	a cover over the		21.9.35

		sun and two hands below, darkly profound		
míng	名	that personal name given in childhood and still whispered by moonlight		47.6.32 44.1.1 41.18.88 37.7.34 37.6.30 34.8.47 34.6.35 34.4.21 32.8.44 32.7.43 32.1.4 25.8.40 25.6.32 21.14.54 14.11.46 14.6.19 14.4.12 14.2.5 1.12.47 1.6.20 1.5.14 1.4.12 1.3.9 1.3.7
míng	明	as bright as dawn rising on a		65.2.9 55.11.60

		crescent moon, enlightened		52.13.64 52.11.53 41.6.36 33.2.8 36.9.36 27.13.58 24.3.13 22.10.33 16.10.39 10.11.42
mìng	命	what has to be, destiny like a command from a magistrate speaking, joining from three sides over a kneeling person		51.9.33 16.9.33 16.8.31
mò	莫	like the sun sinking down in four bushes… you must not be—cannot be, eh?—		78.8.35 78.7.32 78.3.13 78.1.3 70.4.14 70.3.11 69.10.35 66.10.74 59.6.37 59.5.33

				59.1.5
				51.9.31
				51.5.17
				46.5.33
				46.4.26
				46.3.20
				38.9.55
				32.6.34
				32.2.10
				22.18.57
				9.6.21
mò	沒	no longer—as if diving into the water, knife in hand, it's gone—		52.4.26 16.19.64
mò	末	tip-top, tree-top		64.8.35
móu	謀	plotting a scheme, like speaking with a certain humble so- and-so sweet-in- the- mouth plum tree		73.10.56 64.2.9

mù	目	where the eye sees		49.12.60 12.9.44 12.1.5
mù	木	tree branches and roots		76.8.46 76.3.15 64.7.31
mû	母	suckling, a woman kneeling with breasts full of milk		59.7.48 52.4.25 52.3.13 52.2.9 25.5.27 20.28.132 1.6.24
mû	牡	a bull soil, 'male parts'		61.4.19 55.6.33
nài	奈	how, how, indeed is he bearing it, a great big person on an altar		74.2.5 26.7.28
nâi	乃	only then do you get		65.16.66 54.8.57 54.7.48 54.6.40

				54.5.32
				54.4.24
				28.17.63
				16.18.62
				16.17.59
				16.16.56
				16.15.53
				16.14.50
nán	難	solid (like that hard yellow earth with two little grass tufts next to River Han, where "short-tailed birds" find no food)		75.6.26 75.4.16 73.6.32 65.4.17 64.20.102 63.17.78 63.16.73 63.15.67 63.8.30 63.6.19 2.4.27 12.6.28 3.3.10
nè	訥	words entering a city through its outskirts, mumbling or stammering		45.7.28
néng	能	using that legendary Hybrid		78.8.36 78.3.15

		Power of a mythical bear-like animal who has the legs of a deer for		77.11.51
				70.4.15
				70.3.12
				67.15.63
				67.14.54
				67.13.50
				66.10.75
				66.3.17
				66.1.5
				63.13.53
				37.3.12
				34.10.58
				32.3.17
				32.2.11
				23.6.26
				22.18.58
				15.17.93
				15.14.73
				15.13.65
				14.20.87
				10.12.46
				10.10.38
				10.8.30
				10.6.22
				10.4.14
				10.2.6
				9.6.23
				8.11.40

				7.10.46 7.4.20 7.2.9
nián	年	years of carrying wheat upon one's back		30.5.32
niâo	鳥	a bird with a dangling tail, paying attention already		55.4.20
níng	寧	being as settled as when a married woman visits her parents" home, her heart under their roof with food and wine, and she exhales		39.10.54 39.3.15
nù	怒	angry like the heart beneath a hand capturing a woman to be a slave		68.2.11

nuò	諾	assenting by speaking out loud like A Certain Someone compliantly combing her loose hair saying, "this seems is as if, yeah, definitely"		63.14.59
pàn	泮	dissolving as half a beef in the river (as our "Zhou" dynasty's school is named)		64.3.13
pèi	配	matching with the right mix (kneeling by an alcohol vat to allocate, arrange, and prepare, like you would a compounded prescription or the perfect dish to go with rice)		68.7.39
pēng	烹	boiling alive, a baby crying over the fire		60.1.5

pì	譬	metaphorically speaking, ruling over the words coming out of your mouth like a ruler with that chisel used to mark slaves and criminals, making them do what you want,		32.11.59
piān	偏	an assistant, a person just inscribing on the door, flat like bamboo tablets		31.14.86
piāo	飄	two hands placing a cover on an altar, making a swift mark, doing some kind of business that's blowing wind as a male, majestic, legendary bird, fluttering animals and insects adrift like a whirlwind		23.2.6

pín	貧	being separated by a knife from cowry- riches, poor		57.6.32
pìn	牝	the spoon of a cow or 'a woman's valley'		61.4.14 61.3.13 55.6.32 6.3.10 6.2.8
píng	平	pacified, divided and leveled as with a pestle until made even		35.2.12
pû	樸	that 'piece of wood' in the dense, unpolished, sticking, natural state of a thicket of oak trees		57.14.88 37.7.36 37.6.32 32.2.5 28.19.69 28.18.68 19.9.41 15.10.53

pû	普	the general, the universal, the vast lusterlessness of two arrows blocking the sun, (a different "pû")		54.8.58
qí	其	what it holds a basket of...		39.8.41 80.15.56 80.14.53 80.13.50 80.12.47 78.4.17 77.15.75 77.2.4 76.4.21 76.2.7 75.8.33 75.5.19 75.2.5 74.11.57 73.5.25 72.4.16 72.3.11 71.6.22 67.7.22 66.9.68

				66.2.12
				65.5.20
				64.4.14
				64.3.10
				64.2.5
				64.1.1
				63.13.55
				63.7.26
				63.6.21
				61.14.75
				60.6.28
				60.5.22
				60.4.18
				60.3.13
				59.6.39
				59.5.35
				58.12.47
				58.8.33
				58.7.31
				58.4.13
				58.3.9
				58.2.5
				58.1.1
				57.4.19
				56.7.25
				56.6.22
				56.5.19
				56.4.16

				56.3.13
				56.2.10
				54.8.55
				54.7.46
				54.6.38
				54.5.30
				54.4.22
				52.13.63
				52.13.59
				52.9.44
				52.8.41
				52.6.34
				52.5.31
				52.4.24
				52.4.20
				52.3.16
				52.3.12
				50.15.77
				50.13.71
				50.12.65
				50.11.59
				50.7.32
				49.12.58
				49.11.52
				48.7.32
				47.4.17
				47.3.13
				45.4.13

				45.2.5
				42.14.66
				38.23.123
				38.22.119
				38.21.116
				38.20.112
				35.5.26
				34.10.60
				34.9.51
				34.2.5
				33.7.29
				30.3.13
				29.2.11
				28.14.51
				28.13.48
				28.8.28
				28.7.25
				28.2.5
				28.1.2
				27.16.82
				27.16.78
				25.13.70
				25.6.31
				24.7.29
				21.14.53
				21.12.45
				21.11.41
				21.10.37

				21.8.29
				21.6.21
				20.23.105
				20.12.51
				20.8.31
				17.6.31
				17.4.17
				17.3.13
				17.2.7
				16.6.22
				15.12.61
				15.11.56
				15.10.51
				15.8.39
				14.17.76
				14.16.70
				14.10.38
				14.9.34
				11.6.33
				11.4.20
				11.2.8 9.8.31
				9.2.7
				7.10.48
				7.9.41
				7.7.34
				7.5.28
				7.3.15
				5.6.25

	.			4.8.26 4.7.23 4.6.20 4.5.17 3.11.44 3.10.41 3.9.38 3.8.35 1.10.39 1.8.31
qí	奇	remarkably cunning like a great big person atop that very one shouldering a weapon that tastes lip-smackingly genuinely like the one		74.4.19 58.9.39 57.8.45 57.2.6
qì	泣	sobbing a river		31.17.109
qì	氣	that vital qì energy, the breath of life, that air flow that's		55.13.67 42.6.22 10.3.11

		like a gift of rice		
qì	棄	tossing out, two hands throwing a baby from a basket		62.7.33 27.12.53 27.10.45 19.5.19 19.3.11 19.1.3
qí	豈	What? How? Is this 'mountains from beans?!'		22.20.70
qì	器	set of highly regarded vessels with lots of capacity, worthy of a guard dog		80.2.10 67.15.65 57.7.36 41.15.74 36.12.51 31.7.40 31.6.35 31.1.8 29.3.18 28.19.73 11.4.23 11.3.18
qì	契	engraving, this great big person		79.6.28 79.4.19

		carving agreements or contracts like a blade cutting weeds		
qî	企	a person on tiptoes		24.1.1
qî	起	rising up, taking off like a young man who will die young in the womb		64.10.40 57.8.48
qī	其	what it holds a basket of...		
qián	前	at the front (that place in battle where a step could mean your feet get cut off as punishment)		66.7.53 38.17.96 2.8.43
qiān	千	where a person reaches when extending their		64.11.44

		counting, that is, one thousand		
qiáng	強	revolving around oneself as a powerful bow broadening, strengthening, stiff, hard, and compelling as a rice weevil, like a tiny venomous snake— thwang!—		78.5.25 78.2.11 76.9.50 76.8.47 76.7.42 76.5.28 76.2.11 55.13.69 52.12.57 42.14.61 30.12.63 30.7.42 25.8.37 15.5.21 36.10.41 36.4.15 33.6.22 33.4.17 30.2.10 29.9.42 3.11.43
qiâo	巧	the craftiness of a bladed tool on exhaled air		57.8.44 45.6.22 19.5.18

qiê	且	lasting over time as the erect manhood of a male ancestor		67.18.78 67.17.74 67.16.70 41.19.94 7.2.11
qín	勤	exerting with force, working hard with the strong force of an arm, a bladed tool, or a plow on the soil		52.7.39 41.1.5 6.6.25
qīn	親	intimate one, a beloved whose suffering, like from that chisel used to mark slaves and criminals, you see up close with one big eye for a head		79.8.36 56.9.36 44.1.5 18.3.14 17.2.9
qīng	輕	a lightweight (like a light carriage, portable, running through the whole like a lengthwise warp thread of something woven, like		75.9.40 75.7.30 69.11.40 69.10.38 63.14.58 26.9.40 26.8.37 26.1.3

		menses, like a classic text)		
qīng	傾	a person leaning toward that mythical loose-haired head buck creature, separated by an arrow, adoring, emptying all their resources (a king!)		2.6.38
qīng	清	the clarity of still bright blue-green water, the color resembling the growth of that sedative cinnabar plant		45.10.35 39.9.47 39.2.10 15.13.71
qióng	窮	thoroughly used up and destitute, like your pregnant self buried with a bow		45.4.16 5.9.41
qiú	求	looking for, coveting like a centipede,		75.8.34 62.15.68

qù	取	getting hold of, grabbing the ear of		38.24.128 72.11.44 61.11.53 61.10.49 61.9.42 61.7.32 57.3.12 30.7.41 29.1.3 12.10.48
qù	去	leaving, a person with a cave mouth between their legs		72.11.42 38.24.126 29.13.57 29.12.55 29.11.53 21.14.56 20.5.18 20.3.10 12.10.46 2.16.88
qû	取	obtaining like taking the ear of an enemy and carrying it in your hand		48.6.24 48.8.38
qū	屈	bending like one who represents the dead in a rite,		45.5.20 5.7.33

		flexing to step out of a cave		
qū	曲	bent and segmented like a river or a song		22.19.66 22.1.1
quán	全	whole like a piece of pure jade, entire as it arrived		55.6.37 22.21.75 22.19.68 22.1.3
quân	犬	a dog		80.17.63
què	卻	withdrawing like a kneeling person from within that valley mouth between two mountains		46.1.5
quē	缺	a lidded earthen pot with a gap broken by a resolute hand with a fork, incomplete and		58.4.16 58.4.15 45.1.4

		lacking		
rán	然	accomplishing this thus, as naturally as dog meat over a fire		77.9.42 73.10.53 65.16.64 64.22.121 57.4.20 54.14.88 53.1.4 51.9.37 26.6.27 25.17.85 23.1.4 17.8.44
ràng	攘	a hand rolling up a sleeve, helping to undress		69.7.25 38.10.59
rè	熱	a hot fire under a tree tipped and planted by a person in the clay soil		45.9.34
rén	仁	a kernel of humanity —a person seated over not just one but two, a different èr		38.13.76 38.12.74 38.7.35 19.3.10 18.1.5 8.8.31 5.3.14 5.1.4

rén	人	that person	乀	27.8.38
				81.11.51
				81.9.39
				81.8.32
				81.7.26
				79.9.40
				79.5.24
				79.4.16
				78.9.41
				77.13.65
				77.9.37
				76.1.1
				73.6.30
				72.7.30
				71.5.18
				70.11.43
				68.6.34
				68.4.20
				66.6.45
				66.4.25
				64.21.111
				64.20.96
				64.15.63
				63.16.71
				63.12.47
				62.6.28
				62.5.27
				62.3.13

				62.2.8
				61.13.69
				61.12.61
				60.7.38
				60.7.34
				60.6.32
				60.5.26
				59.1.2
				58.13.54
				58.11.44
				57.10.59
				57.8.41
				50.4.17
				49.13.62
				49.9.41
				49.1.2
				47.5.24
				42.12.53
				42.7.26
				36.13.56
				33.3.10
				33.1.2
				31.17.103
				31.11.66
				31.10.62
				30.1.4
				29.11.52
				28.20.75

				27.15.73
				27.15.70
				27.14.65
				27.14.61
				27.10.46
				27.9.42
				26.3.12
				25.14.73
				23.7.31
				22.7.22
				20.27.128
				20.25.114
				20.21.96
				20.19.88
				20.17.79
				20.15.68
				20.9.36
				20.6.21
				12.8.39
				12.7.33
				12.5.24
				12.3.16
				12.2.10
				12.1.4 8.4.15
				7.5.26
				5.3.12
				3.7.31
				2.9.50

rèn	刃	a blade		50.13.72
réng	扔	a hand unexpectedly throwing away what it holds		69.8.28 38.10.62
rì	日	the entire day— the full sun—		58.12.48 55.8.44 48.2.7 48.1.3 26.3.14 23.3.15
róng	榮	brilliantly flourishing—like two torches atop a tree—		26.5.22
róng	容	an outward public container of private parts, like a building housing an important, older man who's 'got balls,' a duke		50.13.70 28.13.49 21.1.4 16.14.49 16.13.48 15.5.24
róng	戎	armed with a		46.2.14

		shield and a weapon on a pole		
róu	柔	softening to be as supple as a tree that can be cut with a spear		78.6.26 78.1.4 76.10.54 76.6.33 76.3.19 76.1.5 55.5.26 52.12.55 43.1.5 36.10.37 10.3.13
rú	如	a kneeling woman with breasts doing as told		64.18.87 62.12.52 39.22.133 39.21.129 20.13.54 20.11.43 20.10.39 9.2.6 5.10.43
rù	入	are entering like an arrowhead inserting or maybe like joining the imperial		61.13.67 50.10.49 50.1.3 43.3.15

		government		
rû	辱	hanging from a cliff above a hand underneath, shaking, humiliated		44.6.31 41.10.55 28.14.52 13.7.30 13.3.13 13.1.2
ruì	銳	a person speaking like an axe being sharpened on metal, pointed		56.4.17 4.5.18
ruò	若	A Certain Someone compliantly combing her loose hair seems to be saying this is as if		78.14.63 74.3.11 67.5.18 60.1.4 59.1.6 45.7.27 45.6.23 45.5.19 45.3.11 45.1.3 41.13.67 41.12.63 41.11.58 41.10.54 41.9.50 41.8.46

Pinyin	MC	Translation	Bronze Inscription Glyphs	Spots in the text
				41.7.42
				41.6.38
				41.2.15
				41.2.13
				37.3.11
				32.3.16
				20.24.110
				20.23.106
				20.16.75

				20.14.63
				20.5.19
				15.12.62
				15.11.57
				15.10.52
				15.9.44
				15.8.40
				15.7.33
				15.6.27
				13.15.77
				13.13.66
				13.8.38
				13.7.31
				13.6.25
				13.5.21
				13.3.14
				13.2.8
				13.1.3
				8.1.3 6.5.20

Pinyin	MC	Translation	Bronze Inscription Glyphs	Spots in the text
ruò	弱	shaking, a pair of fragile bows		78.5.22 78.1.5 76.10.55 76.6.34 76.1.6 55.5.24 40.2.6 36.10.38 36.3.11 3.10.40
sāi	塞	both hands stuffing items into the house, cramming full		56.2.9 52.5.30
sàn	散	scattered like a pair of bamboo stalks atop the crescent moon, tapped lightly by a tutoring cane		64.4.17 28.19.70

Pinyin	MC	Translation	Bronze Inscription Glyphs	Spots in the text
sān	三	three		14.7.23 67.12.40 67.8.28 62.9.41 50.5.27 50.3.16 50.2.10 42.4.10 42.3.9 19.7.26 11.1.1
sāng	喪	many mouths clamoring on a mulberry tree, grieving the dead		69.11.43 31.18.114 31.16.98
sè	色	coloring, hand-clawing a kneeling person and tinting their complexion as a feminine charm albeit sometimes to a perverted countenance		12.1.2

Pinyin	MC	Translation	Bronze Inscription Glyphs	Spots in the text
sè	嗇	like someone stockpiling wheat in a granary rather than letting it flow, as if there's not enough of what they cherish		59.2.10 59.1.7
shà	嗄	hoarse as the mouth of a man under a scorching sun		55.8.48
shā	殺	killing, like impaling a boar by hand		74.8.40 74.8.38 74.7.34 74.7.32 74.5.25 73.1.5 31.17.102 31.11.65 31.10.61

Pinyin	MC	Translation	Bronze Inscription	Spots in the text

			Glyphs	
shàn	善	the traditionally virtuous, offering up a ram's head while speaking back and forth, tongues waggling		81.4.16
				81.3.9
				79.9.39
				79.3.12
				73.10.55
				73.8.45
				73.7.40
				68.4.18
				68.3.12
				68.2.7
				68.1.1
				66.2.13
				65.1.3
				62.6.31
				62.3.12
				62.2.7
				58.10.40
				54.2.6
				54.1.1
				50.8.39
				49.5.25
				49.4.22
				49.4.18
				49.3.15
				49.3.12

				41.19.92
				30.6.33
				27.15.72
				27.15.69
				27.14.64
				27.14.60
				27.11.48
				27.9.40
				27.6.26
				27.4.17
				27.3.11
				27.2.6
				27.1.1
				20.4.13
				15.1.3
				8.12.42
				8.11.39
				8.10.36
				8.9.33
				8.8.30
				8.7.27
				8.6.24 8.2.6
				8.1.2 2.2.20
				2.2.17 2.2.14
shàng	上	up above		76.10.57
				75.5.20
				75.2.6

			一（一）	71.1.4 66.6.47 66.4.27 41.9.48 41.1.1 38.9.50 38.8.42 38.7.34 38.5.18 38.1.1 14.9.35 31.15.91 31.8.50 17.1.2 8.1.1
shàng	尚	nobly assisting the emperor, dividing up and differentiating what's faced with admiration and echoed in that place	尚	31.13.84 31.12.80 23.6.24 3.1.2
shāng	傷	falling ill, injured like someone in front of that male principle of the sun shining on a	傷	74.11.56 60.8.43 60.7.37 60.6.31 60.5.25

		sacrificial altar		
shâo	少	belittled, considered to be insignificant as four tiny dots like a young master's youthful period		63.4.13 47.4.20 22.5.13 19.10.42
shé	蛇	a serpent, a snake as crooked as certain gentlemen or emperors		55.3.12
shè	涉	wading, one foot in front of the other, through a watery		15.6.29
shè	攝	taking well in hand, hearing three times over,		50.8.40
shè	社	the god of the soil to whom we build altars		78.11.49
shê	舍	stopping, like at a thatched inn (usually located		67.18.76 67.17.72 67.16.68

		every 30 of the ancient miles), humble		
shē	奢	a gluttonous great big person stewing noodles or sugar cane		29.12.56
shén	神	that magical god spirit "lightning," the divine spark		60.4.21 39.11.58 60.3.16 60.6.29 60.5.23 39.4.16 29.3.17 6.1.2
shèn	甚	pairing like one-half of a double-yoked harness as pleasant as something sweet in the mouth and therefore extra		70.2.6 70.1.3 53.8.30 53.7.27 53.6.24 53.4.17 44.4.18 29.11.54 21.11.43
shèn	慎			64.18.85

shēn	身	your pregnant self		66.5.39
				54.9.63
				54.9.61
				54.4.21
				52.14.67
				52.10.47
				52.7.37
				52.4.27
				44.2.6
				44.1.3
				7.7.35
				7.8.37
				26.8.36
				16.19.65
				13.14.73
				13.12.62
				13.11.54
				13.10.50
				13.8.39
				13.2.9
				9.9.35
				7.6.31
				7.5.29
shēn	深	deep as far water		65.14.56
				59.8.55

				15.3.11
shéng	繩	a skein of silk around a striving toad		80.10.42 27.6.29 14.11.43 14.11.42
shèng	聖	an ideal grounded sage known for his civilian petition to authority, standing straight, speaking, and being listened to		81.11.50 81.7.25 79.4.15 78.9.40 77.13.64 73.6.29 72.7.29 71.5.17 70.11.42 66.6.44 66.4.24 64.20.95 64.15.62 63.16.70 63.12.46 60.7.33 58.13.53 57.10.58 49.13.61 49.9.40 49.1.1

				47.5.23
				29.11.51
				28.20.75
				27.8.37
				26.3.11
				22.7.21
				19.1.2
				12.8.38
				7.5.25
				5.3.11
				3.7.30
				2.9.49
shèng	勝	able to withstand entirely, to be victorious as a splendid piece of jewelry , an omen or the royal "We" mending something on a boat with two hands by the strength of an arm, bladed tool, or a plow		76.7.45
				78.6.28
				78.5.24
				78.3.16
				73.7.41
				69.13.53
				68.3.13
				67.20.87
				61.4.18
				45.9.33
				45.8.30
				33.4.15
				33.3.9
				36.10.39
				31.18.112
				31.9.51

shèng	乘	four-horse military carriage		80.7.28 26.7.31
shēng	生	sprouting, like a bud from the ground		76.6.36 76.3.17 76.1.3 75.11.53 75.10.46 75.8.35 72.4.18 64.8.32 59.9.60 55.12.62 51.15.57 51.10.40 51.1.2 50.8.41 50.7.34 50.7.33 50.4.19 50.2.5 50.1.2 46.2.16 42.4.11 42.3.8 42.2.5 42.1.2

				40.4.19
				40.3.15
				39.13.76
				39.6.31
				34.3.14
				30.4.23
				25.2.8
				15.14.80
				10.14.54
				10.13.50
				7.4.22
				7.3.18
				2.12.68
				2.3.26
shēng	聲	the many sounds you hear as hitting chimes with a weapon in your right hand, going right through a person		80.17.65 41.16.80 2.7.40
shí	時	seasonally timely as the sunny spot where you measures your pulse, between the footprint and the hand		8.12.43

shí	食	eating, mouth over a bowl of rice on a stand		80.12.48 75.2.7 53.11.40 24.8.35 20.28.131
shí	識	intimately known, speaking of what's gathered with a tone from the mouth by a dagger- ax, marked and remembered		38.17.97 15.4.19 15.3.14
shí	實	filling, like a truly rich building crammed with jade and cowry-shells		38.22.120 3.9.37
shí	十	ten		50.5.25 50.3.14 50.2.8 11.1.2
shí	石	in a habitable cave in a rock cliff, that gem		39.22.134
shí	什	ten people		80.2.7

shì	事	their task, what it is they do with a weapon, flag, or pen in hand		70.6.20 64.19.92 64.17.77 63.10.39 63.8.31 63.2.6 63.2.4 61.13.68 59.1.3 57.13.77 57.3.11 52.9.45 48.7.34 48.6.30 31.13.83 31.12.79 30.3.14 23.8.35 17.7.36 8.11.38 2.9.55
shì	逝	passing on, slowly walking with the footprint of a hand and axe severing		25.10.46 25.9.45

		life early, the left leg leading the way		
shì	恃	a mother—the heart grabbed like by the hand of a government office or temple worker that was usually a eunuch in the old days		77.13.69 51.16.64 34.3.11 10.15.61 2.13.75
shì	示	being displayed on an altar		36.13.55
shì	士	ax-wielding bachelor-soldier-scholar-official appointed by the emperor		68.1.3 41.3.18 41.2.10 41.1.2 15.1.5
shì	釋	distinguishing the sight of the opposite, the upside-down version of a running man who will die young, spying on good		15.9.48

		luck or an emperor's personal favor, in other words, melting		
shì	視	regarded as by one big eye for a head kneeling at an altar		59.9.62 35.6.29 14.1.1
shì	式	a model example, like a bladed tool and a retrievable arrow attached to a string for effective shooting and catching		65.12.49 65.11.45 28.10.37 28.9.33 22.8.28
shì	是	this baby footprint on bamboo-slip pages,		79.4.13 78.13.56 78.11.47 78.9.38 77.13.62 76.7.39 75.11.49 75.9.38 75.6.24 75.3.11 74.9.41 73.6.27

				72.7.27
				72.6.23
				71.7.25
				71.4.13
				70.11.40
				70.8.27
				69.6.20
				68.7.37
				68.6.31
				68.5.25
				66.8.58
				66.6.42
				66.4.22
				65.13.50
				64.20.93
				64.15.60
				63.16.68
				63.12.44
				59.8.53
				59.2.11
				58.13.51
				56.8.27
				53.13.45
				53.3.13
				52.15.69
				51.18.69
				51.5.13
				47.5.21

				44.4.16
				43.4.18
				39.17.100
				38.19.106
				38.4.14
				38.2.5
				22.11.36
				36.9.33
				31.10.59
				30.14.68
				29.11.49
				27.18.88
				27.13.55
				27.8.35
				26.3.9
				24.4.15
				22.7.19
				21.2.7
				16.8.28
				14.21.91
				14.15.62
				14.13.52
				13.7.27
				12.8.36
				10.17.66
				7.5.23
				6.4.13
				6.2.5 3.7.28

				2.16.85
				2.9.47
shì	室	a living space where a wife comes to live		11.5.31
shì	勢	planting power like holding a forceful arm, a bladed tool, or a plow on the soil to seed like testicles		51.4.10
shì	螫	stinging—both armpits sweat this too!—as when hit lightly by a snake		55.3.14
shì	市	a marketplace (like a bustling city at the forked tree)		62.4.21
shî	始	conceiving, a woman kneeling, happy, speaking of gathering oneself from three sides		64.18.88
				64.12.48
				52.1.4
				38.18.105
				32.7.40
				14.20.90
				1.5.18

shì	室	a living space where a wife comes to live		11.5.31
shì	勢	planting power like holding a forceful arm, a bladed tool, or a plow on the soil to seed like testicles		51.4.10
shì	螫	stinging—both armpits sweat this too!—as when hit lightly by a snake		55.3.14
shì	市	a marketplace (like a bustling city at the forked tree)		62.4.21
shî	始	conceiving, a woman kneeling, happy, speaking of gathering oneself from three sides		64.18.88 64.12.48 52.1.4 38.18.105 32.7.40 14.20.90 1.5.18
shì	室	a living space where a wife		11.5.31

		comes to live		
shì	勢	planting power like holding a forceful arm, a bladed tool, or a plow on the soil to seed like testicles		51.4.10
shì	螫	stinging—both armpits sweat this too!—as when hit lightly by a snake		55.3.14
shì	市	a marketplace (like a bustling city at the forked tree)		62.4.21
shǐ	始	conceiving, a woman kneeling, happy, speaking of gathering oneself from three sides		64.18.88 64.12.48 52.1.4 38.18.105 32.7.40 14.20.90 1.5.18
shì	室	a living space where a wife comes to live		11.5.31

shì	勢	planting power like holding a forceful arm, a bladed tool, or a plow on the soil to seed like testicles		51.4.10
shì	螫	stinging—both armpits sweat this too!—as when hit lightly by a snake		55.3.14
shì	市	a marketplace (like a bustling city at the forked tree)		62.4.21
shî	始	conceiving, a woman kneeling, happy, speaking of gathering oneself from three sides		64.18.88 64.12.48 52.1.4 38.18.105 32.7.40 14.20.90 1.5.18
shì	室	a living space where a wife comes to live		11.5.31

shì	勢	planting power like holding a forceful arm, a bladed tool, or a plow on the soil to seed like testicles		51.4.10
shì	螫	stinging—both armpits sweat this too!—as when hit lightly by a snake		55.3.14
shì	市	a marketplace (like a bustling city at the forked tree)		62.4.21
shǐ	始	conceiving, a woman kneeling, happy, speaking of gathering oneself from three sides		64.18.88 64.12.48 52.1.4 38.18.105 32.7.40 14.20.90 1.5.18
shì	室	a living space where a wife comes to live		11.5.31

shì	勢	planting power like holding a forceful arm, a bladed tool, or a plow on the soil to seed like testicles		51.4.10
shì	螫	stinging—both armpits sweat this too!—as when hit lightly by a snake		55.3.14
shì	市	a marketplace (like a bustling city at the forked tree)		62.4.21
shǐ	始	conceiving, a woman kneeling, happy, speaking of gathering oneself from three sides		64.18.88 64.12.48 52.1.4 38.18.105 32.7.40 14.20.90 1.5.18
shì	室	a living space where a wife comes to live		11.5.31

shì	勢	planting power like holding a forceful arm, a bladed tool, or a plow on the soil to seed like testicles		51.4.10
shì	螫	stinging—both armpits sweat this too!—as when hit lightly by a snake		55.3.14
shì	市	a marketplace (like a bustling city at the forked tree)		62.4.21
shǐ	始	conceiving, a woman kneeling, happy, speaking of gathering oneself from three sides		64.18.88 64.12.48 52.1.4 38.18.105 32.7.40 14.20.90 1.5.18
shǐ	使	a low-ranking government official, his hand		80.10.38 80.4.14 80.2.5

		holding a pen, sent as a messenger or an envoy, is putting to work, using in every way you can think of, directing		74.3.12 55.13.66 53.1.1 3.13.53 3.12.47 3.6.23 3.4.14 3.2.4
shî	室	such a living space (where a wife comes to live)		11.6.36
shī	師	army of 2,500 soldiers stationed on a soil mound hill		30.4.17 27.16.79 27.14.67
shī	失	dropped from one's hand		73.12.64 64.16.73 64.14.58 38.14.80 38.13.75 38.12.70 38.11.65 38.3.12 33.7.28 29.6.29 26.10.46 26.9.42

				23.17.76 23.16.74 23.11.53 23.11.49 13.6.23
shī	施	flying flags over—yes, that too, 'female funnel'—spreading, reproducing		53.3.12
shòu	壽	longevity, an old man, 'Lâo,' sheltering many mouths		33.8.38
shòu	獸	a predator like a dog attacking an animal		55.4.16
shòu	受	receiving and bearing (a hand over a commonplace bucket with a hand below, on bottom)		78.12.52 78.10.43
shôu	守	hand-defending this building		67.21.89 52.12.54

				52.4.23
				37.3.13
				32.3.18
				28.14.50
				28.8.27
				28.2.4
				16.2.4
				9.6.24
				5.10.44
shôu	首	the face of the mythical loose-haired head buck creature		38.16.95 14.16.71
shôu	手	their expert, convenient hand		74.11.58
shú	孰	which kneeling person using both arms for paying tribute to an ancestral shrine		77.11.50 74.6.27 73.5.23 58.7.29 44.3.14 44.2.9 44.1.4 23.4.16 15.14.72 15.13.64

shû	數	adding up (tapping lightly with a tutoring cane up through the stack... from a kneeling woman to a round center drum with a flagpole and then a suckling mother)		5.9.40 39.20.121 27.3.12
shû	屬	joining and submitting to the category to which they were born (the most recent or 'tail- end' person, 'a silkworm caterpillar on a hollyhock leaf," as we call the Shû province)		19.8.37
shū	疏	thinned, obstructions cleared—fully enough, like a complete leg and foot, an upside-		73.12.61 56.10.41

		down baby is upside down with amniotic fluid streaming below,		
shuâng	爽	invigoratingly clear and broken, possibly angry as a great big person with a pair of cut hatch-marks on each side of the chest in the style of that ancient women's chest tattoo		12.3.18
shuí	誰	the one of whom 'the short-tailed bird' speaks, who		4.11.36
shuì	稅	open mouthed like a smiling, breathy older brother next to a rice plant, that is, charging tax		75.2.8
shuî	水	water flowing right in the center of a river, spraying up on both sides		78.1.7 8.2.5 8.1.4

shùn	順	smoothly going along like the loose- haired head buck kneeling at a river		65.16.69
shuâng	爽	invigoratingly clear and broken, possibly angry as a great big person with a pair of cut hatch-marks on each side of the chest in the style of that ancient women's chest tattoo		12.3.18
shuí	誰	the one of whom 'the short-tailed bird' speaks, who		4.11.36
shuì	稅	open mouthed like a smiling, breathy older brother next to a rice plant, that		75.2.8

		is, charging tax		
shuî	水	water flowing right in the center of a river, spraying up on both sides		78.1.7 8.2.5 8.1.4
shùn	順	smoothly going along like the loose- haired head buck kneeling at a river		65.16.69
sì	四	from all four directions		25.13.65 15.7.35 10.11.44
sì	似	like how a person and a turned fetus, side-by-side, resemble one another		67.4.15 67.2.8 4.4.11 20.26.122 4.10.30
sì	兕	fearsome buffalo		50.11.55 50.9.47
sì	祀	sacrificing with something like a fetus upon an altar		54.3.15

sì	肆	undisciplined as long hair that must be brushed by hand		58.16.66
sì	駟	driving (like handling four horses that pull a chariot)		62.11.49
sǐ	死	dying, a person turning to a pile of bones		80.18.71 80.4.17 76.5.30 76.4.22 76.2.8 75.9.41 75.7.31 74.3.16 74.2.8 74.1.4 67.19.80 50.15.79 50.4.22 50.3.11 50.1.4 42.14.67 33.8.33 6.1.4
sī	斯	what that holds a basket of is lopped		2.2.18 2.1.9

		off, thereby defining whatever remains as 'not-that' but rather as		
sī	私	your personal concerns, turning about your own private grain supply		19.10.43 7.10.49 7.9.43
sī	司	a reversed royal speaker like a queen or king		79.7.31 79.6.27 74.8.37 74.7.31
sú	俗	in the common practices of the people from that difficult position in the valley between two mountains		80.15.57 41.9.51 20.21.95 20.19.87
sù	素	some plain, unprocessed white silk being braided by two hands		19.9.39
suí	隨	accompanying one another single file near soil mountains, slowly walking with the		29.7.36 14.17.72 2.8.46

		footprint of a meat-handling Being, the left leg leading the way		
suì	遂	slowly walking with the footprint of post-harvest time after you've divided up the pigs, the left leg leading the way		17.7.37 9.9.34
suī	雖	immediately adjacent (like a venomous snake with "a short-tailed bird," right next to it)		80.8.30 80.6.22 62.10.43 32.2.6 27.17.84 26.5.20
sŭn	損	diminishing, like hands and fingers injured by the top edge of the cauldron that is the monarchy government		77.10.43 77.7.30 77.5.20 48.3.12 48.3.9 48.2.8 42.11.52 42.10.44
sūn	孫	infant boy, maybe a grandson like a thin silk skein as		54.3.12

		tiny as three grains of sand		
suô	所	"that place" being intentionally created like any household gate hewn with an axe		80.9.35 80.7.27 73.4.21 72.4.17 72.3.12 66.1.3 64.21.113 62.13.59 62.3.15 61.14.76 58.6.27 58.5.21 50.13.69 50.12.63 50.11.57 42.12.55 42.7.28 33.7.30 30.4.19 22.19.64 20.14.65 20.6.23 19.8.36 13.9.41 8.4.17 7.2.7

tái	臺	a lookout tower from which a person can shoot an arrow		20.11.46
tái	台	what it says, revolving around itself, as its place name		64.9.39
tài	太	the quite greatest biggest person—period!—		35.2.13 20.10.41 17.1.1
tài	忒	shooting a retrievable arrow attached to a string into the heart, catching and changing		28.11.41
tài	泰	the excessively extravagant (a great big person trying to clasp both arms around a flowing stream)		29.13.58
táng	堂	a palace courtyard		9.5.20

tián	畋	tilling a field, hitting it lightly, marking it up like a tattoo,		12.4.21
tián	恬	quietly, a heart licked by a forked tongue emerging upward from a mouth		31.8.47
tián	田	a field		53.7.26
tiān	天	the heavenly from high above this great big person		81.10.43 79.8.33 78.13.58 78.7.30 78.1.1 77.11.56 77.7.27 77.1.1 73.11.57 73.7.34 73.4.19

				70.3.9
				68.7.40
				67.22.92
				67.15.59
				67.12.45
				67.1.1
				66.10.72
				66.8.60
				63.10.36
				63.8.28
				62.17.78
				62.8.38
				61.3.10
				61.2.6
				60.2.11
				59.1.4
				57.6.24
				57.3.13
				56.15.64
				54.14.86
				54.13.80
				54.13.77
				54.8.53
				52.2.7
				52.1.1
				49.10.49
				49.9.43
				48.8.39

				48.6.25
				47.2.11
				47.1.5
				46.2.10
				46.1.1
				45.10.38
				43.7.35
				43.2.8
				43.1.1
				40.3.11
				39.9.44
				39.7.38
				39.2.6
				37.9.46
				35.1.4
				32.11.63
				32.5.25
				32.2.8
				31.11.75
				30.2.11
				29.3.15
				29.1.4
				28.16.58
				28.15.54
				28.10.35
				28.9.31
				28.4.12
				28.3.8

				26.8.38
				25.16.79
				25.15.78
				25.12.55
				25.5.25
				25.2.6
				23.6.22
				23.5.20
				22.18.55
				22.8.26
				16.17.58
				16.16.57
				16.5.15
				13.15.80
				13.14.75
				13.13.69
				13.12.64
				10.9.34
				9.10.37
				7.2.5
				7.1.1 6.4.15
				5.5.21 5.1.1
				2.1.1 1.5.15
tíng	亭	sheltering like a person in a pavilion or in a checkpoint		51.13.49
tīng	聽	hearing, an ear		35.7.34

tōu			listening to voices, perhaps heeding, allowing, or handling matters of state	14.3.8
tóng	同		what's known as 'Fán, one and the same," when spoken of as ordinarily and generally as any commonplace bucket	56.8.30 56.7.24 23.16.72 23.14.63 23.12.54 23.11.51 23.10.46 23.9.41 4.8.25 1.13.48 1.11.43
tōng	通		walking right between two walls, patiently, slowly, the left leg leading the way	15.2.10
tóu	投		throwing expertly by hand like handling a shū weapon	50.11.58
tōu	偷		covertly sneaking, a person standing with their back to	41.12.64

		someone gathering themselves together from three sides after a blade cut off their foot as punishment, like from adultery		
tú	徒	walking with the footprint of merely a foot soldier, afoot on the clay soil		76.6.38 76.5.32 50.3.13 50.2.7
tú	圖	charting, like drawing a city wall around a lowly rural granary,		63.6.18
tǔ	土	clay soil		64.10.43
tuì	退	withdrawing, walking with the footprint of a person slowly retreating from the table after eating, like the ending of a		69.5.18 41.7.43 9.9.36

		thread in a knot, their eye looking backward, the left leg leading the way		
tuī	推	promoting along like hand-pushing that "short-tailed bird"		66.8.63
tuó	橐	a bellows		5.6.27
tuō	託	caring for something like a blade of grass with words from your mouth, trusted with		13.15.79
tuō	脫	freely exchanging the meat of their matter, stripping themself like a smiling breathy older brother		54.2.10 36.11.45
wā	窪	hollow as a watery sinkhole (as a Royal Jade River		22.3.7

		or"River Guī") behind the two-winged flap covering a cave		
wài	外	'outside' or foreign, as the relatives of a mother, sister, and daughter who divine by the moon		7.7.33
wán	頑	obstinate as a head above the kneeling the mythical loose-haired head buck creature who differentiates right from wrong		20.26.121
wàn	萬	the medicine-dancing-scorpion insect swarm of		76.3.12 64.22.117 62.1.3 51.5.15 42.5.14 42.4.12 40.3.13 39.13.72 39.6.26 37.4.15 34.7.38

				34.5.25
				34.3.9
				32.4.20
				26.7.30
				16.3.7 8.2.8
				5.2.6 4.4.12
				2.11.61
				1.6.21
wân	晚	in late evening when the sun on a man in a hat is being removed		41.15.75
wáng	王	the king with his ceremonial jade axe or crown connecting the three levels of heaven, man, and earth		78.13.60 66.3.21 66.1.9 42.9.36 39.17.103 39.14.81 39.7.33 37.3.10 32.3.15 25.13.68 25.12.59 16.16.55 16.15.54
wáng	亡	someone gone, absent because they've perished or		44.5.27 44.3.13 41.2.16

		fled by a knife's edge		33.8.36
wáng	妄	improper and willful, reckless as a kneeling woman fleeing		16.12.43
wàng	望	gazing from a distance like a good human standing on soil below the cutting edge of a knife and the crescent moon		80.16.61
wâng	往	a person is walking slowly toward you with the luxurious footprint of a king, the left leg leading the way		80.19.74 35.2.7 35.1.6
wâng	枉	bending like a tree king connecting heaven, man, and earth		22.2.4
wâng	網	thin silk webbing		73.11.58

wéi	為	creating something by hand, carving an elephant likeness of good fortune and royal power		81.11.54
				81.8.31
				79.3.11
				77.13.66
				75.10.47
				75.5.23
				74.4.18
				69.3.11
				69.2.8
				68.4.22
				68.1.2
				67.15.58
				67.12.44
				66.3.18
				66.1.6
				65.1.4
				64.22.125
				64.15.65
				64.13.52
				64.5.18
				63.12.50
				63.7.23
				63.1.3
				63.1.1
				62.17.77

				61.15.81
				61.5.22
				58.10.42
				58.9.38
				57.11.63
				56.15.63
				52.15.70
				52.2.6
				51.16.61
				49.10.48
				49.2.10
				48.5.23
				48.5.19
				48.4.17
				48.2.5
				48.1.1
				47.7.34
				45.10.37
				43.6.32
				43.4.23
				42.15.71
				42.9.39
				42.6.24
				41.4.29
				39.18.114
				39.16.98
				39.15.93
				39.7.37

				38.9.52
				38.8.49
				38.8.44
				38.7.41
				38.7.36
				38.6.33
				38.6.28
				38.5.25
				38.5.21
				37.2.8
				37.1.4
				34.9.55
				34.8.48
				34.7.44
				34.5.29
				31.8.49
				29.5.23
				29.4.21
				29.1.7
				28.21.79
				28.19.72
				28.16.57
				28.15.53
				28.10.34
				28.9.30
				28.4.11
				28.3.7
				26.2.6

				26.1.2
				25.8.38
				25.5.24
				23.4.17
				22.8.25
				21.3.11
				19.7.29
				15.5.22
				15.1.4
				14.8.32
				13.14.74
				13.12.63
				13.10.47
				13.4.17
				12.9.43
				12.9.40
				11.8.48
				11.7.42
				11.5.30
				11.3.17
				10.15.58
				10.10.39
				5.4.18 5.2.8
				3.14.63
				3.14.61
				3.13.59
				3.4.17
				2.13.72

				2.9.53
				2.2.16 2.1.7
wéi	唯	'oh, YES, Ma'am,' says the 'short-tailed bird'		20.2.5
				22.17.51
				15.16.89
				15.4.16
				77.12.58
				75.10.43
				72.5.20
				71.3.10
				70.7.24
				67.3.12
				59.2.9
				53.3.11
				42.8.30
				41.19.90
				21.4.15
				21.4.13
				21.2.5
				8.13.45
				2.15.82
wèi	謂	by the nitty-gritty, grinding gizzard of a fowl, what that's called		39.17.105
				78.13.57
				78.11.48
				74.9.42
				69.6.21
				68.7.38
				68.6.32

				68.5.26
				67.1.4
				65.13.51
				59.8.54
				59.3.17
				59.2.12
				56.8.28
				55.15.74
				53.13.46
				51.18.70
				36.9.34
				30.14.69
				27.18.89
				27.13.56
				22.19.65
				17.8.41
				16.8.29
				14.21.92
				14.15.63
				14.13.53
				13.8.34
				13.7.28
				13.3.11
				10.17.67
				6.4.14 6.2.6
				1.13.49
wèi	味	tasting, reflecting on a flavor in the		63.3.9
				63.3.7

		mouth which is still forming like a tree whose top branches are not yet fully grown		35.5.28 12.3.14
wèi	畏	scared—like of a ghost with a stick—of		74.3.15 74.1.3 72.1.3 53.3.14 20.7.28 20.6.24 17.3.15 15.7.34
wèi	未	like a tree whose top branches aren't yet fully grown, not yet		64.6.26 64.5.21 64.2.6 55.6.30 20.13.58 20.12.52 20.8.32
wèi	衛	guarding like with footsteps around an enclosure at a public crossroads		67.23.98
wêi	偽	fronting the hand-making of an elephant likeness, that kind of creating		18.2.12

		happening right behind them		
wēi	微	"trifling," a slight thing, this admired beauty wearing a ram's horn headdress and stepping slowly with only the left leg leading, a tutoring cane lightly tapping their hair, combing out or "splitting hairs," not having much		64.4.15 36.9.35 15.2.7 14.6.21
wēi	威	intimidating pomp as powerful as an axe over a kneeling woman		72.2.7 72.1.4
wén	文	is covering with this pattern, like a tattoo on the chest of a great big man		53.9.33 19.7.30
wén	聞	heard at the two-winged gateway and famously reported on		80.17.67 50.8.38 41.3.19 41.2.11

				41.1.3 35.7.38 14.3.11
wò	握	gripping—grasping as onto a room, a roof covering an arrow straight in the clay soil, having arrived at the end, in the extreme climax—		55.5.28
wô	我	I, holding a rake-like weapon to defend myself and my opinion		70.10.37 70.9.33 70.8.29 67.8.26 67.1.5 57.14.82 57.13.75 57.12.68 57.11.61 53.1.2 42.13.57 20.27.124 20.26.119 20.22.99 20.20.91 20.17.77 20.16.73

				20.12.47
				17.8.42
wú	吾	counting up on all five fingers, isn't it me		42.15.68
				43.4.18
				74.5.21
				70.1.1
				69.11.44
				69.2.5
				57.4.15
				54.14.82
				49.7.34
				49.6.28
				49.4.20
				49.3.14
				4.11.33
				29.2.9
				37.6.24
				25.6.28
				21.16.61
				16.4.11
				13.11.55
				13.11.52
				13.10.48
				13.9.40
wú	無	a shamanic dancer with animal tails flowing from her wrists, "Wú,"		2.3.24
				80.9.34
				80.7.26
				79.8.35

		that is to say, "Not-Having"		79.7.29
				78.4.18
				75.10.44
				72.4.14
				72.3.9
				70.7.25
				69.9.32
				69.8.29
				69.7.26
				69.6.23
				64.19.90
				64.16.72
				64.16.69
				64.15.67
				64.15.64
				63.17.77
				63.3.8
				63.2.5
				63.1.2
				59.5.29
				59.4.26
				58.8.34
				57.14.83
				57.13.76
				57.11.62
				57.3.10
				52.14.65
				50.15.78

				50.13.68
				50.12.62
				50.11.56
				49.1.3
				48.6.29
				48.5.21
				48.5.18
				48.4.16
				46.2.12
				43.6.31
				43.4.22
				43.3.16
				43.3.13
				41.18.87
				41.17.83
				41.14.71
				40.4.21
				39.20.123
				39.14.82
				39.13.74
				39.12.66
				39.11.59
				39.10.52
				39.9.45
				38.7.39
				38.5.23
				38.5.20
				38.4.16

				37.7.40
				37.7.33
				37.6.29
				37.2.6
				37.1.3
				35.5.27
				34.6.32
				32.1.3
				28.12.45
				27.12.52
				27.10.44
				27.6.28
				27.4.19
				27.2.8
				27.1.3
				24.5.22
				20.24.111
				20.14.64
				20.1.3
				19.6.23
				14.14.58
				14.13.54
				14.12.50
				13.11.53
				11.8.45
				11.6.34
				11.4.21
				11.2.9

				10.12.47
				10.8.31
				10.6.23
				10.2.7
				8.14.49
				7.9.42
				3.15.65
				3.14.62
				3.12.51
				3.12.49
				2.9.52
				1.7.27
				1.5.13
wú	蕪	thick as a pair of grass sprouts growing from Not-Being, dancing with long tails flowing from her wrists like turnips from an unused field		53.7.28
wù	惡	llike a tomb built over a heart		73.4.22 42.7.29 31.2.11 24.9.40
wù	物	matter outside one's body, "cut		76.3.13 65.15.61

		from the cow" by a bloodied blade		64.22.118
				62.1.4
				57.8.46
				55.14.70
				51.5.16
				51.3.7
				42.10.42
				42.5.15
				42.4.13
				40.3.14
				39.13.73
				39.6.27
				37.4.16
				34.7.39
				34.5.26
				34.3.10
				32.4.21
				31.2.9
				30.13.64
				29.7.32
				27.12.54
				27.11.50
				25.1.2
				24.9.38
				21.8.32
				21.3.12
				16.5.16
				16.3.8

				14.14.59 14.12.51 8.2.9 5.2.7 4.4.13 2.11.62 1.6.22
wù	勿	do not—seriously as a bloodied blade, don't be		30.12.62 30.10.53 30.9.49 30.8.45
wû	侮	ridiculed and disgraced as a person whose lush flourishing sprouts out of a kneeling, suckling woman		17.4.19
wû	五	five times		12.3.13 12.2.7 12.1.1
wû	吾	I/we—our five mouths—		
wû	武	setting out by foot with spear as one for a long journey		68.1.6

		like the military		
xí	襲	an inherited, raiding pattern (superposed atop, like something received from the clothing or placenta of a flying dragon) for		27.13.57
xí	熙	bright as the flame of a healthy fetus, nourished like a beautiful broad chin		20.9.38 20.9.37
xí	習	is fluttering both wings high above the sun, learning to fly, a loyal follower practicing		52.15.71
xì	細	is a small skein-of-silk fontanelle		67.7.23 63.11.43 63.7.27
xî	徙	moving, shifting, migrating like		80.5.21

		feces leaving a living person representing the dead in a rite		
xī	歙	sucking in, coming together as a kneeling person with their mouth open, their back toward one open mouth atop another mouth above a pair of little wings		49.10.46 49.10.45 36.1.3
xī	谿	in a valley mouth between two mountains with the tiniest little silk string of a child between a claw-like hand grabbing from above and a great big person below		28.4.14 28.3.10
xī	希	"barely there," as sparse as the few interconnecting threads in the		74.11.53 70.9.35 43.7.37 41.16.79

| | | gendered head-cloth we wear after reaching adulthood, rarely seen or heard | | 23.1.1
14.4.14 |
| xī | 兮 | hmmm—like wind through tree branches!— | 兮 | 58.6.24
58.5.18
30.4.24
23.18.88
23.18.84
17.5.28
17.5.24
15.6.26
34.1.4
25.3.12
25.3.10
20.24.109
20.18.86
20.14.62
20.12.50
20.8.30
17.6.30
21.9.36
21.9.34
21.7.28
21.7.26
21.5.20
21.5.18 |

				20.23.104
				15.12.60
				15.11.55
				15.10.50
				15.9.43
				15.8.38
				15.7.32
				4.9.29
				4.3.10
xī	昔	ancient times, when floods covered the sun,		39.1.1
xiá	瑕	is like a king who borrowed or forged a gem, a flaw		27.2.9
xiá	狎	behaving intimately (maybe disrespectfully, teasingly, or improperly so, like a dog with a turtle shell),		72.3.10
xià	下	now here down below		29.1.5
				78.13.59
				78.7.31

				78.1.2
				77.11.57
				77.4.13
				76.9.53
				70.3.10
				68.4.24
				67.15.60
				67.12.46
				67.1.2
				66.10.73
				66.8.61
				66.4.32
				66.2.14
				64.12.51
				63.10.37
				63.8.29
				62.17.79
				61.15.82
				61.11.51
				61.10.47
				61.8.38
				61.6.28
				61.5.23
				61.3.11
				61.2.7
				61.1.4
				60.2.12
				57.6.25

				57.3.14
				56.15.65
				54.14.87
				54.13.81
				54.13.78
				54.8.54
				52.2.8
				52.1.2
				49.10.50
				49.9.44
				48.8.40
				48.6.26
				47.1.6
				46.2.11
				46.1.2
				45.10.39
				43.7.36
				43.2.9
				43.1.2
				41.3.17
				40.3.12
				39.16.97
				39.7.39
				38.6.26
				38.3.9
				37.9.47
				35.1.5
				32.11.64

				32.2.9
				31.11.76
				30.2.12
				29.3.16
				28.16.59
				28.15.55
				28.10.36
				28.9.32
				28.4.13
				28.3.9
				26.8.39
				25.5.26
				22.18.56
				22.8.27
				17.1.3
				14.10.39
				13.15.81
				13.14.76
				13.13.70
				13.12.65
				13.4.18
				2.6.36 2.1.2
xián	賢	their eye cleverly, solidly looking down from atop cowry- like riches		77.15.79 75.11.50 3.1.3
xiān	先	leading, long		67.18.79

		before, stepping off from this footprint an ancestor		67.15.61 67.12.47 66.5.35 62.11.48 25.2.5 7.6.32 4.12.42
xiān	鮮	a delicacy such as fresh fish or ram's head		60.1.7
xiang	享	enjoying a tribute offering at the ancestral shrine, a baby, a mouth, a cap on it		20.10.40
xiáng	祥	an omen like a ram's head at an altar		78.12.55 55.12.64 31.6.33 31.1.6
xiàng	象	like an elephant skeleton to a living elephant, it's bearing a likeness to something		41.17.82 35.1.3 21.6.24 14.14.61 4.12.39
xiāng	相	like a seen tree and the eye		80.19.73 80.17.66

		seeing it (or like a well-tended lord and his attentive attendant), when taken together, create this singular phenomenon		80.16.60 69.12.49 60.8.42 2.4.29 32.5.27 20.5.17 20.3.9 2.8.45 2.7.41 2.6.37 2.5.33 2.3.25
xiāng	鄉	a village, a rural community where people face one another over a food vessel, feasting		54.11.71 54.11.69 54.6.37
xiào	孝	doing their filial duty as a loose-haired elder leaning over a baby, filled with piety or, at times, mourning		19.4.15 18.3.18
xiào	笑	laughing like a dog in a pair of grass sprouts		41.4.25 41.3.22

xiào	肖	like our tiny dear little one, three grains of sand being the likeness of meat		67.5.19 67.4.17 67.2.10
xiâo	小	our tiny dear little one, like three grains of sand		80.1.1 63.4.11 61.13.62 61.8.35 61.7.33 61.6.29 60.1.6 52.11.51 34.6.37 32.2.7
xié	歇	fading, a mouth begging for alms behind a kneeling person with their mouth open		39.11.64
xìn	信	giving one's word to a person		81.2.8 81.1.1 63.14.62 49.8.39 49.7.36 49.7.32 49.6.29 49.6.26

				38.15.89
				23.18.87
				23.18.81
				21.12.48
				17.5.27
				17.5.21
				8.9.34
xīn	新	having the look of a freshly chopped hazelnut tree axed by that chisel used to mark slaves and criminals, like someone newly married, recently		22.4.12 15.17.96
xīn	心	in their heart		55.13.65 49.11.53 49.2.11 49.2.9 49.1.5 20.17.81 12.5.25 8.7.26 3.8.36 3.6.25
xíng	形	shaping as finely and level as two shields side by		51.3.8 41.17.84 2.5.34

		side with measuring lines of three hairs' breadth		24.8.37
xíng	行	but out in public at the crossroads, being good, doing one's work		78.8.37 70.4.16 70.2.8 69.6.24 69.6.22 64.11.47 62.5.23 53.2.7 50.9.44 47.5.26 41.1.7 33.6.23 29.7.34 27.1.2 26.3.15 25.4.18 24.2.8 12.7.34 2.10.56
xìng	興	lifting it together, clasping two pairs of hands together in front of ones' chests and		36.6.23

		together carrying ones' shields		
xìng	姓	family names that a kneeling woman sprouts from the ground		49.12.55 49.2.8 17.8.39 5.4.17
xióng	雄	maleness, 'a short- tailed bird' with the left hand flipped, revolving around oneself		28.1.3
xiōng	凶	unlucky as a hole in the ground with rock, mud, or bamboo in the bottom		31.13.82 30.5.31 16.12.45
xiū	修	if a person develops (warned, built, mended, embellished by being lightly hitting on the back with a tutor cane and three strands of hair)		54.8.50 54.7.42 54.6.34 54.5.26 54.4.18
xú	徐	the quiet composure of the		15.14.79 15.13.70

		left side of the royal 'I' used by the Shang Dynasty kings		
xù	畜	tying animals and raising them in a pen		51.11.43 51.2.5
xū	歔	snorting through the nose at nothing like a person with their mouth yawning and empty kneeling before a tiger head on a hill with grass coming through the bottom		29.8.38
xū	虛	empty, like a tiger head upon a mound,		53.8.31 5.7.30 22.20.71 16.1.2 3.8.34
xuán	玄	this hard-to-see structure of a double-looped, figure-eight skein of string-dyed-		65.14.54 65.13.52 56.8.29 51.18.71 15.2.9

		black		10.17.68
				10.5.20
				6.3.9 6.2.7
				1.14.55
				1.14.52
				1.13.51
xué	學	learning and understanding with divination or tally marks held between one's hands and a child safe beneath a roof,		64.21.108
				64.21.106
				48.1.2
				20.1.2
yán	言	speaking out loud		81.2.6
				81.1.2
				78.14.62
				73.8.43
				70.5.17
				70.1.2
				69.1.4
				66.4.31
				62.4.18
				56.1.5
				56.1.4
				43.5.28
				41.5.33
				31.16.96

				27.2.7 23.1.2 22.20.72 17.6.33 8.9.32 5.9.39 2.10.58
yán	埏	molding clay on a potter's wheel		11.3.14
yàn	燕	calmly as the swallow for whom the kingdom Yàn is named		26.6.24
yàn	厭	sated like a dog with meat in its mouth, fed up		72.6.26 72.5.22 72.4.15 66.8.66 53.11.38
yǎn	儼	respectful, making oneself listen even when someone's too chatty		15.8.37
yān	焉	here, straightening things out for "nailing" that first		60.9.48 49.10.47 34.7.41

		footstep of a journey on the back of this yellow bird with the "dangling tail" that lives around the Yangtze and Huai Rivers— right here, huh!—		25.13.72 2.11.64
yáng	陽	the male yáng principle of sun shining on a big soil mound		42.5.20
yáng	殃	harmed by evil misfortune, the bone remnants of a pleading person with their head in the middle of a pole over their shoulders with two things on either end,		52.14.68
yâng	養	feeding a meal, mouth over a rice bowl, as beautiful as a ram's head		51.14.53 34.5.24

yāng	央	really in the middle of it like a person with a pole over their shoulders, one thing on either end, their head in the center		20.8.33
yào	要	demanding something vital as a woman with both hands pointing to her waist		27.18.90
yào	燿	brilliant as that shining fire over the head of a kneeling person when it's like the plumes of a long-tailed cock pheasant		58.17.70
yào	窈	profoundly secluded behind the two- winged flap covering a cave, harboring the strength of an arm, a bladed tool, or a plow caring for an infant as		21.9.33

		fragile as one fine silk thread, hard to see, dim and quiet		
yāo	妖	spooky and evil as gorgeous demons, a kneeling woman chased by a running young man who will die young		58.10.43
yé	邪	as unwholesome in nature as the disease-causing environment around Elephant Tusk Town, Lángyá		62.16.75 39.18.116 7.9.44
yê	也	—yes, that too, oh "female funnel!"—		76.4.23 76.3.18 76.2.9 76.1.4 67.7.24 55.9.52 55.7.42 53.14.51 32.2.13 29.4.22

				24.7.32 20.17.82 3.13.60
yí	以	this is cultivating, like a plow...		
yí	夷	'foreign,' part of the great barbarian tribe of the east carrying bows, leveling and razing		53.4.18 41.8.44 14.2.7
yí	遺	walking with the footprint of someone slowly leaving behind cowry-like riches after dying, the left leg leading the way with two hands wrapped around them, dragging them off		52.14.66 20.16.76 9.8.30
yí	盈	full to overflowing its vessel		

yí	宜	two pieces of meat on a sacrificial altar, seemingly, properly		61.15.80
yì	異	a person wearing a mask, hiding		20.27.126 1.12.46
yì	亦	—both armpits sweat this too!—		65.11.43 60.7.35 50.5.24 49.7.35 49.4.21 42.13.58 37.7.38 32.9.49 32.8.45 25.12.60 23.17.77 23.15.68 23.13.59
yì	易	easily changeable as switching from saying 'don't,' serious as three drops of blood on a blade, to shining		78.4.20 70.2.7 70.1.4 64.4.16 64.3.12 64.2.8

		like the sun		64.1.3 63.15.64 63.9.35 63.6.22 2.4.28
yì	義	sacrificing a ram with that rake-like weapon we use to defend ourselves and our opinions, righteous		38.13.79 38.14.81 38.8.43 19.3.12 18.1.6
yì	益	overflowing like water from a vessel		55.12.61 48.1.4 43.6.34 43.4.26 42.11.49 42.10.47
yì	抑	suppressing like a hand pushing down on a kneeling person		77.3.11
yǐ	矣	—I swear, an arrow revolving around oneself, that's it!		74.11.59 69.13.54 67.19.81 67.6.21 65.15.63 65.14.59 65.14.57

				63.17.79 46.7.45 31.11.77
yî	巳	already finishing it in the womb		55.16.81 31.8.43 30.15.75 30.11.59 30.6.37 29.2.14 9.2.8 2.2.21 2.1.11
yî	以	this is cultivating, like a plow		37.6.28 81.9.37 81.8.30 79.4.14 79.3.10 78.9.39 78.4.19 77.13.63 77.11.54 77.10.46 76.7.40 75.10.45 75.9.39 75.8.32 75.6.25 75.5.18 75.3.12

				75.2.4
				74.2.7
				73.6.28
				72.7.28
				72.6.24
				71.7.26
				71.6.21
				71.4.14
				70.11.41
				70.8.28
				67.23.96
				67.21.88
				67.20.84
				66.9.67
				66.8.59
				66.6.43
				66.5.38
				66.4.30
				66.4.23
				66.2.11
				66.1.4
				65.8.32
				65.6.24
				65.5.19
				65.3.12
				65.2.8
				64.22.115
				64.20.94

				64.15.61
				63.16.69
				63.12.45
				63.5.16
				62.16.73
				62.15.69
				62.13.60
				62.11.47
				62.5.25
				62.4.20
				61.10.48
				61.8.37
				61.6.27
				61.5.20
				61.4.16
				60.2.8
				59.7.50
				59.6.42
				58.13.52
				57.5.22
				57.4.17
				57.3.9
				57.2.5
				57.1.1
				54.15.90
				54.14.84
				54.13.76
				54.12.72

				54.11.68
				54.10.64
				54.9.60
				54.3.13
				52.3.14
				52.2.5
				51.5.14
				50.15.76
				50.7.31
				49.2.6
				48.8.37
				48.6.28
				48.4.13
				47.5.22
				46.1.8
				44.8.37
				43.4.20
				42.15.70
				42.9.38
				42.6.23
				41.4.28
				39.18.112
				39.17.101
				39.16.96
				39.15.91
				39.14.83
				39.13.75
				39.12.67

				39.11.60
				39.10.53
				39.9.46
				39.7.36
				39.6.30
				39.5.24
				39.4.19
				39.3.14
				39.2.9
				38.19.107
				38.8.48
				38.7.40
				38.6.32
				38.4.15
				38.2.6
				36.13.54
				37.8.44
				34.9.50
				32.10.56
				32.5.29
				31.18.113
				31.17.106
				31.16.97
				31.11.71
				30.7.40
				30.2.8
				30.1.1
				29.11.50

				27.8.36
				26.8.35
				26.3.10
				25.5.23
				22.7.20
				21.17.70
				21.16.63
				21.15.57
				20.25.117
				19.7.28
				16.4.12
				15.14.75
				15.13.67
				14.19.82
				13.14.72
				13.12.61
				13.9.42
				12 8 37
				11.8.47
				11.7.41
				11.5.29
				11.3.16
				7.9.40
				7.5.24
				7.3.14 7.2.8
				5.4.15 5.2.5
				3.7.29
				2.16.86

				2.9.48 1.10.36 1.8.29
yî	故	anciently, for ten generations, this taps lightly by a tutoring cane and leaves a mark of reason		13.12.59
yî	倚	leaned on, relied on by a person who's as remarkable as the great big person that—mwah!—tastes truly like the one		58.5.22
yī	衣	clothing, like draping with a robe as the placental afterbirth hanging from a recently pregnant woman		34.5.23
yī	一	The One		67.10.34 42.2.4 42.1.3 39.7.35 39.6.29

				39.5.23
				39.4.18
				39.3.13
				39.2.8
				39.1.4
				25.13.71
				22.7.24
				14.8.33
				11.1.5 10.1.5
yǐn	隱	hides, secreted behind a soil mound as careful and compassionate as a claw-like hand grabbing from above the real work of the force of a bladed tool over a pig-head heart		41.18.86
yǐn	飲	drinking, leaning over a vase for making alcohol with one's mouth		53.11.39
yīn	音	singing one tone from your mouth		41.16.78 12.2.8 2.7.39

yīn	陰	the feminine yīn principle, what's hidden and overcast as when what's being said in the mouth now, in modern times, is said when it's dusky, when clouds are covering a big soil mound		42.5.17
yíng	盈	full to overflowing its vessel		45.3.10 39.12.68 39.5.25 22.3.9 15.16.91 15.15.87 9.1.3 4.2.8
yíng	迎	welcoming, a real hero's parade, slowly walking with the footprint of an admired one, the left leg leading the		14.16.66

		way		
yîng	營	the spiritual soul, that light of a palatial womb's crossed torches,		10.1.2
yīng	嬰	an infant, a kneeling young mother's wealth as surely as two cowry-like riches around her neck		28.6.22 20.13.55 10.4.15
yīng	應	agreeably echoing an answer like a heart in a habitable cliff cave with a bird of prey, a bird with a dangling tail together with a small-tailed bird		73.8.46 38.9.57
yòng	用	doing truly useful work like a water bucket, by means of carrying-capacity		80.11.44 80.3.13 69.1.1 68.6.33 68.4.19 57.2.7 52.13.58 45.4.14

				45.2.6
				40.2.10
				35.8.39
				31.8.45
				31.5.25
				28.20.76
				27.3.14
				11.8.49
				11.6.38
				11.4.25
				11.2.13
				6.6.22 4.1.4
yông	勇	like the handle of a bell, being courageous and sturdy as a soldier, strong as an arm, bladed tool, or plow		73.2.6 73.1.1 67.16.71 67.13.51
yóu	猶	in the same manner as the unlikely rise of a dog monkey to the top of the alcohol vat to become chief of brewing, it's like		77.2.5 73.6.31 63.16.72 32.12.65 15.7.31 5.6.26
yóu	尤	is like a hand with		8.14.50

		a wart: particularly strangely outstanding		
yòu	又	again, on the right hand,		48.3.11 1.14.54
yòu	右	a priority position, right hand over mouth		31.13.85 34.2.8 31.15.95 31.5.29
yôu	有	flesh-and-meat-body-handling "Yôu," that is to say, "Being,"		81.8.35 80.8.31 80.6.23 80.2.6 79.6.25 79.2.5 77.12.59 77.11.52 77.10.48 77.7.31 77.5.17 75.5.22 74.11.54 74.7.30 70.6.21 70.5.18

				69.1.3
				67.8.27
				64.5.22
				62.16.71
				62.10.44
				62.7.35
				59.7.45
				59.6.43
				57.9.56
				53.12.43
				53.1.5
				52.1.3
				51.15.60
				50.5.26
				50.3.15
				50.2.9
				48.7.33
				46.1.3
				43.4.25
				43.3.14
				41.5.34
				40.4.18
				40.3.17
				38.8.47
				38.6.31
				38.2.7
				34.4.22
				33.6.25

				33.3.12
				32.8.47
				32.7.42
				31.3.14
				30.6.34
				30.5.30
				26.5.21
				25.13.64
				25.1.1
				24.10.43
				23.18.85
				22.14.43
				21.12.47
				21.10.39
				21.8.31
				21.6.23
				20.25.116
				20.15.70
				19.8.35
				19.6.24
				18.4.24
				18.3.17
				18.2.10
				18.1.4
				17.5.25
				17.1.5
				14.19.86
				13.11.56

				13.10.49
				13.9.43
				11.7.39
				11.6.35
				11.4.22
				11.2.10
				10.14.57
				2.12.71
				2.3.23
				1.9.34
				1.6.19
yôu	牖	a window, like a boudoir window's sliver of wood that's half of a two-winged gateway and lets the moon shine in on the family's primordial father, ten spindles hanging		47.2.9 11.5.28
yōu	憂	grieving, their heart under the moon inside the backward footprint of returning		20.1.4
yōu	悠	distant and leisurely, like a		17.6.29

		person having water gently poured over their back, purifying their heart		
yú	餘	having leftover excess food remains in their house		79.2.6 77.11.53 77.10.49 77.7.32 77.5.18 54.5.33 53.12.44 24.8.34 20.15.71
yú	於	in this place and time, oh, black, icy raven sun:		34.6.36 79.5.23 78.1.6 75.11.51 73.2.7 73.1.2 69.10.37 64.17.79 64.12.49 64.10.41 64.8.33 64.6.25 64.5.20 63.11.42

				23.9.42 23.8.36 23.7.30 20.27.127 14.12.49 8.5.21
yú	愚	a heart like that trampling monkey with the head of a ghost,		65.3.13 38.18.103 20.17.78
yú	魚	fish		36.11.42
yú	隅	in a corner, that remote place by the big soil mound with that trampling monkey with the head of a ghost		41.14.72
yú	輿	carried in a carriage's sedan chair supported on shoulders, upheld by two hands like the territory and the public		39.20.124 39.20.122 80.6.25

yù	玉	a pure jade totem		70.12.47 39.21.130 9.5.18
yù	御	"you, royal sir," with a person kneeling before a pestle in welcome, managing		14.19.83
yù	欲	missing, kneeling with a yawning mouth before a ravine eroded between two mountains, wanting, lacking		77.15.77 66.5.34 66.4.26 64.20.99 64.20.97 61.14.77 61.13.66 61.12.58 57.14.84 46.5.36 46.3.24 39.21.126 37.8.43 37.7.41 37.5.22 36.7.26 36.5.18 36.3.10 36.1.2

				34.6.33 29.1.2 19.10.45 15.15.86 3.12.52 3.5.22 1.7.28 1.9.35
yù	愈	a person after an illness who is gathering themself together from three sides by moonlight over their heart after a blade cut off their foot as punishment, and now they've recovered,		81.9.41 81.8.34 5.8.36
yù	豫	a content countenance, two hands trading something for an elephant		15.6.25
yù	譽	receiving praise, famously spoken of as participating with someone, a		17.2.11

		'biting tooth' lifted by two hands onto strong shoulders, perhaps interfering with or perhaps supporting		
yù	域	the soil of this particular territory, this enclave defended by a weapon on a pole		25.13.62
yù	遇	walking slowly with the footprint of that trampling monkey with the head of a ghost, the left leg leading the way		50.9.46
yù	育	birthing an upside down baby below the moon		51.12.47
yû	與	participating with (a "biting tooth" lifted by a pair of hands onto strong shoulders, perhaps interfering with or perhaps		81.9.38 79.9.38 77.2.8 68.3.17 66.10.76 65.15.60 44.3.12

		supporting)		44.2.7
				44.1.2
				8.8.29
				36.8.31
				35.3.15
				22.18.59
				20.4.15
				20.2.7
yû	雨	cloudbursts of rain		23.3.12
yū	渝	as changeable as a river flowing against someone gathering themselves together from three sides after a blade cut off their foot as punishment, like from adultery		41.13.68
yuàn	怨	full of resentment (the heart under an animal lying down to die)		79.2.7 79.1.3 63.5.15
yuân	遠	the much distant,		80.5.20

		not intimate or near but profound way of slowly walking with the footprint of a big round spindle with a long robe hanging like the afterbirth from a postpartum woman, the left leg leading the way		65.14.58 47.3.16 25.11.49 25.10.48
yuān	淵	deep water		36.11.47 8.7.28 4.3.9
yuè	閱	a person smiling, exhaling, exchanging through the two-winged gateway, experiencing and reviewing		21.15.58
yuè	籥	flute that you blow into, made of bamboo slips with three mouth frets		5.6.28
yuē	曰	what that's called		67.12.41

				67.11.38
		when issued on a breath from the mouth		67.10.35
				62.14.67
				55.13.68
				55.12.63
				55.11.59
				55.10.55
				52.12.56
				52.11.52
				25.11.50
				25.10.47
				25.9.44
				25.8.41
				25.7.35
				24.7.33
				16.10.38
				16.9.34
				16.7.26
				14.6.20
				14.4.13
				14.2.6
yuē	約	binding it like a skein of silk keeping something in the ladle		27.6.30
yún	芸	quick-growing, voluminous and numerous as a		16.5.18
				16.5.17

		pair of rapeseed plant sprouts ('cloud- grass,' that source of the personal lubricant canola oil)		
yún	云	saying like a cloud		78.9.42 57.10.60
zài	在	its existing sprouting of seedlings and talents, here on earth, of		49.9.42 32.11.62 24.7.30
zâi	宰	dominating as the house of that chisel used to mark slaves and criminals		51.17.68 10.16.65
zāi	載	carrying and protecting a chariot load of sprouting seeds and talents, guarding with a weapon on a pole		10.1.1
zāi	哉	I say, "Oh, indeed,		57.4.21

		that hurts, a weapon on a pole wounding sprouting seeds and talents."		54.14.89 53.14.52 22.20.73 21.16.69 20.17.83 20.8.34
zào	躁	fidgety, impetuous as the footprint of three birds chirping in a tree		45.8.29 26.10.44 26.2.7
zào	鑿	chiseling with that tool used to mark slaves and criminals		11.5.26
zâo	早	early, premature as sunrise above an acorn on the jujube, that thorny plant that's used for insomnia and contraception and causes midterm miscarriages		59.3.15 59.2.13 55.16.80 30.15.74
zé	則	after following this sacrificial blade-and-cauldron-like ritual regulation		77.9.40 76.8.48 76.7.43 73.2.10

				73.1.4
				72.2.5
				70.10.36
				67.21.90
				67.20.86
				64.19.89
				61.9.41
				61.7.31
				59.5.32
				59.4.25
				55.14.72
				38.10.58
				31.11.68
				31.5.27
				31.4.22
				30.13.66
				28.21.78
				28.19.71
				26.10.45
				26.9.41
				22.19.67
				22.6.17
				22.5.14
				22.4.11
				22.3.8
				22.2.5
				22.1.2
				3.15.64

zé	責	poked as if by a tree with thorns over cowry-riches, interrogated, or ordered to do things		79.5.22
zéi	賊	using a weapon on a pole to harm that sacrificial blade-and-cauldron-like ritual regulation, like an insect that eats at the joints and roots of a plant, destroying		65.7.30 57.9.54 19.6.22
zhàn	湛	profound, clear, joyous—that river as pleasant as something sweet in the mouth tucked into the ends of folded cloth		4.9.28
zhàn	戰	battling, using a net for catching animals against a weapon on a pole		68.2.8 67.20.85 31.18.111
zháng	長	lengthing as long		51.17.65

		as hair that has to be tied with a brooch, as a loose-haired old man		51.12.45 28.21.81
zhàng	丈	respected man or husband from whom one maintains a distance of ten feet		38.19.109
zhǎng	長	lengthing as long as hair that has to be tied with a brooch, as a loose-haired old man		24.6.28 22.16.49 10.16.62
zhāng	張	stretching out, lengthening like a bow string		77.2.6 36.2.7
zhāng	彰	shining forth as obviously clear and 'enlightened' as the hair on a person standing on the ground in the early morning		57.9.52 24.4.18 22.12.38

		sun over the thorny jujube plant that's used for insomnia and contraception and causes midterm miscarriages		
zhào	爪	a claw like a hand grabbing from above		50.12.66
zhâo	兆	an omen, the cracks on a divination shell		64.2.7 20.12.53
zhāo	昭	bright, bright as a blade-like imperial summons		20.19.90 20.19.89
zhāo	召	convening when an imperial summons calls everyone together like a blade out of a mouth		73.9.48
zhé	謫	speaking of the base stem of the		27.2.10

		stalk, exiling a high- ranking person to a lowly outlying post		
zhé	折	breaking off, a tree cut in half with an axe		76.8.49
zhê	者	—this is boiling sugarcane with fire as follows!—		81.6.22 81.5.18 81.4.14 81.3.10 78.2.12 77.12.61 77.6.24 77.5.19 77.4.14 77.3.10 76.6.35 76.5.29 75.10.48 74.10.52 74.8.39 74.7.33 74.4.20 73.3.14 70.10.38 70.9.34

				69.13.52
				68.4.21
				68.3.15
				68.2.9
				68.1.4
				66.1.10
				65.10.42
				65.1.6
				64.14.57
				64.13.53
				62.13.64
				62.1.2
				61.15.79
				61.14.72
				61.1.3 56.1.6
				56.1.2
				54.2.8
				54.1.3
				50.8.42
				49.7.33
				49.6.27
				49.4.19
				49.3.13
				42.14.63
				40.2.7
				40.1.2
				39.1.5
				38.17.98

				38.15.87
				33.8.37
				33.7.31
				33.6.24
				33.5.20
				33.4.16
				33.3.11
				33.2.7
				33.1.3
				31.11.67
				31.10.58
				31.6.31
				31.3.16
				31.1.4 30.1.6
				29.6.28
				29.5.24
				27.15.71
				27.14.62
				27.1.4
				24.10.45
				24.6.26
				24.5.21
				24.4.16
				24.3.11
				24.2.6
				4.1.2
				23.16.75
				23.14.66

				23.12.57
				23.11.50
				23.10.45
				23.9.40
				23.8.38
				23.4.19
				22.19.69
				19.7.27
				15.15.84
				15.1.6
				14.7.24
				13.9.46
				7.2.13
				3.13.56
				1.11.42
zhèn	鎮	calming, sedating, chilling with genuine ancient axed- copper-alloy divination spoon and cauldron for a long time		37.6.26
zhēn	真	genuinely getting into it, like using a fork to get food right from the cauldron		54.4.25 41.13.66 21.11.44
zhēn	貞	like an ancient		39.7.40

		divination cauldron, faithful, pure, and chaste as a proper woman		
zhèng	正	straightening up, straightening things out for 'nailing' that first footstep of a journey		78.14.61 58.9.36 58.8.35 57.12.74 57.1.2 45.10.40 8.10.35
zhèng	政	governing or editing, tapping lightly with a tutoring cane to straighten up and "nail" setting out by foot on a long journey or campaign, preparing the ground for it		58.3.10 58.1.2
zhēng	爭	competing, two hands clawing over a plowshare		81.11.57 73.7.38 68.5.28 66.10.78 66.9.70 22.18.61

				22.17.53
				8.13.47
				8.3.12 3.2.7
zhí	直	looking straight on, straight ahead		58.16.63
				45.5.18
				22.2.6
zhí	埴	clay that looks straight on, up and down		11.3.15
zhí	執	a kneeling person, arrested and held, arms outstretched in handcuffs		79.4.17
				74.5.23
				69.9.31
				64.16.70
				64.14.56
				35.1.1
				29.6.27
				14.18.78
zhì	致	thoroughly delivering, exhausting, arriving at the extreme (like an arrow stuck in the ground and tapped lightly with a		39.20.120
				39.8.42
				16.1.1
				14.7.27
				10.3.12

		tutoring cane so as to leave a mark)		
zhì	志	their will, stepping off from the heart's footprint here		33.6.26 31.11.73 3.10.42
zhì	治	flowing the River Happy, speaking of gathering oneself from three sides, managing		75.6.27 75.4.17 65.8.34 65.6.26 65.4.18 64.6.23 60.1.1 59.1.1 57.1.3 10.7.28 8.10.37 3.15.67 3.7.33
zhì	智	oh, so very pleasantly speaking pleasantly speaking with that wise knowledge passed on from a great big person to a baby, as if		65.8.33 65.6.25 65.5.21 33.1.4 27.17.85 19.1.4 18.2.8 3.13.55

		something sweet in the mouth		
zhì	制	ruler edicts, like saying, 'cut that tree!' as was done for parent-mourning rituals		32.7.41 28.22.84

Pinyin	MC	Translation	Bronze Inscription Glyphs	Spots in the text
zhì	質	what matters with the keen and weighty quality of two axes over a cowry, held as hostage		41.13.65
zhì	至	in arriving at the end, the extreme climax, like an arrow straight into the clay soil		80.18.69 72.2.8 65.16.67 55.9.51 55.7.41 48.4.14 43.2.11 43.1.4
zhì	置	putting in place, like a webbed net over an eye directed straight forward		62.9.40
zhǐ	止	halting right here in this footprint		44.7.33 35.3.19 32.10.54 32.9.52 20.24.112

zhī	知	speaking as a great big person to a baby, distinguishing, imparting, and administering wisdom confidently and intimately, like it's something sweet in the mouth		81.6.24
				81.5.17
				78.7.34
				73.5.24
				72.7.32
				71.2.7 71.2.6
				71.1.3 71.1.1
				70.9.32
				70.8.31
				70.7.26
				70.3.13
				70.1.5
				65.12.47
				65.10.39
				59.6.38
				59.5.34
				58.7.30
				57.4.18
				56.1.8
				56.1.1.
				55.11.57
				55.10.53
				55.6.31
				54.14.85
				53.1.6
				52.4.19
				52.3.15
				47.5.28

				47.4.18
				47.1.4
				46.6.39
				46.4.30
				44.7.32
				44.6.28
				43.4.21
				2.2.13 2.1.4
				33.5.18
				33.2.6
				33.1.1
				32.10.53
				32.9.51
				28.13.47
				28.7.24
				28.1.1
				25.6.30
				21.16.64
				17.1.4
				16.13.46
				16.11.41
				16.10.36
				14.20.88
				10.12.48
				10.8.32
				4.11.35
				3.12.50

zhī	之	what it has, stepping on from this footprint, it has this		39.8.43
				64.22.119
				81.11.52
				81.10.44
				80.17.64
				80.11.45
				80.9.37
				80.7.29
				80.2.9
				78.10.45
				78.6.27
				78.5.23
				78.4.21
				78.3.14
				77.9.38
				77.7.28
				77.6.26
				77.5.21
				77.4.16
				77.3.12
				77.1.2
				76.6.37
				76.5.31
				76.3.16
				76.1.2
				75.8.36
				75.7.29
				75.5.21

				75.4.15
				75.2.9
				75.1.2
				74.5.26
				74.2.10
				73.7.35
				73.6.33
				73.4.20
				68.8.42
				68.6.35
				68.5.29
				68.4.23
				67.23.99
				67.22.95
				67.9.33
				66.10.77
				66.5.41
				66.4.33
				66.2.15
				65.9.37
				65.7.29
				65.4.16
				65.3.14
				65.1.2
				64.21.112
				64.20.104
				64.17.84
				64.17.75

				64.14.59
				64.13.55
				64.11.46
				64.9.38
				64.7.30
				64.6.24
				64.5.19
				63.16.74
				62.13.58
				62.7.34
				62.6.29
				62.3.14
				62.2.9
				62.1.5
				61.3.12
				61.2.8
				59.9.63
				59.7.47
				59.3.18
				58.11.45
				58.6.26
				58.5.20
				55.15.75
				55.9.50
				55.7.40
				55.6.34
				55.1.3
				54.8.51

				54.7.43
				54.6.35
				54.5.27
				54.4.19
				51.14.56
				51.14.54
				51.13.52
				51.13.50
				51.12.48
				51.12.46
				51.11.44
				51.10.41
				51.9.32
				51.8.28
				51.7.25
				51.4.12
				51.3.9
				51.2.6
				51.1.3
				50.7.35
				50.4.21
				50.4.18
				50.3.12
				50.2.6
				49.13.65
				49.7.37
				49.6.30
				49.4.23

				49.3.16
				48.3.10
				46.6.41
				43.7.39
				43.6.33
				43.5.29
				43.4.24
				43.2.10
				43.1.3
				42.13.60
				42.12.54
				42.11.50
				42.10.45
				42.7.27
				41.5.35
				41.3.23
				41.1.8
				40.2.9
				40.1.4
				39.1.2
				38.18.104
				38.17.100
				38.16.94
				38.15.90
				25.8.39
				38.10.63
				38.9.56
				38.9.53

				38.8.45
				38.7.37
				38.6.29
				36.12.49
				37.7.35
				37.6.31
				37.6.27
				36 8 32
				36.7.28
				36.6.24
				36.5.20
				36.4.16
				36.3.12
				36.2.8
				36.1.4
				35.8.40
				35.7.35
				35.6.30
				35.4.21
				34.3.12
				32.12.68
				32.11.61
				32.6.35
				32.3.19
				31.18.117
				31.17.110
				31.17.104
				31.16.101

				31.10.57
				31.8.46
				31.7.39
				37.3.14
				31 6 34
				31.2.12
				31.1.7
				30.5.27
				30.4.18
				29.6.30
				29.5.26
				29.1.8
				28.20.77
				27.15.74
				27.14.66
				26.7.32
				25.7.34
				24.9.41
				23.17.80
				23.15.71
				23.13.62
				22.21.78
				22.19.63
				22.18.60
				21.16.67
				21.3.10.
				21.1.3
				20.17.80

				20.6.22
				20.4.14
				20.2.6
				17.4.20
				17.3.16
				17.2.12
				17.1.6
				15.14.78
				15.13.69
				15.9.46
				15.5.23
				15.1.2
				14.19.85
				14.18.80
				14.17.73
				14.16.67
				14.14.60
				14.13.56
				14.5.16
				14.3.9
				14.1.2
				13.6.24
				13.5.20
				12.6.30
				11.4.24
				11.6.37
				11.7.40
				11.2.12

				10.13.53
				10.13.51
				9.10.38
				9.6.22
				9.3.12 9.1.4
				8.4.16
				6.6.23
				6.3.11
				5.5.23
				4.12.41
				4.11.37
				4.4.14 4.1.5
				3.7.32
				3.3.12
				2.10.59
				2.9.54
				2.2.15 2.1.6
				1.15.58
				1.14.53
				1.13.50
				1.6.23
				1.5.17
zhòng	眾	the sun, shining down like an eye on the people, sees all this, sees		64.21.110
				31.17.105
				21.16.65
				21.15.59
				20.25.113
				20.15.67

				20.9.35 8.4.14 1.15.56
zhòng	重	the seriously heavy (like a bag so weighty that a man has to kneel to put it on his back)		80.4.16 66.6.51 59.4.22 59.3.19 26.4.19 26.1.1
zhōng	中	in the center, that drum with a flagpole placed in the middle of a field to gather the people and detect wind		41.2.9 25.13.63 21.12.46 21.10.38 21.8.30 21.6.22 5.10.45
zhōng	忠	a centered heart, like that drum with a flagpole placed in the middle of a field to gather the people		38.15.88 18.4.25
zhōng	終	ending like the knot at the end of a thick silk skein, like winter		64.18.86 63.17.76 63.12.48 55.8.43 52.10.46 52.7.36

				34.9.52
				26.3.13
				23.3.14
				23.2.9
zhòu	驟	sudden as your horse moving sharply when you're gathering and carrying in your hand the ear of an enemy people, quickly		23.3.11
zhōu	周	meticulously organizing something into compartments, like space into circuits, time into weekly structure, money into allotments that can be distributed to help people, or 'Zhōu' as our dynasty is called		25.4.17
zhōu	舟	riding in a boat, a dugout canoe		80.6.24

zhù	注	fills it, like a river and you, honored senior official master, owner and host of the lamp's flame, or your spouse or princess daughter, with		49.12.57
zhǔ	主	you, "oh, honored senior official master," owner, and host of the flame		78.11.51 69.2.9 34.7.45 34.5.30 30.1.5 26.7.33
zhuān	專	monopolizing like a big round spindle rolling over an inch-sized spot as small as that spot on your forearm where your pulse beats strong		10.3.10
zhuàng	狀	in this shape		30.13.65

				21.16.68
		(differently formed like the way a piece of chopped wood can be sculpted in the shape of a dog)		14.13.57 14.13.55
zhuàng	壯	strong as a high-ranking bachelor soldier-scholar-official, appointed by the emperor, like battle-axe-hewn- wood, like one burn of a moxa in moxibustion		55.14.71
zhuì	贅	marrying a woman for their family riches and living there (playing around, tapping lightly with a tutoring cane a feathered headdress who died before taking the throne and		24.8.36

		therefore had no posthumous name) with superfluous cowry-like riches		
zhuó	濁	yellow water like that of the far western sub-state Shū whose name means 'a silkworm caterpillar on a hollyhock leaf,' that all-seing eye above a wiggly body		15.13.66 15.12.63
zhuō	銳	grinding that axe between two blocks of metal to a sharp point		9.3.11
zhuō	拙	clumsy, stepping out of their cave all hands and fingers		45.6.24
zhuō	斲	chopping like a keen axe cutting a stone flagon		74.10.51 74.9.46

zí	泫	is flowing a river of hard-to-see dark structure, a figure- eight skein of string-dyed- black, crying tears, glistening like dews		57.8.47
zì	自	one's self personally, right on the nose		73.9.50 72.10.39 72.9.36 72.8.34 72.7.31 64.22.120 57.14.87 57.13.80 57.12.73 57.11.66 51.9.36 39.17.104 37.9.49 37.4.18 34.9.54 33.4.14 33.2.5

				32.6.38
				32.4.23
	資			25.17.84
				24.6.24
				24.5.19
				24.4.14
				24.3.9
				23.1.3
				22.15.46
				22.13.40
				22.11.35
				22.9.30
				21.13.49
				17.8.43
				9.8.29
				7.3.17
zì	字	"Zì," its public courtesy name, received as a baby under the family roof from their parents or first tutor but not used until a man reaches age 20 or a woman is married		25.7.33
zī	資	supporting		27.16.83

		material, second-tier cowry- like riches		27.15.75
zī	子	a baby with arms wide open and legs swaddled, Zī		62.8.39 55.2.8 54.3.11 52.4.21 52.3.17 31.7.38 31.4.20 4.11.38
zī	輜	a curtained carriage carrying items over field and stream, like for military supply		26.4.18
zī	滋	increasing as a river of double the hard- to-see dark structure, two figure-eight skeins of string- dyed- black		57.9.51 57.7.39
zōng	宗	ancestral temple		70.5.19 4.4.15

zôu	走	taking off, rising up, possibly passing on early like a young man running over a snake		46.1.6
zú	足	fully enough, like the whole leg as well as the footprint		77.10.45 77.8.36 77.6.23 64.12.50 48.8.36 46.7.44 46.6.42 46.6.40 46.4.31 44.6.29 41.11.60 41.4.27 35.8.42 35.7.37 35.6.32 33.5.19 28.17.64 23.18.83 19.7.32 17.5.23
zuì	罪	guilty, suffering, sinful, or even		62.16.72 46.3.19

		criminal, with a webbed net over two wings wrung backwards		
zūn	尊	honoring, like offering by hand the ritual alcohol vessel with the chief in charge of its preparation		62.5.22 51.7.26 51.6.19
zuò	作	recently, exactly, having immediately folded from one straight rod into two		63.11.41 63.9.33 55.6.38 37.5.23 16.12.44 16.3.10 2.11.63
zuò	坐	sitting, two people staying there, on the ground of		62.12.53
zuǒ	左	an inferior aide position, doing left- handed work as with a bladed tool		79.4.18 34.2.7 31.14.90 31.12.81 31.4.24
zuô	佐	a person in an inferior aide		30.1.3

		position, providing left-handed help with work as with a bladed tool, assisting		

www.ingramcontent.com/pod-product-compliance
Lightning Source LLC
Chambersburg PA
CBHW050942210726
48287CB00004B/1104